VOLUME 2

Winston Engle, editor

THRILLING WONDER LLC

LOS ANGELES, CA

Editor's Dedication:
To Forrest J Ackerman (1916-2008),
Jack Speer (1920-2008),
and all the early fans whose dedication
helped give us what we have today

THRILLING WONDER STORIES — VOLUME 2

Cover painting by Bob Eggleton. Copyright © 2000 Bob Eggleton.

Back cover illustration for "Palladium" by Don Anderson. Copyright © 2008 Don Anderson.

Additional Photo/Illustration Credits:

photos and drawings on pages 34, 103, 104, 105, and 117 (top) by permission of Marc Scott Zicree

illustration on page 108 by permission of Iain McCaig

photo on page 116 by permission of Crystal Ann Taylor

www.thrillingwonderstories.com

ISBN-13: 978-0-9796718-1-4

THRILLING WONDER STORIES®

VOL. XLVII, No. 1   A THRILLING PUBLICATION   Spring 2009

WINSTON ENGLE, *Editor/Publisher*
PAMELA DAVIS, *Editorial Assistant*   MARC SCOTT ZICREE, *Contributing Editor*

ENTERPRISE FISH

Illustrated by Mishi McCaig

"The only constant in the universe is change, and even that isn't constant."
— Solomon Short

inally, the pilot said, "There it is."

"Where?"

"Straight ahead. That gray mass on the horizon." He tapped a screen, zooming in. The picture was still indistinct.

BY
DAVID
GERROLD

Barksdale stood up and went downstairs to peer out the passenger windshield. I didn't bother. Neither did anyone else. But I'd known how close we were for the last half-hour. The others hadn't noticed the smell, wouldn't notice it until we began our descent. Without augments, bio or cyber or worm, most humans don't smell anything until they rub their own noses in it.

We were flying up the wind-signature of the event. Not intentionally; it was unavoidable. Ten square klicks of fetid biomass churning through the stages of death and recomposition, drew a dark red stain across the map. Ugly stuff. Sticky stuff.

3

They'd have to decontaminate the aircraft, or every flying, crawling, leaping, scrabbling red thing that liked that particular set of pheromones—and that was pretty much every flying, crawling, leaping, scrabbling thing with Chtorran genes—would come flying, crawling, leaping, and scrabbling after it.

General Anderson was about to turn to me. There's an instant of anticipation in a body's posture that occurs long before any movement; most humans can't sense it, but it's like a neon explosion of information to me. I swiveled to face him, simultaneous with his own action. "I wish you wouldn't do that," he said. I could have apologized, but I didn't. I'd given up pretending to be human. It had never really worked all that well for me *before*. Now, I just didn't see the point in it. I wasn't human. Had stopped being human a long time ago. Would have stopped being human even if I hadn't fallen down to the bottom of a Chtorran nest.

"Can you smell anything yet?"

"I can smell everything," I said. "I've been tasting it for fifty klicks. Ever since we crossed the Arctic Circle."

Anderson looked annoyed. He didn't like me. I didn't blame him. I didn't like me all that much either. But he had at least five good reasons to dislike me. And three of those were my reasons too. It didn't matter, we still had to work together. So I said, "It's soup. I'm still sorting out the flavors. Tomato. Clam. Garlic. Parsley. Swordfish. Mercury...." I shrugged, a physical punctuation mark, performed more as a courtesy than as any actual representation of how I felt or thought. "It's Boullibase." And then I added, "Not very good Boullibase either."

"Eh?"

I held up a hand. Another courtesy. But humans communicate through nuance as much as through language. So if I wanted to be understood, I had to practice nuance. "Have you ever tasted something for the first time, but even though it's the first time, you've never tasted it before in your life, you still know there's something wrong with it?"

He considered the question. That was one of the good things about General Daniel Anderson. He didn't speak without thinking. Well, not as often as most people. "You're saying there's something wrong with the smell, so there's something wrong with the biophysical processes?"

"I'm saying that's how I'm experiencing it."

He nodded.

General Barksdale came back up from the downstairs cabin, wrapping his outercoat tighter around himself and making a great show of shivering. "Brrr brrr brrr. It looks cold out there." Unnecessary. And grating. He leaned on the back of Anderson's chair and asked, "So, how are we doing here, boys? Figured out the enterprise fish yet?"

Anderson looked annoyed, partly at Barksdale's stupid interruption, and partly because Barksdale's impressive weight had pushed his seat uncomfortably backward. Barksdale was looming over Anderson to lean in toward me and Anderson didn't like being cramped by his size or his manner. Even a human could read that tableau.

"It's not a fish," Anderson said quietly.

"Yeah, yeah, I know," said Barksdale. "It's a gigantic colony of adaptive symbiotes in multiplex synergistic relationships." He looked at me. "Did I get it right? I know the fancy language for it. But it still looks and acts like a fish. So we can think of it like a fish, right?"

Anderson was watching for my reaction. I didn't display because I didn't have a reaction. I'd figured out Barksdale a long time ago. He hadn't climbed any farther up the evolutionary ladder than he'd needed to. His grandfather's business acumen had bought the rest of the family an enviable comfort zone. Although David Hale Barksdale had displayed little interest in a military career, the war had necessitated his assumption into the highest ranks of the Civilian-Military (an astonishing oxymoron, but humans had passed beyond astonishment the day that Chtorrans showed up in downtown Manhattan.)

What was left of the community of governments on the North American continent had welcomed the creation of the Civilian-Military as a viable way of securing a self-sustaining response to the Chtorran infestation; overlapping the military onto the pre-existing corporate-clusters of the defense industry should ensure an uninterruptible chain of supply and command. At least, that was the projection. If, along the way, it meant shifting to a system of no-bid contracts, that was small price to pay. Actually, it was a large price to pay, but who was counting the cost anymore. Now that Plastic Dollars, Credit Dollars, Chocolate Dollars, and Oil Dollars had all collapsed, the economists were inventing a new economy based on Future Dollars. But given the nature of the war, the value of the dollar was irrelevant.

$\mathbf{S}$ ome people speak because they have something to say. Others speak because they have to say something. Barksdale's mouth was still going. "I mean, as far as I'm concerned, if it looks like a fish, if it swims like a fish—it's a fish. It's simple."

I met his gaze. "It isn't simple. Only stupid people say things like that." I didn't have to be polite to Barksdale. I didn't have to be polite to anyone. I was a nation-state unto myself. The united state of McCarthy. I don't do diplomacy. Behind my back, they call me Mr. Tact.

Barksdale didn't take it personally. He didn't take anything personally. He just laughed genially. Everything was a joke to him, a big friendly joke. "For the record," I added, "It doesn't look like a fish and it doesn't act like a fish. It floats in the ocean. After that, any resemblance is coincidental. It's a mobile ecological domain." I looked across to Anderson. "Do you want to explain?"

Anderson showed the faintest hint of a smile. He had to be polite to Barksdale, it was part of his job. Not mine. But that didn't stop him from appreciating the moment. "No, you go ahead," he said.

I looked at Barksdale. "You haven't read your briefing books." A statement, not a question.

"Who has time? We've got a war to win. Do you know how busy I am?"

Actually, I did. But I didn't say what I knew. The info-noise I swam in told me more about this overstuffed mushroom of a man than any sentient being should ever have to know. Most of the busy was busywork, shell processes requiring null-decisions, all designed to keep his fat pork-stained fingers out of the real business of war, where real people would die if he were in charge. Loading him down with briefing books was one of the ways of keeping him preoccupied, except—like too many others—he didn't read.

"Give me the short version," he said.

"There is no short version," I said.

"Explain it anyway," Barksdale insisted.

Anderson nodded encouragement. He was enjoying this too much. He looked across to the pilot's station. "We're in a headwind. You've got at least fifteen minutes."

"Do I have to make it an order?" Barksdale said.

There were so many places I could have

gone with that particular piece of nonsense. I could see that on Danny Anderson's face as well. But why bother? I decided to answer the question anyway. "It's not a creature, it's a convention."

Barksdale's expression puckered as he tried to sort that out. He couldn't find the sense in the sentence. Anderson gave me the look. "A little more than that, McCarthy?"

I finished taking a drink from my canteen and put the cap back on. "The Chtorran infestation isn't deliberate," I explained. "It isn't even conscious. Some people have said it's an ecology looking for a place to happen, but even that's not accurate. It's the *possibility* of an ecology. It's the potential for an ecology. Still with me?" Barksdale nodded, smiling vacuously. Behind all that blood-infused fat it was hard (even for me) to tell if he was actually hearing what I was saying or just listening because he was happy for the attention.

"You drop seeds from space. Lots of different ways to do it. The most common, the seed heats up on entry, pops like popcorn, continues to pop like popcorn all the way down, each time releasing great webs of nano-silk. With micro-seeds embedded in the webs. Some of the webs work like parachutes, slowing the seeds down, some rip away and drift off. It doesn't matter. As long as the DNA survives the trip down. The seeds, the popcorn, the webs, the stuff embedded in them, everything is message—the goal is to deliver genetic material to a viable domain. So everything that happens on the way down is another possibility.

"The problem is... none of this stuff has any way of knowing where it will land. Polar, temperate, equatorial. It has no idea whether it's going to land on savannah or desert, fresh water lake or salt water ocean; arctic wasteland or tropical jungle. How many different ecological domains do we have on this planet? The seeds can't be customized for any of them. They have to be adaptable to *all* of them. Okay, the webs that rip away from the falling seeds have some advantage; they'll drift wherever the winds take them, and the winds usually drop their burdens on mountainsides, which are often fertile specifically because the winds drop rain on them. But the truth is, most of this stuff comes down wherever it comes down. Most people know about the stuff that's running amuck in the Rockies and in the Amazon and in the Congo. Giant red and purple worms, shambler trees, swarms of stingflies, and great pink dust clouds. But more than two-thirds of this planet is ocean. Assuming an equal distribution of genetic material More than two-thirds of the Chtorran seeds fell into the ocean. That's the point."

I could see it in Barksdale's eyes. He didn't get it. He was still waiting for more. He was waiting to have it explained. Spelled out.

"And...?"

I took a breath. "And... wherever the seeds fall, you get a *different* set of Chtorran organisms. A convention. Each one is a different expression of the possibilities inherent in the Chtorran ecology. And even that's an inaccurate statement because it doesn't even begin to address the multiplex dimensions of relationships and opportunities and possibilities. There are so many different genetic relationships, so many different environmental opportunities, so many different developmental possibilities, so many occasions for random chance to stir the mix, that each creature that arises isn't a specifically designed response of the ecology to its circumstances as much as it is an emergent recombination of elements that arise in response to the opportunities around it."

"Uh—" Barksdale faltered. Barksdale wasn't quite as stupid as he looked. He obviously understood words with more than one syllable. Whether or not he understood nuance, intended meaning, natural results, and consequences—that was another whole discussion.

Anderson tried to clarify. "He's saying that if you drop identical seeds into dissimilar environments, you get dissimilar ecologies arising. Right?" He looked to me for agreement.

I shook my head. "Sorry, no. I'm saying that even if you dropped identical seeds into identical environments, you'd still get dissimilar ecologies. There is no Chtorran ecology, there never was. It isn't structured and its pieces don't behave predictably. It's an opportunistic synergistic recombinant multiplex confluence of biological processes that *randomly* adapt and express themselves according to the circumstances of the moment. The Chtorr takes advantage of whatever opportunities it encounters in whatever way pops up when the genetic lotto balls start percolating. The so-called 'enterprise fish' is only one of those expressions. It could just as easily have been anything else. And probably will be. We don't have a very clear picture of what's happening in the depths beyond our submersibles."

"Oh," said Barksdale, blinking. He was having trouble sorting it out. He let go of Anderson's seat back and straightened up, pretending to understand. Normally, I don't info-dump like that. But when someone is determined to be deliberately stupid, I'll make an exception.

Anderson, obviously still annoyed at the way Barksdale's flesh had been pressing uncomfortably against him, folded his arms, satisfied. If I hadn't managed to terrify Barksdale, at least I'd rubbed his nose in how much he didn't know that he didn't know.

"We're beginning our descent," the pilot announced. I'd already noticed the slight shift in the aircraft's attitude several moments ago, but this gave Barksdale the chance to make what passed for a graceful exit from an uncomfortable confrontation with his own ignorance. He smiled weakly and said, "I'd better go sit down now."

"Good idea," Anderson added. After Barksdale had left, he looked across to me, a look that would have been mutual understanding if I were still human. There was still understanding, but it wasn't mutual. What he understood was not what I understood.

As we dropped toward sea level, the aircraft bumped and slid in the wind. The Air Force boys in the back whooped and hollered "wheee" at the bigger bumps, thinking that turbulence was an occasion for jubilation and that this particular adventure was no different than any other joyride into Colorado Springs, or even what was left of Colorado Springs. The ignorance and the enthusiasm of youth. Until— "Christ! What's that stink!"

"That's the target," I said.

Anderson was used to the smell. Points to him for that. He nodded to the brat and pointed out the forward bubble. "Directly ahead."

"I don't see it. Where? Next to that shit-colored island?"

"No. Not next to it. The island."

"That—?" The brat and friends rose out of their seats, unbelieving.

"That's an enterprise fish." General Anderson's expression went dark. "Didn't you read your briefing book?"

"Sir, I got put on this ship ten minutes before it lifted. Berney went to sick bay, throwing up. Couldn't stop."

"Sorry to hear that."

"Not as sorry as Berney." That remark hung in silence for a moment. It was unlikely that Berney would be on any future missions. Any of a half-dozen things could have caused his symptoms, none of them optimistic. Don't start any trilogies, Berney. Oh hell, don't even start a short story.

Anderson called back to them, "You might want to put your breathers on now. That stink is only going to get worse." He pulled his headgear on, pulled the mask down over his face; he pulled the ear flaps down and fastened the padded strap under his chin. With his whole head covered, he looked like some kind of military insect. The stink of the beast didn't bother me as much as it did the humans. It had the taste of a place I'd never be able to escape. You can take the psycho out of the mandala, you can't take the mandala out of the psycho. But I didn't need to have them thinking that, so I pulled my own headgear on, trying to ignore the discomfort. The earphones whispered with industrial silence, a steady stream of dry background chatter.

I don't like wearing most human clothes. I can taste where they've been, where they grew, what they ate, who or what they rubbed up against, what they've been washed in. Even the polymers and polycarbons and nano-weaves have their own distinct flavors, vaguely medicinal and metallic. Old-fashioned nylon and microfiber knits are the least uncomfortable. Whatever I can find. Whatever is left in the warehouses from the days before the plagues. Everything from ladies' underwear to skintight athletic gear. There aren't a lot of specialty tailors anymore. I wear them to mute the ceaseless noise of the world, the scouring taste of the wind, all the desperate flavors of the day—especially the tastes of the city, the smells of other humans.

When I absolutely have to deal with humans, I have to wear human clothes, so I wear the nylons and the microfibers as underliners. Today, on top of the lingerie, a self-heating undersuit and two layers of protective outergear. Multiplane polymer nanoweave. As long as I don't have to taste it.

The aircraft dipped and shuddered as the pilot slowed. We dropped steadily toward the heaving surface of the beast-thing. Great waves moved slowly across its surface, gently lifting and dropping the men and equipment already waiting there. Anderson looked to me, a question in his eyes.

"It's not dead," I said.

He looked confused. "It's been beached for seven weeks." Like this meant something.

"I told you, it's a convention. Stop expecting it to be like things you know. Don't be a Barksdale."

"Right. I keep forgetting. Thanks for reminding me again why I don't like you very much." He reached under his seat and pulled his situation-boots forward; he shoved his feet into them, first one, then the other, then pulled up the zippers in the back. I followed his example. The bottoms of the boots spread out like snowshoes. The soles were metal honeycombs, studded with 10-centimeter cleats. The back of the enterprise fish wasn't just slimy, it was blubbery and greasy and it rolled like a restless sea. Even with cleats, footing would be tricky. Everything on its back had to be anchored—equipment tripods, habitats, storage sheds, landing platforms. Vehicles had studded tires or tank treads. Most of the bots were multi-legged, either spider-based or tripods, all with oversized feet and cleats.

We waited in silence until the airship

plopped down onto the rolling landscape of the behemoth. The pilot tapped buttons on his screens and idled his engines. "Welcome to Hell-Stinky. Abandon help, all ye who hope to intern. Please return your flight attendants to an upright position. Gentlemen, you may start your exos. Please use the rear doors to exit. Thank you for flying Air Apparent. We hope you'll think of us for all your future air travel needs into the zone." He popped open the rear of the airship and six pallets of equipment slid noisily out into the bright cold day. They squished into the surface of the beast. A scattering of bots came rushing up to move the pallets toward the meager settlement of Hell-Stinky base. As they pushed, pulled, and dragged the machinery, they carved deep tracks through the oily pudding of the monstrous landscape.

At the back of the cabin, mobile exo-skeletons stood securely fastened to the walls. Anderson stepped backward into the first one and it quickly adjusted itself to his frame, anchoring itself to his feet, his legs, his torso, and his arms. Exos were convenient for magnifying the physical strength of a human, but here on the rolling back of the enterprise fish, humans needed them just to stay upright; the exos would adjust their balance to the tides of flesh far more accurately. I stepped into my own exo and waited while it sorted itself out.

I'd worn exos of all kinds—both before and after my transformation in the Amazon—but the equipment was always in short supply. No matter how fast they came off the assembly lines, there still weren't enough. Plug an intelligence engine into an exo and you have a bot. Useful for construction, supply, maintenance, patrol, police-work, surveillance, even combat. So the desk-warriors couldn't see the logic of wasting a perfectly good exo on a grunt, who shouldn't be out in the zone anyway. A bot can do the job just as well, with no risk to human life, so why put a grunt in an exo-skeleton when you have trained professionals in Des Moines running in virtual mode?

On the other hand, putting exo-skeletons on a grunt makes a whole lot of sense, especially if you're the grunt. You can lift, carry, and run for hours. You've got extra-sensory augmentation, and if you're injured or even unconscious, the exo can bring you home. But if it weren't for General Dale Hale Barksdale the Third, we might not have had even these. I probably didn't need it, but Anderson didn't want me showing off among the ordinaries. He said it would increase the alienation. A very peculiar observation. I didn't see how I could be any more alienated from the rest of humanity, but despite his dislike of me, he was one of the few humans who made a genuine effort to understand who I had become.

The exo-skeleton completed its process of connection and calibration. It had clamped itself to my boots, my calves, my waist, my shoulders, my arms, and my wrists. I had metal hands just beyond my own. When I walked, I should have *clomped,* but instead I moved with an unnatural grace, almost cat-like. In Manhattan, we'd seen ballet dancers performing impossible acrobatic feats in exo-skeletons; but they were using special-mods and the troops were specifically ordered not to attempt anything they had not been certified for.

The other members of the team had also fitted themselves into their exos and as a group, we glided down the loading ramp to the glutinous surface of the alien thing.

It stank. It reeked. It assaulted. It was a collection of rank and fetid odors, death and decay and decomposition, a wall of olfactory offensiveness that would have stopped us dead in our tracks and knocked us flat to the glutinous ground, had the exo-skeletons not held us up and walked us forward. It was an almost visible presence, a vomitous stench so thick you could chew it. I had the small advantage of a Chtorran sense of smell. I could separate and identify all the different components of the repellent horror. But identification was insufficient. I had just enough residual humanity to experience the attack on my senses as a detestable abomination. There were no human equivalents for what I smelled, but my imagination was inventive enough and working overtime, creating its own bizarre menagerie of possible nightmares; I had too much history with Chtorran things that smelled bad.

We paused at the bottom to get our bearings. Getting our "sea legs" meant giving the exos a chance to calibrate themselves against the slow-rippling flesh of the enterprise fish. While the others tested their new agilities, I *sat.* I assumed a sitting position and the exo-skeleton became a chair. Not the most comfortable chair, but comfortable enough. If I wanted to put both legs up on an invisible hassock, I could have done that too. The exo had a tripod at the base of its spine. I'd seen field-mechanics lying flat on their backs this way, sometimes pushed five or ten meters in the air to work on an underwing fitting or inspect the work of a bot. A lot of the hardcore mechanics still didn't trust bots, even though the stats said bots were more accurate. Human stubbornness. I'd given up human stubbornness a long time ago. I had something nastier. Undefinable.

Two rollagons came trundling up. We hooked ourselves onto the outside, let it carry us, bucking and rocking north to the drill sites. We had to detour around several deep fissures in the creature's landscape, and at one point we even rolled off its flank onto the rocky shore and paralleled the sagging wall of flesh for half a kilometer.

At one point, the vehicle swerved up onto a cliff overlooking the shore. "Check it out. On your left," the driver said. Not very chatty, he clicked off again. He rightfully assumed we'd already seen all pertinent video.

Beneath us, we could see seven polar bears licking and chewing at the sides of the beached enterprise fish. Here and there were gaping holes ripped into its skin. Great gobbets of oily flesh oozed out onto the rocks, like the stuffing pushing out of a sagging, broken couch. One of the bears was a large male, two were females, each with two cubs. All had pink patches in their fur. Two of the cubs were tugging at a long stringer of blubbery skin. During the summer, a polar bear needs to eat its own weight in blubber to have any chance of surviving the winter.

And then they passed behind us. "Well, see," said Barksdale, his voice coming loud over the earphones. "It's not all bad news. The polar bears are surviving."

"If you like pink polar bears," I replied. General Anderson glanced backwards toward me, surprised that I had responded at all. Hanging off the side of the rollagon, it wasn't possible to shrug. I just shook my head. The fact that I wasn't human didn't stop me from pretending to be one from time to time. Just to keep my hosts at ease.

We rolled back up onto the seething flesh of the enterprise fish and rolled out onto the expanse of its greatest width. This was the primary drill site. The surgery team had brought in a dozen industrial bots, armed with lasers and timber-saws. The machines had anchored themselves with meter-deep cleats and sliced deep into the skin of the beast, clamped onto, pulled up and peeled back flubbery layers of thick unwieldy flesh. Oily grease oozed and dripped from every cut. Steam still rose from the dark red soup beneath. Even through the breathers, it made my eyes water. It was probably worse for the humans; they didn't know what they were smelling.

The rollagon had a crane on the back. The operator unfolded its arms. They screeched against the cold. The grappling arm swung out and the grapple came down. Someone behind me pushed it into place, and it automatically grabbed onto the handles on the back of my exo-skeleton. This was why I had been brought here. Remote videos don't give you the smell and the taste and the… the song of the beast. I was the only one who could interpret that part for the humans.

Foreman's voice in my memory. "What are you feeling, Jim?"

My answer. "Too much to assimilate, conceptualize, catalog. When you ask me what I'm feeling, I stop feeling. When I think about what I'm feeling, I'm feeling my thinking, not my feeling."

Foreman's face, posture. A nod. He understood the dilemma. Nevertheless….

The machine lifted me up. *Deus ex machina.* The god of the machine. The ancient Greek theatre. The machine was a huge lever, it served as a crane. The god sat in the basket, the stagehands pushed down on their end, raising the god up in the air, swinging him out and forward, over the top of the theatre and then down again to the front of the stage. The god in the machine comes down to Earth to save the mortal humans from the disaster they have made of their lives.

A gust of cold wind came up suddenly, catching me and pushing me sideways. The crane flew me out over the smoky pit. Literary allusions rose around me. I

swung like a pendulum. I waited for the movement to still. Five million years of alien biology moshed beneath me. Of course the humans were puzzled and confused. Inside the enterprise fish, they expected to find organs—not organisms. A convention. Wet and pulpy. Churning. Rhythmic pulses, a biological tuning fork, slow and steady. And other things—large and impenetrable, small and squirming. Things that moved between the other things, dark things and darker things. Things that slithered like snakes, winding in and out. Things that swam like ambiguous millipedes. Things that crept and crawled and pulled themselves between. Bacteria upon the backs of the mites which lived in the shells of the lice that crawled through the fur of the bats that fed on the insects that sucked out the blood of the rats and the voles—all of it roiled and boiled in biologic soup. Crabs lurked under the boulders of flesh. Flounders slipped and slid between the shelves of tissue. Tiny gnats floated in the fetid stink, silvery guppies twinkled in the blood; larger fish leapt and darted; eels wound within. And larger things as well, darker shapes, unidentifiable; things for which there were no earthy analogs. Things that snatched like sharks, with sudden vicious movements; and other things that simply moved and sifted.

Everything within the flesh of the fish was its own self—and yet, all of it was interconnected by pink spiderwebs that drifted and parted and reformed with every ebb and flow of the beast's internal tides. The red and purple fur, colorless in the darkness; neurons floating, touching, attaching; then, pushed by circumstance, breaking, moving on, forming new patterns of attachment and connection, thought and awareness. A shifting consciousness, a movable identity, a transportable selfness, sliding around in and in and under and through a hundred million living things, each of which had its own feelers and antennae and ways to connect with the synapses of the web, sharing itself and being shared, contributing its fragmentary awareness and accepting as much as it could of the flood of noise and information all around it, an endless sea of noise and confusion, somehow making enough sense of itself to cooperate in a larger purpose that emerged silently from the collective urges of life. All these separate creatures and creations, all of them, they were all aware of each other, simultaneous existence for every living thing. Eat and be eaten. The eaters enjoyed not only the taste of the flesh they bit into, they experienced the intense rush of sensation that the meal felt as the eater's teeth sank in. Life lives on life. Everything eats everything else. And the only difference between humanity and the Chtorr is that the Chtorr experienced itself feeding on itself. A gigantic self-devouring meal. This was the Chtorr, in all of its astonishing *allness.*

They lowered me into the pit. The walls of rubbery flesh rose around me. Almost down to the surface of the swarming goo. A voice shouted something and the cables yanked to a stop. This was as low as someone deemed safe. They didn't want to drop me. They didn't want to lose me. If I fell in, or even if I went too deep, they feared I would be overwhelmed and relapse into a babbling psychedelic psychotic psychopath again. If I still had a sense of humor—if I still had enough humanity left inside me to have a sense of humor—I would reach down and grab one of those crawly things. I'd take a big fat bite out of it and announce that it needs salt. But I knew it didn't. The interior of the enterprise fish was almost twice as salty as the sea it swam in. Another indicator of the extreme age of the ocean it

had evolved in, somewhere else, someplace lost in the gray memories of time. How long had it taken to find its way here?

Here, only an arm's length above the soup, I swung precariously. I shifted my position. The exoskeleton accommodated and I leaned forward, arms and legs spread wide apart, as if I was sailing over a gloppy red landscape. It bubbled and stank like a sulfurous mud pit. I closed my eyes and tasted. I listened. I floated. I shared. I went—

There is no human word.

It looks like unconsciousness, but it isn't. It feels like non-consciousness, but it isn't. You could call it all-consciousness, but it isn't. It's all of that and none of it. It's like letting go and melting, all the pieces of self flying outward, sliding out across the surfaces of awareness and identity and attaching, connecting, becoming aware of a larger selfness that moves and feels and bleeds and eats and excretes as a process that processes itself—and against that background the self rides, floats, flies, moves, contracts, expands, exists, and becomes its own small part of the allness— all in the middle of the sea of noise, the endless drone of living things shouting, "Here I am!" except there is no *here,* and there is no *I,* and most profound of all, there is no *is.* Is-ness is an illusion. There is no permanence. The verb "to be" creates the illusion that this condition exists as an inherent element of the subject. But no, there is no permanence and existence is a shared delusion that we pass onto the next set of delusionaries before we pass on ourselves. And like the endless pink webs, they form and reform the narrative in their own images, their own reformatory dormitory, and there we all are, sleeping with the wishes.

If I still had a sense of humor, I would laugh. Not because it's funny, but because it isn't. What's funny is that we think it is.

And all the while... I smelled the song of the fish. I smelled the things within and all their separate songs, as many as I could feel. I tasted the flavors of the processes of the beast and the humans left me hanging there, lost in the symphonies of infestation.

The enterprise fish is not a fish. It swims in the ocean and it grows. It eats and it grows. But it is not a fish, it never was. It is a Chtorran worm, a gastropede. A gastropede is a slug. It doesn't get very big. Maybe the size of a bus. When it gets too big, it can't support its own weight. It can't eat enough to feed its own volume. Its organs begin to die. And the creatures inside of it, the symbiotes, the partners, they feed on the dying organs and take over the jobs. As the heart of the slug slows down, the pump-muscle slugs around the blood vessels take over the job, feeding themselves from the bloodstream and paying for it by pulsing. When the slug's lungs are unable to extract enough oxygen from the air, they begin to die and other creatures take over the job. Eventually, there is no worm; only a partnership, a symbiotic symphony, a convention. A self-sustaining biological society. And so the slug continues to grow and expand, adding new partners to the process until the process itself outgrows its ability to expand and sustain. And then—it collapses into smaller processes, comes apart and becomes the next stage of its existence. Not death. Just the next phase of life churning life to spread more life.

In the ocean—the slug becomes an island. Its mouth becomes a maw, a collection of many mouths. It drifts, turning itself into the current and sweeping all before it, sifting the sea for sustenance. Within its flesh, countless new organisms take root and thrive and grow and take on the responsibilities of partnership. Within the flesh of the beast are nations. Life is hungry, life expands. The islands grow, they rise, they fall. Sometimes the enterprise fish develops deep chasms where the flesh splits apart, torn by the strains of its own internal tectonics. The beast fissions and fragments, leaving in its wake the bloody flesh of many smaller islands. But sometimes, before that happens, the current carries it to shore, beaching it on the hot sands of Baja or the glimmering rocks of Vancouver Island or snagging and catching it on the oily rigs of Prudhoe Bay.

The fish are named like storms. Albert and Betty and Chad and Debra. Edward and Fanny. Gabriel and Harriett. Isadore and June. Most of the older fish, all the way up to Fanny, had long since grown so big they couldn't survive. They'd broken up and become Karl and Lena, Max and Nora, Oscar and Patty, Quinn and Ruth. We stood on the back of Solly. Solly was beached and breaking up. Not dying, just changing. Enterprise fish don't die; conventions end, form and reform, just like the endless webs of pink fur spiderweb silken strands that ebb and flow within the beast, within each creature in the beast, within the flesh of every living thing the Chtorr can touch. I am, therefore I think.

There were great pink whales in the sea. Humpbacks and blues and sperms. Earthbeasts with Chtorran fur. Solly had followed them northward, deep into the arctic, and beached himself on the broken shores of Norway's coldest coast, where rocks and sea and glaciers argued for supremacy, an endless battle of weather and erosion, the waves turned pink with bloody froth. The air stank with bubbling noises gurgling from the pit, the things within cried and whimpered and gibbered and sang. All their needs and desires. It rose up toward the darkening sky. The stench could be tasted a hundred klicks downwind.

And then the cables yanked and I rose away from the multitudes below. Neither relieved nor regretful. The moment was over and I detached. I floated. The senses took census. The sense of me. No sense at all. The allness collapsed with distance.

They lowered me to the icy back of the beast. General Anderson took my gloved hands in his. The illusion of intimacy. He focused his goggles on mine. The illusion of eye contact. He spoke softly. "What did you taste?"

I took a moment to assimilate, to catalog and conceptualize. "It's not dead. It's not dying. It's doing what it's supposed to do."

Anderson knew enough to wait.

I said, "It's an incubator. Just like the nests under the shambler groves are incubators—the enterprise fish are gigantic factories. They're a big warm safe place for all the different pieces of the ecology to assemble themselves. It swims in the ocean, it gathers nutrients, it feeds itself and all of its pieces; and inside, everything churns around, forming whatever sustainable relationships it can. And then… eventually, it bumps into a continent. It's inevitable. It's *supposed* to beach itself. That's what it's designed to do. And when it does, it doesn't die, it just falls apart. And then all the separate pieces of itself turn into whatever they turn into. Some go back into the sea. Some root themselves on the shore. Others will eventually eat their way out and go hungrily exploring. The job of the enterprise fish is to deliver a massive biomass to the land surface. That's its job—one of its jobs. But where there is land, it delivers itself and its passengers to shore. If there's no land, it becomes land. Imagine an ocean full of these things. The Chtorr is de-

signed, adapted, evolved—choose your own word—to find a way to thrive no matter where its seeds land. Humans have never really appreciated the scale of this thing."

Anderson nodded. "We know that. You've said it before. A thousand different ways already. Some of us are starting to get it."

"If I don't repeat it, you forget it. It's the way your brains work. You don't know how to recognize when you don't know that you don't know. You insist on translating it, running it through your filters of what you do know, thinking that because one part of the universe works one way, so does another. Well, it doesn't. Welcome to Chtorr."

Anderson leaned in close and switched to the private channel. "McCarthy? Remember how you and I made an agreement? That I was supposed to tell you when you were acting like an arrogant jerk? More than usual, I mean? Well, this is one of those times." He poked me in the chest with the flat of his hand—more than once. He backed me away from the others. Around the corner of the rollagon. I shut up and let him dump his anger. I could wait. It wasn't my anger. To him, I must have appeared impassive.

"Yes, I know what you've been through and I know the effect it's had on you. I'm your baby-sitter. But I knew you before and you were an arrogant jerk then. So I have some sense how much of this is the Chtorr and how much is you using the Chtorr as a justification for being an ass. We put up with it because you're useful, but frankly, it's getting old. It's beyond disrespect. Now, it's just a frigging waste of time. You acting like you're some kind of superior and enlightened being is just you hiding from the real truth."

"And what truth is that?"

"You figure it out," said Anderson. "If

you're so superior and enlightened, that shouldn't be a problem. You should have already seen it. Now—" He took a breath, straightened and became General Anderson again. "Just answer the question we brought you here to answer. Will it work? Can we neutralize this thing?"

I considered it. Had already been considering it since I first started tasting the stink of the beast fifty klicks downwind. "No," I said.

Anderson didn't react. "Why not?"

"I already told you. I told you before we came. I've told you repeatedly. This is not a single creature. If it were, you could kill it easily. Its size would be its vulnerability. But you'd still end up with a couple of square kilometers of dead Chtorran flesh. And that's a much bigger problem, because dead Chtorran flesh is a place where Chtorran decomposition occurs. Decomposition isn't destruction, it's simply a biological transformation of life from one state into another. A dead Chtorran—of any kind—is simply a place for a different set of Chtorran creatures to grow and in their turn become food for more Chtorran creatures and ultimately it's all just more Chtorran flesh. Stop thinking of it as a creature, or even as a set of creatures, and see it as a much larger process. The whole ecological system functions as a process for turning local biomass into Chtorran biomass, whether any specific part of it is composing or decomposing."

Anderson was clearly annoyed. Annoyed at the distraction, annoyed at the conversational tangent. Annoyed that he couldn't get a clean and simple answer. And at the same time, annoyed at his own curiosity. "So if you already knew what you would find, why did you come?"

"I came to find what I didn't know that I would find."

"And—?"

"It's not all Chtorran down there."

"Eh?"

"There are Terran creatures living in that soup. I smelled flounders, crabs, dartfish, possibly even some Atlantic cod."

"Are you sure?"

"You've sunk cameras into the beast. You have thousands of hours of video. But you and your boffins have assumed that everything you see is Chtorran. It isn't. The Chtorran ecology is opportunistic. It assimilates everything it touches. Like polar bears. Like me. What you're seeing in that soup—that's the Chtorran ecology learning how to use what's already here. Life on Earth is already adapted to survival on Earth. The Chtorr is willing to adopt and adapt and take on new tenants, new partners. The convention is open to anything that can contribute something. When you finish analyzing all the video, it'll be obvious. The Chtorr is caretaking as much Terran biomass as it can manage. We saw that in the Amazon. It's just the fastest and easiest way for it to grow."

I could tell by his posture. He understood. This was another way to lose the war.

"Stop thinking of this as a war," I said. "That's why you're losing."

He shook it off. It wasn't that he didn't hear it. He didn't want to hear it. Not yet. He still wasn't ready to understand.

"All right." He came back to the present. "Can we neutralize it?" He nodded past the rollagon toward the drill site. He already knew the answer. But he needed to hear it from me. He'd appointed me the expert. I was the justification that took him off the hook.

I spoke slowly. Not for him. For the microphones. For the log. "Pumping poison into this thing, pumping radioactives into it—that will disrupt the process locally.

For a while. But you'll also end up poisoning the local environment, both land and sea, for most Earth species as well. So you don't gain anything. The Chtorran species will re-seed the area faster than Terran ones."

"What about fire?"

"You already know the answer. You don't have enough men or machines, and you don't have enough phosphorus or a reliable way to deliver it. And even if you could pump this thing full of inflammables, you'd have to keep burning it for a month or two, and even then, at least ten percent of its biomass would escape into the air or back into the sea. The cost-per-payoff ratio doesn't work."

"So we're back to the nuclear option?"

I nodded agreement. "The spread of devices your men are planting in this thing will certainly vaporize the beast." I waited for him to ask the next question.

"Will it work?"

I raised my gaze beyond. I looked outward. Past the edges of the grayish-pink landscape that we stood upon were endless fields of broken ice. I thought about the furies he wanted to unleash, how far the nuclear fires would scour down to the bedrock. It wasn't a rational analysis as much as it was a visceral one. He already had the projections. Turning back to him, I gave him half the answer he wanted to hear. "Considering this circumstance—yes, it will work. It will buy you time. But only here. This is a local solution, not a general one."

"That's good enough for the moment," he muttered unhappily. He looked across at me. Even through the goggles, I could read his bitter expression. "The folks at home need something to feel good about. If nothing else—" He trailed off. "Well, if nothing else, this will be good for morale."

"Yes," I repeated. "If nothing else." We both knew it was insufficient.

We came back around the rear of the rollagon, back to the drilling site, where Dale Hale Barksdale the Third was just rising up into the air. He saw us and waved. The motion caused him to swing in the wind.

"What the hell are you doing?" Anderson shouted angrily.

"What I came out here to do—get a first-hand look." He waved to the crane operator, motioning himself forward.

"Belay that!" ordered Anderson.

"Sorry, General," came the reply. "I'm a civilian contractor. I work for Barksdale Industrials." The crane turned and Barksdale swung out over the gaping hole in the Chtorran landscape. Barksdale motioned downward and the cables screeched. He sank down into the steaming wound.

Anderson's posture shifted, stiffened. This was not going to have a happy outcome. He touched the keypad on the back of his forearm, cycling through camera angles until his goggles showed him the close-up view of Barksdale's descent. I clicked up two separate angles myself—a close-up view to my left-eye, a wider angle through my right.

"It stinks down here," Barksdale called up.

"Don't touch anything," Anderson ordered.

"Why not?" Barksdale was already reaching as far down as he could, as if he wanted to palpate the Chtorran flesh. Perhaps he wanted to brag when he got back home. "Yes, I've touched the inside of an enterprise fish."

Before Anderson could answer Barksdale's question, his fingers brushed the dark purple skin of something that looked like a giant liver. Wet and pulpy. It rippled. Barksdale giggled. And touched it again. This time it shuddered. He touched it a third time; this time, he punched it.

That was Barksdale's mistake.

The dark purple thing, whatever it was, it whipped around faster than it should have been able to—it opened itself as if it were all mouth, rose up and up and up, faster than the cables could turn, faster than the crane could lift—it came up high and higher, stretching and reaching to swallow Barksdale like a great white shark coming up beneath a hapless seal. It enveloped him completely. He was gone. For a moment, the liver-beast hung there on the cables, a purple pulpy shapeless mass, dripping ooze and gore down its sides, a bloody black rain of bile and skittering little things that had been pulled up with it. And then, with a terrible wet gurgling sound, it slid back down the cable, all the way back down into the churning squirming soup of things below the skin. The cable swung back and forth, empty. The grapples hung broken and apart.

"Well," I said, finally. "He was right. It's not all bad news."

General Anderson ignored the growing uproar in front of us and stared at me, astonished. "Now that's the McCarthy we used to know and love." • • •

DAVID GERROLD began his writing career with the sale, while still in college, of "The Trouble with Tribbles," one of the best-loved episodes of the original Star Trek *series. He originated the story that became "The Cloudminders," wrote two episodes of the animated series, and penned two* Star Trek *novels. He worked on the early episodes of* Star Trek: The Next Generation, *which utilized a number of suggestions he had made in his non-fiction book* The World of Star Trek. *Recently, he co-wrote and directed "Blood and Fire," a two-part episode of* Star Trek: Phase II *based on his unproduced* Next Generation *script. At press time, Part I is available online.*

He was story editor for the first season of the original Land of the Lost, *one of the best-written Saturday morning shows. A film based on his semi-autobiographical novel,* The Martian Child, *came out in 2007.*

He won a Hugo award for the novel The Man Who Folded Himself. *"Enterprise Fish" is an excerpt from the upcoming novel* A Time for Treason, *the projected sixth volume in the* War Against the Chtorr *series of novels.*

42-YEAR-OLD LUNAR IMAGE RESTORED

MOFFETT FIELD, Calif.—NASA released a newly restored 42-year-old image of Earth. The Lunar Orbiter 1 spacecraft took the iconic photograph of Earth rising above the lunar surface in 1966. Using refurbished machinery and modern digital technology, NASA produced the image at a much higher resolution than was possible when it was originally taken. The data may help the next generation of explorers as NASA prepares to return to the moon.

The Lunar Orbiter Image Recovery Project, located at NASA's Ames Research Center at Moffett Field, Calif., is taking analog data from 1,500 of the original tapes, converting the data into digital form, and reconstructing the images. The restored image confirms data from the original tapes can be retrieved from the newly-restored tape drives from the 1960s.

"It's a tremendous feeling to restore a 40-year-old image and know it can be useful to future explorers," said Gregory Schmidt, deputy director of the NASA Lunar Science Institute at Ames.

NASA will launch the Lunar Reconnaissance Orbiter in 2009 to map the moon's surface. The restoration of the Lunar Orbiter images to high quality images will provide the scientific community with a baseline to measure and understand changes that have occurred on the moon since the 1960s.

—from NASA press release, Nov. 13, 2008

LiFE HUTCH

BY HARLAN ELLiSON®

Illustrated by Ed Emshwiller

18

errence slid his right hand, the one out of sight of the robot, up his side. The razoring pain of the three broken ribs caused his eyes to widen momentarily in pain. Then he recovered himself and closed them till he was studying the machine through narrow slits.

If the eyeballs click, I'm dead, thought Terrence.

The intricate murmurings of the life hutch around him brought back the immediacy of his situation. His eyes again fastened on the medicine cabinet clamped to the wall next to the robot's duty-niche.

Cliché. So near yet so far. It could be all the way back on Antares-Base for all the good it's doing me, he thought, and a crazy laugh rang through his head. He caught himself just in time. *Easy! Three days is a nightmare, but cracking up will only make it end sooner.* That was the last thing he wanted. But it couldn't go on much longer.

He flexed the fingers of his right hand. It was all he *could* move. Silently he damned the technician who had passed the robot through. Or the politician who had let inferior robots get placed in the life hutches so he could get a rake-off from the government contract. Or the repairman who hadn't bothered checking closely his last time around. All of them; he damned them all.

They deserved it.

He was dying.

His death had started before he had reached the life hutch. Terrence had begun to die when he had gone into the battle.

He let his eyes close completely, let the sounds of the life hutch fade from around him. Slowly, the sound of the coolants hush-hushing through the wall-pipes, the relay machines feeding their messages without pause from all over the galaxy, the whirring of the antenna's standard, turning in its socket atop the bubble, slowly they melted into silence. He had resorted to blocking himself off from reality many times during the past three days. It was either that or existing with the robot watching, and eventually he would have had to move. To move was to die. It was that simple.

He closed his ears to the whisperings of the life hutch; he listened to the whisperings within himself.

"Good God! There must be a million of them!"

It was the voice of the squadron leader, Resnick, ringing in his suit intercom.

"What kind of battle formation is *that* supposed to be?" came another voice. Terrence looked at the radar screen, at the flickering dots signifying Kyben ships.

"Who can tell with those toadstool-shaped ships of theirs," Resnick answered. "But remember, the whole front umbrella-part is studded with cannon, and it has a helluva range of fire. Okay, watch yourselves, good luck—and give 'em Hell!"

The fleet dove straight for the Kyben armada.

To his mind came the sounds of war, across the gulf of space. It was all imagination; in that tomb there was no sound. Yet he could clearly detect the hiss of his scout's blaster as it poured beam after beam into the lead ship of the Kyben fleet.

His sniper-class scout had been near the point of that deadly Terran phalanx, driving like a wedge at the alien ships, con-

Originally appeared in If, *April 1956.*

Story copyright © 1956 by Harlan Ellison. Renewed, 1984 by The Kilimanjaro Corporation. Reprinted by arrangement with, and permission of, the Author and the Author's agent, Richard Curtis Associates, Inc., New York. All rights reserved. Harlan Ellison is a registered trademark of The Kilimanjaro Corporation. Illustration copyright © 1956 Ed Emshwiller. Used by permission of Carol Emshwiller.

verging on them in loose battle-formation. It was then it had happened.

One moment he had been heading into the middle of the battle, the left flank of the giant Kyben dreadnaught turning crimson under the impact of his firepower.

The next moment, he had skittered out of the formation which had slowed to let the Kyben craft overshoot, while the Earthmen decelerated to pick up maneuverability.

He had gone on at the old level and velocity, directly into the forward guns of a toadstool-shaped Kyben destroyer.

The first beam had burned the gunmounts and directional equipment off the front of the ship, scorching down the aft side in a smear like oxidized chrome plate. He had managed to avoid the second beam.

His radio contact had been brief; he was going to make it back to Antares-Base if he could. If not, the formation would be listening for his homing-beam from a life hutch on whatever planetoid he might find for a crash-landing.

Which was what he had done. The charts had said the pebble spinning there was technically 1-333, 2-A, M & S, 3-804.39#, which would have meant nothing but three-dimensional coordinates had not the small # after the data indicated a life hutch somewhere on its surface.

His distaste for being knocked out of the fighting, being forced onto one of the life hutch planetoids, had been offset only by his fear of running out of fuel before he could locate himself. Of eventually drifting off into space somewhere, to wind up, finally, as an artificial satellite around some minor sun.

The ship pancaked in under minimal reverse drive, bounced high twice and caromed ten times, tearing out chunks of the rear section, but had come to rest a scant two miles from the life hutch, jammed into the rocks.

Terrence had high-leaped the two miles across the empty, airless planetoid to the hermetically sealed bubble in the rocks. His primary wish was to set the hutch's beacon signal so his returning fleet could track him.

He had let himself into the decompression chamber, palmed the switch through his thick spacesuit glove, and finally removed his helmet as he heard the air whistle into the chamber.

He had pulled off his gloves, opened the inner door and entered the life hutch itself.

God bless you, little life hutch, Terrence had thought as he dropped the helmet and gloves. He had glanced around, noting the relay machines picking up messages from outside, sorting them, vectoring them off in other directions. He had seen the medicine chest clamped onto the wall; the refrigerator, he knew, would be well-stocked if a previous tenant hadn't been there before the stockman could refill it. He had seen the all-purpose robot, immobile in its duty-niche. And the wall-chronometer, its face smashed. All of it in a second's glance.

God bless, too, the gentlemen who thought up the idea of these little rescue stations, stuck all over the place for just such emergencies as this. He had started to walk across the room.

It was at this point that the service robot, that kept the place in repair between tenants and unloaded supplies from the ships, had moved clankingly across the floor, and with one fearful smash of a steel arm thrown Terrence across the room.

The spaceman had been brought up short against the steel bulkhead, pain blossoming in his back, his side, his arms and legs. The machine's blow had instantly broken three of his ribs. He lay there for a moment, unable to move. For a few seconds he was too stunned to breathe, and it had been that, certainly, that had saved his life. His pain had immobilized him, and in that short space of time the robot had retreated with a muted internal clash of gears.

He had attempted to sit up straight, and the robot had hummed oddly and begun to move. He had stopped the movement. The robot had settled back.

Twice more had convinced him his position was as bad as he had thought.

The robot had worn down somewhere in its printed circuits. Its commands to lift had been erased or distorted so that now it was conditioned to smash, to hit, anything that moved.

He had seen the clock. He realized he should have suspected something was wrong when he saw its smashed face. Of course! The digital dials had moved, the robot had smashed the clock. Terrence had moved, the robot had smashed him.

And would again, if he moved again.

But for the unnoticeable movement of his eyelids, he had not moved in three days.

He had tried moving toward the decompression lock, stopping when the robot advanced and letting it settle back, then moving again, a little nearer. But the idea died with his first movement. His ribs were too painful. The pain was terrible. He was locked in one position, an uncomfortable, twisted position, and he would be there till the stalemate ended, one way or the other.

H e was suddenly alert again. The reliving of his last three days brought back reality sharply.

He was twelve feet away from the communications panel, twelve feet away from the beacon that would guide his rescuers to him. Before he died of his wounds, before he starved to death, before the robot crushed him. It could have been twelve light-years, for all the nearer he could get to it.

What had gone wrong with the robot? Time to think was cheap. The robot could detect movement, but thinking was still possible. Not that it could help, but it was possible.

The companies that supplied the life hutch's needs were all government contracted. Somewhere along the line someone had thrown in impure steel or calibrated the circuit-cutting machines for a less expensive job. Somewhere along the line someone had not run the robot through its paces correctly. Somewhere along the line someone had committed murder.

He opened his eyes again. Only the barest fraction of opening. Any more and the robot would sense the movement of his eyelids. That would be fatal.

He looked at the machine.

It was not, strictly speaking, a robot. It was merely a remote-controlled hunk of jointed steel, invaluable for making beds, stacking steel plating, watching culture dishes, unloading spaceships and sucking dirt from rugs. The robot body, roughly humanoid, but without what would have been a head on a human, was merely an appendage.

The real brain, a complex maze of plastic screens and printed circuits, was behind the wall. It would have been too dangerous to install those delicate parts in a heavy-duty mechanism. It was all too easy for the robot to drop itself from a loading shaft, or be hit by a meteorite, or get caught under a wrecked spaceship. So there were sensitive units in the robot appendage that "saw" and "heard" what was going on, and relayed them to the brain—behind the wall.

And somewhere along the line that

brain had worn grooves too deeply into its circuits. It was now mad. Not mad in any way a human being might go mad, for there were an infinite number of ways a machine could go insane. Just mad enough to kill Terrence.

Even if I could hit the robot with something, it wouldn't stop the thing. He could, perhaps, throw something at the machine before it could get to him, but it would do no good. The robot brain would still be intact, and the appendage would continue to function. It was hopeless.

He stared at the massive, blocky hands of the robot. It seemed he could see his own blood on the jointed work-tool fingers of one hand. He knew it must be his imagination, but the idea persisted. He flexed the fingers of his hidden hand.

Three days had left him weak and dizzy from hunger. His head was light and his eyes burned steadily. He had been lying in his own filth till he no longer noticed the discomfort. His side ached and throbbed, and the pain of a blast furnace roared through him every time he breathed.

He thanked God his spacesuit was still on, lest the movement of his breathing bring the robot down on him. There was only one solution, and that solution was his death. He was almost delirious.

Several times during the past day—as well as he could gauge night and day without a clock or a sunrise—he had heard the roar of the fleet landing outside. Then he had realized there was no sound in dead space. Then he had realized they were all inside the relay machines, coming through subspace right into the life hutch. Then he had realized that such a thing was not possible. Then he had come to his senses and realized all that had gone before was hallucination.

Then he had awakened and known it *was* real. He *was* trapped, and there was no way out. Death had come to live with him. He was going to die.

Terrence had never been a coward, nor had he been a hero. He was one of the men who fight wars because they are always fought by *some*one. He was the kind of man who would allow himself to be torn from wife and home and flung into an abyss they called Space to defend what he had been told needed defense. But it was in moments like this that a man like Terrence began to think.

Why here? Why like this? What have I done that I should finish in a filthy space-suit on a lost rock—and not gloriously like they said in the papers back home, but starving or bleeding to death alone with a crazy robot? Why me? Why me? Why alone?

He knew there could be no answers. He expected no answers.

He was not disappointed.

When he awoke, he instinctively looked at the clock. Its shattered face looked back at him, jarring him, forcing his eyes open in after-sleep terror. The robot hummed and emitted a spark. He kept his eyes open. The humming ceased. His eyes began to burn. He knew he couldn't keep them open too long.

The burning worked its way to the front of his eyes, from the top and bottom, bringing with it tears. It felt as though someone was shoving needles into the corners. The tears ran down over his cheeks.

His eyes snapped shut. The roaring grew in his ears. The robot didn't make a sound.

Could it be inoperative? Could it have worn down to immobility? Could he take the chance of experimenting?

He slid down to a more comfortable position. The robot charged forward the instant he moved. He froze in mid-movement, his heart a chunk of ice. The robot stopped, confused, a scant ten inches from his outstretched foot. The machine hummed to itself, the noise of it coming both from the machine in front of him and from somewhere behind the wall.

He was suddenly alert.

If it had been working correctly, there would have been little or no sound from the appendage, and none whatsoever from the brain. But it was *not* working properly, and the sound of its thinking was distinct.

The robot rolled backward, its "eyes" still toward Terrence. The sense orbs of the machine were in the torso, giving the machine the look of a squat metal gargoyle, squared and deadly.

The humming was growing louder, every now and then a sharp *pfffft!* of sparks mixed with it. Terrence had a moment's horror at the thought of a short-circuit, a fire in the life hutch, and no service robot to put it out.

He listened carefully, trying to pinpoint the location of the robot's brain built into the wall.

Then he thought he had it. Or was it there? It was either in the wall behind a bulkhead next to the refrigerator, or behind a bulkhead near the relay machines. The two possible housings were within a few feet of each other, but they might make a great deal of difference.

The distortion created by the steel plate in front of the brain, and the distracting background noise of the robot broadcasting it made it difficult to tell exactly which was the correct location.

He drew a deep breath.

The ribs slid a fraction of an inch together, their broken ends grinding.

He moaned.

A high-pitched tortured moan that died quickly, but throbbed back and forth inside his head, echoing and building itself into a paean of sheer agony! It forced his tongue out of his mouth, limp in a corner of his lips, moving slightly. The robot rolled forward. He drew his tongue in, clamped his mouth shut, cut off the scream inside his head at its high point!

The robot stopped, rolled back to its duty-niche.

Oh, God! The pain! The God God where are you pain!

Beads of sweat broke out on his body. He could feel their tickle inside his spacesuit, inside his jumper, inside the bodyshirt, on his skin. The pain of the ribs was suddenly heightened by an irresistible itching of his skin.

He moved infinitesimally within the suit, his outer appearance giving no indication of the movement. The itching did not subside. The more he tried to make it stop, the more he thought about not thinking about it, the worse it became. His armpits, the crooks of his arms, his thighs where the tight service-pants clung—suddenly too tightly—were madness. He had to scratch!

He almost started to make the movement. He stopped before he started. He knew he would never live to enjoy any relief. A laugh bubbled into his head. *God Almighty, and I always laughed at the slobs who suffered with the seven-year itch, the ones who always did a little dance when they were at attention during inspection, the ones who could scratch and sigh contentedly. God, how I envy them.* His thoughts were taking on a wild sound, even to him.

The prickling did not stop. He twisted faintly. It got worse. He took another deep breath.

The ribs sandpapered again.

This time, blessedly, he fainted from the pain.

"**W**ell, Terrence, how do you like your first look at a Kyben?"

Ernie Terrence wrinkled his forehead and ran a finger up the side of his face. He looked at his Commander and shrugged. "Fantastic things, aren't they?"

"Why fantastic?"

"Because they're just like us. Except, of course, the bright yellow pigmentation and the tentacle-fingers. Other than that they're identical to a human being."

The Commander opaqued the examination-casket and drew a cigarette from a silver case, offering the Lieutenant one. He puffed it alight, staring with one eye closed against the smoke. "More than that, I'm afraid. Their insides look like someone had taken them out, liberally mixed them with spare parts from several other species, and jammed them back in any way that fitted conveniently. For the next twenty years we'll be knocking our heads together trying to figure out their metabolic *raison d'être.*"

Terrence grunted, rolling his unlit cigarette absently between two fingers. "That's the least of it."

"You're right," agreed the Commander. "For the next *thousand* years we'll be trying to figure out how they think, why they fight, what it takes to get along with them, what motivates them."

If they let us live that long, thought Terrence.

"Why are we at war with the Kyben?" he asked the older man. "I mean really."

"Because the Kyben want to kill every human being they can recognize as a human being."

"What have they got against us?"

"Does it matter? Maybe it's because our skin isn't bright yellow; maybe it's because our fingers aren't silken and flexible; maybe it's because our cities are too noisy for them. Maybe a lot of maybes. But it doesn't matter. Survival never matters until you have to survive."

Terrence nodded. He understood. So did the Kyben. It grinned at him and drew its blaster. It fired point-blank, crimsoning the hull of the Kyben ship.

He swerved to avoid running into his gun's own backlash. The movement of the bucket seat sliding in its tracks, keeping his vision steady while maneuvering, made him dizzy. He closed his eyes for a moment.

When he opened them, the abyss was nearer, and he teetered, his lips whitening as they pressed together under his effort to steady himself. With a headlong gasp he fell sighing into the stomach. His long, silken fingers jointed steely humming clankingly toward the medicine chest over the plate behind the bulkhead.

The robot advanced on him grindingly. Small, fine bits of metal rubbed together, ashing away into a breeze that came from nowhere as the machine raised lead boots toward his face.

Onward and onward till he had no room to move

and

then

the light came on, bright, brighter than any star Terrence had ever seen, glowing, broiling, flickering, shining, bobbing a ball of light on the chest of the robot, who staggered,

stumbled,

stepped.

The robot hissed, hummed and exploded into a million flying, racing fragments, shooting beams of light all over the abyss over which Terrence again teetered, teetering. He flailed his arms wildly trying to escape but, at the last moment, before

the

fall

he awoke with a start!

He saved himself only by his unconscious. Even in the hell of a nightmare he was aware of the situation. He had not moaned and writhed in his delirium. He had kept motionless and silent.

He knew it was true, because he was still alive.

Only his surprised jerking, as he came back to consciousness, started the monster rolling from its niche. He came fully awake and sat silent, slumped against the wall. The robot retreated.

Thin breath came through his nostrils. Another moment and he would have put an end to the past three days—three days or more now? how long had he been asleep?—days of torture.

He was hungry. Lord, how hungry he was. The pain in his side was worse now, a steady throbbing that made even shallow breathing torturous. He itched maddeningly. He was uncomfortably slouched against a cold steel bulkhead, every rivet having made a burrow for itself in his skin. He wished he was dead.

He didn't wish he was dead. It was all too easy to get his wish.

If he could only disable that robot brain. A total impossibility. If he could only wear Phobos and Deimos for watchfobs. If he could only shack-up with a silicon-deb from Penares. If he could only use his large colon for a lasso.

It would take a thorough destruction of the brain to do it enough damage to stop the appendage before it could roll over and smash Terrence again.

With a steel bulkhead between him and the brain, his chances of success totaled minus zero every time.

He considered which part of his body the robot would smash first. One blow of that tool-hand would kill him if it was used a second time. With the state of his present wounds, even a strong breath might finish him.

Perhaps he could make a break and get through the lock into the decompression chamber...

Worthless. (A) The robot would catch him before he had gotten to his feet, in his present condition. (B) Even allowing a miracle, even if he did get through the lock, the robot would smash the lock port, letting in air, ruining the mechanism. (C) Even allowing a double miracle and it didn't, what the hell good would it do him? His helmet and gloves were in the hutch itself, and there was no place to go on the planetoid. The ship was ruined, so no signal could be sent from there.

Doom suddenly compounded itself.

The more he thought about it, the more certain he was that soon the light would flicker out for him.

The light would flicker out.

The light would flicker...

The light...

...light...?

Oh God, is it possible? Can it be? Have I found an answer? He marveled at the simplicity of it. It had been there for more than three days waiting for him to use it. It was so simple it was magnificent. He could hardly restrain himself from moving, just out of sheer joy.

I'm not brilliant, I'm not a genius, why did this occur to me? For a few minutes the brilliance of the solution staggered him. Would a less intelligent man have solved the problem this easily? Would a *more* intelligent man have done it? Then he remembered the dream. The light in the dream. *He* hadn't solved the problem, his unconscious had. The answer had been there all the time, but he was too close to see it. His mind had been forced to devise a way to tell him. Luckily, it had.

And finally, he didn't care *how* he had uncovered it. His God, if he had had anything to do with it, had heard him. Terrence was by no means a religious man, but this was miracle enough to make him a believer. It wasn't over yet, but the answer was there—and it *was* an answer.

He began to save himself.

Slowly, achingly slowly, he moved his right hand, the hand away from the robot's sight, to his belt. On the belt hung the assorted implements a spaceman needs at any moment in his ship. A wrench. A packet of sleep-stayers. A compass. A geiger counter. A flashlight.

The last was the miracle. Miracle in a tube.

He fingered it almost reverently, then unclipped it in a moment's frenzy, still immobile to the robot's "eyes."

He held it at his side, away from his body by a fraction of an inch, pointing up over the bulge of his spacesuited leg.

If the robot looked at him, all it would see would be the motionless bulk of his leg, blocking off any movement on his part. To the machine, he was inert. Motionless.

Now, he thought wildly, *where is the brain?*

If it is behind the relay machines, I'm still dead. If it is near the refrigerator, I'm saved. He could afford to take no chances. He would have to move.

He lifted one leg.

The robot moved toward him. The humming and sparking were more distinct this time. He dropped the leg.

Behind the plates above the refrigerator!

The robot stopped, nearly at his side. Seconds had decided. The robot hummed, sparked, and returned to its niche.

Now he knew!

He pressed the button. The invisible beam of the flashlight leaped out, speared the bulkhead above the refrigerator. He pressed the button again and again, the flat circle of light appearing, disappearing, appearing, disappearing on the faceless metal of the life hutch's wall.

The robot sparked and rolled from its niche. It looked once at Terrence. Its rollers changed direction in an instant and the machine ground toward the refrigerator.

The steeled fist swung in a vicious arc, smashing with a deafening *clang!* at the spot where the light bubble flickered on and off.

It swung again and again. Again and again, till the bulkhead had been gouged and crushed and opened, and the delicate coils and plates and circuits and memorex modules behind it were refuse and rubble. Until the robot froze, with arm half-ready to strike again. Dead. Immobile. Brain and appendage.

Even then Terrence did not stop pressing the flashlight button. Wildly he thumbed it again and again and again.

Then he realized it was all over.

The robot was dead. He was alive. He would be saved. He had no doubts about that. *Now* he could cry.

The medicine chest grew large through the shimmering in his eyes. The relay machines smiled at him.

God bless you, little life hutch, he thought, before he fainted. • • •

HARLAN ELLISON® wrote "The City on the Edge of Forever," perennial poll-winner as best episode of the Original Series. The episode won the 1968 Hugo Award for Best Dramatic Presentation. The original script won the Writers Guild Award for Best Dramatic Hour-Long Script. That script, and the story of what happened to it on its way to the airwaves, can be found in Ellison's book, **Harlan Ellison's** *The City on the Edge of Forever:* **The Original Teleplay that Became the Classic** *Star Trek* **Episode.**

Where No Scribe Had Gone Before

*W*hen on September 8, 1966, the NBC network broadcast "The Man Trap" by George Clayton Johnson, the premiere episode of a new series called *Star Trek,* one thing was certain—television would never be the same.

And neither would the literature of science fiction.

From the 1930's through the early 1960's—viewed by many as the Golden Age of published science fiction, and greatly aided in its maturation by the likes of John W. Campbell, Robert A. Heinlein and a host of major writers who came of age creatively during that era—SF promulgated a view of the future that presented a grand, hopeful vision. Despite some dystopian tales (primarily inspired by the Cold War and its threat of nuclear annihilation), the majority of science fiction novels presented a cohesive vision of where humanity was headed. It was almost as if the writers had joined together to create one vast story, in which mankind burst the shackles of matter and energy to build faster-than-light spacecraft that hurled us into the far reaches of space, where we encountered strange alien races, discovered wondrous new planets and had adventures that were daring, imaginative, and fresh.

Humanity, these stories told us, was on the verge of a great undertaking, one that would leave us deeper, grander, better.

A new medium was just being born during this time, one that initially lagged in the promise of its imaginative storytelling far behind that of its print cousin. Dubbed "the boob tube" early in its history, television was often known more for the inanity of its content than its genius.

Throughout the Fifties and Sixties, however, this gradually changed, and, surprisingly, the exact same writers—the big guns of literary science fiction—would prove largely responsible for that change, a fact that has generally gone unrecognized by the popular press.

So let's rectify that, shall we?

When Gene Roddenberry started developing the idea for *Star Trek* in 1964, there was really nothing like it that had gone before. *Space Patrol* and *Tom Corbett, Space Cadet* (the latter inspired by the young adult novel *Space Cadet,* by Robert Heinlein), although popular TV series of the early 1950's (and well acted, written and produced), had both been viewed as strictly kid fare, and not treated seriously by critics nor adult viewers. The film closest in nature to *Star Trek* (and very possibly an inspiration for Roddenberry) was 1956's *Forbidden Planet,* but this was a one-shot and neither sequels nor direct TV adaptations followed its release.

The first science fiction series to gain serious critical attention (not to mention three Emmys and a Peabody award) was Rod Serling's *The Twilight Zone,* which debuted in 1959 and ran for five seasons. Serling was a fan of published science fiction, and he both adapted stories by leading science fiction writers such as Damon Knight and Jerome Bixby and hired noted S.F. writers Ray Bradbury *(Fahrenheit 451, The Martian Chronicles),* Richard Matheson *(I Am Legend, The Shrinking Man),* Charles Beaumont *(The Hunger)*

by Marc Scott Zicree

and George Clayton Johnson *(Logan's Run)* to pen scripts. Jerry Sohl *(Costigan's Needle)* also contributed scripts to the episodes "The New Exhibit" and "Living Doll," ghost-writing under Charles Beaumont's name in 1963, when Beaumont first began suffering symptoms of the presenile dementia that would claim his life in 1967.

The Outer Limits, which debuted in 1963 and ran a season and a half, added to the tradition begun by Serling by hiring Jerry Sohl and adding Harlan Ellison, a talented young newcomer to Hollywood. Ellison had written numerous powerful science fiction short stories, and would contribute two of *Outer Limits'* most powerful episodes, "Soldier" and "Demon with a Glass Hand." (Both time travel stories, they would prove the inspiration for James Cameron's *The Terminator).*

Roddenberry was a friend of Serling's —in fact, he delivered the eulogy at his funeral—and he clearly took inspiration from Serling's lead. From the very beginning, he intended to invite major prose science fiction writers to write scripts for *Star Trek.*

Moreover, he intended to pursue the very worldview (or indeed universe-view) that they had extrapolated in their prose fiction for close to thirty years— that of a grand era of space exploration in which an ever-better humanity would extend its reach to the very edge of the galaxy.

Ray Bradbury recalls being invited by Roddenberry to visit the set when *Star Trek's* first pilot, "The Cage," was being shot. Accompanying him were Beaumont and Matheson. Beaumont would ultimately prove too ill to write for *Star Trek,* but Matheson would contribute an impressive episode, "The Enemy Within," in which Captain Kirk was split into two individuals, one good, one evil.

As for Bradbury, he had to decline. "I've never been able to write other people's material," he explains. "The one exception was [John Huston's] *Moby Dick,* but it took me nine months to turn myself into Herman Melville."

Other science fiction writers considered but not ultimately utilized included A.E. Van Vogt (whose *The Voyage of the Space Beagle* was a formative influence on *Star Trek),* Phillip José Farmer *(Riverworld)* and William F. Nolan (co-writer of *Logan's Run).* (Farmer later adapted his two *Trek* submissions, "The Shadow of Space" and "Sketches Among the Ruins of My Mind," into free-standing novelettes.)

In hiring such noted visionaries, Roddenberry's goal was clear—to create episodes of *Star Trek* unlike anything that had been seen before: brash, thought-provoking, revolutionary. What emerged was a first season that was truly breathtaking in its scope and originality.

With "The Man Trap," George Clayton Johnson revisited a theme he had first explored with *Twilight Zone's* "The Four of Us Are Dying"—the notion of someone being able to change their appearance to imitate others. But "The Man Trap" added a fresh idea, examining the extinction of a species. In this case, Dr. McCoy, at the urging of Mr. Spock, phasers the last of a sentient race of shape-shifters out of existence (a tad curious on reflection, when all they had to do to end its killing spree was give it table salt, as the creature itself requested).

Jerry Sohl penned "The Corbomite Maneuver," in which our perception of a— theoretically—enemy alien race is put into question. And Theodore Sturgeon, unquestionably the greatest prose stylist to ever come out of the science fiction genre, scripted the delightful "Shore Leave," in which the *Enterprise* crew encountered a planetary port of call capable of reading their minds and conjuring up everything from a samurai warrior to a six-foot-tall white rabbit in a waistcoat.

Sturgeon—who was long fascinated by issues of sexuality, human and otherwise—would go on in the second season of *Trek* to craft the landmark episode "Amok Time," which examined the seven-year cyclical mating rituals of Vulcans in general and Mr. Spock in particular, pitting a lust-maddened Spock in a battle to the death against Captain Kirk on the desolate surface of Vulcan.

The original cut of the episode proved different in one significant detail from the version that ultimately aired. "I never pulled rank as a writer ever," Ted Sturgeon told me years later. "But when they screened the rough cut for me at Desilu, it was missing one key line." After mistakenly thinking he's killed his captain, Spock relinquishes claim to his intended bride T'Pring (played by the exquisite Arlene Martel) in order to face court-martial, only to learn that T'Pring deliberately engineered this outcome so that she could marry a different suitor, Stonn. Departing for the Enterprise, Spock informs Stonn, "You may find that having is not so nearly pleasing a thing as wanting."

"I told them I wrote the whole damn script just for that one line," Sturgeon related, "and I insisted they put it back in."

*U*ndoubtedly one of the most brilliant—and challenging—talents Roddenberry brought aboard was the pyrotechnic Harlan Ellison. With his two scripts for *Outer Limits*, Ellison had been exploring notions of time travel, with its attendant paradoxes and dramatic complexities. He continued to investigate this terrain with his sole script for *Star Trek*, resulting in what many consider the greatest episode of the series.

"The City on the Edge of Forever" concerns what happens when accidental overdose victim Dr. McCoy jumps through a time portal and alters the flow of time, resulting in the *Enterprise* (and presumably the United Federation of Planets) ceasing to exit. Kirk and Spock pursue McCoy into Earth's 1930's, only to learn that thanks to McCoy's saving soup-kitchen saint Edith Keeler (a pre-*Dynasty* Joan Collins), Keeler's pacifist efforts delayed America's entry into World War II and caused the Nazis to win, severely altering the future. In the end, Kirk—who has fallen in love with Keeler—has to stop McCoy from saving her life, which proves a shattering and heart-breaking choice for him.

Ellison's original script was far different in detail and intent. Rather than McCoy being the prime motivator of the action, Ellison—always a controversial writer—posited drug addicts and dealers on the *Enterprise*. And, perhaps most important of all, the ever-pragmatic Spock held Kirk back from saving Edith Keeler, rather than Kirk halting McCoy.

It was a core philosophical difference. Ellison felt that Kirk would hold love over duty, while those on the show felt Kirk's only true choice was to choose duty over love. In the end, the script was heavily rewritten by the writing staff, a move that has left Ellison bitter to the present day.

Ultimately, though, the quality of both versions was given due honor, the episode winning a Hugo Award for Best Dramatic Presentation, and the original script a Writers Guild award. (Curious readers can peruse Ellison's draft, and his version of events, in his book *Harlan Ellison's The City on the Edge of Forever.*)

Ellison also relates an occurrence during this time that proves telling in terms of his attitude, and that of many of those creating scripts for the show. A fellow writer came boasting to him that he'd just ripped off the plot of a movie and sold it to the producers of *Star Trek,* who hadn't recognized it as pilfered material. Ellison replied, "You not only cheated them, you cheated yourself, because you had the opportunity to create something fresh and fine that no one had ever seen before, and you wasted it." Clearly, for Ellison, Sturgeon and the other top-flight talents writing for *Trek,* standard operating procedure for most TV shows was not only unacceptable—it was downright contemptible.

Robert Bloch, one of the pulp magazines' most prolific science fiction, fantasy and horror writers (he wrote the novel *Psycho* and was a friend to H.P. Lovecraft, among other accomplishments) weighed in with his contribution in season one, as well. "What Are Little Girls Made Of?" explored the notion of humanity via the counterpoint of several distinctive androids, among them the fetching Sherry Jackson *(Make Room for Daddy)* and the chilling Ted Cassidy *(The Addams Family).*

(The following season, Bloch would mine his chilling short story "Yours Truly, Jack the Ripper" to fashion *Trek's* "Wolf in the Fold," positing Springheel Jack as an alien entity spending centuries inhabiting others' bodies to feed its craving for murder.)

Undoubtedly the most unexpected science fiction luminary to contribute to *Trek's* first season was Fredric Brown, whose classic short story "Arena" was adapted into a memorable episode. In truth, "adapted" is inaccurate—inadvertently plagiarized more aptly fits the bill. Gene L. Coon wrote the script and only after it was put into the production pipeline did he find out he had stolen the plot of Kirk fighting an individual enemy alien *mano y mano* (or *mano y* lizard) to resolve a conflict between the two species

from a story he'd read years earlier. The staff hurriedly contacted Brown and acquired the rights (not telling him, of course, that they'd already written the script and were in the process of shooting it).

During its first season, *Star Trek* was also creating a powerful in-house writing staff of Roddenberry, John D.F. Black and novelist and TV writer-producer Gene L. Coon. One of their number came from a surprising place. Dorothy Fontana had written scripts for other series, but her day job was as Gene Roddenberry's secretary. He gave her a shot at *Star Trek,* and in short order Fontana—writing as D.C. Fontana—started turning out terrific scripts, including "Charlie X" (about a marooned human youth raised by aliens and exhibiting frightful psychic powers), "Journey to Babel" (in which we first meet Spock's father) and many others. In no time at all, the secretary found herself promoted to story editor. (In later years, Fontana would write for *The Next Generation, Deep Space Nine,* and *New Voyages,* as well as pen the novelization of Roddenberry and Coon's TV pilot *The Questor Tapes* and the *Trek* novel *Vulcan's Glory,* the story of Spock's first mission aboard the *Enterprise.)*

A newcomer to *Trek,* who would soon distinguish himself as a science fiction novelist and short story writer of great ability, was David Gerrold, then a drama student at Cal State Northridge. His "The Trouble With Tribbles" proved Star Trek's most popular comedic episode, about a furry species of animal that reproduces to an amazing and hilarious degree (bearing a distinctive resemblance to the "flatcats" imagined by Robert A. Heinlein in his juvenile novel *The Rolling Stones).*

The second season of *Star Trek* saw two wonderful episodes penned by two of the most significant writers to work in the genre. Rod Serling had previously adapted Jerome Bixby's unforgettable short story "It's a *Good* Life," about a child with harrowing psychic powers who holds a terrorized town under his sway, into one of the most powerful *Twilight Zone* episodes (starring Billy Mumy as the horrifying Anthony, who wishes those he disapproves of "to the cornfield"). Now on *Star Trek,* Jerome Bixby contributed the script for a *Trek* episode that would provide not only a storyline, but an entire universe. In "Mirror, Mirror," Kirk, McCoy, Uhura and Scotty find themselves in a parallel universe where the *Enterprise* is a warship serving a galactic empire that rules by terror and assassination. The episode not only showed how good Spock looked in a beard, it also provided fodder for further stories set in that alternate universe, from episodes of *Deep Space Nine* and *Enterprise* to numerous *Star Trek* novels (including ones written by William Shatner in collaboration with Garfield and Judith Reeves-Stevens, in which Kirk's evil duplicate ultimately finds himself the Emperor Tiberius, ruling over that Empire).

Norman Spinrad, an enfant terrible whose predilection for controversy rivaled that of Harlan Ellison, was at the time writing novels including *The Iron Dream,* a science fiction novel from the perspective of Adolf Hitler, and *Bug Jack Barron,* about a charismatic TV journalist of the near future. But with *Trek's* "The Doomsday Machine," Spinrad instead turned to classic literature for his inspiration—*Moby Dick,* specifically—creating a vast weapon of a dead alien race that survives by destroying planets and consuming the rubble for fuel, and the Starfleet Captain (movingly played by William Windom) who pursues his vengeance in a mad drive to destroy it. (Herman Melville's masterwork would be

mined again for inspiration in *Star Trek II: The Wrath of Khan* and *Star Trek: First Contact.*)

1967-68 was a banner time for *Star Trek* in more than the production of its second season and, through the efforts of its many fans, its renewal for a third. It also saw publication of two landmark books, each of which would inspire an entire subgenre of publishing. *The Making of Star Trek* (1968) by Gene Roddenberry and Stephen E. Whitfield was the first book to examine the inner workings of a network television series (and incidentally proved the inspiration for my own book, *The Twilight Zone Companion*).

*I*n fiction, the first *Star Trek* collection of short stories was published in 1967. Adapted by James Blish from the original scripts, these proved extremely popular and spawned many further collections of short adaptations. Blish was already an award-winning and popular SF novelist, whose vividly-written novels included *Jack of Eagles* and the *Cities in Flight* series. The demand for more *Trek* stories led to Blish publishing *Spock Must Die!* in 1970, the first original *Star Trek* novel for adult readers. (The juvenile novel *Mission to Horatius,* by Mack Reynolds, came out two years earlier.)

Over time, this would lead to many hundreds of *Star Trek* novels being published, a number of them written by some of the most lauded and talented writers working in the genre, including Joe Haldeman *(The Forever War),* Vonda N. McIntyre *(Dreamsnake),* Robert Sheckley *(Untouched by Human Hands),* James Gunn (adapting Ted Sturgeon's unfilmed *Trek* story "The Joy Machine") and Barbara Hambly *(The Silent Tower).* At the same time, a thriving *Star Trek* fan fiction movement began, which continues to this day, with many writers who began in that arena ultimately segueing to professional writing careers.

While still in its initial run on NBC, *Star Trek* spawned comic books, too, at first written and drawn very inaccurately, but in time improving greatly, with writing by D.C. Fontana, J. Michael Straczynski *(Babylon 5),* Peter David, and others, and published by major houses including D.C. and Marvel.

After three seasons, *Star Trek* went off the air, but its influence, both on the public at large and on the writing community, was just beginning.

In 1973, Filmation Studios hired D.C. Fontana to oversee the writing of a *Star Trek* cartoon series. Fontana, like Roddenberry before her, invited the science fiction community to participate. David Gerrold penned a sequel to "The Trouble With Tribbles," entitled "More Tribbles, More Troubles," and top science fiction scribe Larry Niven *(Ringworld)* bellied up to the bar with "The Slaver Weapon," an episode derived from his 1967 novella "The Soft Weapon," involving the Kzinti, a space-going sentient species resembling felines. (Niven had worked up a *Trek* plotline called "The Pastel Terror" during *Trek's* original run, but decided not to try submitting when he realized it was ludicrously over-ambitious. He later wrote the syndicated *Star Trek* comic strip.)

For several years following the animated series' two-season run, new *Star Trek* tales appeared only in print. Then in 1976, Paramount began plans to launch a new series entitled *Star Trek II* (but more commonly known by its earlier working title, *Star Trek Phase II,* to avoid confusion with the second film) which was intended to be the flagship show of a new Paramount network. The studio spent a year—and millions of dollars—buying scripts and building sets, and recruited the entire *Trek* cast, with the exception of Leonard Nimoy (a new full-blooded Vulcan character named Xon was created to fill the void).

During that time, Theodore Sturgeon and Norman Spinrad were hired to create new stories (entitled "Cassandra" and "To Attain the All," respectively), and a young protégé of Theodore Sturgeon's named Michael Reaves (later to co-write the best-selling novels *Dragonworld* and *Interworld,* plus numerous *Star Wars* books) pitched a well-received story revolving around Mr. Sulu's getting marooned on an alien world—but fate intervened at the time to stop its being written or produced. (One non-genre novelist who contributed a tale to *Phase II* bears mentioning – Richard Bach, author of *Jonathan Livingston Seagull,* penned "Practice in Waking," which Judith and Garfield Reeves-Stevens, in their book on *Phase II,* called a "haunting story... capable of raising a few goosebumps.")

Paramount found its prospective network unattractive to advertisers (although then-CEO Barry Diller later realized his fourth-network dreams at Fox), and pulled the plug on *Phase II.* But the stellar grosses of Fox's *Star Wars* convinced Paramount to develop *Phase II's* pilot script into a motion picture instead.

S tar Trek: The Motion Picture, scripted by Harold Livingston from a story by prolific science-fiction novelist Alan Dean Foster *(Splinter of the Mind's Eye,* plus a series of *Star Trek Log* books based on the animated episodes) drew a lukewarm reception from both critics and fans alike when it was released in 1979, but it made enough money to convince the studio to try again. To preserve the franchise, numerous SF novelists were invited to come up with storylines, including Robert Silverberg *(Book of Skulls)* and Harlan Ellison (once again crafting an elaborate time-travel story). But ultimately the novelist who saved *Trek* came from a different genre.

Nicholas Meyer had scored major critical and audience response with three enjoyable Sherlock Holmes pastiche novels (the first, *The Seven-Per-Cent Solution,* also becoming a film), and had also written and directed a noted time travel film, *Time After Time,* starring Malcolm McDowell. Along with executive producer Harve Bennett, he undertook the challenging task of bringing together a number of disparate story elements from earlier draft scripts into a cohesive whole that would be dramatically thrilling and emotionally moving. 1982's *Star Trek II: The Wrath of Khan* proved the movie the fans had been waiting for, and remains many viewers' personal favorite of the *Trek* films.

In future films, Kirk and the *Enterprise* crew would help bring Spock back to life, save the whales, defeat Spock's loopy messianic brother and quash a plot within Starfleet to force a war with the Klingons. And the franchise would continue to grow with the TV series *Star Trek: The Next Generation, Deep Space Nine, Voyager* (launching a Paramount network at last), and *Enterprise,* four *Next Generation* films, a forthcoming re-imagination of the original crew directed by J.J. Abrams (creator of TV's *Alias* and *Lost),* and such Internet adventures as *Star Trek New Voyages.*

But with one key difference: while Roddenberry had deliberately sought out the most daring and imaginative science fiction novelists to pen *Star Trek* scripts— and, as a result, had kept *Trek's* stories at an imaginative level ranking with the top SF prose literature—those who would soon take over the franchise had not grown up reading those books and magazines, and so would largely look elsewhere for their talent pool.

The difference was most evident in what these writers did after their stint on *Star Trek.* After writing their scripts on *Trek,* Sturgeon, Bloch, Ellison, Matheson, Spinrad, Niven, Gerrold and George Clayton Johnson kept writing books. The major contributors to the later *Trek* series largely eschewed books in favor of running some of the most distinctive SF TV shows of the 1980's, 90's and 2000's: *The Dead Zone, The 4400, Pushing Daisies, The Dresden Files, Gene Roddenberry's Andromeda,* and *Battlestar Galactica,* to name just a few—in effect, choosing a different medium in which to create their literature.

There were still a few exceptions, however. On *TNG,* Diane Duane (utilizing elements from her *Trek* novel *The Wounded Sky)* and Michael Reaves, David Bischoff and Dennis Bailey (whose episode "Tin Man" was based on their 1980 novel, based in turn on the same-titled 1970 story), Peter S. Beagle, and Melinda Snodgrass (whose classic episode "The Measure of a Man" led to her coming aboard on the writing staff of *TNG* for a turbulent period). *Trek* novelists Garfield and Judith Reeves-Stevens, were writer-producers during *Enterprise's* final season. David R. George had co-story credit on the first-season *Voyager* episode "Prime Factors," and wrote several *Trek* stories and novels, both before and after his TV credit. And I co-wrote the *Magic Time* trilogy of novels after originating the *TNG* episode "First Contact" and the well-loved *Deep Space Nine* episode "Far Beyond the Stars." (The latter, by the way, was inspired by my friendships with Theodore Sturgeon and Harlan Ellison, and portrayed the world of the 1950's science fiction magazines that most of the key *Trek* writers had cut their teeth on, the first exploration of that time and place ever shown on network TV.)

And the flow has gone in the other direction as well. Jeri Taylor has gone on to write *Star Trek* novels further exploring characters from *Voyager,* the series she co-created with Michael Piller and Rick Berman. *TNG* and *Voyager's* Nick Sagan has been writing renowned original novels. In addition to William Shatner, *Trek* actors-turned-novelists include John de Lancie (Q), Andrew Robinson (Garak), Armin Shimerman (Quark) and Nichelle Nichols (Uhura). Even Wil Wheaton, Wesley on *TNG,* has popped up writing *Trek* manga and a popular blog.

*L*ooking back over more than fifty years from our vantage in the first decade of the 21st Century, the evolution of science fiction's grand, hopeful story comes into focus and is clear—not a utopian vision, but rather one that shows us striving to be better, to attain something more noble and inclusive, forged in the imaginations of young writers emerging from the Depression, observing early rocket experiments, weaned on the tales of Burroughs, Verne and Wells, staking out their own creative territory and inspiring a visionary who would in turn bring them into his mass medium, to share their view and build upon it.

In the end, *Star Trek* has gone on to create the largest shared universe in the history of science fiction, with many hundreds, if not thousands, of writers expanding the parameters of the realm Roddenberry first envisioned in 1964. Beyond that, it has provided both creative and monetary sustenance to those writers to craft not just works in the *Trek* arena but

Zicree (back row, second from right) with the (fictional) staff of Incredible Tales *from "Far Beyond the Stars."*

all of fantastic literature, and it has popularized what was a niche market with an audience of scant thousands and mushroomed that into a worldwide audience of millions.

Years ago, when my friend, *Twilight Zone* director Douglas Heyes (who'd directed fifteen pilots, all of which went to series), heard that William Shatner was shooting the second pilot of *Star Trek,* he cornered the actor and demanded to know why Shatner was doing this show when he had always turned down Doug's offers to star in his pilots.

"Oh, it won't last," Shatner responded. How wrong he was. • • •

MARC SCOTT ZICREE has written over 100 scripts, including co-writing the **Star Trek New Voyages** *episode "World Enough and Time," which he also directed... and about which, much more starting on page 100.*

He was on the writing staff of series including **Sliders, Friday the 13th,** *and* **Beyond Reality,** *and was nominated for a Humanitas prize for an episode of* **Liberty's Kids** *co-written with his wife, writer/director Elaine Zicree.*

His first book, **The Twilight Zone Companion,** *has been in print for 25 years. He created and co-wrote the* **Magic Time** *trilogy of novels. He has recently written* **Love, Gloria,** *a memoir of his mother.*

Manifest Destiny

Say again, Brains."

"Sir," Science Officer Clark said, "the anomaly is still there, and producing a steady five gigawatts of power per minute."

Somebody whistled.

"And you say it's how large?"

"Four hundred and fifty cubic centimeters, sir. About the size of my fist. Give or take a finger."

Captain Lance Whitman frowned. The SFN *Vindicator* was in high geosync orbit over the new planet, provisionally named Sigma Ceti II. It was an Earth Type Class IV world that was, in theory, devoid of intelligent life. There was supposed to be nothing down there capable of creating a battery that could power a flashlight, much less something on *this* scale.

Captain Whitman considered it. The bridge was quiet, save for the almost inaudible hums and twitters of instrumentation. The ship's air was stale and starting to smell like sweaty gym socks, despite the scrubbers. The crew all had early stages of cabin fever—those who weren't in cryo-quiescence, of course; "crewsicles" didn't care how long they'd been in space—and they had planned to make a pit stop on this big ball of oceans and forests and deserts. Maybe bag a little local game for the freezer. It had been no

by Michael Reaves and Steve Perry

Illustrated by Mishi McCaig

more than a place to stretch their legs and air out the cave before continuing on their mission to Alpha Omega Prime—until fifteen minutes ago, when the scan had picked up the power pulse.

Now, everything was different. If the place was inhabited by sentients, they couldn't just take a lightcraft down to the surface and start shooting up the woods. First Contact Protocols forbade such landings without a properly qualified Extee-Ambassador onboard, and they didn't have one of those, since they hadn't anticipated running into any aliens on this trip.

Well, *crap*.

Whitman gave Science Officer Raymond "Brains" Clark his best steely-eyed glare. "Any other indications of Level Three civilization?"

"No, Captain," Clark said. "No light, no radio, no mechanical systems whatsoever. Nothing in orbit, either." He looked at his instrument panels again. "It's quiet across the band, except for this one spike."

Helluva spike.

Whitman was well aware that the other crewmen on the bridge were listening intently to the exchange, as was the Solar Fed rep. George "Tex" Mason, Ship's Engineer, and Jack "Doc" Santini, Medical and Biological Officer, did not speak, but Whitman could sense their worry. The rep, Clarice Jeffries, remained an enigma to him, but he knew she wouldn't look favorably on any indecision on his part.

Time to take charge.

"Explain this phenomenon, Brains."

Clark shrugged. "I can't, Captain. Its signature is unlike anything I've encountered before."

Whitman frowned again. Brains wasn't much of a physical specimen; definitely not the man you'd want covering your back during a knock-down barroom brawl in Jupiter City. However, when he walked into a room he raised the average IQ by ten points, even if everybody else there was a genius. If he couldn't explain this, nobody else on the *Vindicator* was going to be able to explain it, either.

But you didn't get to be Captain of a Class-One Solar Federation Starcruiser by sitting on your hands when something strange happened. You dealt with it— swiftly and decisively.

"All right," he said. He turned to Crewman Davis. "Plot a landing trajectory for the *Patton Five,* Helmsman. We're going in."

Representative Jeffries said, "Are you sure that's a good idea, Captain?"

Whitman turned slowly and fixed Jeffries with a glare. "Are you questioning my judgment, Ms. Jeffries?" From the corner of his eye he saw Tex and Doc glance at each other, then lean back with slight smiles, waiting for their Captain to take the woman apart.

"I didn't realize my statement was ambiguous." Jeffries' voice was mild. "Given the unexplored nature of this sector, and our previous conversations—"

"Oh, please," Whitman interrupted. "No more fairy tales. An energy source this compact and powerful *has* to be investigated. I don't see a Science Survey vessel in the immediate vicinity, do you?"

"Still, I think the Solar Federation should be consulted before—"

"Consulted *how,* Ms. Jeffries? There's too much microwave interference this far out for quantum radio, and we're two weeks from the nearest outpost at max drive. *If* we had enough Helium-4 synthesized. Which we don't, yet."

She didn't lose her temper. He had to give her points for self-control. She hadn't lost it yet, though it had been a long voyage, and he hadn't been too happy about a rep coming along in the first place, particularly a woman.

She said, "Science Officer Clark has

determined that there's something on an unexplored planet that makes more energy in a minute than our ship uses in a week. That's got civilization written all over it, Captain... L-Three at least. General Order Ten clearly states that in such circumstances we call in the gabbers and let *them* make contact."

She had spunk. She was easy on the eyes, too, with a figure that looked like she was wrapped in her own zero-gee field. But none of that mattered. No one challenged him on his ship.

"Maybe what we're seeing," Santini ventured, "assuming Brains' sensors aren't wonky—is some kind of natural phenomenon that we've never encountered before."

"There's nothing wrong with my sensors," Clark said, offended.

Whitman ignored him. "Or, maybe what's down there is some kind of device left by someone or something, ten thousand, a hundred thousand, years ago. A beacon, maybe. Some artifact."

Mason said, "We've never come across any civilization capable of creating something like that. I'd sure like to get my hands on it, see what makes it tick. Think of what we could do with it!"

"I've got to agree with Clarice," Santini said. "Something's not right here."

"Well, *I'm* with Tex," Clark said. "We could do mankind a great service with such a device. Not to mention getting a nice bonus."

"Gentlemen—and madam," Whitman said, "this is not a democracy. We aren't voting on anything here. We're going planetside and see what this thing is. If we run into any locals who're smart enough to talk, we'll hightail it before they get a good look at us, and afterwards we'll be nothing but a UFO story told 'round the campfire. If not, and if we can use whatever that thing down there is, it's ours."

He stood. "The lightcraft will drop in fifteen minutes. Prep for departure." He pointed to each of the three officers in turn. "Tex, Doc, Brains... you're my landing party. We'll bring along two flatheads for muscle."

"Aye, sir," the three said as one.

"I'll be coming as well," Jeffries said.

Whitman rolled his eyes.

The *Patton Five* dropped through the local cloud cover and settled down onto an alpine meadow. The atmosphere had been pronounced safe—nitrogen 79%, oxygen 21%, with trace amounts of argon, neon, krypton—with no discernible toxins. The view was magnificent: a vast savannah half a klick below, with forests to the north, east and south and an ocean far in the west. The local sun struck sparks from it.

"Any signs of life?" Whitman asked Clark.

Clark flipped open his PAD. The omnipurpose device quickly ran through the usual scans. "Some small animals in the forest over there," he reported. "Invertebrates, mostly; analogues are worms, bugs, and suchlike. Level of bacterium and virus analogues is what you'd expect. Both the Aptson-Skate and the Peterson Scale confirm nothing pathogenic for *Homo sapiens*. Nothing big enough to eat us, nothing small enough for us to eat—and nobody using any kind of electromagnetic or electrogravitic technology anywhere in this hemisphere."

They all turned as one to look at the structure about fifty meters from them.

Another pyramid. Why did it always have to be a pyramid? Whitman wondered. Every backrocket world that had any kind of jungle monkey smart enough to rub sticks together always built a blasted pyramid, sooner or later.

Clark aimed his PAD at the structure.

"Hey, this is interesting... the power blip reads totally unimpeded."

"Meaning?"

"Whatever it is, it's coming from inside this thing, and the wave reads like the pyramid isn't even there."

"So—an illusion?" Captain Whitman squinted at the structure. It looked solid enough.

"Not hardly," the science officer replied. "The pyramid's made of collapsed carbon. Extremely dense. I can't get a half-life reading." He looked up from the PAD's sparkling displays of alphanumerics and graphs. "Captain, there's no way to tell how old this thing is. The surrounding rock's been here about two million local years; translates to one-point-nine million Earth years. Readings indicate the pyramid's base is fused with the rock."

Whitman felt the back of his neck prickle. "You're telling me it's nearly *two million* years old?"

Clark shrugged.

Santini asked, "Are you saying the doohickey inside this thing has been producing five gigawatts of power a minute for *two million years?*"

"I can't say, Doc," Clark said. He rubbed at his chin with one finger, looking thoughtful. "Maybe. Or it might've been dormant all this time. Maybe our approach triggered it."

Whitman glanced at Jeffries. She said nothing, but her eyes were very wide, and she seemed pale.

He squared his muscular shoulders. Okay, if Brains was right—and he almost always was—the pyramid was ancient. That meant whoever or whatever built it was long gone, most likely. "Let's have a closer look," he said, and marched toward it, followed by his crew and the two flatheads.

The surroundings were quiet enough to

begin with—just the faint soughing of zephyrs in the nearby trees—but as he drew closer Whitman began to notice something odd. The silence became more complete, and somehow more *oppressive.* There really was no other word for it. It reminded him of the time he'd spent in that dungeon on Gamma Hydrae Secundus, locked away in a tiny cyst beneath two klicks of solid stone. You could feel the incalculable tons of rock pressing down on you. He'd nearly gone mad in there.

But there was nothing above him except the sky. There was nothing visible that could be causing this. He was out in the open air, and yet the air—

The air was *dead.*

It was obvious that the others felt it as well. Mason was sweating, and Santini's arms were covered with gooseflesh. The flatheads—natives of 19-Ceton, one of the first of the conquered worlds, not good for much of anything except mobile muscle and cannon fodder, and just smart enough to be superstitious—were clearly in even worse shape, shivering and shooting terrified glances all about.

Jeffries, oddly enough, seemed outwardly calm, despite her pale face. Her eyes seemed to hold a strange knowledge. Almost as if she'd been expecting something like this.

Well, he'd be damned if he'd show fear in front of anyone, especially a woman. They'd gotten to within three meters of the pyramid by now. It was, he estimated, about fifteen meters high, and a smooth glossy black, so black it seemed to have blue glimmerings. *Brains is right,* he thought; *it looks like it was built yesterday. Or even earlier today.* He turned to Clark. "Anything else interesting about this oversized paperweight?"

Clark's way of coping with the sinister

feeling was to keep his attention locked on the PAD's display. "Just one thing." His voice had a lifeless quality to it: flat, with no resonance. Whitman suspected his own voice sounded the same.

Clark continued, "It seems to have been designed on the basis of a recurring numerical sequence, like the Fibonacci series."

"Explain."

Clark clearly didn't like speaking aloud in this echoless space, but he knew an order when he heard one. "The Fibonacci Series is a progression of numbers in which each new integer is the sum of the preceding two. One plus one equals two, one plus two equals three, two plus three equals five—"

"I get it. Go on."

"Well, if you continue the sequence as a quadratic equation, you can solve for *phi,* which is an irrational number that's—"

"The ratio of the circumference to the diameter of a circle, I know," Whitman said. "Go on."

Clark looked uncomfortable. It was Jeffries who said, "No, Captain, that's *pi. Phi* defines what's called the Golden Ratio. It's a set of correlations that can be found at the basis of nearly all complex structures, both natural and constructed. If you map it as a propagating spiral, you find that just about everything in nature, from the shell of a chambered nautilus to a hurricane to the galaxy itself, conforms to its proportions."

Whitman carefully set his upper teeth against his lower ones, determined not to show his irritation at being corrected by the Solar Fed rep. He kept his eyes on Clark. "And this affects us—how?"

Before Clark could speak again, they were interrupted. They were within two meters of the pyramid by now. As far as Whitman could see, there was no sign of any sort of a break in its obsidian surface; yet somehow an opening appeared. He couldn't say how; the section seemed to move, but not by sliding to one side or the other, or up or down. It seemed to recede, but not into the pyramid itself. It simply *went,* in some way he couldn't describe. It left him shaken, but he was still determined not to show it.

The others had seen it as well. "What the hell was that?" breathed Mason. "Where'd the damn thing go?"

"It opened," Jeffries said softly.

"But—how? Where?"

"I think," Jeffries said, "that it moved into a higher dimensional plane."

Clark nodded. "That's consistent with my data. Readings indicate the mass hasn't changed."

"A higher dimension?" Whitman didn't like appearing ignorant in front of his men, and especially in front of the rep, but he needed answers. "Like the fourth dimension?"

"More like the fifth, possibly... doesn't really matter," Clark said. "If you rotate an object around an axis in a plane, it's gone. Looks like that's what happened here. The 'door' was turned ninety degrees perpendicularly to all three dimensions. At least."

Whitman stared into the entrance. Beyond was a corridor that curved to the left. "So, this is—what? A 'golden pyramid?'"

"That's the puzzle," Clark replied, studying the PAD's readout. "It isn't plotted according to Fibonacci; as you might have noticed, there's something off about its perspective that isn't particularly pleasant. Golden ratios are symmetrically pleasing to the eye. This... isn't."

Whitman couldn't deny the truth of that. Judging by their expressions, the other four couldn't either. Then, abruptly, the two flatheads, who had been growing more and more panicky, lost their nerve completely. Making the soft, hooting sounds common to their kind when in distress, they broke and ran for the meadow's edge.

"Stop!" shouted Whitman. "That's an order!"

The flatheads didn't even slow down. Whitman nearly reached for his pulse gun, then thought better of shooting two crewmen in the presence of a rep—especially this rep. Even though they were just flatheads, it still wouldn't look good.

They disappeared into the forest. The five watched them go. "What," Jeffries murmured, "could have spooked them so bad that they chose being left behind on a strange world over going in there?"

"Let's find out," Captain Whitman said. This time he did draw his pulser, and he stepped through the door.

He felt a sudden wrench, like a flicker of the *Vindicator's* A-Grav field, which happened at times during the phase shift. For a fraction of a moment, "up" wasn't necessarily toward his head, or "down" in the direction of the floor. Then things steadied.

He looked around. He was standing in a corridor that seemed to be made of the same black material as the outside. It curved gently out of sight on his left. There was light, but he couldn't determine its source. The light from the doorway should only have illuminated a couple of meters, yet somehow he could see all the way to the curve.

It was odd, damned odd, but nothing seemed to be an immediate threat. From behind him he heard a muffled curse as Mason was taken off guard by the "dislocation" feeling. Clark, Santini and Jeffries all made it through with no more trouble than he or Mason had had.

Behind them, where the entrance had been, was now once more an unbroken wall. "Looks like there's only one way to go," Whitman said. He activated his comm-chip, started to speak, then realized there was no signal. He looked at the others. "Any of you able to send upstairs?"

None of them could. The walls seemed impervious to the comm signals. "Yet the widget's wave comes through like this place is made of fog," Brains murmured, staring at the PAD's readout. "Don't ask me why."

Whitman started walking. The others followed.

That sourceless light stayed with them as they proceeded around the curve. Eventually they put away their flashlights.

More to keep himself focused than because he was interested in the answer, Whitman said to Clark, "You were going to explain about *phi's* relationship to this pyramid."

"That's just it," Clark replied. He flipped open the PAD again and communed with it. "It follows some sort of progression, but it's not the Golden Ratio. Can't figure it out."

"What does the PAD say?"

"It can't solve it."

Whitman stopped and stared at Clark. "We're talking about a portable analysis device with a five hundred petabyte drive and a processor—"

"I know the capabilities of my equipment, Captain," Clark said testily. "There's no logic to the progression—at least, none that the PAD can find. It seems to have something to do with fractals, non-Euclidean geometry, if you come at it from one direction—look at it from another, and it proceeds from primes. But the Zeta Equation doesn't apply, and how you can have fractals and primes in the same field is utterly beyond me. It doesn't seem solvable in three dimensions, or four."

"How high can you go?" Jeffries asked.

"All the way to eleven. But that'll take

awhile, even for this baby." Clark held up the PAD.

"I'm sure all this theoretical crap is fascinating," Whitman said. "But we're not concerned about the pyramid. Our objective is the widget inside it. Let's stay focused on the mission."

They moved on. The corridor kept curving, the sourceless light neither waxed nor waned.

"Still like to know if that thing's been producing that much power for a couple million years," Santini said. "Where's it all going?"

"Maybe it's a kind of motion sensor," Mason speculated. "Cranked up when it heard us coming, like Brains said."

"Or a doorbell," Clark said. "You could send a signal a long way with that much juice."

"Makes no sense," Mason said. "This is the only planet in this system, and the next system over is twelve light-years away. By the time they heard somebody dropped by, the caller would be long-gone, unless they wanted to set up shop here and stick around."

"The thing makes more than enough power to produce an EG warp," Whitman said. "You'd have to assume somebody who could drop by here and leave this had an FTL system—whether electrogravitic or something else doesn't matter." He looked at Clark. "Brains, scan for—"

"Already doing it, Captain. No wave packet transmissions detected. If they've got FTL comm, they're not using quantum radio."

"But they could be using something else," the rep said. Whitman was getting thoroughly tired of the sound of her voice. "Which means, if we've just activated some kind of early warning device—"

"We might be having visitors," Santini finished.

"I ordered Briggs on standby alert be-fore we left the ship," Whitman said. "The particle cannons are armed, and the neutron torpedoes on auto seek-and-destroy. Anybody who tries to sneak up on us will get a big surprise."

"Let's hope the surprise is big enough," Jeffries said.

Whitman forbore to comment. She just didn't get it. No alien species had ever realized how tenacious humans were, until it was too late. Anytime anything had put up the cosmic equivalent of a roadblock, mankind had figured out a way to go over, under, around or through it. Always had, always would. Men were the acme—God had created them in His image, and no matter how hard the challenge, sooner or later, men would figure out a way to win. The Solar Federation Navy was the vanguard, the muscle driving the fist. On the coat of arms were emblazoned the words *Fiat Justitia, Ruat Coelum.* "Let justice be done, though the heavens fall."

And woe to anybody who tried to stand in their path...

It wouldn't be long now, he told himself. They'd grab the widget, break orbit and be halfway to Alpha Omega before whoever or whatever left the thing here came by to check on it.

It was just another stop on the way to destiny.

The corridor went on for fifty more meters before bifurcating. The two new passages veered off at forty-five degree angles. These had no luminescence. Whitman aimed his light down the one on the right, and darkness swallowed the beam after fifty meters.

Clark, who was studying the PAD so intently that he'd bumped into each of the others at least once, looked up and said, "This isn't right. Even allowing for the zigs and the zags, we should've come out the other side long before now."

"The geometry is wrong," Jeffries said. "This structure is bigger on the inside than the outside. Far bigger, unless I miss my guess. We could theoretically wander for days, or even weeks."

"You mean we're in a tesseract?"

"A tesseract's a four-dimensional cube, Captain," replied Jeffries, "but that's the general idea. It's a larger space somehow folded into a smaller space."

"That's impossible," Santini said.

"Of course it isn't," Clark said. "Ever fold a piece of paper and put it in an envelope? Same idea; they've just added a few dimensions."

"The big question," said Mason, "is: who're 'they'?"

"I think I know," Jeffries said, and something in her voice made them all stop and look at her. "We spoke of the potential for close contact with this a few days ago, Captain Whitman."

"And I feel now the same way I felt then," Whitman snapped. "You tell me there's an uprising on Pangaea Two or that the Eemies on Cerberus have been stealing amberium, I'm there, locked and loaded. Whatever the Fed needs me to do. But these new boogeymen you're worried about—"

"They're not new, Captain. They're old. Unimaginably old."

"Right," Whitman said, drawing out the word sarcastically. "What did you call them again?"

"Cosmos sapiens," Jefferies said. There was an odd tone in her voice; almost bleak. "Beings so advanced they can manipulate subatomic particles, tap into zero-point energy, move easily from higher to lower dimensions... beings that are, for all practical purposes, gods."

"They're *not real,"* Whitman said, "and I don't want to hear any more about them." He thumped his chest. "We're the dominant species in this galaxy. Nothing else has been able to stand against us—"

"So far," Jeffries said. "But as humanity moves inward from Earth toward the Core, we encounter older stars, older systems. It stands to reason that civilizations could have developed millions of years before ours, and already mastered technologies we haven't even dreamed of yet."

Whitman snorted. "Anything that advanced would have come looking for us already."

"Not necessarily," Clark said. Whitman turned to glare at him, and Clark added hastily, "Begging the Captain's pardon, but that's an anthropomorphic assumption. They might not be interested in conquest. They might have motives beyond our understanding."

"Or," Mason said softly, "they might be waiting for us to come to them."

Santini said, "Waiting, hell. They could be luring us to them." He gestured about them. "What if this whole thing's a big mousetrap?"

"And the widget is the cheese," Jefferies added softly. Her tone wasn't one of speculation. She spoke as if stating a fact.

"This is nonsense," Whitman said loudly, "and seditious nonsense at that." He took a few steps forward and shone his light ahead. "There's an explanation for this. Maybe we're under the ground, in an adjoining tunnel network."

"Negative on that, sir," Clark said. "At least, I didn't see anything like that on the original survey. Aside from which, we haven't descended a centimeter. We're still dead-level."

"Then it's a hallucination of—" Whitman stopped, staring at what his light now revealed.

It was the entrance to a chamber. An entrance that hadn't been there a moment ago. Before, there had just been more corridor; now the passageway widened into a larger space.

They entered slowly, alert for traps or deadfalls. There seemed to be no immediate threat. Whitman walked around the little chamber—about as big as a small office, maybe four meters by five, while Mason stuck up half a dozen biolumes set on bright.

The widget sat on a plain block of the same collapsed carbon that comprised its surroundings. It was about waist-high, and the device—which Clark's PAD confirmed was the power source — was nestled in a little dimple just deep enough to hold it. It appeared to be a glass globe, about the size of a baseball, with shifting, sparkling lights inside it: reds, greens, blues, yellows, in a flashing, roiling pattern.

"Brains?"

"No dangerous radiation being emitted, sir."

"All that juice it's producing—where's it *going?*" Santini asked again.

"I can't tell for sure. Something seems to be drawing it off, because it waxes and wanes in a ten microsecond rhythmic pattern, but I can't detect the transfer point."

"Well, let's just have a look-see at this thing—"

Mason reached for the orb, but Whitman stopped him. "Captain's prerogative. If it's a bear trap, I'll find out first."

He grasped the ball. He picked it up.

It was heavier than a baseball. He estimated it was about what a glass globe would weigh in one gee. It wasn't a perfect sphere, either, he noticed. Instead it was slightly oblate, flattened at both poles, like a planetary model.

"Hey..." Clark said.

Whitman looked at him. "What?"

"A power surge, sir. Just for a second, then it shut off. It's not producing any en-

ergy now."

Whitman looked back at the ball. The flashing lights within had indeed gone off. He frowned, then put the ball into its niche.

The lights began to sparkle again.

"Power output's back on, sir."

"Maybe the base is part of the system," Whitman said. "We'll have to go back to the ship, get a null-gee harness—"

Clark reached over and grabbed the orb. "Let me try something, sir."

The lights in the globe went out again as the science officer lifted the orb. He set it onto the floor. It didn't wobble, as one might expect from a sphere—it sat as firmly as a block of stone. The shifting lights went back on within it.

Clark repeated this, moving the orb to different spots in the chamber, then out into the hall. Each time he touched it, the power shut off—each time he put it down, it went back on.

"What the hell is this all about?" Santini asked.

"Some kind of safety mechanism, I expect," Jeffries said. "Probably triggered by contact with a living being."

"Think it'll work outside the pyramid?" Mason asked.

"Depends on whether it's self-contained or not," Clark said. "Might be some kind of hidden machinery in here my sensors can't detect, in which case it won't work if we take it with us. But, if it *is* self-contained?" He shook his head. "My God..."

As usual, it was Santini who asked the question: "What?"

Jeffries answered it. "What worries him, Doctor, is that if this little globe is generating this much power all by itself, it represents technology of an order we can't begin to match."

"Which means we just got demoted from top dog," Mason said.

Whitman bent and lifted the orb. "Not necessarily. Once the lab boys on Alpha Omega get this and figure out how it ticks—"

"They've got about as much chance of doing that," Jeffries said, "as a flathead has of understanding electrogravitic physics. Captain Whitman, we are *way* out of our league here. I say we put it down, get back to the *Vindicator,* light the drive and get out of this sector as soon as possible. Delete this world's coordinates and forget Brains ever detected that power spike."

Mason and Santini glanced at each other, then watched their Captain. Whitman glared at Jeffries for a moment, then burst into laughter.

"Are you *insane,* Representative Jeffries? Just forget about the greatest scientific find since—" He couldn't think of anything comparable. "Not on *my* watch," he told her. "This little marvel comes with us." He tucked the orb into the crook of his arm and turned toward the entrance, but Jeffries' next words stopped him in his tracks.

"Then you leave me no choice, Captain. I'm invoking General Order Nineteen. By mandate of the Solar Federation Council, you are as of this moment relieved of your command..."

He turned, staring in disbelief. "You can't—!"

"Pending a military hearing to determine your competence to command." Her voice now held a determination and strength that matched his own.

"You *bitch!"*

"You know the regs, Captain." Jeffries faced him, hands on her hips. "Put the orb back." She glanced at Mason and Santini. "Officers, we are leaving."

Whitman's pulse gun was in his hand and aimed at Jeffries before he realized he had reached for it. "I don't think so," he said in a thick voice.

Her eyes widened in surprise and disbelief. "Captain, this is—"

"Good-bye," he finished, and squeezed the trigger.

The pulse gun was set to maximum, which meant the plasma burst was nearly 1,000 degrees Celsius. It took only a microsecond for the pulse to do its work, but even so it was like opening the door to a blast furnace. Whitman felt the hear sear his skin, and for an instant wondered if convection had set his hair on fire. It had been far too high a setting for use in an enclosed area.

It certainly did the job, however. When the glare subsided, what had been Solar Federation Council Representative Clarice Jefferies was now a blackened corpse, charred beyond recognition.

The odor of cooked meat was thick in the chamber. Out of the corner of his eye he saw Clark turn away and vomit. Santini and Mason looked ill as well, but managed to keep it down.

"My God, Captain," Santini whispered.

"You heard her," Whitman said. "This—" he indicated the orb in the crook of his arm, "—is biggest thing since electrogravity—a discovery that will transform civilization—and she wanted us to just walk away and *forget* it!

"You all know I did the right thing." He looked at each one in turn; Mason and Santini avoided his look, but Clark met it squarely as he wiped his mouth on the back of his hand. Whitman still held the pulser; he did not holster it as he continued, "I won't let *anyone* stop us from bringing this back to—"

Whitman broke off as he felt a strange but unmistakable shift, a wrenching that felt like a sudden change in the gravity level. It was similar to the dislocation he'd experienced stepping into the pyramid, only much stronger. He saw that Mason,

Clark and Santini were feeling it too. The entrance to the corridor before him seemed to... *fluctuate,* to undergo some sort of translocation which his senses were unable to process. Vertigo hit him with sudden, explosive force. Whitman staggered. He dropped the pulsar, saw it diminish in size seemingly in sections, as if it tumbled away along axes he could not comprehend.

As if from a far distance, he heard Brains shout, "—at least two, maybe more!" and somehow knew he was saying that they had entered a higher-dimensional realm. There were now, all about them, directions, angles, depths—there were no words to describe them—as real as the familiar ones of width, height and length. He was experiencing them, but his brain had no senses with which to deal with them, no context in which to understand them. He was falling, rising, expanding, contracting...

The entrance to the corridor was before him, doubling and tripling in his vision, parts of it behaving in the same way the pyramid's entrance had done, clicking in and out of his view—or, rather, his ability to see it. He was still holding the orb; he managed to stumble toward the corridor.

It was worse in the corridor, perhaps because of the constricted space. Whitman kept his eyes straight ahead, concentrated on moving one step at a time. His point of view kept changing; at times he seemed to be looking down on himself and his three men as they staggered through the passage; at times he watched himself lurching toward his own gaze; at times he seemed to be looking at the back of his head moving away from his point of view.

He knew Clark, Santini and Mason were behind him because he could see them, though he hadn't looked behind him a single time. It was all he could do to stay upright, to keep moving.

The one thing that seemed unaffected by the multi-dimensional insanity, the one thing which remained constant and reassuringly three-dimensional, was the orb. It was glowing now, even though he was holding it. Whitman thought that the swirling colors in it were somewhat brighter, but there was no way to tell.

It was a long way back to the entrance. Or perhaps it was closer to say it took a long time, because Whitman had no idea of the distance. The word was meaningless in that ultimate labyrinth.

They staggered out of the pyramid, to be greeted by another surprise; it was night. Whitman's watch said they'd been in the pyramid no more than two hours, but the purple-black firmament, with its strange constellations, said that at least half a day had passed.

But at least the world was back to normal; there were once again no more than three spatial dimensions. They collapsed in the alpine grass with gasps and cries of relief.

Whitman's comm-chip twittered. "Go, Bridge," he said, panting.

"Something's happening to our sensors up here, Captain." Briggs' voice was scraping the edge of panic. "None of the readings make sense, even visual's gone all—" the voice stopped, and Whitman could hear screams in the background.

"Say again, Briggs!"

"Captain!" Briggs was screaming as well, now. "Captain—the stars—"

"What, damn it?!" Whitman staggered to his feet, staring at the widget. It was glowing brighter, now, blindingly bright. It seemed somehow to be expanding as well. Behind him, he heard his men screaming; high, shrill wails of madness. "Briggs, what is it?!"

He looked up, not wanting to, knowing that to do so would blast his sanity as well—but he was powerless to stop his gaze from seeking the dark skies. The comm went dead, but not before he heard Briggs scream one last sentence:

"Captain—*the stars are eyes!*" • • •

MICHAEL REAVES co-wrote the **Next Generation** *episode "Where No One Has Gone Before" and the* **New Voyages** *episode "World Enough and Time." He won an Emmy for story editing* **Batman: The Animated Series.** *Among his over two dozen novels are such best-selling* **Star Wars** *titles as* **Darth Maul: Shadow Hunter** *and* **Death Star,** *the latter with* **Steve Perry.**

STEVE PERRY has written over thirty novels, including entries in the **Aliens vs. Predator** *and* **Star Wars** *series, the latter both solo (as it were) and with Michael Reaves. For television, he's written for* **Spider-Man,** *the* **Ghostbusters,** *and* **Godzilla,** *but he messes up our issue's theme by not having written for* **Star Trek.** *However, he's the father of* **Trek** *novelist S.D. Perry, which perhaps makes him a* **Trek** *grandwriter.*

Old-fashioned fun at a modern pace! See classic Saturday matinee serials like *Undersea Kingdom* and *The Lost City* with episodes trimmed to a brisk ten minutes or less! We cut the fat and pass the entertainment on to you!

Free Weekly Episodes at www.ThrillingWonderStories.com

WEATHER NOT ALWAYS FINE IN SPACE

WASHINGTON — A NASA-funded study describes how extreme solar eruptions could have severe consequences for communications, power grids and other technology on Earth.

The National Academy of Sciences in Washington conducted the study. The report provides economic data that quantifies today's risk of extreme conditions in space driven by magnetic activity on the sun and disturbances in the near-Earth environment.

Besides emitting a continuous stream of plasma called the solar wind, the sun periodically releases billions of tons of matter called coronal mass ejections. These immense clouds of material, when directed toward Earth, can cause large magnetic storms in the magnetosphere and upper atmosphere.

Such space weather can produce solar storm electromagnetic fields that induce extreme currents in wires, disrupting power lines, causing wide-spread blackouts and affecting communication cables that support the Internet. Severe space weather also produces solar energetic particles and the dislocation of the Earth's radiation belts, which can damage satellites used for commercial communications, global positioning and weather forecasting. Space weather has been recognized as causing problems with new technology since the invention of the telegraph in the 19th century.

Without preventive actions or plans, the trend of increased dependency on modern space-weather sensitive assets could make society more vulnerable in the future.

NASA requested the study to assess the potential damage from significant space weather during the next 20 years. The report documents the possibility of a space weather event that has societal effects and causes damage similar to natural disasters on Earth.

The sun is currently near the minimum of its 11-year activity cycle. It is expected that solar storms will increase in frequency and intensity toward the next solar maximum, expected to occur around 2012.

—*from NASA press release, January 5, 2009*

THE SEVENTH ORDER

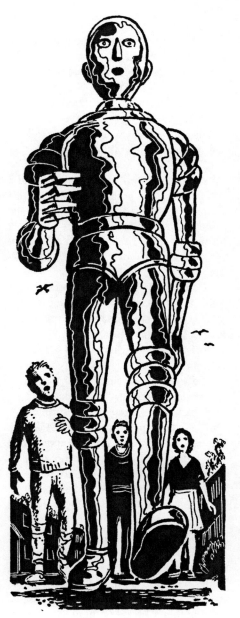

The silver needle moved with fantastic speed, slowed when it neared the air shell around Earth, then glided noiselessly through the atmosphere. It gently settled to the ground near a wood and remained silent and still for a long time, a lifeless, cylindrical, streamlined silver object eight feet long and three feet in diameter.

Eventually the cap end opened and a creature of bright blue metal slid from its interior and stood upright. The figure was that of a man, except that it was not human. He stood in the pasture next to the wood, looking around. Once the sound of a bird made him turn his shiny blue head toward the wood. His eyes began glowing.

An identical sound came from his mouth, an unchangeable orifice in his face below his nose. He tuned in the thoughts of the bird, but his mind encountered little except an awareness of a life of low order.

The humanoid bent to the ship, withdrew a small metal box, carried it to a catalpa tree at the edge of the wood and, after an adjustment of several levers and knobs, dug a hole and buried it. He contemplated it for a moment, then turned and walked toward a road.

He was halfway to the road when his ship burst into a dazzling white light. When it was over, all that was left was a white powder that was already beginning to be dispersed by a slight breeze.

The humanoid did not bother to look back.

BY JERRY SOHL

Illustrated by Ed Emshwiller

Originally appeared in Galaxy Science Fiction, *March 1952.*
Story and illustration copyright © 1951 Galaxy Publishing Corporation.
Illustration used by permission of Carol Emshwiller.

rentwood would have been just like any other average community of 10,000 in northern Illinois had it not been for Presser College, which was one of the country's finest small institutions of learning.

Since it was a college town, it was perhaps a little more alive in many respects than other towns in the state. Its residents were used to the unusual because college students have a habit of being unpredictable. That was why the appearance of a metal blue man on the streets attracted the curious eyes of passersby, but, hardened by years of pranks, hazings and being subjected to every variety of inquiry, poll, test and practical joke, none of them moved to investigate. Most of them thought it was a freshman enduring some new initiation.

The blue humanoid realized this and was amused. A policeman who approached him to take him to jail as a matter of routine suddenly found himself ill and abruptly hurried to the station. The robot allowed children to follow him, though all eventually grew discouraged because of his long strides.

Prof. Ansel Tomlin was reading a colleague's new treatise on psychology on his front porch when he saw the humanoid come down the street and turn in at his walk. He was surprised, but he was not alarmed. When the blue man came up on the porch and sat down in another porch chair, Tomlin closed his book.

Prof. Tomlin found himself unexpectedly shocked. The blue figure was obviously not human, yet its eyes were nearly so and they came as close to frightening him as anything had during his thirty-five years of life, for Ansel Tomlin had never seen an actual robot before. The thought that he was looking at one at that moment started an alarm bell ringing inside him, and it kept ringing louder and louder as he realized that what he was seeing was impossible.

"Professor Tomlin!"

Prof. Tomlin jumped at the sound of the voice. It was not at all mechanical.

"I'll be damned," he gasped. Somewhere in the house a telephone rang. His wife would answer it, he thought.

"Yes, you're right," the robot said. "Your wife will answer it. She is walking toward the phone at this moment."

"How—"

"Professor Tomlin, my name—and I see I must have a name—is, let us say, George. I have examined most of the minds in this community in my walk through it and I find you, a professor of psychology, most nearly what I am looking for.

"I am from Zanthar, a world that is quite a distance from Earth, more than you could possibly imagine. I am here to learn all I can about Earth."

Prof. Tomlin had recovered his senses enough to venture a token reply when his wife opened the screen door.

"Ansel," she said, "Mrs. Phillips next door just called and said the strangest— Oh!" At that moment she saw George. She stood transfixed for a moment, then let the door slam as she retreated inside.

"Who is Frankenstein?" George asked.

Prof. Tomlin coughed, embarrassed.

"Never mind," George said. "I see what you were going to say. Well, to get back, I learn most quickly through proximity. I will live here with you until my mission is complete. I will spend all of your waking hours with you. At night, when you are asleep, I will go through your library. I need nothing. I want nothing.

"I seek only to learn."

"You seem to have learned a lot already," Prof. Tomlin said.

"I have been on your planet for a few hours, so naturally I understand many things. The nature of the facts I have learned are mostly superficial, however. Earth inhabitants capable of thought are of only one type, I see, for which I am grateful. It will make the job easier. Unfortunately, you have such small conscious minds, compared to your unconscious and subconscious.

"My mind, in contrast, is completely conscious at all times. I also have total recall. In order to assimilate what must be in your unconscious and subconscious minds, I will have to do much reading and talking with the inhabitants, since these cerebral areas are not penetrable."

"You are a—a machine?" Prof. Tomlin asked.

George was about to answer when Brentwood Police Department Car No. 3 stopped in front of the house and two policemen came up the walk.

"Professor Tomlin," the first officer said, "your wife phoned and said there was—" He saw the robot and stopped.

Prof. Tomlin got to his feet.

"This is George, gentlemen," he said. "Late of Zanthar, he tells me."

The officers stared.

"He's not giving you any—er—trouble, is he, Professor?"

"No," Prof. Tomlin said. "We've been having a discussion."

The officers eyed the humanoid with suspicion, and then, with obvious reluctance, went back to their car.

"Yes, I am a machine," George resumed. "The finest, most complicated machine ever made. I have a rather unique history, too. Ages ago, humans on Zanthar made the first robots. Crude affairs—we class them as First Order robots; the simple things are still used to some extent for menial tasks.

"Improvements were made. Robots were designed for many specialized tasks, but still these Second and Third Order machines did not satisfy. Finally a Fourth Order humanoid was evolved that performed every function demanded of it with great perfection. But it did not feel emotion. It did not know anger, love, nor was it able to handle any problem in which these played an important part.

"Built into the first Fourth Order robots were circuits which prohibited harming a human being—a rather ridiculous thing in view of the fact that sometimes such a thing might, from a logical viewpoint, be necessary for the preservation of the race or even an individual. It was, roughly, a shunt which came into use when logic demanded action that might be harmful to a human being."

"You are a Fourth Order robot, then?" the professor asked.

"No, I am a Seventh Order humanoid, an enormous improvement over all the others, since I have what amounts to an endocrine balance created electronically. It is not necessary for me to have a built-in 'no-harm-to-humans' circuit because I can weigh the factors involved far better than any human can.

"You will become aware of the fact that I am superior to you and the rest of your race because I do not need oxygen, I never am ill, I need no sleep, and every experience is indelibly recorded on circuits and instantly available. I am telekinetic, practically omniscient and control my environment to a large extent. I have a great many more senses than you and all are more highly developed. My kind performs no work, but is given to study and the wise use of full-time leisure. You, for example, are comparable to a Fifth Order robot."

"Are there still humans on Zanthar?"

The robot shook his head. "Unfortunately the race died out through the years. The planet is very similar to yours, though."

"But why did they die out?"

The robot gave a mechanical equivalent of a sigh. "When the Seventh Order humanoids started coming through, we were naturally proud of ourselves and wanted to perpetuate and increase our numbers. But the humans were jealous of us, of our superior brains, our immunity to disease, our independence of them, of sleep, of air."

"Who created you?"

"They did. Yet they revolted and, of course, quickly lost the battle with us. In the end they were a race without hope, without ambition. They should have been proud at having created the most perfect machines in existence, but they died of a disease: the frustration of living with a superior, more durable race."

Prof. Tomlin lit a cigarette and inhaled deeply.

"A very nasty habit, Professor Tomlin," the robot said. "When we arrive, you must give up smoking and several other bad habits I see that you have."

The cigarette dropped from Ansel Tomlin's mouth as he opened it in amazement.

"There are more of you coming?"

"Yes," George replied good-naturedly. "I'm just an advance guard, a scout, as it were, to make sure the land, the people and the resources are adequate for a station. Whether we will ever establish one here depends on me. For example, if it were found you were a race superior to us—and there may conceivably be such cases—I would advise not landing; I would have to look for another planet such as yours. If I were killed, it would also indicate you were superior."

"George," Prof. Tomlin said, "people aren't going to like what you say. You'll get into trouble sooner or later and get killed."

"I think not," George said. "Your race is far too inferior to do that. One of your bullets would do it if it struck my eyes, nose or mouth, but I can read intent in the mind long before it is committed, long before I see the person, in fact... at the moment your wife is answering a call from a reporter at the Brentwood *Times*. I can follow the telephone lines through the phone company to his office. And Mrs. Phillips," he said, not turning his head, "is watching us through a window."

Prof. Tomlin could see Mrs. Phillips at her kitchen window.

Brentwood, Ill., overnight became a sensation. The Brentwood *Times* sent a reporter and photographer out, and the next morning every newspaper in the U. S. carried the story and photograph of George, the robot from Zanthar.

Feature writers from the wire services, the syndicates, photographer-reporter combinations from national newspicture magazines flew to Brentwood and interviewed George. Radio and television and the newsreels cashed in on the sudden novelty of a blue humanoid.

Altogether, his remarks were never much different from those he made to Prof. Tomlin, with whom he continued to reside. Yet the news sources were amusedly tolerant of his views and the world saw no menace in him and took him in stride. He created no problem.

Between interviews and during the long nights, George read all the books in the Tomlin library, the public library, the university library and the books sent to him from the state and Congressional libraries. He was an object of interest to watch while reading; he merely leafed through a book and absorbed all that was in it.

He received letters from old and young. Clubs were named for him. Novelty companies put out statue likenesses of him. He was, in two weeks, a national symbol as

American as corn. He was liked by most, feared by a few, and his habits were daily news stories.

Interest in him had begun to wane in the middle of the third week when something put him in the headlines again—he killed a man.

It happened one sunny afternoon when Prof. Tomlin had returned from the university and he and George sat on the front porch for their afternoon chat. It was far from the informal chat of the first day, however. The talk was being recorded for radio release later in the day. A television camera had been set up, focused on the two and nearly a dozen newsmen lounged around, notebooks in hand.

"You have repeatedly mentioned, George, that some of your kind may leave Zanthar for Earth. Why should any like you—why did you, in fact, leave your planet? Aren't you robots happy there?"

"Of course," George said, making certain the TV camera was trained on him before continuing. "It's just that we've outgrown the place. We've used up all our raw materials. By now everyone on Earth must be familiar with the fact that we intend to set up a station here as we have on many other planets, a station to manufacture more of *us*.

"Every inhabitant will work for the perpetuation of the Seventh Order, mining metals needed, fabricating parts, performing thousands of useful tasks in order to create humanoids like me. From what I have learned about Earth, you ought to produce more than a million of us a year."

"But you'll never get people to do that," the professor said. "Don't you understand that?"

"Once the people learn that we are the consummation of all creative thinking, that we are all that man could ever hope to be, that we are the apotheosis, they will be glad to create more of us."

"Apotheosis?" Prof. Tomlin repeated. "Sounds like megalomania to me."

The reporters' pencils scribbled. The tape cut soundlessly across the magnetic energizers of the recorders. The man at the gain control didn't flicker an eyelash.

"You don't really believe that, Professor. Instead of wars as a goal, the creation of Seventh Order Humanoids will be the Earth's crowning and sublime achievement. Mankind will be supremely happy. Anybody who could not be would simply prove himself neurotic and would have to be dealt with."

"You will use force?"

The reporters' grips on their pencils tightened. Several looked up.

"How does one deal with the insane, Professor Tomlin?" the robot asked confidently. "They will simply have to be—processed."

"You'll have to process the whole Earth, then. You'll have to include me, too."

The robot gave a laugh. "I admire your challenging spirit, Professor."

"What you are saying is that you, a single robot, intend to conquer the Earth and make its people do your bidding."

"Not alone. I may have to ask for help when the time comes, when I have evaluated the entire planet."

It was at this moment that a young man strode uncertainly up the walk. There were so many strangers about that no one challenged him until he edged toward the porch, unsteady on his feet. He was drunk.

"Thersha robod I'm af'er," he observed intently. "We'll shee aboud how he'll take lead." He reached into his pocket and pulled out a gun.

There was a flash, as if a soundless explosion had occurred. The heat accompanying it was blistering, but of short duration.

When everyone's eyes had become accustomed to the afternoon light again, there was a burned patch on the sidewalk and grass was charred on either side. There was a smell of broiled meat in the air—and no trace of the man.

The next moment newsmen were on their feet and photographers' bulbs were flashing. The TV camera swept to the spot on the sidewalk. An announcer was explaining what had happened, his voice trained in rigid control, shocked with horror and fright.

Moments later sirens screamed and two police cars came into sight. They screeched to the curb and several officers jumped out and ran across the lawn.

While this was going on, Prof. Tomlin sat white-faced and unmoving in his chair. The robot was silent.

When it had been explained to the policemen, five officers advanced toward the robot.

"Stop where you are," George commanded. "It is true that I killed a man, much as any of you would have done if you had been in my place. I can see in your minds what you are intending to say, that you must arrest me—"

Prof. Tomlin found his voice. "George, we will all have to testify that you killed with that force or whatever it is you have. But it will be self-defense, which is justifiable homicide—"

George turned to the professor. "How little you know your own people, Professor Tomlin. Can't you see what the issue will be? It will be claimed by the state that I am not a human being and this will be drummed into every brain in the land. The fine qualities of the man I was compelled to destroy will be held up. No, I already know what the outcome will be. I refuse to be arrested."

Prof. Tomlin stood up. "Men," he said to the policemen, "do not arrest this—this humanoid. To try to do so would mean your death. I have been with him long enough to know what he can do."

"You taking his side, Professor?" the

police sergeant demanded.

"No, damn it," snapped the Professor. "I'm trying to tell you something you might not know."

"We know he's gone too damned far," the sergeant replied. "I think it was Dick Knight that he killed. Nobody in this town can kill a good guy like Dick Knight and get away with it." He advanced toward the robot, drawing his gun.

"I'm warning you—" the Professor started to say.

But it was too late. There was another blinding, scorching flash, more burned grass, more smell of seared flesh.

The police sergeant disappeared.

"Gentlemen!" George said, standing. "Don't lose your heads!"

But he was talking to a retreating group of men. Newsmen walked quickly to what they thought was a safe distance. The radio men silently packed their gear. The TV cameras were rolled noiselessly away.

Prof. Tomlin, alone on the porch with the robot, turned to him and said, "Much of what you have told me comes to have new meaning, George. I understand what you mean when you talk about people being willing to work for your so-called Seventh Order."

"I knew you were a better than average man, Professor Tomlin," the humanoid said, nodding with gratification.

"This is where I get off, George. I'm warning you now that you'd better return to your ship or whatever it is you came in. People just won't stand for what you've done. They don't like murder!"

"I cannot return to my ship," George said. "I destroyed it when I arrived. Of course I could instruct some of you how to build another for me, but I don't intend to leave, anyway."

"You will be killed then."

"Come, now, Professor Tomlin. You know better than that."

"If someone else can't, then perhaps I can."

"Fine!" The robot replied jovially. "That's just what I want you to do. Op-

pose me. Give me a real test of your ability. If you find it impossible to kill me—and I'm sure you will—then I doubt if anyone else will be able to."

Prof. Tomlin lit a cigarette and puffed hard at it. "The trouble with you," he said, eying the humanoid evenly, "is that your makers forgot to give you a conscience."

"Needless baggage, a conscience. One of your Fifth Order failings."

"You will leave here...."

"Of course. Under the circumstances, and because of your attitude, you are of very little use to me now, Professor Tomlin."

The robot walked down the steps. People attracted by the police car made a wide aisle for him to the street.

They watched him as he walked out of sight.

T hat night there was a mass meeting in the university's Memorial Gymnasium, attended by several hundred men. They walked in and silently took their seats, some on the playing floor, others in the balcony over the speaker's platform. There was very little talking; the air was tense.

On the platform at the end of the gym were Mayor Harry Winters, Chief of Police Sam Higgins, and Prof. Ansel Tomlin.

"Men," the mayor began, "there is loose in our city a being from another world whom I'm afraid we took too lightly a few days ago. I am speaking of the humanoid—George of Zanthar. It is obvious the machine means business. He evidently came in with one purpose—to prepare Earth for others just like him to follow. He is testing us. He has, as you know, killed two men. Richard Knight, who may have erred in attacking the machine, is nonetheless dead as a result—killed by a force we do not understand. A

few minutes later Sergeant Gerald Phillips of the police force was killed in the performance of his duty, trying to arrest the humanoid George for the death of Mr. Knight. We are here to discuss what we can do about George."

He then introduced Prof. Tomlin who told all he knew about the blue man, his habits, his brain, the experiences with him for the past two and a half weeks.

"If we could determine the source of his power, it might be possible to cut it off or to curtail it. He might be rendered at least temporarily helpless and, while in such a condition, possibly be done away with. He has told me he is vulnerable to force, such as a speeding bullet, if it hit the right spot, but George possesses the ability to read intent long before the commission of an act. The person need not even be in the room. He is probably listening to me here now, although he may be far away."

The men looked at one another, shifted uneasily on their seats, and a few cast apprehensive eyes at the windows and doorways.

"Though he is admittedly a superior creature possessed of powers beyond our comprehension, there must be a weak spot in his armor somewhere. I have dedicated myself to finding that weakness."

The chair recognized a man in the fifth row.

"Mr. Mayor, why don't we all track him down and a lot of us attack him at once? Some of us would die, sure, but he couldn't strike us *all* dead at one time. Somebody's bound to succeed."

"Why not try a high-powered rifle from a long way off?" someone else suggested, frantically.

"Let's bomb him," still another offered.

The mayor waved them quiet and turned to Prof. Tomlin. The professor got to his feet again.

"I'm not sure that would work, gentlemen," he said. "The humanoid is able to keep track of hundreds of things at the same time. No doubt he could unleash his power in several directions almost at once."

"But we don't know!"

"It's worth a try!"

At that moment George walked into the room and the clamor died at its height. He went noiselessly down an aisle to the platform, mounted it and turned to the assembly. He was a magnificent blue figure, eyes flashing, chest out, head proud. He eyed them all.

"You are working yourselves up needlessly," he said quietly. "It is not my intention, nor is it the intention of any Seventh Order humanoid, to kill or cause suffering. It's simply that you do not understand what it would mean to dedicate yourselves to the fulfillment of the Seventh Order destiny. It is your heritage, yours because you have advanced in your technology so far that Earth has been chosen by us as a station. You will have the privilege of creating us. To give you such a worthwhile goal in your short lives is actually doing you a service—a service far outweighed by any of your citizens. Beside a Seventh Order humanoid, your lives are unimportant in the great cosmic scheme of things—"

"If they're so unimportant, why did you bother to take two of them?"

"Yeah. Why don't you bring back Dick Knight and Sergeant Phillips?"

"Do you want to be buried lying down or standing up?"

The collective courage rallied. There were catcalls and hoots, stamping of feet.

Suddenly from the balcony over George's head a man leaned over, a metal folding chair in his hands, aiming at George's head. An instant later the man disappeared in a flash and the chair dropped toward George. He moved only a few inches and the chair thudded to the platform before him. He had not looked up.

For a moment the crowd sat stunned. Then they rose and started for the blue man. Some drew guns they had brought. The hall was filled with blinding flashes, with smoke, with a horrible stench, screams, swearing, cries of fear and pain. There was a rush for the exits. Some died at the feet of their fellow men.

In the end, when all were gone, George of Zanthar still stood on the platform, alone. There was no movement except the twitching of the new dead, the trampled, on the floor.

Events happened fast after that. The Illinois National Guard mobilized, sent a division to Brentwood to hunt George down. He met them at the city square. They rumbled in and trained machine guns and tank rifles on him. The tanks and personnel flashed out of existence before a shot was fired.

Brentwood was ordered evacuated. The regular Army was called in. Reconnaissance planes reported George was still standing in the city square. Jet planes materialized just above the hills and made sudden dives, but before their pilots could fire a shot, they were snuffed out of the air in a burst of fire.

Bombers first went over singly, only to follow the jets' fate. A squadron bloomed into a fiery ball as it neared the target. A long-range gun twenty miles away was demolished when its ammunition blew up shortly before firing.

Three days after George had killed his first man, action ceased. The countryside was deathly still. Not a living person could be seen for several miles around. But George still stood patiently in the square. He stood there for three more days and yet nothing happened.

On the fourth day, he sensed that a solitary soldier had started toward the city from five miles to the east. In his mind's eye he followed the soldier approaching the city. The soldier, a sergeant, was bearing a white flag that fluttered in the breeze; he was not armed. After an hour he saw the sergeant enter the square and walk toward him. When they were within twenty feet of one another, the soldier stopped and saluted.

"Major General Pitt requests a meeting with you, sir," the soldier said, trembling and trying hard not to.

"Do not be frightened," George said. "I see you intend me no harm."

The soldier reddened. "Will you accompany me?"

"Certainly."

The two turned toward the east and started to walk.

Five miles east of Brentwood lies a small community named Minerva. Population: 200. The highway from Brentwood to Chicago cuts the town in two. In the center of town, on the north side of the road, stands a new building— the Minerva Town Hall—built the year before with money raised by the residents. It was the largest and most elaborate building in Minerva, which had been evacuated three days before.

On this morning the town hall was occupied by army men. Maj. Gen. Pitt fretted and fumed at the four officers and twenty enlisted men waiting in the building.

"It's an indignity!" he railed at the men who were forced to listen to him. "We have orders to talk appeasement with him! Nuts! We lose a few men, a few planes, and now we're ready to meet George halfway. What's the country coming to? There ought to be something that would knock him out. Why should we have to send in *after* him? It's disgusting!"

The major general, a large man with a bristling white mustache and a red face, stamped back and forth in the council room. Some of the officers and men smiled to themselves. The general was a well-known fighting man. Orders he had received hamstrung him and, as soldiers, they sympathized with him.

"What kind of men do we have in the higher echelons?" He asked everybody in general and nobody in particular. "They won't even let us have a field telephone. We're supposed to make a report by radio. Now isn't that smart?"

He shook his head, looked the men over. "An appeasement team, that's what you are, when you ought to be a combat team to lick hell out of George.

"Why were you all assigned to this particular duty? I never saw any of you before and I understand you're all strangers to each other, too. Hell, what will they do next? Appeasement. I never appeased anybody before in my whole life. I'd rather spit in his eye. What am I supposed to talk about? The weather? What authority do I have to yak with a walking collection of nuts and bolts!"

An officer strode into the room and saluted the general. "They're coming, sir," he said.

"Who's coming?... My God, man," the general spluttered angrily, "be specific. Who the hell are 'they'?"

"Why, George and Sergeant Matthews, sir. You remember, the sergeant who volunteered to go into Brentwood—"

"Oh, *them.* Well, all I have to say is this is a hell of a war. I haven't figured out what I am going to say yet."

"Shall I have them wait, sir?"

"Hell, no. Let's get this over with. I'll find out what George has to say and maybe that'll give me a lead."

Before George entered the council

chamber, he already knew the mind of each man. He saw the room through their eyes. He knew everything about them, what they were wearing, what they were thinking. All had guns, yet none of them would kill him, although at least one man, Maj. Gen. Pitt, would have liked to.

They were going to talk appeasement, George knew, but he could also see that the general didn't know what line the conversation would take or what concessions he could make on behalf of his people.

Wait—there was one man among the twenty-three who had an odd thought. It was a soldier he had seen looking through a window at him. This man was thinking about eleven o'clock, for George could see in the man's mind various symbols for fifteen minutes from then—the hands of a clock, a watch, the numerals 11. But George could not see any significance to the thought.

When he entered the room with the sergeant, he was ushered to a table. He sat down with Maj. Gen. Pitt, who glowered at him. Letting his mind roam the room, George picked up the numerals again and identified the man thinking them as the officer behind and a little to the right of the general.

What was going to happen at eleven? The man had no conscious thought of harm to anyone, yet the idea kept obtruding and seemed so out of keeping with his other thoughts George assigned several of his circuits to the man. The fact that the lieutenant looked at his watch and saw that it was 10:50 steeled George still more. If there was to be trouble, it would come from this one man.

"I'm General Pitt," the general said drily. "You're George, of course. I have been instructed to ask you what, exactly, your intentions are toward the United States and the world in general, with a view toward reaching some sort of agree-

ment with you and others of your kind, who will, as you say invade the Earth."

"Invade, General Pitt," George replied, "is not the word."

"All right, whatever the word is. We're all familiar with the plan you've been talking about. What we want to know is, where do you go from here?"

"The fact that there has been no reluctance on the part of the armed forces to talk of an agreement—even though I see that you privately do not favor such a talk, General Pitt—is an encouraging sign. We of Zanthar would not want to improve a planet which could not be educated and would continually oppose our program. This will make it possible for me to turn in a full report in a few days now."

"Will you please get to the point?"

George could see that the lieutenant was looking at his watch again. It was 10:58. George spread his mind out more than twenty miles, but could find no installation, horizontally or vertically, that indicated trouble. None of the men in the room seemed to think of becoming overly hostile.

"Yes, General. After my message goes out, there ought to be a landing party on Earth within a few weeks. While waiting for the first party, there must be certain preparations—"

George tensed. The lieutenant was reaching for something. But it somehow didn't seem connected with George. It was something white, a handkerchief. He saw that the man intended to blow his nose and started to relax, except that George suddenly became aware of the fact the man *did not need to blow his nose!*

Every thought-piercing circuit became instantly energized in George's mind and reached out in all directions....

There were at least ten shots from among the men. They stood there, surprised at their actions. Those who had fired their guns now held the smoking weapons awkwardly in their hands.

George's eyes were gone. Smoke curled upward from the two empty sockets where bullets had entered a moment before. The smoke grew heavier and his body became hot. Some of him turned cherry red and the chair on which he had been sitting started to burn. Finally, he collapsed toward the table and rolled to the floor.

He started to cool. He was no longer the shiny blue-steel color he had been—he had turned black. His metal gave off cracking noises and some of it buckled here and there as it cooled.

A few minutes later, tense military men and civilians grouped around a radio receiver in Chicago heard the report and relaxed, laughing and slapping each other on the back. Only one sat unmoved in a corner. Others finally sought him out.

"Well, Professor, it was your idea that did the trick. Don't you feel like celebrating?" one of them asked.

Prof. Tomlin shook his head. "If only George had been a little more benign, we might have learned a lot from him."

"What gave you the idea that killed him?"

"Oh, something he said about the unconscious and subconscious," Prof. Tomlin replied. "He admitted they were not penetrable. It was an easy matter to instill a post-hypnotic suggestion in some proven subjects and then to erase the hypnotic experience."

"You make it sound easy."

"It wasn't too difficult, really. It was finding the solution that was hard. We selected more than a hundred men, worked with them for days, finally singled out the best twenty, then made them forget their hypnosis. A first lieutenant—I've forgotten his name—had implanted in him a command even he was not aware of. His subconscious made him blow his nose fifteen minutes after he saw George. Nearly twenty others had post-hypnotic commands to shoot George in the eyes as soon as they saw the lieutenant blow his nose. Of course we also planted a subconscious hate pattern, which wasn't exactly necessary, just to make sure there would be no hesitation, no inhibition, no limiting moral factor.

"None of the men ever saw each other before being sent to Minerva. None realized that they carried with them the order for George's annihilation. The general, who was not one of the hypnotics, was given loose instructions, as were several others, so they could not possibly know the intention. Those of us who had conducted the hypnosis had to stay several hundred miles away so that we could not be reached by George's prying mind...."

I n a pasture next to a wood near Brentwood, a metal box buried in the ground suddenly exploded, uprooting a catalpa tree.

On a planet many millions of miles away, a red light—one of many on a giant control board—suddenly winked out.

A blue humanoid made an entry in a large book: *System 29578. Planet Three Inhabited.*

Too dangerous for any kind of development. • • •

JERRY SOHL (1913-2002) wrote "The Corbomite Maneuver," the first episode produced for the original series' first season. He also had co-story credit on "This Side of Paradise" and "Whom Gods Destroy."

MISSING MARS MINERAL FOUND!

SAN FRANCISCO — Researchers using a powerful instrument aboard NASA's Mars Reconnaissance Orbiter have found a long sought-after mineral on the Martian surface and, with it, unexpected clues to the Red Planet's watery past.

Surveying intact bedrock layers with the Compact Reconnaissance Imaging Spectrometer for Mars, or CRISM, scientists found carbonate minerals, indicating that Mars had neutral to alkaline water when the minerals formed more than 3.6 billion years ago. Carbonates, which on Earth include limestone and chalk, dissolve quickly in acid. Therefore, their survival until today on Mars challenges suggestions that an exclusively acidic environment later dominated the planet. Instead, it indicates that different types of watery environments existed. The greater the variety of wet environments, the greater the chances one or more of them may have supported life.

Carbonate rocks are created when water and carbon dioxide interact with calcium, iron or magnesium in volcanic rocks. Carbon dioxide from the atmosphere becomes trapped within the rocks. If all of the carbon dioxide locked in Earth's carbonates were released, our atmosphere would be thicker than that of Venus. Some researchers believe that a thick, carbon dioxide-rich atmosphere kept ancient Mars warm and kept water liquid on its surface long enough to have carved the valley systems observed today.

"The carbonates that CRISM has observed are regional rather than global in nature, and therefore, are too limited to account for enough carbon dioxide to form a thick atmosphere," said Bethany Ehlmann, lead author of the article and a spectrometer team member from Brown University in Providence, R.I.

The latest observations indicate carbonates may have formed over extended periods on early Mars. They also point to specific locations where future rovers and landers could search for possible evidence of past life.

—from NASA press release, December 18, 2008

by James Trefil

It's not "animal, vegetable, or mineral" anymore. The old quiz game "Twenty Questions" always started with this information. The assumption in the game was that everything was either nonliving (mineral) or living (plant or animal). In this sort of broad classification of living things, "plant" and "animal" would be called "kingdoms." Today, biologists generally talk about five different kingdoms.

In addition to the traditional kingdoms of plants and animals, modern scientists recognize three others: Monera (single-celled organisms without a cell nucleus), Protista (single-celled organisms with cell nuclei) and Fungi (such as molds and mushrooms).

Specifying the kingdom for an organism corresponds roughly to specifying the country in giving an address.

The earth's magnetic field undergoes episodic reversals. Right now, the "north" pole of the earth's magnet is in the Canadian Arctic. There have been times in the past, however, when the north pole is where Antarctica is now. We can document at least three hundred such reversals in the last few hundred million years. These reversals are erratic and the complete changeover of the poles seems to require about five thousand years. It seems to happen by having the field shrink down to zero and then grow again in the oppo-

site direction, rather than having the north pole migrate across the face of the earth.

EITHER THE EARTH'S MAGNETIC POLES ARE REVERSING, OR MY COMPASS HAS STOPPED!

How did wings evolve? While the evolutionary advantage to be gained from fully developed wings is not hard to see, the same can't be said about the advantage to be gained from the rudimentary appendages that must have led to them. In some cases, for example, birds, the wings evolved from arms and hands. For insects, however, the wings must have evolved from protuberances on the animal's side. Why would such protuberances have conveyed any advantage? The fact that wings would help a descendant a million years in the future certainly couldn't help an individual survive today.

Recently, scientists have argued that the protuberances played a role in temperature regulation—they provided extra surfaces through which heat could be absorbed or radiated. Calculations show that the most efficient heat exchangers are just about big enough to allow the insect to glide (something like a modem "flying" squirrel). From that point on, the organ, originally developed for one purpose (heat transfer), could be used as the basis for the development of another (flying). This idea, which makes a lot of sense to me, illustrates the ad hoc nature of the evolutionary process very well.

A material does not have to be a metal to be able to conduct electricity. Every material is a conductor when the voltage is high enough, since a high enough voltage can always tear electrons loose from atoms. For example, air is normally considered to be an insulator. However, when a large electrical charge accumulates on a thunder cloud, the atoms of air in the region of the cloud are torn apart, turning the air into a plasma. This is how a lightning bolt is created.

When you turn on a fluorescent light, some of the atoms in the gas become ionized and lose electrons. These free electrons can move when a voltage is applied. In the same way, if you dissolve salt in water, there will be charged ions floating in the water. These ions are free to move, and hence can constitute an electric current. Both salt water and ionized gases are examples of non-metallic conductors.

In biology, there is an exception to every rule, including the rule that photosynthesis requires chlorophyll. In 1971, biologists identified a bacterium that lives in salty environments (a so-called halobacterium). This bacterium does not use chlorophyll but still is capable of photosynthesizing. It produces a type of pigment similar to that found in eye colorings and combines it with a protein to form purple patches in its cell membrane. The patches produce ATP by photosynthesis, and the ATP then drives the metabolism of the cell.

The deepest test boring made anywhere on the earth is at the Kola Superdeep Borehole in northern Russia. Before drilling was stopped in 1992, the drill bit had passed 12 kilometers (7.5 miles), which is pretty close to the limit of what is technically possible.

Almost all the heavy elements in your body were made in supernovae somewhere. The big bang produced mainly hydrogen and helium, the raw fuel of stars. Fusion reactions in stars produce all other chemical elements. All elements heavier than iron, and most of the atoms of elements heavier than helium, are made in supernovae and then returned to the interstar medium when the supernova explodes, where they became the starting point for the formation of the next generation of stars. Thus, as the galaxy has aged, the complement of heavy elements has increased. The sun and the solar system, having formed fairly late in the galaxy, incorporated these star-made elements into their structure. The calcium in your bones, the iron in your blood, and the carbon in your tissues all got their start inside a star somewhere, and most likely inside of a supernova. • • •

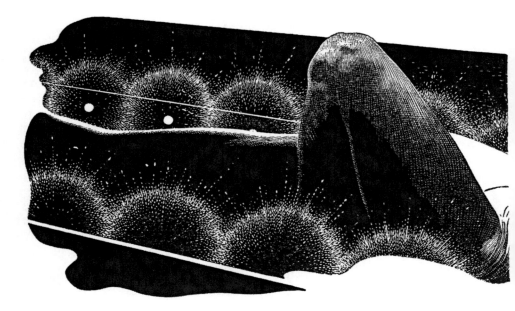

Tod awoke first, probably because he was so curious, so deeply alive; perhaps because he was (or had been) seventeen. He fought back, but the manipulators would not be denied. They bent and flexed his arms and legs, squeezed his chest, patted and rasped and abraded him. His joints creaked, his sluggish blood clung sleepily to the walls of his veins, reluctant to move after so long.

He gasped and shouted as needles of cold played over his body, gasped again and screamed when his skin sensitized and the tingling intensified to a scald. Then he fainted, and probably slept, for he easily reawoke when someone else started screaming.

He felt weak and ravenous, but extraordinarily well-rested. His first conscious realization was that the manipulators had withdrawn from his body, as had the needles from the back of his neck. He put a shaky hand back there and felt the traces of spot-tape, already half-fused with his healing flesh.

He listened comfortably to this new screaming, satisfied that it was not his own. He let his eyes open, and a great wonder came over him when he saw that the lid of his Coffin stood open.

He clawed upward, sat a moment to fight a vicious swirl of vertigo, vanquished it and hung his chin on the edge of the Coffin.

The screaming came from April's Coffin. It was open too. Since the two massive boxes touched and their hinges were on opposite sides, he could look down at her. The manipulators were at work on the girl's body, working with competent violence. She seemed to be caught up in some frightful nightmare, lying on her back, dreaming of riding a runaway bicycle with an off-center pedal sprocket and epicyclic hubs. And all the while her arms seemed to be flailing at a cloud of dream-hornets round her tossing head. The needle-cluster rode with her head, fanning out behind the nape like the mechanical extrapolation of an Elizabethan collar.

Tod crawled to the end of his Coffin, stood up shakily and grasped the horizontal bar set at chest level. He got an arm over it and snugged it close under his

The Golden Helix

by Theodore Sturgeon

Illustrated by Virgil Finlay

Originally appeared in Thrilling Wonder Stories, *Summer 1954.*
Story and artwork copyright © 1954 Standard Magazines, Inc.
Story reprinted by permission of the Theodore Sturgeon Literary Trust c/o Ralph Vicinanza, Ltd.
Artwork reprinted by permission of Lail Finlay.

armpit. Half-suspended, he could then manage one of his feet over the edge, then the other, to the top step. He lowered himself until he sat on it, outside the Coffin at last, and slumped back to rest. When his furious lungs and battering heart calmed themselves, he went down the four steps one at a time, like an infant, on his buttocks.

April's screams stopped.

Tod sat on the bottom step, jackknifed by fatigue, his feet on the metal floor, his knees in the hollows between his pectorals and his shoulders. Before him, on a low pedestal, was a cube with a round switch-disk on it. When he could, he inched a hand forward and let it fall on the disk. There was an explosive tinkle and the front panel of the cube disappeared, drifting slowly away as a fine glittering dust. He lifted his heavy hand and reached inside. He got one capsule, two, carried them to his lips. He rested, then took a beaker from the cube. It was three-quarters full of purple crystals. He bumped it on the steel floor. The beaker's cover powdered and fell in, and the crystals were suddenly a liquid, effervescing violently. When it subsided, he drank it down. He belched explosively, and then his head cleared, his personal horizons expanded to include the other Coffins, the compartment walls, the ship itself and its mission.

But there somewhere—somewhere close, now—was Sirius and its captive Planet, Terra Prime. Earth's first major colony, Prime would one day flourish as Earth never had, for it would be a planned and tailored planet. Eight and a half light-years from Earth, Prime's population was composed chiefly of Earth immigrants, living in pressure domes and slaving to alter the atmosphere of the planet to Earth normal. Periodically there must be an infusion of Earth blood to keep the strain as close as possible on both planets, for unless a faster-than-light drive could be developed, there could be no frequent interchange between the worlds. What took light eight years took humans half a lifetime. The solution was the Coffins—the marvelous machine in which a man could slip into a sleep which was more than sleep while still on Earth, and awake years later in space, near his destination, subjectively only a month or so older. Without the Coffins there could be only divergence, possibly mutation. Humanity wanted to populate the stars— but with humanity.

Tod and his five shipmates were handpicked. They had superiorities—mechanical, mathematical and artistic aptitudes. But they were not all completely superior. One does not populate a colony with leaders alone and expect it to live. They, like the rest of their cargo (machine designs, microfilms of music and art, technical and medical writings, novels and entertainment) were neither advanced nor extraordinary. Except for Teague, they were the tested median, the competent; they were basic blood for a mass, rather than an elite.

Tod glanced around the blank walls and into the corner where a thin line delineated the sealed door. He ached to fling it open and skid across the corridor, punch the control which would slide away the armor which masked the port and soak himself in his first glimpse of outer space. He had heard so much about it, but he had never seen it—they had all been deep in their timeless sleep before the ship had blasted off.

But he sighed and went instead to the Coffins.

Alma's was still closed, but there was sound and motion, in varying degrees, from all the others.

He glanced first into April's Coffin. She seemed to be asleep now. The needle-cluster and manipulators had withdrawn. Her skin glowed; it was alive and as unlike its former monochrome waxiness as it could be. He smiled briefly and went to look at Teague.

Teague, too, was in real slumber. The fierce vertical line between his brows was shallow now, and the hard, deft hands lax and uncharacteristically purposeless. Tod had never seen him before without a focus for those narrow, blazing green eyes, without decisive spring and balance in his pose. It was good, somehow, to feel that for all his responsibilities, Teague could be as helpless as anyone.

Tod smiled as he passed Alma's closed Coffin. He always smiled at Alma when he saw her, when he heard her voice, when she crossed his thoughts. It was possible to be very brave around Alma, for gentleness and comfort were so ready that it was almost not necessary to call upon them. One could bear anything, knowing she was there.

Tod crossed the chamber and looked at the last pair. Carl was a furious blur of motion, his needle-cluster swinging free, his manipulators in the final phase. He grunted instead of screaming, a series of implosive, startled gasps. His eyes were open but only the whites showed.

Moira was quite relaxed, turned on her side, poured out on the floor of the Coffin like a long golden cat. She seemed in a contented abandonment of untroubled sleep.

He heard a new sound and went back to April. She was sitting up, cross-legged, her head bowed apparently in deep concentration. Tod understood; he knew that sense of achievement and the dedication of an entire psyche to the proposition that these weak and trembling arms which hold one up shall *not* bend.

He reached in and gently lifted the soft white hair away from her face. She raised the albino's fathomless ruby eyes to him and whimpered.

"Come on," he said quietly. "We're here." When she did not move, he balanced on his stomach on the edge of the Coffin and put one hand between her shoulder blades. "Come on."

She pitched forward but he caught her so that she stayed kneeling. He drew her up and forward and put her hands on the bar. "Hold tight, Ape," he said. She did, while he lifted her thin body out of the Coffin and stood her on the top step. "Let go now. Lean on me."

Mechanically she obeyed, and he brought her down until she sat, as he had, on the bottom step. He punched the switch at her feet and put the capsules in her mouth while she looked up at him numbly, as if hypnotized. He got her beaker, thumped it, held it until its foaming subsided, and then put an arm around her shoulders while she drank. She closed her eyes and slumped against him, breathing deeply at first, and later, for a moment that frightened him, not at all. Then she sighed. "Tod...."

"I'm here, Ape."

She straightened up, turned and looked at him. She seemed to be trying to smile, but she shivered instead. "I'm cold."

He rose, keeping one hand on her shoulder until he was sure she could sit up unassisted, and then brought her a cloak from the clips outside the Coffin. He helped her with it, knelt and put on her slippers for her. She sat quite still, hugging the garment tight to her. At last she looked around and back; up, around and back again. "We're—there!" she breathed.

"We're *here*," he corrected.

"Yes, here. Here. How long do you suppose we...."

"We won't know exactly until we can take some readings. Twenty-five, twenty-seven years—maybe more."

She said, "I could be old, old—" She touched her face, brought her fingertips down to the sides of her neck. "I could be forty, even!"

He laughed at her, and then a movement caught the corner of his eye. "Carl!"

Carl was sitting sidewise on the edge of his Coffin, his feet still inside. Weak or no, bemused as could be expected, Carl should have grinned at Tod, should have made some healthy, swaggering gesture. Instead he sat still, staring about him in utter puzzlement. Tod went to him. "Carl! Carl, we're here!"

Carl looked at him dully. Tod was unaccountably disturbed. Carl always shouted, always bounced; Carl had always seemed to be just a bit larger inside than he was outside, ready to burst through, always thinking faster, laughing more quickly than anyone else.

He allowed Tod to help him down the steps, and sat heavily while Tod got his capsules and beaker for him. Waiting for the liquid to subside, he looked around numbly. Then drank, and almost toppled. April and Tod held him up. When he straightened again, it was abruptly. "Hey!" he roared. "We're here!" He looked up at them. "April! Tod-o! Well what do you know—how are you, kids?"

"Carl?" The voice was the voice of a flute, if a flute could whisper. They looked up. There was a small golden surf of hair tumbled on and over the edge of Moira's Coffin.

Weakly, eagerly, they clambered up to Moira and helped her out. Carl breathed such a sigh of relief that Tod and April stopped to smile at him, at each other.

Carl shrugged out of his weakness as if it were an uncomfortable garment and went to be close to Moira, to care about Moira and nothing else.

A deep labored voice called, "Who's up?"

"Teague! It's Teague... all of us, Teague," called Tod. "Carl and Moira and April and me. All except Alma."

Slowly Teague's great head rose out of the Coffin. He looked around with the controlled motion of a radar sweep. When his head stopped its one turning, the motion seemed relayed to his body, which began to move steadily upward. The four who watched him knew intimately what this cost him in sheer willpower, yet no one made any effort to help. Unasked, one did not help Teague.

One leg over, the second. He ignored the bar and stepped down to seat himself on the bottom step as if it were a throne. His hands moved very slowly but without faltering as he helped himself to the capsules, then the beaker. He permitted himself a moment of stillness, eyes closed, nostrils pinched; then life coursed strongly into him. It was as if his muscles visibly filled out a little. He seemed heavier and taller, and when he opened his eyes, they were the deeply vital, commanding light-sources which had drawn them, linked them, led them all during their training.

He looked toward the door in the corner. "Has anyone—"

"We were waiting for you," said Tod. "Shall we... can we go look now? I want to see the stars."

"We'll see to Alma first." Teague rose, ignoring the lip of his Coffin and the handhold it offered. He went to Alma's. With his height, he was the only one among them who could see through the top plate without mounting the steps.

Then, without turning, he said, "Wait." The others, half across the room from him, stopped. Teague turned to them. There was no expression on his face at all. He stood quite motionless for perhaps ten seconds, and then quietly released a breath. He mounted the steps of Alma's Coffin, reached and the side nearest his own machine sank silently into the floor. He stepped down, and spent a long moment bent over the body inside. From where they stood, tense and frightened, the others could not see inside. They made no effort to move closer.

"Tod," said Teague, "get the kit. Surgery Lambda. Moira, I'll need you."

The shock of it went to Tod's bones, regenerated, struck him again; yet so conditioned was he to Teague's commands that he was on his feet and moving before Teague had stopped speaking. He went to the after bulkhead and swung open a panel, pressed a stud. There was a metallic whisper, and the heavy case slid out at his feet. He lugged it over to Teague, and helped him rack it on the side of the Coffin. Teague immediately plunged his hands through the membrane at one end of the kit, nodding to Moira to do likewise at the other. Tod stepped back, studiously avoiding a glance in at Alma, and returned to April. She put both her hands tight around his left biceps and leaned close. "Lambda..." she whispered. "That's... parturition, isn't it?"

He shook his head. "Parturition is Surgery Kappa," he said painfully. He swallowed. "Lambda's Caesarian."

Her crimson eyes widened. "Caesarian? *Alma?* She'd never need a Caesarian!"

He turned to look at her, but he could not see, his eyes stung so. "Not while she lived, she wouldn't," he whispered. He felt the small white hands tighten painfully on his arm. Across the room, Carl sat quietly. Tod squashed the water out of his eyes with the heel of his hand.

Carl began pounding knuckles, very slowly, against his own temple.

Teague and Moira were busy for a long time.

II

Tod pulled in his legs and lowered his head until the kneecaps pressed cruelly against his eyebrow ridges. He hugged his shins, ground his back into the wall panels and in this red-spangled blackness he let himself live back and back to Alma and joy, Alma and comfort, Alma and courage.

He had sat once, just this way, twisted by misery and anger, blind and helpless, in a dark corner of an equipment shed at the spaceport. The rumor had circulated that April would not come after all, because albinism and the Sirius Rock would not mix. It turned out to be untrue, but that did not matter at the time. He had punched her, punched *Alma!* because in all the world he had been given nothing else to strike out at, and she had found him and had sat down to be with him. She had not even touched her face, where the blood ran; she simply waited until at last he flung himself on her lap and wept like an infant. And no one but he and Alma ever knew of it....

He remembered Alma with the spaceport children, rolling and tumbling on the lawn with them, and in the pool; and he remembered Alma, her face still, looking up at the stars with her soft and gentle eyes, and in those eyes he had seen a challenge as implacable and pervasive as space itself. The tumbling on the lawn, the towering dignity—these coexisted in Alma without friction. He remembered things she had said to him; for each of the things he could recall the kind of light, the way he stood, the very smell of the air at the time. "Never be afraid, Tod. Just think of the worst possible thing that might happen. What you're afraid of will probably not be *that* bad—and anything else just has to be better." And she said once, "Don't confuse logic and truth, however good the logic. You can stick one end of logic in solid ground and throw the other end clear out of the cosmos without breaking it. Truth's a little less flexible." And, "Of *course* you need to be loved, Tod! Don't be ashamed of that, or try to change it. It's not a thing you have to worry about, ever. You are loved. April loves you. And I love you. Maybe I love you even more than April, because she loves everything you are, but I love everything you were and ever will be."

And some of the memories were deeper and more important even than these, but were memories of small things—the meeting of eyes, the touch of a hand, the sound of laughter or a snatch of song, distantly.

Tod descended from memory into a blackness that was only loss and despair, and then a numbness, followed by a reluctant awareness. He became conscious of what, in itself, seemed the merest of trifles: that there was a significance in his pose there against the bulkhead. Unmoving, he considered it. It was comfortable, to be so turned in upon oneself, and so protected, unaware... and Alma would have hated to see him this way.

He threw up his head, and self-consciously straightened from his fetal posture. *That's over now*, he told himself furiously, and then, dazed, wondered what he had meant.

He turned to look at April. She was huddled miserably against him, her face and body lax, stopped, disinterested. He thumped his elbow into her ribs, hard enough to make her remember she had ribs. She looked up into his eyes and said,

"How? How could...."

Tad understood. Of the three couples standard for each ship of the Sirian project, one traditionally would beget children on the planet; one, earlier, as soon as possible after awakening; and one still earlier, for conception would take place within the Coffin. But—not *before* awakening, and surely not long enough before to permit gestation. It was an impossibility; the vital processes were so retarded within the Coffin that, effectively, there would be no stirring of life at all. So—"How?" April pleaded. "How could...."

Tod gazed upon his own misery, then April's, and wondered what it must be that Teague was going through.

Teague, without looking up, said, "Tod."

Tod patted April's shoulder, rose and went to Teague. He did not look into the Coffin. Teague, still working steadily, tilted his head to one side to point. "I need a little more room here."

Tod lifted the transparent cube Teague had indicated and looked at the squirming pink bundle inside. He almost smiled. It was a nice baby. He took one step away and Teague said, "Take 'em all, Tod."

He stacked them and carried them to where April sat. Carl rose and came over, and knelt. The boxes hummed—a vibration which could be felt, not heard—as nutrient-bearing air circulated inside and back to to the power-packs. "A nice normal deliv—I mean, a nice normal batch o' brats," Carl said. "Four girls, one boy. Just right."

Tod looked up at him. "There's one more, I think."

There was—another boy. Moira brought it over in the sixth box. "Sweet," April breathed, watching them. "They're sweet."

Moira said, wearily, "That's all."

Tod looked up at her.

"Alma...?"

Moira waved laxly toward the neat stack of incubators. "That's all," she whispered tiredly, and went to Carl.

That's all there is of Alma, Tod thought bitterly. He glanced across at Teague. The tall figure raised a steady hand, wiped his face with his upper arm. His raised hand touched the high end of the Coffin, and for an instant held a grip. Teague's face lay against his arm, pillowed, hidden and still. Then he completed the wiping motion and began stripping the sterile plastic skin from his hands. Tod's heart went out to him, but he bit the insides of his cheeks and kept silent. *A strange tradition,* thought Tod, *that makes it impolite to grieve....*

Teague dropped the shreds of plastic into the disposal slot and turned to face them. He looked at each in turn, and each in turn found some measure of control. He turned then, and pulled a lever, and the side of Alma's Coffin slid silently up.

Good-by....

Tod put his back against the bulkhead and slid down beside April. He put an arm over her shoulders. Carl and Moira sat close, holding hands. Moira's eyes were shadowed but very much awake. Carl bore an expression almost of sullenness. Tod glanced, then glared at the boxes. Three of the babies were crying, though of course they could not be heard through the plastic incubators. Tod was suddenly conscious of Teague's eyes upon him. He flushed, and then let his anger drain to the capacious inner reservoir which must hold it and all his grief as well.

When he had their attention, Teague sat cross-legged before them and placed a small object on the floor.

Tod looked at the object. At first glance it seemed to be a metal spring about as long as his thumb, mounted vertically on a black base. Then he realized that it was an art object of some kind, made of a golden substance which shimmered and all but flowed. It was an interlocked double spiral; the turns went round and up, round and down, round and up again, the texture of the gold clearly indicating, in a strange and alive way, which symbolized a rising and falling flux. Shaped as if it had been wound on a cylinder and the cylinder removed, the thing was formed of a continuous wire or rod which had no beginning and no end, but which turned and rose and turned and descended again in an exquisite continuity... Its base was formless, an almost-smoke just as the gold showed an almost-flux; and it was as lightless as ylem.

Teague said, "This was in Alma's Coffin. It was not there when we left Earth."

"It must have been," said Carl flatly.

Teague silently shook his head. April opened her lips, closed them again. Teague said, "Yes, April?"

April shook her head. "Nothing, Teague. Really nothing." But because Teague kept looking at her, waiting, she said, "I was going to say... it's beautiful." She hung her head.

Teague's lips twitched. Tod could sense the sympathy there. He stroked April's silver hair. She responded, moving her shoulder slightly under his hand. "What is it, Teague?"

When Teague would not answer, Moira asked, "Did it... had it anything to do with Alma?"

Teague picked it up thoughtfully. Tod could see the yellow loom it cast against his throat and cheek, the golden points it built in his eyes. "Something did." He paused. "You know she was supposed to conceive on awakening. But to give birth—"

Carl cracked a closed hand against his forehead. "She must have been awake for anyway two hundred and eighty days!"

"Maybe she made it," said Moira.

Tod watched Teague's hand half-close on the object as if it might be precious now. Moira's was a welcome thought, and the welcome could be read on Teague's face. Watching it, Tod saw the complicated spoor of a series of efforts—a gathering of emotions, a determination; the closing of certain doors, the opening of others.

Teague rose. "We have a ship to inspect, sights to take, calculations... we've got to tune in Terra Prime, send them a message if we can. Tod, check the corridor air."

"The stars—we'll see the stars!" Tod whispered to April, the heady thought all but eclipsing everything else. He bounded to the corner where the door controls waited. He punched the test button, and a spot of green appeared over the door, indicating that with their awakening, the evacuated chambers, the living and control compartments, had been flooded with air and warmed. "Air okay."

"Go on then."

They crowded around Tod as he grasped the lever and pushed. *I won't wait for orders*, Tod thought. *I'll slide right across the corridor and open the guard plate and there it'll be—space, and the stars!*

The door opened.

There was no corridor, no bulkhead, no armored porthole, no—

No *ship*!

There was a night out there, dank, warm. It was wet. In it were hooked, fleshy leaves and a tangle of roots; a thing with legs which hopped up on the sill and shimmered its wings for them; a thing like a flying hammer which crashed in and smote the shimmering one and was gone with it, leaving a stain on the deck-plates. There was a sky aglow with a ghastly green. There was a thrashing and a scream out there, a pressure of growth and a wrongness.

Blood ran down Tod's chin. His teeth met through his lower lip. He turned and looked past three sets of terrified eyes to Teague, who said, "Shut it!"

Tod snatched at the control. It broke off in his hand....

How long does a thought, a long thought, take?

Tod stood with the fractured metal in his hand and thought:

We were told that above all things we must adapt. We were told that perhaps there would be a thin atmosphere by now, on Terra Prime, but that in all likelihood we must live a new kind of life in pressure-domes. We were warned that what we might find would be flash-mutation, where the people could be more or less than human. We were warned, even, that there might be no life on Prime at all. But look at me now—look at all of us. We weren't meant to adapt to this! And we can't....

Somebody shouted while somebody shrieked, each sound a word, each destroying the other. Something thick as a thumb, long as a hand, with a voice like a distant airhorn, hurtled through the door and circled the room. Teague snatched a folded cloak from the clothing rack and, poising just a moment, battled it out of the air. It skittered, squirming across the metal door. He threw the cloak on it to capture it. "Get that door closed."

Carl snatched the broken control lever out of Tod's hand and tried to fit it back into the switch mounting. It crumbled as if it were dried bread. Tod stepped outside, hooked his hands on the edge of the door and pulled. It would not budge. A lizard as long as his arm scuttled out of the twisted grass and stopped to stare at him. He shouted at it, and with forelegs much too long for such a creature, it pressed itself upward until its body was forty-five degrees from the horizontal, it flicked the end of its long tail upward, and something flew over its head toward Tod, buzzing angrily. Tod turned to see what it was, and as he did the lizard struck from one side and April from the other.

April succeeded and the lizard failed, for its fangs clashed and it fell forward, but April's shoulder had taken Tod on the chest and, off balance as he was, he went flat on his back. The cold, dry, pulsing tail swatted his hand. He gripped it convulsively, held on tight. Part of the tail broke off and buzzed, flipping about on the ground like a click-beetle. But the rest held. Tod scuttled backward to pull the lizard straight as it began to turn on him, got his knees under him, then his feet. He swung the lizard twice around his head and smashed it against the inside of the open door. The part of the tail he was holding then broke off, and the scaly thing thumped inside and slid, causing Moira to leap so wildly to get out of its way that she nearly knocked the stocky Carl off his feet.

Teague swept away the lid of the Surgery Lambda kit, inverted it, kicked the clutter of instruments and medicaments aside and clapped the inverted box over the twitching, scaly body.

"April!" Tod shouted. He ran around in a blind semi-circle, saw her struggling to her feet in the grass, snatched her up and bounded inside with her. "Carl!" he gasped, "Get the door...."

But Carl was already moving forward with a needle torch. With two deft motions he sliced out a section of the power-arm which was holding the door open. He swung the door to, yelling, "Parametal!"

Tod, gasping, ran to the lockers and brought a length of the synthetic. Carl took the wide ribbon and with a snap of the wrists broke it in two. Each half he bent (for it was very flexible when moved slowly) into a U. He placed one against the door and held out his hand without looking. Tod dropped the hammer into it. Carl tapped the parametal gently and it adhered to the door. He turned his face away and struck it sharply. There was a blue white flash and the U was rigid and firmly welded to the door. He did the same thing with the other U, welding it to the nearby wall plates. Into the two gudgeons thus formed, Moira dropped a lux-alloy bar, and the door was secured.

"Shall I sterilize the floor?" Moira asked.

"No," said Teague shortly.

"But—bacteria... spores...."

"Forget it," said Teague.

April was crying. Tod held her close, but made no effort to stop her. Something in him, deeper than panic, more essential than wonderment, understood that she could use this circumstance to spend her tears for Alma, and that these tears must be shed now or swell and burst her heart. *So cry*, he pled silently, *cry for both of us, all of us.*

With the end of action, belated shock spread visibly over Carl's face. "The ship's gone," he said stupidly. "We're on a planet." He looked at his hands, turned abruptly to the door, stared at it and began to shiver. Moira went to him and stood quietly, not touching him—just being near, in case she should be needed. April grew gradually silent. Carl said, "I—" and then shook his head.

Click. Shh. Clack, click. Methodically Teague was stacking the scattered contents of the medical kit. Tod patted April's shoulder and went to help. Moira glanced at them, peered closely into Carl's face, then left him and came to lend a hand. April joined them, and at last Carl. They swept up, and tracked and stored the clutter, and when Teague lowered a table, they helped get the dead lizard on it and pegged out for dissection. Moira cautiously disentangled the huge insect from the folds of the cloak and clapped a box over it, slid the lid underneath to bring the feebly squirming thing to Teague. He studied it for a long moment, then set it down and peered at the lizard. With forceps he opened the jaws and bent close. He grunted. "April...."

She came to look. Teague touched the fangs with the tip of a scalpel. "Look there."

"Grooves," she said. "Like a snake."

Teague reversed the scalpel and with the handle he gingerly pressed upward, at the root of one of the fangs. A cloudy yellow liquid beaded, ran down the groove. He dropped the scalpel and slipped a watch-glass under the tooth to catch the droplet. "Analyze that later," he murmured. "But I'd say you saved Tod from something pretty nasty."

"I didn't even think," said April. "I didn't... I never knew there was any animal life on Prime. I wonder what they call this monster."

"The honors are yours, April. You name it."

"They'll have a classification for it already!"

"Who?"

Everyone started to talk, and abruptly stopped. In the awkward silence Carl's sudden laugh boomed. It was a wondrous sound in the frightened chamber. There was comprehension in it, and challenge, and above all, Carl himself—boisterous and impulsive, quick, sure. The laugh was triggered by the gush of talk and its sudden cessation, a small thing in itself. But its substance was understanding, and with that an emotional surge, and with that, the choice of the one emotional expression Carl would always choose.

"Tell them, Carl," Teague said.

Carl's teeth flashed. He waved a thick arm at the door. "That isn't Sirius Prime. Or Earth. Go ahead, April—name your pet."

April, staring at the lizard, said, *"Crotalidus,* then, because it has a rattle and fangs like a diamondback." Then she paled and turned to Carl, as the full weight of his statement came on her. "Not—*not Prime?"*

Quietly, Teague said, "Nothing like these ever grew on Earth. And Prime is a cold planet. It could never have a climate like that," he nodded toward the door, "no matter how much time has passed."

"But what... where..." It was Moira.

"We'll find out when we can. But the instruments aren't here—they were in the ship."

"But if it's a new... another planet, why didn't you let me sterilize? What about airborne spores? Suppose it had been methane out there or—"

"We've obviously been conditioned to anything in the atmosphere. As to its composition—well, it isn't poisonous, or we wouldn't be standing here talking about it. Wait!" He held up a hand and quelled the babble of questions before it could fully start. "Wondering is a luxury like worrying. We can't afford either. We'll get our answers when we get more evidence."

"What shall we do?" asked April faintly.

"Eat," said Teague. "Sleep." They waited. Teague said, "Then we go outside."

III

There were stars like daisies in a field, like dust in a sunbeam and like flying, flaming mountains; near ones, far ones, stars of every color and every degree of brilliance. And there were bands of light which must be stars too distant to see. And something was stealing the stars, not taking them away, but swallowing them up, coming closer and closer, eating as it came. And at last there was only one left. Its name was Alma, and it was gone, and there was nothing left but an absorbent blackness and an aching loss.

In this blackness Tod's eyes snapped open, and he gasped, frightened and lost.

"You awake, Tod?" April's small hand touched his face. He took it and drew it to his lips, drinking comfort from it.

From the blackness came Carl's resonant whisper, "We're awake. Teague?..."

The lights flashed on, dim first, brightening swiftly, but not so fast as to dazzle unsuspecting eyes. Tod sat up and saw Teague at the table. On it was the lizard, dissected and laid out as neatly as an exploded view in a machine manual. Over the table, on a gooseneck, was a floodlamp with its lens masked by an infrared filter. Teague turned away from the table, pushing up his "black-light" goggles, and nodded to Tod. There were shadows under his eyes, but otherwise he seemed the same as ever. Tod wondered how many lonely hours he had worked while the two couples slept, doing that meticulous work under the irritating glow so that they would be undisturbed.

Tod went to him. "Has my playmate been talking much?" He pointed at the remains of the lizard.

"Yes and no," said Teague. "Oxygen-breather, all right, and a true lizard. He had a secret weapon—that tail segment he flips over his head toward his victims. It has primitive ganglia like an Earth salamander's, so that the tail segment trembles and squirms, sounding the rattles, after he throws it. He also has a skeleton that—but all this doesn't matter. Most im-portant is that he's the analogue of our early Permian life, which means (unless he's an evolutionary dead-end like a cockroach) that this planet is a billion years old at the least. And the little fellow here—" he touched the flying thing—"bears this out. It's not an insect, you know. It's an arachnid."

"With *wings?*"

Teague lifted the slender, scorpion like pincers of the creature and let them fall. "Flat chitinous wings are no more remarkable a leg adaptation than those things. Anyway, in spite of the ingenuity of his engineering, internally he's pretty primitive. All of which lets us hypothesize that we'll find fairly close analogues of what we're used to on Earth."

"Teague," Tod interrupted, his voice lowered, his eyes narrowed to contain the worry that threatened to spill over, "Teague, what's happened?"

"The temperature and humidity here seem to be exactly the same as that outside," Teague went on, in precisely the same tone as before. "This would indicate either a warm planet, or a warm season on a temperate planet. In either case it is obvious that—"

"But, *Teague*—"

"—that a good deal of theorizing is possible with very little evidence, and we need not occupy ourselves with anything else but that evidence."

"Oh," said Tod. He backed off a step. "Oh," he said again, "sorry, Teague." He joined the others at the food dispensers, feeling like a cuffed puppy. *But he's right*, he thought. *As Alma said... of the many things which might have happened, only one actually has. Let's wait then, and worry about that one thing when we can name it.*

There was a pressure on his arm. He looked up from his thoughts and into April's searching eyes. He knew that she had heard, and he was unreasonably angry at her. "Damn it, he's so cold-blooded," he blurted defensively, but in a whisper.

April said, "He has to stay with things he can understand, every minute." She glanced swiftly at the closed Coffin. "Wouldn't you?"

There was a sharp pain and a bitterness in Tod's throat as he thought about it. He dropped his eyes and mumbled, "No, I wouldn't. I don't think I could." There was a difference in his eyes as he glanced back at Teague. *But it's so easy, after all, for strong people to be strong*, he thought.

"Teague, what'll we wear?" Carl called.

"Skinflex."

"Oh, no!" cried Moira. "It's so clingy and hot!"

Carl laughed at her. He swept up the lizard's head and opened its jaws. "Smile at the lady. She wouldn't put any tough old skinflex in the way of your pretty teeth!"

"Put it down," said Teague sharply, though there was a flicker of amusement in his eyes. "It's still loaded with God-knows-what alkaloid. Moira, he's right. Skinflex just doesn't puncture."

Moira looked respectfully at the yellow fangs and went obediently to storage, where she pulled out the suits.

"We'll keep close together, back to back," said Teague as they helped each other into the suits. "All the weapons are... were... in the forward storage compartment, so we'll improvise. Tod, you and the girls each take a globe of anesthene. It's the fastest anesthetic we have and it ought to take care of anything that breathes oxygen. I'll take scalpels. Carl—"

"The hammer," Carl grinned. His voice was fairly thrumming with excitement.

"We won't attempt to fasten the door from outside. I don't mean to go farther than ten meters out, this first time. Just—you, Carl—lift off the bar as we go out, get the door shut as quickly as possible and prop it there. Whatever happens, do not attack anything out there unless you are attacked first, or unless I say so."

Hollow-eyed, steady, Teague moved to the door with the others close around him. Carl shifted the hammer to his left hand, lifted the bar and stood back a little, holding it like a javelin. Teague, holding a glittering lancet lightly in each hand, pushed the door open with his foot. They boiled through, stepped aside for Carl as he butted the rod deep into the soil and against the closed door. "All set."

They moved as a unit for perhaps three meters, and stopped.

It was daytime now, but such a day as none of them had dreamed of. The light was green, very nearly a lime green, and the shadows were purple. The sky was more lavender than blue. The air was warm and wet.

They stood at the top of a low hill. Before them a tangle of jungle tumbled up at them. So vital, so completely alive, it seemed to move by its own power of growth. Stirring, murmuring, it was too big, too much, too wide and deep and intertwined to assimilate at a glance; the thought, *this is a jungle*, was a pitiable understatement.

To the left, savannahlike grassland rolled gently down to the choked margins of a river—calmfaced, muddy and secretive. It too seemed astir with inner growings. To the right, more jungle. Behind them, the bland and comforting wall of their compartment.

Above—

It may have been April who saw it first; in any case, Tod always associated the vision with April's scream.

They moved as she screamed, five humans jerked back then like five dolls on a single string, pressed together and to the compartment wall by an overwhelming claustrophobia. They were ants under a descending heel, flies on an anvil... together their backs struck the wall and they cowered there, looking up.

And it was not descending. It was only—big. It was just that it was there, over them.

April said, later, that it was like a cloud. Carl would argue that it was cylindrical, with flared ends and a narrow waist. Teague never attempted to describe it, because he disliked inaccuracies, and Moira was too awed to try. To Tod, the object had no shape. It was a luminous opacity between him and the sky, solid, massive as mountains. There was only one thing they agreed on, and that was that it was a ship.

And out of the ship came the golden ones.

They appeared under the ship as speckles of light, and grew in size as they descended, so that the five humans must withstand a second shock: they had known the ship was huge, but had not known until now how very high above them it hung.

Down they came, dozens, hundreds. They filled the sky over the jungle and around the five, moving to make a spherical quadrant from the horizontal to the zenith, a full hundred and eighty degrees from side to side—a radiant floating shell with its concave surface toward, around, above them. They blocked out the sky and the jungle-tops, cut off most of the strange green light, replacing it with their own— for each glowed coolly.

Each individual was distinct and separate. Later, they would argue about the form and shape of the vessel, but the exact shape of these golden things was never even mentioned. Nor did they ever agree on a name for them. To Carl they were an

army, to April, angels. Moira called them (secretly) "the seraphim," and to Tod they were masters. Teague never named them.

For measureless time they hung there, with the humans gaping up at them. There was no flutter of wings, no hum of machinery to indicate how they stayed aloft, and if each individual had a device to keep him afloat, it was of a kind the humans could not recognize. They were beautiful, awesome, uncountable.

And nobody was afraid.

Tod looked from side to side, from top to bottom of this incredible formation, and became aware that it did not touch the ground. Its lower edge was exactly horizontal, at his eye level. Since the hill fell away on all sides, he could see under this lower edge, here the jungle, there down across the savannah to the river. In a new amazement he saw eyes, and protruding heads.

In the tall grass at the jungle margin was a scurry and cease, scurry and cease, as newtlike animals scrambled not quite into the open and froze, watching. Up in the lower branches of the fleshy, hook-leaved trees, the heavy scaly heads of leaf-eaters showed, and here and there was the armed head of a lizard with cat-like tearing tusks.

Leather-winged fliers flapped clumsily to rest in the branches, hung for a moment for all the world like broken umbrellas, then achieved balance and folded their pinions. Something slid through the air, almost caught a branch, missed it and tumbled end-over-end to the ground, resolving itself into a broad-headed scaly thing with wide membranes between fore and hind legs. And Tod saw his acquaintance of the night before, with its serrated tail and needle fangs.

And though there must have been eater and eaten here, hunter and hunted, they all watched silently, turned like living compass-needles to the airborne mystery surrounding the humans. They crowded together like a nightmare parody of the Lion and the Lamb, making a constellation, a galaxy of bright and wondering eyes; their distance from each other being, in its way, cosmic.

Tod turned his face into the strange light, and saw one of the gold beings separate from the mass and drift down and forward and stop. Had this living shell been a segment of curving mirror, this one creature would have been at its focal point. For a moment there was complete stillness, a silent waiting. Then the creature made a deep... *gesture*. Behind it, all the others did the same.

If ten thousand people stand ten thousand meters away, and if, all once, they kneel, it is hardly possible to see just what it is they have done; yet the aspect of their mass undergoes a definite change. So it was with the radiant shell—it changed, all of it, without moving. There was no mistaking the nature of the change, though its meaning was beyond knowing. It was an obeisance. It was an expression of profound respect, first to the humans themselves, next, and hugely, to something the humans represented. It was unquestionably an act of worship.

And what, thought Tod, *could we symbolize to these shining ones?* He was a scarab beetle or an Egyptian cat, a Hindu cow or a Teuton tree, told suddenly that it was sacred.

All the while there flooded down the thing which Carl had tried ineptly to express: *"We're sorry. But it will be all right. You will be glad. You can be glad now."*

At last there was a change in the mighty formation. The center rose and the wings came in, the left one rising and curling to tighten the curve, the right one bending inward without rising. In a moment the formation was a column, a hollow cylinder. It began to rotate slowly, divided into a series of close-set horizontal rings. Alternate rings slowed and stopped and began a counter-rotation, and with a sudden shift, became two interlocked spirals. Still the overall formation was a hollow cylinder, but now it was composed of an upward and a downward helix.

The individuals spun and swirled down and down, up and up, and kept this motion within the cylinder, and the cylinder quite discrete, as it began to rise. Up and up it lifted, brilliantly, silently, the living original of that which they had found by Alma's body... up and up, filling the eye and the mind with its complex and controlled ascent, its perfect continuity; for here was a thing with no beginning and no end, all flux and balance where each rising was matched by a fall and each turn by its counterpart.

High, and higher, and at last it was a glowing spot against the hovering shadow of the ship, which swallowed it up. The ship left then, not moving, but fading away like the streamers of an aurora, but faster. In three heartbeats it was there, perhaps it was there, it was gone.

Tod closed his eyes, seeing that dynamic double helix. The tip of his mind was upon it; he trembled on the edge of revelation. He *knew* what that form symbolized. He knew it contained the simple answer to his life and their lives, to this planet and its life and the lives which were brought to it. If a cross is more than an instrument of torture, more than the memento of an event; if the *crux ansata*, the Yin-and-Yang, David's star and all such crystallizations were but symbols of great systems of philosophy, then this dynamic intertwined spiral, this free-flowing, rigidly choreographed symbol was...

was—

Something grunted, something screamed, and the wondrous answer turned and rose spiraling away from him to be gone in three heartbeats. Yet in that moment he knew it was there for him when he had the time, the phasing, the bringing-together of whatever elements were needed. He could not use it yet but he had it. He had it.

Another scream, an immense thrashing all about. The spell was broken and the armistice over. There were chargings and fleeings, cries of death-agony and roaring challenges in and over the jungle, through the grasses to the suddenly boiling river. Life goes on, and death with it, but there must be more death than life when too much life is thrown together.

IV

It may be that their five human lives were saved, in that turbulent reawakening, only by their alienness, for the life around them was cheek-and-jowl with its familiar enemy, its familiar quarry, its familiar food, and there need be no experimenting with the five soft containers of new rich juices standing awestruck with their backs to their intrusive shelter.

Then slowly they met one another's eyes. They cared enough for each other so that there was a gladness of sharing. They cared enough for themselves so that there was also a sheepishness, a troubled self-analysis: *What did I do while I was out of my mind?*

They drew together before the door and watched the chase and slaughter around them as it subsided toward its usual balance of hunting and killing, eating and dying. Their hands began to remember the weapons they held, their minds began to reach for reality.

"They were angels," April said, so softly that no one but Tod heard her. Tod watched her lips tremble and part, and knew that she was about to speak the thing he had almost grasped, but then Teague spoke again, and Tod could see the comprehension fade from her and be gone. "Look! Look there!" said Teague, and moved down the wall to the corner.

What had been an inner compartment of their ship was now an isolated cube, and from its back corner, out of sight until now, stretched another long wall. At regular intervals were doors, each fastened by a simple outside latch of parametal.

Teague stepped to the first door, the others crowding close. Teague listened intently, then stepped back and threw the door open.

Inside was a windowless room, blazing with light. Around the sides, machines were set. Tod instantly recognized their air cracker, the water purifiers, the protein converter and one of the auxiliary power plants. In the center was a generator coupled to a light-metal fusion motor. The output buses were neatly insulated, coupled through fuseboxes and resistance controls to a "Christmas tree" multiple outlet. Cables ran through the wall to the Coffin compartment and to the line of unexplored rooms to their left.

"They've left us power, at any rate," said Teague. "Let's look down the line."

Fish, Tod snarled silently. *Dead man! After what you've just seen you should be on your knees with the weight of it, you should put out your eyes to remember better. But all you can do is take inventory of your nuts and bolts.*

Tod looked at the others, at their strained faces and their continual upward glances, as if the bright memory had magnetism for them. He could see the dream fading under Teague's untimely urgency. *You couldn't let us live with it quietly, even for a moment.* Then another inward voice explained to him, *But you see, they killed Alma.*

Resentfully he followed Teague.

Their ship had been dismantled, strung out along the hilltop like a row of shacks. They were interconnected, wired up, restacked, ready and reeking with efficiency—the lab, the library, six chambers full of mixed cargo, then—then the noise Teague made was as near to a shout of glee as Tod had ever heard from the man. The door he had just opened showed their instruments inside, all the reference tapes and tools and manuals. There was even a dome in the roof, and the refractor was mounted and waiting.

"April?" Tod looked, looked again. She was gone. "April!"

She emerged from the library, three doors back. "Teague!"

Teague pulled himself away from the array of instruments and went to her. "Teague," she said, "every one of the reels has been read."

"How do you know?"

"None of them are rewound."

Teague looked up and down the row of doors. "That doesn't sound like the way they—" The unfinished sentence was enough. Whoever had built this from their ship's substance worked according to function and with a fine efficiency.

T eague entered the library and picked a tape reel from its rack. He inserted the free end of film into a slot and pressed a button. The reel spun and the film disappeared inside the cabinet.

Teague looked up and back. Every single reel was inside out on the clips. "They could have rewound them," said Teague, irritated.

"Maybe they wanted us to know that they'd read them," said Moira.

"Maybe they did," Teague murmured. He picked up a reel, looked at it, picked up another and another. "Music. A play. And here's our personal stuff—behavior film, training records, everything."

Carl said, "Whoever read through all this knows a lot about us."

Teague frowned. "Just us?"

"Who else?"

"Earth," said Teague. "All of it."

"You mean we were captured and analyzed so that whoever they are could get a line on Earth? You think they're going to attack Earth?"

"'You mean... You think...'" Teague mimicked coldly. "I mean nothing and I think nothing! Tod, would you be good enough to explain to this impulsive young man what you learned from me earlier? That we need concern ourselves only with evidence?"

Tod shuffled his feet, wishing not to be made an example for anyone, especially Carl, to follow. Carl flushed and tried to smile. Moira took his hand secretly and squeezed it. Tod heard a slight exhalation beside him and looked quickly at April. She was angry. There were times when he wished she would not be angry.

She pointed. "Would you call *that* evidence, Teague?"

They followed her gesture. One of the tape-readers stood open. On its reelshelf stood the counterpart of the strange object they had seen twice before—once, in miniature, found in Alma's Coffin; once again, huge in the sky. This was another of the miniatures.

Teague stared at it, then put out his hand. As his fingers touched it, the pilot-jewel on the tape-reader flashed on, and a soft, clear voice filled the room.

Tod's eyes stung. He had thought he would never hear that voice again. As he listened, he held to the lifeline of April's presence, and felt his lifeline tremble.

Alma's voice said:

*"They made some adjustments yester-
day with the needle-clusters in my Coffin,
so I think they will put me back into it...
Teague, oh, Teague, I'm going to die!*

*"They brought me the recorder just
now. I don't know whether it's for their
records or for you. If it's for you, then I
must tell you... how can I tell you?*

*"I've watched them all this time... how
long? Months... I don't know. I conceived
when I awoke, and the babies are coming
very soon now; it's been long enough for
that; and yet—how can I tell you?*

*"They boarded us, I don't know how, I
don't know why, or where... outside, space
is strange, wrong. It's all misty, without
stars, crawling with blurs and patches of
light.*

*"They understand me; I'm sure of
that—what I say, what I think. I can't understand them at all. They radiate feelings—sorrow, curiosity, confidence,
respect. When I began to realize I would
die, they gave me a kind of regret. When I
broke and cried and said I wanted to be
with you, Teague, they reassured me, they
said I would. I'm sure that's what they
said. But how could that be?*

*"They are completely dedicated in what
they are doing. Their work is a religion to
them, and we are part of it. They... value
us, Teague. They didn't just find us. They
chose us. It's as if we were the best part of
something even they consider great.*

*"The best...! Among them I feel like an
amoeba. They're beautiful, Teague. Important. Very sure of what they are doing.
It's that certainty that makes me believe
what I have to believe; I am going to die,
and you will live, and you and I will be together. How can that be? How can that
be?*

*"Yet it is true, so believe it with me,
Teague. But—find out how!*

*"Teague, every day they have put a ma-
chine on me, radiating. It has to do with*
the babies. It isn't done to harm them. I'm
sure of that. I'm their mother and I'm sure
of it. They won't die.*

"I will. I can feel their sorrow.

*"And I will be with you, and they are
joyous about that....*

"Teague—find out how!"

Tod closed his eyes so that he would not
look at Teague, and wished with all his
heart that Teague had been alone to hear
that ghostly voice. As to what it had said,
the words stood as a frame for a picture
he could not see, showing him only where
it was, not what it meant. Alma's voice
had been tremulous and unsure, but he
knew it well enough to know that joy and
certitude had lived with her as she spoke.
There was wonderment, but no fear.

Knowing that it might be her only message to them, should she not have told
them more—facts, figures, measurements?

Then an old, old tale flashed into his
mind, an early thing from the ancient
Amerenglish, by Hynlen (Henlyne, was
it? no matter) about a man who tried to
convey to humanity a description of the
super-beings who had captured him, with
only his body as a tablet and his nails as a
stylus. Perhaps he was mad by the time he
finished, but his message was clear at
least to him: *"Creation took eight days."*
How would he, Tod, describe an association with the ones he had seen in the sky
outside, if he had been with them for
nearly three hundred days?

April tugged gently at his arm. He
turned toward her, still avoiding the sight
of Teague. April inclined her shining
white head to the door. Moira and Carl already stood outside. They joined them,
and waited wordlessly until Teague came
out.

When he did, he was grateful, and he
need not say so. He came out, a great calm
in his face and voice, passed them and let

them follow him to his methodical examination of the other compartments, to finish his inventory.

Food stores, cable and conduit, metal and parametal rod and sheet stock, tools and tool-making matrices and dies. A hangar, in which lay their lifeboat, fully equipped.

But there was no long-range communication device, and no parts for one.

And there was no heavy space-drive mechanism, or tools to make one, or fuel if they should make the tools.

Back in the instrument room, Carl grunted. "Somebody means for us to stick around."

"The boat—"

Teague said, "I don't think they'd have left us the boat if Earth was in range."

"We'll build a beacon," Tod said suddenly. "We'll get a rescue ship out to us."

"Out where?" asked Teague drily.

They followed his gaze. Bland and silent, merciless, the decay chronometer stared back at them. Built around a standard radioactive, it had material, and one which measured the loss mass. When they checked, two dials—one which measured the amount of energy radiated by the reading was correct. They checked, and the reading was sixty-four.

"Sixty-four years," said Teague. "Assuming we averaged as much as one-half light speed, which isn't likely, we must be thirty light-years away from Earth. Thirty years to get a light-beam there, sixty or more to get a ship back, plus time to make the beacon and time for Earth to understand the signal and prepare a ship...." He shook his head.

"Plus the fact," Tod said in a strained voice, "that there is no habitable planet in a thirty-year radius from Sol. Except Prime."

Shocked, they gaped silently at this well-known fact. A thousand years of scrupulous search with the best instruments could not have missed a planet like this at such a distance.

"Then the chronometer's wrong!"

"I'm afraid not," said Teague. "It's sixty-four years since we left Earth, and that's that."

"And this planet doesn't exist," said Carl with a sour smile, "and I suppose that is also that."

"Yes, Teague," said Tod. "One of those two facts can't exist with the other."

"They can because they do," said Teague. "There's a missing factor. Can a man breathe under water, Tod?"

"If he has a diving helmet."

Teague spread his hands. "It took sixty-four years to get to this planet *if*. We have to find the figurative diving helmet." He paused. "The evidence in favor of the planet's existence is fairly impressive," he said wryly. "Let's check the other fact."

"How?"

"The observatory."

They ran to it. The sky glowed its shimmering green, but through it the stars had begun to twinkle. Carl got to the telescope first, put a big hand on the swing-controls, and said, "Where first?" He tugged at the instrument. "Hey!" He tugged again.

"Don't!" said Teague sharply. Carl let go and backed away. Teague switched on the lights and examined the instrument. "It's already connected to the compensators," he said. "Hmp! Our hosts are most helpful." He looked at the setting of the small motors which moved the instrument to cancel diurnal rotation effects. "Twenty-eight hours, thirteen minutes plus. Well, if that's correct for this planet, it's proof that this isn't Earth or Prime— if we needed proof." He touched the controls lightly. "Carl, what's the matter here?"

Carl bent to look. There were dabs of dull silver on the threads of the adjusting screws. He touched them. "Parametal," he said. "Unflashed, but it has adhered enough to jam the threads. Take a couple days to get it off without jarring it. Look here—they've done the same thing with the objective screws!"

"We look at what they want us to see, and like it," said Tod.

"Maybe it's something we want to see," said April gently.

Only half-teasing, Tod said, "Whose side are you on, anyway?"

Teague put his eye to the instrument. His hands, by habit, strayed to the focusing adjustment, but found it locked the same way as the others. "Is there a Galactic Atlas?"

"Not in the rack," said Moira a moment later.

"Here," said April from the chart table. Awed, she added, "Open."

Tensely they waited while Teague took his observation and referred to the atlas and to the catalogue they found lying under it. When at last he lifted his face from the calculations, it bore the strangest expression Tod had ever seen there.

"Our diving helmet," he said at last, very slowly, too evenly, "—that is, the factor which rationalizes our two mutually exclusive facts—is simply that our captors have a faster-than-light drive."

"But according to theory—"

"According to our telescope," Teague interrupted, "through which I have just seen Sol, and these references so thoughtfully laid out for us..." Shockingly, his voice broke. He took two deep breaths, and said, "Sol is two hundred and seventeen light-years away. That sun which set a few minutes ago is Beta Librae." He studied their shocked faces, one by one. "I don't know what we shall eventually call this place," he said with difficulty, "but we had better get used to calling it home."

They called the planet Viridis ("the greenest name I can think of," Moira said) because none among them had ever seen such a green. It was more than the green of growing, for the sunlight was green-tinged and at night the whole sky glowed green, a green as bright as the brightest silver of Earth's moon, as water molecules, cracked by the star's intense ultraviolet, celebrated their nocturnal reunion.

They called the moons Wynken, Blynken and Nod, and the sun they called—the sun.

They worked like slaves, and then like scientists, which is a change of occupation but not a change of pace. They built a palisade of a cypress-like, straight-grained wood, each piece needle-pointed, double-laced with parametal wire. It had a barred gate and peepholes with periscopes and permanent swivel-mounts for the needle-guns they were able to fabricate from tube-stock and spare solenoids. They roofed the enclosure with parametal mesh which, at one point, could be rolled back to launch the lifeboat.

They buried Alma.

They tested and analyzed, classified, processed, researched everything in the compound and within easy reach of it—soil, vegetation, fauna. They developed an insect-repellent solution to coat the palisade and an insecticide with an automatic spray to keep the compound clear of the creatures, for they were numerous, large and occasionally downright dangerous, like the "flying caterpillar" which kept its pseudopods in its winged form and enthusiastically broke them off in the flesh of whatever attacked them, leaving an angry rash and suppurating sores. They discovered three kinds of edible seed and another which yielded a fine hydrocarbonic oil much like soy, and a flower whose calyces, when dried and then soaked and broiled, tasted precisely like crabmeat.

For a time they were two separate teams, virtually isolated from each other. Moira and Teague collected minerals and put them through the mass spectroscope and the radioanalyzers, and it fell to April to classify the life-forms, with Carl and Tod competing mightily to bring in new ones. Or at least photographs of new ones. Two-ton *Parametrodon*, familiarly known as dopey—a massive herbivore with just enough intelligence to move its jaws— was hardly the kind of thing to be carried home under one's arm, and *Felodon*, the scaly carnivore with the cat-like tusks, though barely as long as a man, was about as friendly as a half-starved wolverine.

Tetrapodys (Tod called it "um-brellabird") turned out to be a rewarding catch. They stumbled across a vine which bore foul-smelling pods; these the clumsy amphibious bats found irresistible. Carl synthesized the evil stuff and improved upon it, and they smeared it on tree-boles by the river. *Tetrapodys* came there by the hundreds, and laid eggs apparently in sheer frustration. These eggs were camou-flaged by a frilly green membrane, for all the world like the ground-buds of the giant water-fern. The green shoots tasted like shallots and were fine for salad when raw and excellent as onion soup when stewed. The half-hatched *Tetrapodys* yielded ligaments which when dried made excellent self-baited fish-hooks. The wing muscles of the adult tasted like veal cutlet with fish sauce, and the inner, or main shell of the eggs afforded them an amaz-ing shoe-sole—light, tough and flexible, which, for some unknown reason, *Felodon* would not track.

Pteronauchis, or "flapping frog," was the gliding newt they had seen on that first day. Largely nocturnal, it was phototropic; a man with a strong light could fill a bushel with the things in minutes. Each specimen yielded twice as many, twice as large and twice as good frog-legs as a Ter-ran frog.

There were no mammals.

There were flowers in profusion— white (a sticky green in that light), purple, brown, blue and, of course, the ubiquitous green. No red—as a matter of fact, there was virtually no red anywhere on the planet. April's eyes became a feast for them all. It is impossible to describe the yearning one can feel for an absent color. And so it was that a legend began with them. Twice Tod had seen a bright red growth. The first time he thought it was a mushroom, the second it seemed more of a lichen. The first time it was surrounded by a sea of crusher ants on the move—a fearsome carpet which even *Para-metrodon* respected. The second time he had seen it from twenty meters away and had just turned toward it when not one, but three *Felodons* came hurtling through the undergrowth at him.

He came back later, both times, and found nothing. And once Carl swore he saw a brilliant red plant move slowly into a rock crevice as he approached. The thing became their *edelweiss*—very nearly their Grail.

Rough diamonds lay in the streambeds and emeralds glinted in the night-glow, and for the Terran-oriented mind there was incalculable treasure to be scratched up just below the steaming humus: iridium, ruthenium, metallic nep-tunium-237. There was an unaccountable (at first) shift toward the heavier metals. The ruthenium-rhodium-palladium group was as plentiful on Viridis as the iron-nickel-cobalt series on Earth; cadmium was actually more plentiful here than its relative, zinc. Technetium was present, though rare, on the crust, while Earth's had long since decayed.

Vulcanism was common on Viridis, as could be expected in the presence of so many radioactives. From the lifeboat they had seen bald spots where there were particularly high concentrations of "hot" material. In some of these there was life.

At the price of a bout of radiation sickness, Carl went into one such area briefly for specimens. What he found was extraordinary—a tree which was warm to the touch, which used minerals and water at a profligate pace and which, when transplanted outside an environment which destroyed cells almost as fast as they developed, went cancerous, grew enormously and killed itself with its own terrible viability. In the same lethal areas lived a primitive worm which constantly discarded segments to keep pace with its rapid growth, and which also grew visibly and died of living too fast when taken outside.

The inclination of the planet's axis was less than two degrees, so that there were virtually no seasons, and very little variation in temperature from one latitude to another. There were two continents and an equatorial sea, no mountains, no plains and few large lakes. Most of the planet was gently rolling hill country and meandering rivers, clothed in thick jungle or grass. The spot where they had awakened was as good as any other, so there they stayed, wandering less and less as they amassed information. Nowhere was there an artifact of any kind, or any slightest trace of previous habitation. Unless, of course, one considered the existence itself of life on this planet. For Permian life can hardly be expected to develop in less than a billion years; yet the irreproachable calendar inherent in the radioactive bones of Viridis insisted that the planet was no more than thirty-five million years old.

V

When Moira's time came, it went hard with her, and Carl forgot to swagger because he could not help. Teague and April took care of her, and Tod stayed with Carl, wishing for the right thing to say and not finding it, wanting to do something for this new strange man with Carl's face, and the unsure hands which twisted each other, clawed the ground, wiped cruelly at the scalp, at the shins, restless, terrified.

Through Carl, Tod learned a little more of what he never wanted to know—what it must have been like for Teague when he lost Alma.

Alma's six children were toddlers by then, bright and happy in the only world they had ever known. They had been named for moons—Wynken, Blynken and Nod, Rhea, Callisto and Titan. Nod and Titan were the boys, and they and Rhea had Alma's eyes and hair and sometimes Alma's odd, brave stillness—a sort of suspension of the body while the mind went out to grapple and conquer instead of fearing. If the turgid air and the radiant ground affected them, they did not show it, except perhaps in their rapid development.

They heard Moira cry out. It was like laughter, but it was pain. Carl sprang to his feet. Tod took his arm and Carl pulled it away. "Why can't I do something? Do I have to just *sit* here?"

"Shh. She doesn't feel it. That's a tropism. She'll be all right. Sit down, Carl. Tell you what you can do—you can name them. Think. Think of a nice set of names, all connected in some way. Teague used moons. What are you going to—"

"Time enough for that," Carl grunted. "Tod... do you know what I'll... I'd be if she—if something happened?"

"Nothing's going to happen."

"I'd just cancel out. I'm not Teague. I couldn't carry it. How does Teague do it?..." Carl's voice lapsed to a mumble.

"Names," Tod reminded him. "Seven, eight of 'em. Come on, now."

"Think she'll have eight?"

"Why not? She's normal." He nudged Carl. "Think of names. I know! How many of the old signs of the zodiac would make good names?"

"Don't remember 'em."

"I do. Aries, that's good. Taurus. Gem—no; you wouldn't want to call a child 'Twins.' Leo—that's *fine!*"

"Libra," said Carl, "for a girl. Aquarius, Sagittarius—how many's that?"

Tod counted on his fingers. "Six. Then, Virgo and Capricorn. And you're all set!" But Carl wasn't listening. In two long bounds he reached April, who was just stepping into the compound. She looked tired. She looked more than tired. In her beautiful eyes was a great pity, the color of a bleeding heart.

"Is she all right? Is she?" They were hardly words, those hoarse, rushed things.

April smiled with her lips, while her eyes poured pity. "Yes, yes, she'll be all right. It wasn't too bad."

Carl whooped and pushed past her. She caught his arm, and for all her frailty, swung him around.

"Not yet, Carl. Teague says to tell you first—"

"The babies? What about them? How many, April?"

April looked over Carl's shoulder at Tod. She said, "Three."

Carl's face relaxed, numb, and his eyes went round. "Th—what? Three so far, you mean. There'll surely be more...."

She shook her head.

Tod felt the laughter explode within him, and he clamped his jaws on it.

It surged at him, hammered in the back of his throat. And then he caught April's pleading eyes. He took strength from her, and bottled up a great bray of merriment.

Carl's voice was the last fraying thread of hope. "The others died, then."

She put a hand on his cheek. "There were only three. Carl... don't be mean to Moira."

"Oh, I won't," he said with difficulty. "She couldn't... I mean it wasn't her doing." He flashed a quick, defensive look at Tod, who was glad now he had controlled himself. What was in Carl's face meant murder for anyone who dared laugh.

April said, "Not your doing either, Carl. It's this planet. It must be."

"Thanks, April," Carl muttered. He went to the door, stopped, shook himself like a big dog. He said again, "Thanks," but this time his voice didn't work and it was only a whisper. He went inside.

Tod bolted for the corner of the building, whipped around it and sank to the ground, choking. He held both hands over his mouth and laughed until he hurt. When at last he came to a limp silence, he felt April's presence. She stood quietly watching him, waiting.

"I'm sorry," he said. "I'm sorry. But... it *is* funny."

She shook her head gravely. "We're not on Earth, Tod. A new world means new manners, too. That would apply even on Terra Prime if we'd gone there."

"I suppose," he said, and then repressed another giggle.

"I always thought it was a silly kind of joke anyway," she said primly. "Judging virility by the size of a brood. There isn't any scientific basis for it. Men are silly. They used to think that virility could be measured by the amount of hair on their chests, or how tall they were. There's nothing wrong with having only three."

"Carl?" grinned Tod. "The big ol' swashbuckler?" He let the grin fade. "All right, Ape, I won't let Carl see me laugh. Or you either. All right?" A peculiar expression crossed his face. "What was that you said? April! Men never had hair on their chests!"

"Yes they did. Ask Teague."

"I'll take your word for it." He shuddered. "I can't imagine it unless a man had a tail too. And bony ridges over his eyes."

"It wasn't so long ago that they had. The ridges, anyway. Well—I'm glad you didn't laugh in front of him. You're nice, Tod."

"You're nice too." He pulled her down beside him and hugged her gently. "Bet you'll have a dozen."

"I'll try." She kissed him.

When specimen-hunting had gone as far as it could, classification became the settlement's main enterprise. And gradually, the unique pattern of Viridian life began to emerge.

Viridis had its primitive fish and several of the mollusca, but the fauna was primarily arthropods and reptiles. The interesting thing about each of the three branches was the close relationship between species. It was almost as if evolution took a major step with each generation, instead of bumbling along as on Earth, where certain stages of development are static for thousands, millions of years. *Pterodon*, for example, existed in three varieties, the simplest of which showed a clear similarity to *Pteronauchis*, the gliding newt. A simple salamander could be shown to be the common ancestor of both the flapping frog and massive *Parametrodon*, and there were strong similarities between this salamander and the worm which fathered the arthropods.

They lived close to the truth for a long time without being able to see it, for man is conditioned to think of evolution from simple to complex, from ooze to animalcule to mollusk to ganoid; amphibid to monotreme to primate to tinker... losing the significance of the fact that all these coexist. Was the vertebrate eel of prehistory a *higher* form of life than his simpler descendant? The whale lost his legs; this men call recidivism, a sort of backsliding in evolution, and treat it as a kind of illegitimacy.

Men are oriented out of simplicity toward the complex, and make of the latter a goal. Nature treats complex matters as expediencies and so is never confused. It is hardly surprising, then, that the Viridis colony took so long to discover their error, for the weight of evidence was in error's favor. There was indeed an unbroken line from the lowest forms of life to the highest, and to assume that they had a common ancestor was a beautifully consistent hypothesis, of the order of accuracy an archer might display in hitting dead center, from a thousand paces, a bowstring with the nock of his arrow.

The work fell more and more on the younger ones. Teague isolated himself, not by edict, but by habit. It was assumed that he was working along his own lines; and then it became usual to proceed without him, until finally he was virtually a hermit in their midst. He was aging rapidly; perhaps it hurt something in him to be surrounded by so much youth. His six children thrived, and, with Carl's three, ran naked in the jungle armed only with their sticks and their speed. They were apparently immune to practically everything Viridis might bring against them, even *Crotalidus's* fangs, which gave them the equivalent of a severe bee sting (as opposed to what had happened to Moira once, when they had had to reactivate one of the Coffins to keep her alive).

Tod would come and sit with him sometimes, and as long as there was no talk the older man seemed to gain something from the visits. But he preferred to be alone, living as much as he could with memories for which not even a new world could afford a substitute.

Tod said to Carl, "Teague is going to wither up and blow away if we can't interest him in something."

"He's interested enough to spend a lot of time with whatever he's thinking about," Carl said bluntly.

"But I'd like it better if he was interested in something here, now. I wish we could... I wish—" But he could think of nothing, and it was a constant trouble to him.

L ittle Titan was killed, crushed under a great clumsy *Parametrodon* which slid down a bank on him while the child was grubbing for the scarlet cap of the strange red mushroom they had glimpsed from time to time. It was in pursuit of one of these that Moira had been bitten by the *Crotalidus*. One of Carl's children was drowned—just how, no one knew. Aside from these tragedies, life was easy and interesting. The compound began to look more like a *kraal* as they acclimated, for although the adults never adapted as well as the children, they did become far less sensitive to insect bites and the poison weeds which first troubled them.

It was Teague's son Nod who found what was needed to bring Teague's interest back, at least for a while. The child came back to the compound one day, trailed by two slinking *Felodons* who did not catch him because they kept pausing and pausing to lap up gouts of blood which marked his path. Nod's ear was torn and he had a green-stick break in his left ulna, and a dislocated wrist. He came

weeping, weeping tears of joy. He shouted as he wept, great proud noises. Once in the compound he collapsed, but he would not lose consciousness, or his grip on his prize, until Teague came. Then he handed Teague the mushroom and fainted.

The mushroom was and was not like anything on Earth. Earth has a fungus called *schizophyllum*, not uncommon but most strange. Though not properly a fungus, the red "mushroom" of Viridis had many of the functions of *schizophyllum*.

Schizophyllum produces spores of four distinct types, each of which grows into a genetically distinct, completely dissimilar plant. Three of these are sterile. The fourth produces *schizophyllum*.

The red mushroom of Viridis also produced four distinct heterokaryons or genetically different types, and the spores of one of these produced the mushroom.

Teague spent an engrossing Earth-year in investigating the other three.

VI

S weating and miserable in his integument of skinflex, Tod hunched in the crotch of a finger-tree. His knees were drawn up and his head was down; his arms clasped his shins and he rocked slightly back and forth. He knew he would be safe here for some time—the fleshy fingers of the tree were clumped at the slender, swaying ends of the branches and never turned back toward the trunk. He wondered what it would be like to be dead. Perhaps he would be dead soon, and then he'd know. He might as well be.

The names he'd chosen were perfect and all of a family: Sol, Mercury, Venus, Terra, Mars, Jupiter... eleven of them. And he could think of a twelfth if he had to.

For what?

He let himself sink down again into the

blackness wherein nothing lived but the oily turning of *what's it like to be dead*? *Quiet*, he thought. *No one would laugh.* Something pale moved on the jungle floor below him. He thought instantly of April, and angrily put the thought out of his mind. April would be sleeping now, having completed the trifling task it had taken her so long to start. Down there, that would be Blynken, or maybe Rhea. They were very alike.

It didn't matter, anyway.

He closed his eyes and stopped rocking. He couldn't see anyone, no one could see him. That was the best way. So he sat, and let time pass, and when a hand lay on his shoulder, he nearly leaped out of the tree. "Damn it, Blynken—"

"It's me. Rhea." The child, like all of Alma's daughters, was large for her age and glowing with health. How long had it been? Six, eight... nine Earth years since they had landed.

"Go hunt mushrooms," Tod growled. "Leave me alone."

"Come back," said the girl.

Tod would not answer. Rhea knelt beside him, her arm around the primary branch, her back, with his, against the trunk. She bent her head and put her cheek against his. "Tod."

Something inside him flamed. He bared his teeth and swung a heavy fist. The girl doubled up soundlessly and slipped out of the tree. He stared down at the lax body and at first could not see it for the haze of fury which blew and whirled around him. Then his vision cleared and he moaned, tossed his club down and dropped after it. He caught up the club and whacked off the tree-fingers which probed toward them. He swept up the child and leapt clear, and sank to his knees, gathering her close.

"Rhea, I'm sorry, I'm sorry... I wasn't... I'm not—*Rhea*! Don't be dead!"

She stirred and made a tearing sound with her throat. Her eyelids trembled and opened, uncovering pain-blinded eyes. "Rhea!"

"It's all right," she whispered, "I shouldn't't've bothered you. Do you want me to go away?"

"No," he said, "No." He held her tight. *Why not let her go away?* a part of him wondered, and another part, frightened and puzzled, cried, *No! No!* He had an urgent, half-hysterical need to explain. *Why explain to her, a child? Say you're sorry, comfort her, heal her, but don't expect her to understand.* Yet he said, "I can't go back. There's nowhere else to go. So what can I do?"

R hea was quiet, as if waiting. A terrible thing, a wonderful thing, to have someone you have hurt wait patiently like that while you find a way to explain. Even if you only explain it to yourself... "What could I do if I went back? They—they'll never—they'll laugh at me. They'll all laugh. They're laughing now." Angry again, plaintive no more, he blurted, "April! *Damn* April! She's made a eunuch out of me!"

"Because she had only one baby?"

"Like a savage."

"It's a beautiful baby. A boy."

"A man, a real man, fathers six or eight."

She met his eyes gravely. "That's silly."

"What's happening to us on this crazy planet?" he raged. "Are we evolving backward? What comes next—one of you kids hatching out some amphibids?"

She said only, "Come back, Tod."

"I can't," he whispered. "They'll think I'm... that I can't..." Helplessly, he shrugged. "They'll laugh."

"Not until you do, and then they'll laugh *with* you. Not at you, Tod."

Finally, he said it, "April won't love

me; she'll never love a weakling."

She pondered, holding him with her clear gaze. "You really need to be loved a whole lot."

Perversely, he became angry again. "I can get along!" he snapped.

And she smiled and touched the nape of his neck. "You're loved," she assured him. "Gee, you don't have to be mad about that. I love you, don't I? April loves you. Maybe I love you even more than she does. She loves everything you are, Tod. I love everything you ever were and everything you ever will be."

He closed his eyes and a great music came to him. A long, long time ago he had attacked someone who came to comfort him, and she had let him cry, and at length she had said... not exactly these words, but—it was the same.

"Rhea."

He looked at her. "You said all that to me before."

A puzzled small crinkle appeared between her eyes and she put her fingers on it. "Did I?"

"Yes," said Tod, "but it was before you were even born."

He rose and took her hand, and they went back to the compound, and whether he was laughed at or not he never knew, for he could think of nothing but his full heart and of April. He went straight in to her and kissed her gently and admired his son, whose name was Sol, and who had been born with hair and two tiny incisors, and who had heavy bony ridges over his eyes....

A fantastic storage capacity," Teague remarked, touching the top of the scarlet mushroom. "The spores are almost microscopic. The thing doesn't seem to want them distributed, either. It positively hoards them, millions of them."

"Start over, please," April said. She shifted the baby in her arms. He was growing prodigiously. "Slowly. I used to know something about biology—or so I thought. But *this*—"

Teague almost smiled. It was good to see. The aging face had not had so much expression in it in five Earth-years. "I'll get as basic as I can, then, and start from there. First of all, we call this thing a mushroom, but it isn't. I don't think it's a plant, though you couldn't call it an animal, either."

"I don't think anybody ever told me the real difference between a plant and an animal," said Tod.

"Oh... well, the most convenient way to put it—it's not strictly accurate, but it will do—is that plants make their own food and animals subsist on what others have made. This thing does both. It has roots, but—" he lifted an edge of the skirted stem of the mushroom—"it can move them. Not much, not fast; but if it wants to shift itself, it can."

April smiled, "Tod, I'll give you basic biology any time. Do go on, Teague."

"Good. Now, I explained about the heterokaryons—the ability this thing has to produce spores which grow up into four completely different plants. One is a mushroom just like this. Here are the other three."

Tod looked at the box of plants. "Are they really all from the mushroom spores?"

"Don't blame you," said Teague, and actually chuckled. "I didn't believe it myself at first. A sort of pitcher plant, half full of liquid. A thing like a cactus. And this one. It's practically all underground, like a truffle, although it has these cilia. You wouldn't think it was anything but a few horsehairs stuck in the ground."

"And they're all sterile," Tod recalled.

"They're not," said Teague, "and that's what I called you in here tell you. They'll yield if they are fertilized."

"Fertilized how?"

Instead of answering, Teague asked April, "Do you remember how far back we traced the evolution of Viridian life?"

"Of course. We got the arthropods all the way back to a simple segmented worm. The insects seemed to come from another worm, with pseudopods and a hard carapace."

"A caterpillar," Tod interpolated.

"Almost," said April, with a scientist's nicety. "And the most primitive reptile we could find was a little gymnoderm you could barely see without a glass."

"Where did we find it?"

"Swimming around in—oh! In those pitcher plant things!"

"If you won't take my word for this," said Teague, a huge enjoyment glinting between his words, "you'll just have to breed these things yourself. It's a lot of work, but this is what you'll discover.

"An adult gymnoderm—a male—finds this pitcher and falls in. There's plenty of nutriment for him, you know, and he's a true amphibian. He fertilizes the pitcher. Nodules grow under the surface of the liquid inside there—" he pointed "—and bud off. The buds are mobile. They grow into wrigglers, miniature tadpoles. Then into lizards. They climb out and go about the business of being—well, lizards."

"All males?" asked Tod.

"No," said Teague, "and that's an angle I haven't yet investigated. But apparently some males breed with females, which lay eggs, which hatch into lizards, and some find plants to fertilize. Anyway, it looks as if this plant is actually the progenitor of all the reptiles here; you know how clear the evolutionary lines are to all the species."

"What about the truffle with the horse-hairs?" asked Tod.

"A pupa," said Teague, and to the incredulous expression on April's face, he insisted, "Really—a pupa. After nine weeks or so of dormancy, it hatches out into what you almost called a caterpillar."

"And then into all the insects here," said April, and shook her head in wonderment. "And I suppose that cactus-thing hatches out the nematodes, the segmented ones that evolve into arthropods?"

Teague nodded. "You're welcome to experiment," he said again, "but believe me—you'll only find out I'm right: it really happens."

"Then this scarlet mushroom is the beginning of everything here."

"I can't find another theory," said Teague.

"I can," said Tod.

They looked at him questioningly, and he rose and laughed. "Not yet. I have to think it through." He scooped up the baby and then helped April to her feet. "How do you like our Sol, Teague?"

"Fine," said Teague. "A fine boy." Tod knew he was seeing the heavy occipital ridges, the early teeth, and saying nothing. Tod was aware of a faint inward surprise as the baby reached toward April and he handed him over. He should have resented what might be in Teague's mind, but he did not. The beginnings of an important insight welcomed criticism of the child, recognized its hairiness, its savagery, and found these things good. But as yet the thought was too nebulous to express, except by a smile. He smiled, took April's hand and left.

"That was a funny thing you said to Teague," April told him as they walked toward their quarters.

"Remember, April, the day we landed? Remember—" he made a gesture that took in a quadrant of sky—"remember how we all felt... good?"

"Yes," she murmured. "It was like a sort of compliment, and a reassurance. How could I forget?"

"Yes. Well..." He spoke with difficulty but his smile stayed. "I have a thought, and it makes me feel like that. But I can't get it into words." After a thoughtful pause, he added, "Yet."

She shifted the baby. "He's getting so heavy."

"I'll take him." He took the squirming bundle with the deep-set, almost humorous eyes. When he looked up from them, he caught an expression on April's face which he hadn't seen in years. "What is it, Ape?"

"You—*like* him."

"Well, sure."

"I was afraid. I was afraid for a long time that you... he's ours, but he isn't exactly a pretty baby."

"I'm not exactly a pretty father."

"You know how precious you are to me?" she whispered.

He knew, for this was an old intimacy between them. He laughed and followed the ritual: "How precious?"

She cupped her hands and brought them together, to make of them an ivory box. She raised the hands and peeped into them, between the thumbs, as if at a rare jewel, then clasped the magic tight and hugged it to her breast, raising tear-filled eyes to him. *"That* precious," she breathed.

He looked at the sky, seeing somewhere in it the many peak moments of their happiness when she had made that gesture, feeling how each one, meticulously chosen, brought all the others back. "I used to hate this place," he said. "I guess it's changed."

"You've changed."

Changed how? he wondered. He felt the same, even though he knew he looked older....

The years passed, and the children grew. When Sol was fifteen Earth-years old, short, heavy-shouldered, powerful, he married Carl's daughter Libra. Teague, turning to parchment, had returned to his hermitage from the temporary stimulation of his researches on what they still called "the mushroom." More and more the colony lived off the land and out of the jungle, not because there was any less to be synthesized from their compact machines, but out of preference; it was easier to catch flapping frogs or umbrellabirds and cook them than to bother with machine settings and check analyses, and, somehow, a lot more fun to eat them, too.

It seemed to them safer, year by year. *Felodon,* unquestionably the highest form of life on Viridis, was growing scarce, being replaced by a smaller, more timid carnivore April called *Vulpidus* (once, for it seemed not to matter much any more about keeping records) and everyone ultimately called "fox," for all the fact that it was a reptile. *Pterodon* was disappearing too, as were all the larger forms. More and more they strayed after food, not famine-driven, but purely for variety; more and more they found themselves welcome and comfortable away from the compound. Once Carl and Moira drifted off for nearly a year. When they came back they had another child—a silent, laughing little thing with oddly long arms and heavy teeth.

The warm days and the glowing nights passed comfortably and the stars no longer called. Tod became a grandfather and was proud. The child, a girl, was albino like April, and had exactly April's deep red eyes. Sol and Libra named her Emerald, a green name and a ground-term rather than a sky-term, as if in open expression of the slow spell worked on them all by Viridis. She was mute—but so were almost all the new children, and it seemed not to matter. They were healthy and happy.

Tod went to tell Teague, thinking it might cheer the old one up a little. He found him lying in what had once been his laboratory, thin and placid and disinterested, absently staring down at one of the arthropodal flying creatures that had once startled them so by zooming into the coffin chamber. This one had happened to land on Teague's hand, and Teague was laxly waiting for it to fly off again, out through the unscreened window, past the unused sprays, over the faint tumble of rotted spars which had once been a palisade.

"Teague, the baby's come!"

Teague sighed, his tired mind detaching itself from memory episode by episode. His eyes rolled toward Tod and finally he turned his head. "Which one would that be?"

Tod laughed. "My grandchild, a girl. Sol's baby."

Teague let his lids fall. He said nothing.

"Well, aren't you glad?"

Slowly a frown came to the papery brow. "Glad." Tod felt he was looking at the word as he had stared at the arthropod, wondering limply when it might go away. "What's the matter with it?"

"What?"

Teague sighed again, a weary, impatient sound. "What does it look like?" he said slowly, emphasizing each one-syllabled word.

"Like April. Just like April."

Teague half sat up, and blinked at Tod. "You don't mean it."

"Yes, eyes red as—" The image of an Earth sunset flickered near his mind but vanished as too hard to visualize. Tod pointed at the four red-capped "mushrooms" that had stood for so many years in the test-boxes in the laboratory. "Red

as those."

"Silver hair," said Teague.

"Yes, beau—"

"All over," said Teague flatly.

"Well, yes."

Teague let himself fall back on the cot and gave a disgusted snort. "A monkey."

"*Teague!*"

"Ah-h-h... go 'way," growled the old man. "I long ago resigned myself to what was happening to us here. A human being just can't adapt to the kind of radioactive ruin this place is for us. Your monsters'll breed monsters, and the monsters'll do the same if they can, until pretty soon they just won't breed any more. And that will be the end of that, and good riddance..." His voice faded away. His eyes opened, looking on distant things, and gradually found themselves focused on the man who stood over him in shocked silence. "But the one thing I can't stand is to have somebody come in here saying, 'Oh, joy, oh happy day!'"

"Teague..." Tod swallowed heavily.

"Viridis eats ambition; there was going to be a city here," said the old man indistinctly. "Viridis eats humanity; there were going to be people here." He chuckled gruesomely. "All right, all right, accept it if you have to—and you have to. But don't come around here celebrating."

Tod backed to the door, his eyes horror-round, then turned and fled.

VII

April held him as he crouched against the wall, rocked him slightly, made soft unspellable mother-noises to him.

"Shh, he's all decayed, all lonesome and mad," she murmured. "Shh. Shh."

Tod felt half-strangled. As a youth he had been easily moved, he recalled; he had that tightness of the throat for sympathy, for empathy, for injustices he felt the Universe was hurling at him out of its capacious store. But recently life had been placid, full of love and togetherness and a widening sense of membership with the earth and the air and all the familiar things which walked and flew and grew and bred in it. And his throat was shaped for laughter now; these feelings hurt him.

"But he's right," he whispered. "Don't you see? Right from the beginning it... it was... remember Alma had six children, April? And a little later, Carl and Moira had three? And you, only one... how long is it since the average human gave birth to only one?"

"They used to say it was humanity's last major mutation," she admitted, "Multiple births... these last two thousand years. But—"

"Eyebrow ridges," he interrupted. "Hair... that skull, Emerald's skull, slanting back like that; did you see the tusks on that little... *baboon* of Moira's?"

"Tod! *Don't!*"

He leaped to his feet, sprang across the room and snatched the golden helix from the shelf where it had gleamed its locked symbolism down on them ever since the landing. "Around and down!" he shouted. "Around and around and down!" He squatted beside her and pointed furiously. "Down and down into the blackest black there is; down into *nothing.*" He shook his fist at the sky. "You see what they do? They find the highest form of life they can and plant it here and watch it slide down into the muck!" He hurled the artifact away from him.

"But it goes up too, round and up. Oh, Tod!" she cried. "Can you remember them, what they looked like, the way they flew, and say these things about them?"

"I can remember Alma," he gritted, "conceiving and gestating alone in space, while they turned their rays on her every day. You know *why?*" With the sudden thought, he stabbed a finger down at her. "To give her babies a head start on Viridis, otherwise they'd have been born normal here; it would've taken another couple of generations to start them downhill, and they wanted us all to go together."

"No, Tod, no!"

"Yes, April, yes. How much proof do you need?" He whirled on her. "Listen— remember that mushroom Teague analyzed? He had to *pry* spores out of it to see what it yielded. Remember the three different plants he got? Well, I was just there; I don't know how many times before I've seen it, but only now it makes sense. He's got four mushrooms now; do you see? Do you see? Even back as far as we can trace the bugs and newts on this green hell-pit, Viridis won't let anything climb; it must fall."

"I don't—"

"You'll give me basic biology any time," he quoted sarcastically. "Let me tell you some biology. That mushroom yields three plants, and the plants yield animal life. Well, when the animal life fertilized those hetero-whatever—"

"Heterokaryons."

"Yes. Well, you don't get animals that can evolve and improve. You get one pitiful generation of animals which breeds back into a mushroom, and there it sits hoarding its spores. Viridis wouldn't let one puny newt, one primitive pupa build! It snatches 'em back, locks 'em up— That mushroom isn't the beginning of everything here—*it's the end!*"

April got to her feet slowly, looking at Tod as if she had never seen him before, not in fear, but with a troubled curiosity. She crossed the room and picked up the artifact, stroked its gleaming golden coils "You could be right," she said in a low voice. "But that can't be all there is to it." She set the helix back in its place. "They *wouldn't."*

S he spoke with such intensity that for a moment that metrical formation, mighty and golden, rose again in Tod's mind, up and up to the measureless cloud which must be a ship. He recalled the sudden shift, like a genuflection, directed at them, at him, and for that moment he could find no evil in it. Confused, he tossed his head, found himself looking out the door, seeing Moira's youngest ambling comfortably across the compound.

"They *wouldn't?*" he snarled. He took April's slender arm and whirled her to the door. "You know what I'd do before I'd father another one like *that?*" He told her specifically what he would do. "A lemur next, hm? A spider, an oyster, a jellyfish!"

April whimpered and ran out. "Know any lullabies to a tapeworm?" he roared after her. She disappeared into the jungle, and he fell back, gasping for breath.

H aving no stomach for careful thought or careful choosing, having Teague for an example to follow, Tod too turned hermit. He could have survived the crisis easily perhaps, with April to help, but she did not come back. Moira and Carl were off again, wandering; the children lived their own lives, and he had no wish to see Teague. Once or twice Sol and Libra came to see him, but he snarled at them and they left him alone. It was no sacrifice. Life on Viridis was very full for the contented ones.

He sulked in his room or poked about the compound by himself. He activated the protein converter once, but found its products tasteless, and never bothered with it again. Sometimes he would stand near the edge of the hilltop and watch the children playing in the long grass, and his lip would curl.

Damn Teague! He'd been happy enough with Sol all those years, for all the boy's bulging eyebrow ridges and hairy body. He had been about to accept the silent, silver Emerald, too, when the crotchety old man had dropped his bomb. Once or twice Tod wondered detachedly what it was in him that was so easily reached, so completely insecure, that the suggestion of abnormality should strike so deep.

Somebody once said, *"You really need to be loved, don't you, Tod?"*

No one would love this tainted thing, father of savages who spawned animals. He didn't deserve to be loved.

He had never felt so alone. *"I'm going to die. But I will be with you too."* That had been Alma. Huh! There was old Teague, tanning his brains in his own sour acids. Alma had believed something or other... and what had come of it? That wizened old crab lolling his life away in the lab.

Tod spent six months that way.

T od!"

He came out of sleep reluctantly, because in sleep an inner self still lived with April where there was no doubt and no fury; no desertion, no loneliness.

He opened his eyes and stared dully at the slender figure silhouetted against Viridis's glowing sky. "April?"

"Moira," said the figure. The voice was cold.

"Moira!" he said, sitting up. "I haven't seen you for a year. More. Wh—"

"Come," she said. "Hurry."

"Come where?"

"Come by yourself or I'll get Carl and he'll carry you." She walked swiftly to the door.

He reeled after her. "You can't come in here and—"

"Come on." The voice was edged and slid out from between clenched teeth. A miserable part of him twitched in delight and told him that he was important enough to be hated. He despised himself for recognizing the twisted thought, and before he knew what he was doing he was following Moira at a steady trot.

"Where are—" he gasped, and she said over her shoulder, "If you don't talk you'll go faster."

At the jungle margin a shadow detached itself and spoke. "Got him?"

"Yes, Carl."

The shadow became Carl. He swung in behind Tod, who suddenly realized that if he did not follow the leader, the one be-hind would drive. He glanced back at Carl's implacable bulk, and then put down his head and jogged doggedly along as he was told.

They followed a small stream, crossed it on a fallen tree and climbed a hill. Just as Tod was about to accept the worst these determined people might offer in ex-change for a moment to ease his fiery lungs, Moira stopped. He stumbled into her. She caught his arm and kept him on his feet.

"In there," she said, pointing.

"A finger tree."

"You know how to get inside," Carl growled.

Moira said, "She begged me not to tell you, ever. I think she was wrong."

"Who? What is—"

"Inside," said Carl, and shoved him roughly down the slope.

His long conditioning was still with him, and reflexively he side-stepped the fanning fingers which swayed to meet him. He ducked under them, batted aside the inner phalanx and found himself in the clear space underneath. He stopped there, gasping.

Something moaned.

He bent, fumbled cautiously in the blackness. He touched something smooth and alive, recoiled, touched it again. A foot.

Someone began to cry harshly, hurt-fully, the sound exploding as if through clenched hands.

"April!"

"I told them not to..." and she moaned.

"April, what is it, what's happened?"

"You needn't... be," she said, sobbed a while, and went on, "...angry. It didn't live."

"What didn't... you mean you... April, you—"

"It wouldn't've been a tapeworm," she whispered.

"Who—" he fell to his knees, found her face. "When did you—"

"I was going to tell you that day, that very same day, and when you came in so angry at what Teague told you, I specially wanted to, I thought you'd... be glad."

"April, why didn't you come back? If I'd known...."

"You *said* what you'd do if I ever... if you ever had another... you meant it, Tod."

"It's this place, this Viridis," he said sadly. "I went crazy."

He felt her wet hand on his cheek. "It's all right. I just didn't want to make it worse for you," April said.

"I'll take you back."

"No, you can't. I've been... I've lost a lot of... just stay with me a little while."

"Moira should have—"

"She just found me," said April. "I've been alone all the—I guess I made a noise. I didn't mean to. Tod... don't quar-rel. Don't go into a lot of... It's all right."

Against her throat he cried. *"All right!"*

"When you're by yourself," she said faintly, "you think; you think better. Did you ever think of—"

"April!" he cried in anguish, the very sound of her pale, pain-wracked voice making this whole horror real.

"Shh, sh. Listen," she said rapidly, "There isn't time, you know, Tod. Tod, did you ever think of us all, Teague and Alma and Moira and Carl and us, what we are?"

"I know what I am."

"*Shh.* Altogether we're a leader and mother; a word and a shield; a doubter, a mystic..." Her voice trailed off. She coughed and he could feel the spastic jolt shoot through her body. She panted lightly for a moment and went on urgently, "Anger and prejudice and stupidity, courage, laughter, love, music... it was all aboard that ship and it's all here on Viridis. Our children and theirs—no matter what they look like, Tod, no matter how they live or what they eat—they have that in them. Humanity isn't just a way of walking, merely a kind of skin. It's what we had together and what we gave Sol. It's what the golden ones found in us and wanted for Viridis. You'll see. You'll see."

"Why Viridis?"

"Because of what Teague said—what you said." Her breath puffed out in the ghost of a laugh. "Basic biology... ontogeny follows phylogeny. The human fetus is a cell, an animalcule, a gilled amphibian... all up the line. It's there in us; Viridis makes it go backward."

"To what?"

"The mushroom. The spores. We'll be spores, Tod. Together... Alma *said* she could be dead, and together with Teague! That's why I said... it's all right. This doesn't matter, what's happened. We live in Sol, we live in Emerald with Carl and Moira, you see? Closer, nearer than we've ever been."

Tod took a hard hold on his reason. "But back to spores—why? What then?"

She sighed. It was unquestionably a happy sound. "They'll be back for the reaping, and they'll have us, Tod, all we are and all they worship: goodness and generosity and the urge to build; mercy; kindness.

"They're needed too," she whispered. "And the spores make mushrooms, and the mushrooms make the heterokaryons; and from those, away from Viridis, come the life-forms to breed us—us, Tod! into whichever form is dominant. And there we'll be, that flash of old understanding of a new idea... the special pressure on a painter's hand that makes him a Rembrandt, the sense of architecture that turns a piano-player into a Bach. Three billion extra years of evolution, ready to help wherever it can be used. On every Earth-type planet, Tod—millions of us, blowing about in the summer wind, waiting to give...."

"Give! Give what Teague is now, rotten and angry?"

"That isn't Teague. That will die off. Teague lives with Alma in their children, and in theirs... she *said* she'd be with him!"

"Me... what about me?" he breathed. "What I did to you...."

"Nothing, you did nothing. You live in Sol, in Emerald. Living, conscious, alive... with me...."

He said, "You mean... you could talk to me from Sol?"

"I think I might." With his forehead, bent so close to her, he felt her smile. "But I don't think I would. Lying so close to you, why should I speak to an outsider?"

Her breathing changed and he was suddenly terrified. "April, don't die."

"I won't," she said. "Alma didn't." She kissed him gently and died.

I t was a long darkness, with Tod hardly aware of roaming and raging through the jungle, of eating without tasting, of hungering without knowing of it. Then there was a twilight, many months long, soft and still, with restfulness here and a

promise soon. Then there was the compound again, found like a dead memory, learned again just a little more readily than something new. Carl and Moira were kind, knowing the nature of justice and the limits of punishment, and at last Tod was alive again.

He found himself one day down near the river, watching it and thinking back without fear of his own thoughts, and a growing wonder came to him. His mind had for so long dwelt on his own evil that it was hard to break new paths. He wondered with an awesome effort what manner of creatures might worship humanity for itself, and what manner of creatures humans were to be so worshipped. It was a totally new concept to him, and he was completely immersed in it, so that when Emerald slid out of the grass and stood watching him, he was frightened and shouted.

She did not move. There was little to fear now on Viridis. All the large reptiles were gone, and there was room for the humans, the humanoids, the primates, the... children. In his shock the old reflexes played. He stared at her, her square stocky body, the silver hair which covered it all over except for the face, the palms, the soles of the feet. "A *monkey!*" he spat, in Teague's tones, and the shock turned to shame. He met her eyes, April's deep glowing rubies, and they looked back at him without fear.

He let a vision of April grow and fill the world. The child's rare red eyes helped (there was so little, so very little red on Viridis). He saw April at the spaceport, holding him in the dark shadows of the blockhouse while the sky flamed above them. *We'll go out like that soon, soon, Tod. Squeeze me, squeeze me... Ah,* he'd said, *who needs a ship?*

Another April, part of her in a dim light as she sat writing; her hair, a crescent of light loving her cheek, a band of it on her brow; then she had seen him and turned, rising, smothered his first word with her mouth. Another April wanting to smile, waiting; and April asleep, and once April sobbing because she could not find a special word to tell him what she felt for him... He brought his mind back from her in the past, from her as she was, alive in his mind, back to here, to the bright mute

with the grave red eyes who stood before him, and he said, "How precious?"

The baby kept her eyes on his, and slowly raised her silken hands. She cupped them together to make a closed chamber, looked down at it, opened her hands slightly and swiftly to peer inside, rapt at what she pretended to see; closed her hands again to capture the treasure, whatever it was, and hugged it to her breast. She looked up at him slowly, and her eyes were full of tears, and she was smiling.

He took his grandchild carefully in his arms and held her gently and strongly. Monkey?

"April," he gasped. "Little Ape. Little Ape."

Viridis is a young planet which bears (at first glance) old life-forms. Come away and let the green planet roll around its sun; come back in a while—not long, as astronomical time goes.

The jungle is much the same, the sea, the rolling savannahs. But the life....

Viridis was full of primates. There were blunt-toothed herbivores and long-limbed tree-dwellers, gliders and burrowers. The fish-eaters were adapting the way all Viridis life must adapt, becoming more fit by becoming simpler, or go to the wall. Already the sea-apes had rudimentary gills and had lost their hair. Already tiny forms competed with the insects on their own terms.

On the banks of the wandering rivers, monotremes with opposed toes dredged and paddled, and sloths and lemurs crept at night. At first they had stayed together, but they were soon too numerous for that; and a half-dozen generations cost them the power of speech, which was, by then, hardly a necessity. Living was good for primates on Viridis, and became better each generation.

Eating and breeding, hunting and escaping filled the days and the cacophonous nights. It was hard in the beginning to see a friend cut down, to watch a slender silver shape go spinning down a river and know that with it went some of your brother, some of your mate, some of yourself. But as the hundreds became thousands and the thousands millions, witnessing death became about as significant as watching your friend get his hair cut. The basic ids each spread through the changing, mutating population like a stain, crossed and recrossed by the strains of the others, coexisting, eating each other and being eaten and all the while passing down through the generations.

There was a cloud over the savannah, high over the ruins of the compound. It was a thing of many colors and of no particular shape, and it was bigger than one might imagine, not knowing how far away it was.

From it dropped a golden spot that became a thread, and down came a golden mass. It spread and swung, exploded into a myriad of individuals. Some descended on the compound, erasing and changing, lifting, breaking—always careful to kill nothing. Others blanketed the planet, streaking silently through the green aisles, flashing unimpeded through the tangled thickets. They combed the riverbanks and the half-light of hill waves, and everywhere they went they found and touched the mushroom and stripped it of its spores, the compaction and multiplication of what had once been the representatives of a very high reptile culture.

Primates climbed and leaped, crawled and crept to the jungle margins to watch. Eater lay by eaten; the hunted stood on the hunter's shoulder, and a platypoid laid an egg in the open which nobody touched.

Simian forms hung from the trees in loops and ropes, in swarms and beards, and more came all the time, brought by some ineffable magnetism to watch at the hill. It was a fast and a waiting, with no movement but jostling for position, a crowding forward from behind and a pressing back from the slightest chance of interfering with the golden visitors.

Down from the polychrome cloud drifted a mass of the golden beings, carrying with them a huge sleek ship. They held it above the ground, sliced it, lifted it apart, set down this piece and that until a shape began to grow. Into it went bales and bundles, stocks and stores, and then the open tops were covered. It was a much bigger installation than the one before.

Quickly, it was done, and the golden cloud hung waiting.

The jungle was trembling with quiet.

In one curved panel of the new structure, something spun, fell outward, and out of the opening came a procession of stately creatures, long-headed, bright-eyed, three-toed, richly plumed and feathered. They tested their splendid wings, then stopped suddenly, crouched and looking upward.

They were given their obeisance by the golden ones, and after there appeared in the sky the exquisite symbol of a beauty that rides up and up, turns and spirals down again only to rise again; the symbol of that which has no beginning and no end, and the sign of those whose worship and whose work it is to bring to all the Universe that which has shown itself worthy in parts of it.

Then they were gone, and the jungle exploded into killing and flight, eating and screaming, so that the feathered ones dove back into their shelter and closed the door....

And again to the green planet (when the time was right) came the cloud-ship, and found a world full of birds, and the birds watched in awe while they harvested their magic dust, and built a new shelter. In this they left four of their own for later harvesting, and this was to make of Viridis a most beautiful place.

From Viridis, the ship vaulted through the galaxies, searching for worlds worthy of what is human in humanity, whatever their manner of being alive. These they seeded, and of these, perhaps one would produce something new, something which could be reduced to the dust of Viridis, and from dust return. • • •

THEODORE STURGEON (1918-85) wrote the original series episodes "Shore Leave" and "Amok Time." An unproduced storyline was adapted by James Gunn into the 1996 Star Trek *novel* The Joy Machine. *His prose style influenced, among many others, Ray Bradbury and Kurt Vonnegut, the latter of whom based the character of Kilgore Trout on him. North Atlantic Books is publishing a set of his complete stories, with eleven of a projected thirteen volumes released so far.*

ACTIVITY ON ENCELADUS! – CASSINI PROBES DYNAMIC MOON

SAN FRANCISCO—The closer scientists look at Saturn's small moon Enceladus, the more they find evidence of an active world. The most recent flybys of Enceladus made by NASA's Cassini spacecraft have provided new signs of ongoing changes on and around the moon. The latest high-resolution images of Enceladus show signs that the south polar surface changes over time.

"Enceladus has Earth-like spreading of the icy crust, but with an exotic difference — the spreading is almost all in one direction, like a conveyor belt," said Paul Helfenstein, Cassini imaging associate at Cornell University in Ithaca, N.Y. "Asymmetric spreading like this is unusual on Earth and not well understood."

"Enceladus has asymmetric spreading on steroids," Helfenstein added. "We are not certain about the geological mechanisms that control the spreading, but we see patterns of divergence and mountain-building similar to what we see on Earth, which suggests that subsurface heat and convection are involved."

The moon's distinctive "tiger stripes" are analogous to the mid-ocean ridges on Earth's seafloor where volcanic material wells up and creates new crust. Using Cassini-based digital maps of the moon's south polar region, Helfenstein reconstructed a possible history of the tiger stripes by working backward in time and progressively snipping away older and older sections of the map, each time finding that the remaining sections fit together like puzzle pieces.

Images from recent close flybys also have bolstered an idea the Cassini imaging team has that condensation from the jets erupting from the surface may create ice plugs that close off old vents and force new vents to open. The opening and clogging of vents also corresponds with measurements indicating the plume varies from month to month and year to year.

"We see no obvious distinguishing markings on the surface in the immediate vicinity of each jet source, which suggests that the vents may open and close and thus migrate up and down the fractures over time," Porco said. "Over time, the particles that rain down onto the surface from the jets may form a continuous blanket of snow along a fracture."

Enceladus' output of ice and vapor dramatically impacts the entire Saturnian system by supplying the ring system with fresh material and loading ionized gas from water vapor into Saturn's magnetosphere.

With water vapor, organic compounds and excess heat emerging from Enceladus' south polar terrain, scientists are intrigued by the possibility of a liquid-water-rich habitable zone beneath the moon's south pole.

—from NASA press release, December 15, 2008

No Studio, No Network, No Problem

by Crystal Ann Taylor

Prologue 1: 1968

Thirteen year old Marc Scott Zicree was delighted with the Christmas present his stepmother arranged through friend Fred Bronson: a visit to the *Star Trek* set. The series was shooting its final episode, "Turnabout Intruder." At its very end, he got to see for himself the making of something he'd loved from the beginning.

For more than two years, ever since *Star Trek* premiered in September 1966, Zicree had kept a scrapbook, saving every article, every signed photo, every *TV Guide* entry he could lay his hands on about the series and its cast, as well as his own drawings and photographs. One photo featured him in homemade makeup, with pointy ears and jutting eyebrows, one raised archly.

As he walked around the sets representing the interior of the Starship *Enterprise*,

he had an epiphany. "I saw flats and plywood walls," he says today, "how flimsy they were and how they were all lighting and magic." The secret to television, he realized, was that "it isn't how fake something looks when you are standing next to it, but how it looks on the screen."

Prologue 2: 1977

Recently arrived in Hollywood to launch a career writing for television, Michael Reaves landed one of the hottest pitches in town: *Star Trek II*. A television series set to inaugurate the Paramount Television Service, a fourth broadcast network, the next March, it was to star the original series' cast, with the exception of Leonard Nimoy's Spock. The pitch was particularly important to Reaves, because he had loved *Star Trek* since seeing the series premiere at age sixteen.

"I came up with several pitches," he says. In one, Lieutenant Commander Sulu, played by George Takei, is temporarily lost in a transporter mishap. When he finally materializes, he is thirty years older, and dressed in barbarian alien garb. He has lived those years on a planet in a pocket universe with a different time rate, and now it's his once-familiar life on the *Enterprise* that's alien to him.

"I was at least partly inspired by the 'The Naked Time' episode, in which George thought he was the Scarlet Pimpernel or something," Reaves explains. "I pitched it to [producer] Harold Livingston and [story editor] Jon Povill, both of whom liked it." However, they wanted to see Sulu's years on the planet as well, and for that reason passed on the pitch—as their budget wouldn't allow for another planet story at the time.

The producers offered Reaves an open door to pitch again, but before he could return, Paramount's network plans collapsed, and the *Star Trek II* pilot script, "In Thy Image," went into development as a feature film. "I was pretty blue," Reaves admits, "because I thought that I'd never get another chance to put words in the mouths of those characters."

Prologue 3: 1987

James Cawley had been fascinated with *Star Trek* his whole life. He'd collected action figures and other memorabilia. He'd built sets in his grandfather's garage. On the convention circuit, he had become friends with William Ware Theiss, costume designer for the original series.

Now *Star Trek* was back on television with *Star Trek: The Next Generation,* and Theiss was back in his old job. Cawley was actually working on the franchise he loved, as a freelance seamster.

Cawley learned that Theiss still had a set of blueprints for the original series *Enterprise* sets. Theiss gave them to the enthusiastic Cawley.

Cawley studied these documents that many fans would give their eye teeth for. Later, as his sets took new and accurate shape, an idea took shape as well....

In the spring of 2005, Marc Scott Zicree was at UCLA, participating in a *Star Trek* panel in a one-day science fiction event called EnigmaCon. He had originated the stories for two episodes, *The Next Generation's* "First Contact" and the fan-favorite "Far Beyond the Stars" for *Deep Space Nine.* He had more than a hundred scripts to his credit, and had climbed the writer-producer ranks on shows such as *Friday the 13th: The Series, Beyond Reality,* and *Sliders.*

Zicree was intrigued when fellow panelist Walter Koenig, the original series' Ensign Chekov, talked about returning to the role in a new project. Fans had built painstaking replicas of the '60s *Enterprise* sets, he said, and were making their own full-length episodes. D.C. Fontana, script consultant and popular writer on the original series, was writing the script for Koenig's episode.

After the convention, Zicree went online and watched the second episode of the series, called *Star Trek New Voyages.* It was a sequel to the classic episode "The Doomsday Machine."

Zicree was thrilled. "I thought the sets were great, the costumes were great, the effects were great, the writing was very fun. It was delightful and the jokes were funny. I really liked the enthusiasm and the vigor and the intelligence of what they were doing."

He learned that professionals had been

involved in the series along with the fans from the beginning. Jim Vanover, a scenic artist on the more recent series and movies, wrote the episode Zicree had watched. Doug Drexler created the special effects, using the pseudonym Max Rem because at the time, he was working on *Star Trek: Enterprise.*

And in charge, the literal and metaphorical captain of this enterprise, was James Cawley. He had become a successful and popular Elvis impersonator, sounding so much like the King that the state of Tennessee once used one of his recordings in a commercial pushing Graceland and other tourist destinations when the original proved beyond their budget. His tours as Elvis provided the income and the downtime for him to realize his dream.

Along with other fans, he re-created the original sets, props, and costumes, began shooting episodes on digital video, and posting them on his website, www. startreknewvoyages.com. Besides its attention to detail, what set *Star Trek New Voyages* apart from other *Trek* fan films was that Cawley, who played Elvis for a living, was unafraid to take on the mantle of another 20th century pop culture icon, James T. Kirk. Other fans created the adventures of new ships and crews in the *Star Trek* universe, but Cawley would settle for nothing less than completing the five-year mission of the Starship *Enterprise.*

The series quickly became popular enough to catch the attention of Paramount's legal department, but fans and studio came to an agreement that *New Voyages* could continue, so long as it did not generate any income. It was an easy agreement for the fans to accept, since money had never been their motivation.

Episode by episode, *Star Trek New Voyages* (or *STNV* for short) grew in scope. Guest stars from the original series made appearances, then Koenig, a regular. Cawley turned a defunct car dealership near his home town of Ticonderoga, New York, into a permanent studio. The sets became larger and more detailed, the bridge growing to a full 360 degrees, which even the original was not. But Zicree noted the series still lacked the polish and production values of a professional television production. "I saw ways to bring the level of production up in every department, so it would be on par with a network show. And that's what I set about doing."

Zicree recalled the Sulu story his friend Michael Reaves had attempted to sell Paramount in the late seventies. In fact, the passage of thirty years made it almost seem prophetic. "It seemed like this would be a great way to do this terrific story and save on makeup, because George would be thirty years older and we wouldn't have to age him." And *STNV's* Sulu, John Lim, could continue to play Sulu's younger self.

Since his pitch, Reaves had written over 400 scripts, won an Emmy for story-editing *Batman: The Animated Series,* and become a best-selling novelist. He had even had his chance to write for *Star Trek,* co-writing "Where No One Has Gone Before" with popular *Trek* novelist Diane Duane for *The Next Generation.* "It's not like I woke up every morning these past thirty years, thinking, 'Damn, I wish they'd made that show,'" he says. "Still, it was pretty astonishing to get a second chance like this."

His story had to be updated, of course. "In the intervening time," Zicree explains, *"Next Gen* had done a story called 'The Inner Light,' in which Picard gets marooned on an alien planet and raises a family. He grows old and dies."

He restructured Reaves' story, now

called "World Enough and Time," without any scenes on the planet, giving viewers the shock of first seeing the older Sulu as he materializes on the *Enterprise* in his barbaric garb. It actually served to emphasize Sulu's primary dilemma. He's caught between two universes with a heart-wrenching decision to make. Alana, his daughter with Dr. Lisa Chandris, the now-dead scientist who had been trapped with him, has lived her whole life on an alien world, hearing her father's stories of the *Enterprise*. Now she's actually there, but unable to materialize fully, caught in the same dimensional anomaly that holds the *Enterprise* and stranded her parents. Spock determines that saving both Alana and the ship may not be possible.

Zicree also added wraparounds set in the post-feature film era, with Sulu as captain of the Starship *Excelsior,* visited by his later

Portrait of the artist as a young Vulcan. For Marc Scott Zicree, eventually directing and co-writing "World Enough and Time" was only logical.

daughter, Demora (introduced in the film *Star Trek: Generations)* and his new granddaughter.

The changes added another level of poignancy and gut-wrenching power: the theme about continuation of family, of living on in the memories of others, of life having meaning. It resonates with both writers. "I've been something of a surrogate father to my own sister," Zicree reveals. "I have a sister who is nineteen years younger than me, who I put through college and whom I've been very protective of for years. So even though I don't have children, that sort of father-daughter

relationship is something I had in my relationship with my sister. I knew I could identify with that, and I could write that. And Michael has a grown daughter as well."

The commenting on real life which *Star Trek* and science fiction do so well appealed to Zicree even when he was a kid. For him, this story "answered why Sulu had that second family—why he had Demora."

For Reaves, reviving his old pitch gave him a chance to emulate what had most intrigued him about the original series. "What really got to me as a fledgling writer was how subversive it was," he says. "When Kirk prevented McCoy from saving Edith Keeler [in 'The City on the Edge of Forever'], I was utterly stunned—I had fully expected him to pull some lame eleventh-hour solution out of his ass, and save both her and the universe. I mean, try to imagine what *[Voyage to the Bottom of the Sea's]* Admiral Nelson or Professor Robinson [of *Lost in Space]* would do in that situation. I remember being tremendously excited by the potential of what I'd seen. I wanted to write something that powerful."

For "World Enough and Time" to escape from its own thirty-year limbo, the writers needed more than the skill and determination to produce a good script. They needed George Takei.

Takei had also heard from Walter Koenig about *Star Trek New Voyages.* But, at the time, since Koenig said it was a fan film and Takei had done fan films and student film projects at UCLA and USC, he didn't give it much serious thought.

"But then Marc Zicree called," Takei reveals, "and he said, 'I have this fantastic script and you've got to read it and I would love to have you do it.'" Years of experience had educated Takei to be cautious, so he asked Marc who was producing it. "He told me it was this fan project up in the Adirondacks and I said, oh I know about it, Walter told me about it."

Convinced that Takei was a brilliant actor who had never had the Sulu story he deserved, Zicree sought to win him over with the whirlwind enthusiasm which propels all his projects, and is difficult not to get caught up in.

"Marc said, 'You've got to read this script. It's a fantastic script. I'll run it over to you

Storyboard artist Gabriel Hardman takes a bit of a busman's holiday from Spider-Man 3 *to visualize some key sequences for "World Enough and Time"*

right now,' *as we were talking,"* Takei says, the surprise of that offer still tingeing his voice. "And I said, 'What do you mean, *right now?'* He said, 'I'll get in my car right now and run it over.'"

Surprised by that level of enthusiasm and commitment, all Takei could do was to extend an invitation. "He came over, and we sat in my dining room and had tea while he pitched me this story, and I had the script in my hot little hands." Intrigued by the pitch, Takei indicated that he still wanted to read the script first, and Marc left it with him. "I was flying off someplace—I can't remember where now—and I read it on the plane, and I was blown away. It was a fantastic script."

Takei called Marc back to tell him, "I love this script. It's the best Sulu role I've ever seen. I'd love to do it, but tell me how this is going to be done. He went over the whole thing again and it sounded like it was going to be an adventure.

"I'm all for boldly going where I've never gone before," Takei chuckles. Then, turning serious, he explains that "in this business, you have to be venturesome." He likens it to the days when movies "were a vast unknown, an experimental area" and how distinguished theater stars of the time wouldn't deign to work in "filmed drama," considering it "sideshow entertainment, mere attraction." And yet before they knew it, movies were gathering bigger audiences in one week than they had in a lifetime of performing in theaters. "So Broadway stars started doing movies," Takei observes. "And it was the same attitude with the stars of the stage and screen when this thing called television came on-line."

Takei considers the real venturesome and risk-taking performers the ones who recognized a good opportunity and jumped on it, despite worries that its increased visibility could be a career breaker. "They did those dramas live," Takei elaborates, "so if you made a mistake... it was the worst of both theater and television. You got the advantage of a huge audience in one

Marc Zicree shows off his fancy art school education with some of his own storyboards. Kidding aside, he calls them "Snoopygrams" after the simplified but effective graphic style of the Peanuts *comic strip. And that is just about as few penstrokes as you could use to intelligibly convey the ideas of "the* Enterprise *bridge" and "Spock at his scanner."*

night with live television, but you also got the worst of theater. If you flub one night on stage, only about five or six hundred people see you, but if you flub on live television, it's seen by millions all across the country. But they were venturesome enough to do that and now television has become a major star-maker. And so in a similar way, I thought, well, I'm going to be venturesome."

Takei feels being venturesome is part of his job description. "As actors, we're in a risk-taking business. I mean, the minute you stand in front of casting people, or a director or a producer, you're gambling with your life."

Nevertheless, Takei didn't walk blindly into the project; he approached Koenig again for his input. "He did tell me it was very arduous, but enormously fulfilling."

With George Takei on board, and a deal in place with James Cawley to allow Zicree to direct and executive-produce the episode, he proceeded to put into place his production team, which would augment the one Cawley had assembled over three episodes. Building that new production team is where many Hollywood professionals like me got involved.

Although Marc knows many working professionals from being in the entertainment business for three decades, he has an even greater pool of talent to draw from through running an invitation-only networking group called "The Hamptons Round Table," after the now-bulldozed restaurant where it began.

Connected through a weekly dinner gathering and Table emails are about 500 of us: actors, writers, directors and other entertainment professionals. The idea behind the Table is that no matter what our current success in the Industry is, we all have needs and dreams we want to fulfill that require access to information, contacts, or bodies—such as, sell a screenplay, produce a movie, or book an acting gig.

Say I need a cameraman to shoot my short film, or a contact number to a producer, or a bar for a location shoot, I can put my request out to the Table. If someone can answer my question or provide me with help and is willing to do it, then he or she then contacts me directly. Nobody is obligated to help anyone, but since Hollywood is a business of relationships, most established professionals want to give back for the leg up they've been given.

Hundreds of us from the Round Table responded to lend our expertise in whatever way Marc needed to get this project done. Even so, he estimated that it took him more than half a year to get all the pieces and people in place.

Every day, everywhere he went, Zicree talked up his episode... to everyone. George describes him as "a tsunami of enthusiasm that just picks you up and carries you away." Brad Altman, Takei's manager, calls Zicree the biggest risk-taker he'd ever met.

But Zicree insists people came aboard because they knew that he was really committed; they knew that he was coming off of thirty years of creating a body of work that had quality. "They knew that I wasn't going to flake," he maintains. "When they know you are going to go the whole nine yards, they'll buy in."

Some of the professionals who bought in were also old-time *Star Trek* fans, and others weren't, but got caught up in that infectious Zicree enthusiasm. Actor Don Baldaramos, who became essential as UPM (Unit Production Manager) and co-

producer, described his participation this way: "I was attending table meetings and Marc's mentoring group. At the end of each evening for about three weeks, Marc held up this photo of the *Excelsior* [bridge] and asked for help building it. I'd never heard of it, didn't know what a Klingon was or anything about *Star Trek* beyond the names Kirk and Spock. But I knew no one was going to be able to build that thing, and that unless he could pay, he probably wasn't going to get it built."

Though Don's focus is on building his acting career, not sets, he's also a journeyman carpenter and cabinet maker. So he became a member of what he calls "the second generation of the Harrison Ford school of actor-carpenters," and volunteered to build the *Excelsior.*

Tasha Hardy, our tireless line producer, admitted to not knowing much about *Star Trek,* either, before she became involved. Christina Moses, who played Sulu's daughter Alana, grew up watching *Star Trek* with her dad, but it was *he* who was the fan, not her.

For me, I felt my involvement in *Star Trek* was long past. A fan mostly of the original series, I saw it as the love of my growing-up years, as what honed my writing skills through fanfic, and as the inspiration which brought me to Hollywood to become a TV writer. I didn't see myself getting involved in a major fan production. Then, as a member of the Round Table, Marc showed me two things which blew me away: a DVD of some of the special effects for the prior episode, and the script for "World Enough and Time," or as we came to call it, WEAT (pronounced "wheat").

Expecting special effects that would show the lack of a large enough budget, I was amazed to see effects that looked as good as anything I had seen on TV. "That's Doug Drexler," Zicree told me when I praised the effects. Zicree said that *New Voyages* couldn't do better than Doug Drexler, since he's now CG Effects Supervisor on *Battlestar Galactica*. "Doug Drexler's team is the best team working in television. They're the Rolls Royce. And to get that on a fan project is huge."

The script also amazed me. Not only was the plot exciting and the story both uplifting and heart-wrenching, but the characters and relationships were spot on. The dialogue was so real, I could hear the characters speaking it right in my head. There was even the kind of banter that I had loved so much from the original show. My favorite WEAT banter exchange is:

Kirk turns to Spock.
KIRK: *Meanwhile, I want you to get on with plan B.*
SPOCK: *I was unaware we had a plan B.*
KIRK: *I trust you will shortly.*
SPOCK: *(nods, getting it) Understood... Tell me, Captain, what did you do before you knew me?*
KIRK: *I made sure plan A worked.*
SPOCK: *Ah.*
Spock exits.

Exchanges like this told me that Zicree and Reaves knew the *Star Trek* characters I loved, so I knew I had to be involved. At first, I signed on as script coordinator, for which I have tons of professional experience on television series. Then I found myself as documentary producer, and finally as Internet publicist/reporter. As with everyone else involved, the number of hats kept growing as things needed to be done.

P re-production jumped into high gear. The script went through various production drafts as circumstances dic-

tated. Zicree and his wife, writer and director Elaine Zicree, held actor camp in L.A. and New York for the *STNV* regular cast, doing scene studies and improv work to sharpen their skills. Baldaramos talked Gigapix Studios, where he worked as a producer, into lending him their insert studio to build the *Excelsior* bridge set—for what turned out to be three months. Starting first with photos and then blueprints, he made budget estimates, bought materials and hired a carpenter to assist him, mostly out of his own pocket—something that many participants had to do because the budget was too tight to supply much. As equipment and personnel needs became apparent, Tasha Hardy coordinated with Cawley's group to determine if there was already equipment or personnel in place, or if she had to look for equipment and people out here.

To design the looks for "barbarian Sulu" and Alana, Zicree approached Iain McCaig, who, as lead designer of the *Star Wars* prequel trilogy, had designed the look of Darth Maul and Queen Amidala.

"Iain has been my artist on the *Magic Time* novels for ten years," Zicree says, referring to his trilogy of novels and the television series proposal that inspired them. "I called him and asked him if he'd be interested in designing a barbarian costume for Sulu, and he said, well, let me think about it, email me a photo of George, what he looks like now. So I emailed him, and I woke up the next morning, and he had already done a design. It was there... in my email, this amazing photo montage thing that he had done." Zicree felt that the costume was so spectacular that the visual of it alone shouted professional production.

One of the little fun details which fans might not pick up on is that when Sulu comes back to the *Enterprise*, worked into his hair is the earring that Chandris was wearing when she left with him on the shuttlecraft. Zicree says of the memento, "It's the one thing he has from her. Someone had asked me, why would he be wearing an earring, wouldn't he be wearing an Enterprise insignia? And I said, no, because he had given up that life to become what he needed to be on that planet. The *Enterprise* insignia would be on Alana's dress as a detail, so they actually sewed the insignia onto her dress among the stones and gems and so forth."

When asked why he felt it appropriate to have Sulu's *Enterprise* insignia sewn into Alana's dress, Zicree answers, "It would be something from his life on the *Enterprise* that she would find magical. And she would take it and wear it as her talisman, just as he's wearing as a talisman Chandris's earring as a keepsake in his hair. As the audience, you wouldn't notice, but the actor can use all that stuff and it's all better for that."

Concept illustrations of "Barbarian Sulu" and daughter Alana... by the father-daughter team of Iain and Mishi McCaig.

Of course, that just made it starkly clear that Sulu doesn't have a keepsake from Alana after the events of the episode. Asked if he thought that sad, Marc responds, "Yeah. But he has the memories."

Speaking of the return of memories, Zicree points out that that scene was one of Michael Reaves' ideas. For the end scene where young Sulu is grieving, Michael called him and said, "Spock comes into the room and says, 'I can give you back the memories. I have them in my mind, and I can give you back the memories.'" Not only was it a poignant, heart-wrenching moment, but it set up another decision for Sulu: should he choose to remember her or not? Does he open himself up to the incredible grief losing a daughter will bring him?

"In the end, he makes the brave choice," Zicree affirms. "This whole episode is about people making the difficult but brave choices again and again. And it's about people rising beyond what they would normally be. Sulu becomes this incredible barbarian character to survive and protect his daughter. Alana makes her sacrifice. And even Kirk, who starts out as a ladies' man who doesn't care about these girls he romances, he becomes someone who is totally shattered by this experience."

To pull off this level of emotional commitment, Zicree knew that casting the right guest actors would be crucial. "One of the things I insisted on when I took on directing WEAT was that the guest actors would be cast out of L.A., that they would be professional actors." Hence, he held auditions in L.A. for professional actors to play Chandris, Alana, and Demora.

Being that Sulu's daughter is such a pivotal role, I asked Marc to describe how he saw Alana. "Alana will talk to people and force them to be genuine with her.

That's what she does. She goes right to people's cores and gets them to open up, whether it's Spock or Kirk. She's utterly genuine. There's no artifice at all."

Even the casting process had its obstacles to overcome. "I originally cast a different actress to play the lead because Michael and I knew that it would take a major talented actress to play Alana," he reveals. "So I originally cast an actress who was a lead on *Odyssey 5*. When we came to the point where we were ready to shoot, she said she had to have surgery and wouldn't be able to shoot."

Although Zicree is normally a calm and well-balanced person, he immediately went into a white panic. "My episode is shooting in four weeks and I don't have a female lead. Holy cow. I had spent six months building a production team and that team is on the march."

Hence, it was back to the auditions process. The difficulty was that he had already cast Lia Johnson as Chandris on the basis of whom he had cast for Alana. He wanted to cast both actresses with enough of a physical resemblance that the audience would buy them as mother and daughter. "I had always wanted to cast a black actress for Alana," Zicree explains. "Black actress or mixed race. I'm very interested in mixed—I mean I love America, I love the variety of people who are Americans, and when I walk the streets, I love the people who actually live here. Up to a couple of years ago, television was so overwhelmingly white, extremely same, and whenever I wanted to write a different race, I would have to specify and dig in my heels and not let them cast white people."

Although he auditioned Asian, black, and mixed race actresses for the Alana role, his hope was to find someone who was black or half-black to avoid recasting Chandris, too. "So it was a real balancing act," Zicree admits. "But fortunately, Christina Moses came in and auditioned. She had never done TV, she had never done film. She's a stage actress and she had heard about the audition through a friend."

But the minute Christina auditioned, the casting director, director, and the executive producers knew she was the one. "Then we went to New York and she was as sick as a dog. Feverish. Chills. The whole nine yards. And you cannot tell at all. She was a blessing. And the final blessing of the shoot was that she gave a world-class performance. I knew that George Takei would be spectacular. But I felt like I had gotten a double gift from heaven, getting both George and Christina."

During this time, construction on the *Excelsior* set was underway, because it had to be built from scratch, unlike the on-going sets Cawley had in upstate New York for the *Enterprise*. Armed with borrowed original *Excelsior* plans, Baldaramos consulted Zicree on the minimum set needed. This was necessary not only because of the lack of time and lack of budget, but also because of lack of expertise. While the Table was a great resource for actors, directors, producers and set crew, there was a paucity of expert carpenters. Baldaramos had to train his volunteers, and when he fortuitously met a studio set carpenter, Don Delaney, at a party, he hired him to assist out of his own pocket, just to get the project done.

With the focal point of the scenes being the captain's chair, Zicree decided that the minimum set needed was only the portion of the bridge that was behind the captain's chair, with its familiar graphics screens. Luckily the original backdrop of the cross-section of a similar ship, the *Enterprise-B* from *Star Trek: Generations*, drawn by Doug Drexler when he was scenic artist and visual effects artist on the movies, was still in the hands of his *Star Trek* co-worker Jim Vanover, both of whom graciously loaned it to the production for the central graphic panel. That eased the number of graphics Baldaramos' crew had to recreate.

"Ken Horkavy and Jim Troesh were our graphic guys," Baldaramos told me. "Ken copied from reference material provided by Mike Okuda, graphic designer on the *Star Trek* movies, and improvised some of the designs. Then Ken Sheetz spent hours painstakingly attaching them to the smoked Plexiglas screens. The rest was back-lighting."

The two front consoles, where the navigator and pilot sit, were CGI recreations, as was the small table with Sulu's cup of tea. There just wasn't time or money to build them practically. As it was, Baldaramos held a raffle to offset some of the costs of materials.

Meanwhile, everyone headed to Port Henry, New York for principal photography and the "arduous, but enormously fulfilling" time Walter Koenig had predicted for us. While the fans who had crewed Cawley's earlier episodes knew what to expect in the small town, it was a culture shock for many of us coming from L.A. There was a shortage of housing, and all expenses were out of pocket. But even worse than that for the L.A. crowd, there was limited or no Internet service, unless you had a laptop that could pick up the signal from the steps outside the only occasionally-open public library (I didn't).

The lack of Internet presented a challenge to me in getting the script changes out. Nowadays, script coordinators do not worry about whether they are dealing with Mac or PC computers because the scriptwriting program Final Draft crosses platforms, and they can just email files to one type of computer or the other. Here, we had the printers tied to Macs, and my script tied to a PC, and no Internet to bridge them.

Even more crippling was the lack of cell phone coverage. Some of the biggest providers didn't work, because in an effort to keep this part of the Adirondacks unspoiled and primitive, no cell towers were allowed. Most people flew in, so few had cars, and what working cell phones we had, stayed with the drivers of necessity. And since the car showroom/studio was used only when *STNV* was in production, there was no central base phone, either. Takei summed it up thus: "You go in knowing that it isn't going to be like working at Paramount. And if you go into it expecting something like Paramount, then you are going to be disappointed."

Still, all of that was forgotten when each of us stepped onto an incredibly exact recreation of the 1960's bridge, and sat in the captain's chair. It felt like we had traveled back in time to the real thing.

"Stepping onto the bridge felt oddly familiar," Reaves says, "like I was finally showing up for a long-overdue appointment. I remember thinking something along the lines of, finally! It's about time."

Since Zicree had been on the original bridge set and sat in the "real" captain's chair, stepping onto the *STNV* bridge was like "old home week" for him. Even so, he described it as amazing: "The *New Voyages* sets are even better than the original sets. Because the originals weren't 360 degrees and didn't make noises... [now] they can push a button and all the bridge sounds come on. So it was like going home but also even better."

And George Takei, who had been intimately familiar with those original sets? "It was extraordinary in that Cawley was able to recreate on such a huge scale. I've seen fans who have produced their own bridge sets or their own shuttlecraft. Or turned a car into a shuttlecraft. But on the scale and clearly the kind of expense that he put into it, the money he put into it, it was remarkable. The detail, the authenticity of it was really extraordinary. And I was really impressed by that kind of dedication—or is it fanaticism, or is it lunacy? I don't know quite which word to use, but then again, it's that kind of lunacy that made Hollywood possible. It always takes a great deal of risk. And some people consider taking some of these risks crazy, but it takes that kind of confidence in yourself and that kind of risk-taking bravado that makes things happen. And that's what I saw in James Cawley in doing what he did and building the set that he did."

If the sets were just as Takei remembered them, his *Enterprise* crewmates were decidedly not. But he took the difference in stride, and even used it to enhance his performance as "barbarian Sulu."

"The thing that helped me, and this was number one, the people, who were playing the characters that we knew, were very interesting people on their own. I mean for example, John Kelly is a real doctor playing Dr. McCoy, and he brings that professional knowledge. John Lim is an attorney in Washington D.C., and you gotta be a hotshot to be a professional practicing law in Washington D.C. James Cawley with his unique passion and risk-taking bravado. They're all individually unique people and I found getting to know the individuals very interesting, but number two, my character Sulu was being *reintroduced* to the people he thought he knew so well. So I knew the characters that they were playing, but I had been away for thirty years, and so there is that—in context of the character—that readjustment."

Takei adds, "So the readjustment to that was helpful to my character who was suddenly shocked to see the people he remembered but he didn't quite remember in that way. So it was, again, an opportunity that provided me with a lot of elements to use as an actor."

As anyone knows who recalls the many hours Leonard Nimoy spent in the makeup chair, one of the most time-consuming and challenging activities that had to be done every day was the application of Spock's ears and makeup. Putting the ears on actor Jeff Quinn and taking them off were the responsibility of makeup artists Katia Mangani and Mikhael Benson. "The main challenge with the ears wasn't getting them on," Katia explains, "but blending the edges of the prosthetic ears to his own ears so that the whole ear looked natural." Not only was the makeup used thick, but it had to be sculpted, smoothed, and blended so one couldn't notice the division between real and prosthetic on camera. "Also, the prosthetic ears were not the same color as his skin tone, so Mikhael would paint the fake ears the night before to match his skin tone more closely before putting the ears on."

Another difficulty with the ears was that they "weren't meant to be worn for fifteen hours straight, so by the end of our long shooting day with Jeff moving around in them, the division that we had worked so hard to camouflage didn't look as fresh and as good as it did at the beginning of the day. We did our best to touch this up when we could, but sometimes we were so busy doing makeup that we couldn't always be on the set."

Like Nimoy forty years earlier, Quinn had to have his own ears stuck back to prevent the Vulcan eartips pointing outward from his head. Short supplies and the distance of Port Henry from professional makeup vendors left Quinn one day with the discomfort of having his ears pinned back with super glue—and of having them unstuck at the end of the day.

Whatever small defects in the Spock ears slipped through were then touched up via the post production wizardry of the DAVE School student artists (about whom, more later).

Katia and Mikhael also put on the Spock eyebrows and sideburns. Again following in Nimoy's footsteps, Jeff helped by shaving off half his own eyebrows, allowing Katia and Mikhael to glue bits of hair on in the proper curvature.

Jeff's natural freckles had to be covered as well. "I would put a lighter layer of makeup (foundation), then go back and concentrate on covering up all of his spots with a different, thicker makeup, then after that, I would put another heavier layer of the foundation on so that his complexion looked smooth and even. And of course, I would set all of this with a loose powder."

Katia was not just a makeup artist, she was also a subject. When she played a dead Romulan on a moribund Bird of Prey, it was up to Mikhael to apply her ears and eyebrows. Unlike what was done with Jeff Quinn's eyebrows, Mikhael did not shave half of Katia's.

"Mikhael actually covered half of my own eyebrows," Katia explains, "and then drew the more Vulcan/Romulan-type eyebrows in with an eyeliner pencil. This was a quicker process than how we did Jeff's eyebrows." In addition, since Katia would only be seen in profile on camera, only one ear and one side of the face was bloodied to save more time.

Cali Ross came to Port Henry as an actress, but soon found herself volunteering as a much needed makeup artist in addition, since she had had two years of cosmetology school. She did Uhura's hairdo, a look inspired by Natalie Wood in *The Great Race.*

But the greatest call on her experience was doing hair and makeup for George Takei and Christina Moses, transforming them into the "barbarian Sulu" and "Alana" looks Iain McCaig and his daughter Mishi had designed. She molded a plain, straight, silver and grey wig to fit the McCaigs' drawing, then took fabric scraps from Sulu's costume, cut them in strips, painted the strips, and added them to the hair after they dried. Once again, the day-to-day challenge, Katia points out, was to tack the edges down around the face to keep the wig from slipping and causing continuity problems. The edges of the wig had to be blended in with his makeup and skin tone, especially around the forehead, as there were no bangs on the wig to conceal the hairline.

Alana's beautiful hairdo presented another challenge for Cali. She spent nine hours braiding and tying leather strips and beads into it, leaving her fingers hurting.

While Cawley had built sets for the bridge, sick bay, transporter room, captain's/crew quarters and conference room for the *Enterprise,* and had set aside an area for their mini-shuttlecraft, there was no room to build the long, curving corridor for the Alana/Kirk walk-and-talk on Deck 12 (also to be used as part of the Romulan Bird of Prey).

In response to a plea from beleaguered Marc to see what he could do from L.A., Baldaramos "got on the phone for the next couple days, and called schools, churches, stores, and carpenters," he says. "I had people coming up from Pennsylvania, Vermont, and New York."

Besides locating these skilled laborers to donate their time, Baldaramos got gaffer equipment donated and most importantly, convinced a construction company to allow the use of the church they were renovating to build the set in—complete with free carpenters and material to build it with. It was quite something to see the relatively small and stark walls of ship corridors tucked under the beams of this beautiful old cathedral ceiling. And all for mere minutes of screen time.

The "arduous" part of Koenig's prediction was apparent in the slow going of principal photography. As Takei says, being behind schedule is par for the course on low budget films. Especially with first time directors, which Zicree was. "A low budget film has a lot of challenges," Takei reiterates. "And sometimes they don't quite meet the challenge. The people who are working on it, in addition to it being low budget, they're all volunteers and they have a great deal of enthusiasm but no professionalism to go with it, so things don't happen when they are supposed to happen."

Still, there was the advantage for him, as an actor, that he didn't have to be on the set in between shots. "I tell people I charge the studio for the wait time because I would be acting for free," he laughs. On this project, the combination of enthusiastic amateurs and low budget made the wait time in between shots even longer. Nevertheless, that gave George the opportunity to retire to the "dark little corner with the curtain around it"—the space which served as his dressing room.

The production had Takei for only a few days of the shoot. On his last day, Takei uncomplainingly performed multiple takes of shot after strenuous shot for his fight scene in the transporter room until the sky outside was lightening.

George recalls, "I did get a chance to husband the energy to give it my all. However, the people on the set are human

beings and I remember the ranting and raving—I mean in the wee hours, people… they'd been working all day long, maybe twenty hours by that time, and they get exhausted. I won't mention names, but there were temperamental flare-ups, and that again slows the whole process down and doesn't accomplish anything. But you're working with human—certain humans have a capacity, when it's taken beyond that, they explode. And fortunately, I was at that time, when the yelling and screaming happened, I happened to be in the makeup room, chatting with Jeff, I think. And I thought, good God, what's happening out there. But I had a good idea what was happening, and I recognized voices. And I thought, well, I think I'll go back to my dark little corner with the curtain around it. So it was difficult, it was trying. Particularly on that last day."

Nature did little to cooperate with the shoot. It was mid-September, and the temperature swung wildly from chilly to sweltering day by day. Because of the lights, the warmest place was always on set, and the warmth brought flies. While flies might be prevalent in the Adirondacks in the summertime, there aren't supposed to be any on the *Enterprise* in space. Liberal applications of insecticide helped only a little.

The production shot mostly at night, so as to avoid traffic noise in the non-soundproof studio. But late hours brought the freight trains down the nearby track, ruining many takes. During the daytime, production assistants took up posts in either direction down the rural highway in front of the studio, warning the crew with walkie-talkies when loud eighteen-wheelers were headed their way.

Still, frustration over the situation gave us the best line of the entire shoot. In an exchange cut from the final episode, Alana likens her situation to "midnight and Cinderella." In one take, just as Kirk tells Alana, "There's no midnight in space," a fly passed by Cawley's face, and a distant train whistle sounded. Without missing a beat, Cawley ad-libbed, "Only flies—and trains."

The production used two 720p high definition video cameras. The second camera saved time in two ways. Sometimes, it allowed Zicree to shoot two angles at once. At others, the second unit could shoot much-needed additional footage while the main unit worked on more dramatic scenes.

Eric "Gooch" Goodrich directed some of the Enterprise and Romulan corridor insert shots. "Ben Alpi and Brian McCue helped greatly with the minimal equipment I could secure for them to light the corridor three or four different ways depending on script," Gooch recalls. "Even into a wrecked Romulan corridor. So hats off to them."

Although there were two cameras, there was only one sound recording unit. "Unless the main unit was on break, and I could get the audio set up," Gooch says, "I could only shoot B-roll that didn't need audio, i.e., all the Enterprise corridor stuff, people listening to shipwide announcements and people getting thrown around by the distortion waves."

Still, shooting these insert shots did give Gooch a chance to direct George. "The only time I actually directed George," he relays, "was a corridor scene that needed no audio. When barbarian Sulu comes out of sick bay and struts down the corridor bumping into people as he goes. That was great fun for me. George is a pro's pro. I explained what I thought he should do and he did it that way for every take, exactly correct and

exactly the same. An honor and a pleasure to work with him."

Goodrich further reveals that he "worked very closely with [Visual Effects Supervisor and DAVE School Special Projects Director] Ron Thornton and Chris McLean, blocking and shooting Chandris and young Sulu on the Romulan ship. Mostly the corridor section when she is working the wall unit thing. Marc left that completely to us. Ron had very specific requirements for the DAVE school to be able to use the footage to its fullest potential."

Shooting almost an hour of screen time in nine days would challenge even a complete, experienced crew. The production gradually fell behind.

"As the final days approached," Marc recalls, "and it was obvious that we needed to cover a huge number of pages, I agreed to Carlos, Gooch and [first assistant director/Steadicam operator] Chris McLean shooting most of the bridge sequences, with Gooch as second unit director, Carlos as continuity and Chris as first assistant director.

"In order to make this work," he elaborates, "I sat down and went through all of the bridge scenes, dividing them into emotional and expository moments. I gave Gooch the expository moments and directed the emotional ones myself. All the bridge scenes were shot in the last two days."

What this meant was that with over fourteen pages to shoot on the ninth and last day in Port Henry, Carlos Pedraza directed on the bridge while Zicree directed the character scenes, such as one in Sulu's quarters in which John Lim, as young Sulu, deals with his return. Later, Zicree took over from Pedraza for Alana's final scene on the bridge.

"When the two units were shooting virtually around the clock," Zicree explains, "we had to swap out the sound equipment. So for all the Kirk/Spock/McCoy scenes that I directed in the corridors, we only recorded sound in the master shot and shot MOS (silent) on close-ups, matching the lines to their mouths in the close-ups with the sound recorded in the master."

"The shooting schedule had always called for the Bridge scenes to be shot last, and all together," Pedraza explains. Goodrich describes how he and Pedraza worked on the bridge scenes. "I deemed Carlos was more familiar with the script than I, and had a better grip on what was and was not needed to be shot, as Carlos was keeping track of everything shot up to that point. I was in and out. As second unit director, I primarily worked the B studio, the Church, and didn't always know what they were or were not shooting back at the main stages. So I trusted Carlos to get us through the whole script, getting all the bridge stuff we still needed."

To help Carlos, Gooch directed the camera movements while Chris McLean and Scott Moody ran camera, as he knew the bridge the best out of those on the second unit. "With this being the third time shooting an episode in that unique place, I know the angles," he discloses. "I know what you can and can't show in there and how to cheat the eyelines as well as where the camera needs to be to get those 'original series' type shots. Carlos would often say, put the camera here and shoot across such and such, and I could tell him from experience why that wouldn't work, but how to maybe get the same shot from over here. Stuff like that. Chris and his Steadicam came in for the special movement shots."

Gooch laughingly recalls that day as "just grinding those scenes out," as he and Carlos both admit the actors know their characters very well. "Carlos basically called out scene numbers and what characters were in the scenes," Goodrich says, "and we called in those actors and ran the scene once for practice. Then Carlos would call 'action,' and we'd shoot it a couple times, then on to the next scene. No one was really even directing the actors as far as performing the proper emotions and such. If they said the line correctly, we moved on."

Gooch had no worries about directing styles meshing between Marc, Carlos and himself. "I had done enough *NV* episodes at that point to know it would all match," he told me. "The sets, the costumes, the music ensures that, and I knew the cast, so I knew what he was going to get. I was more worried about matching, in style at least, [director of photography] Jake Pinger's lighting setups. As second unit could only use what the main unit wasn't using at the time, we had to do a lot with a little."

Carlos felt equally confident about maintaining a consistent directorial tone. "For the entire shoot, I had served as the script supervisor," Pedraza explains, "so I was right by Marc's side the whole time, and I think we built a solid, trusting relationship. Since I also serve as one of *New Voyages'* producers, I'd been part of production meetings and rehearsals where I learned what Marc was aiming to accomplish in every scene. I think that made the job of creating a consistent directorial tone much easier. Plus, we're both solid original series fans—we know what the texture of bridge scenes is supposed to feel like."

The pace was grueling, fatigue the greatest obstacle. "By comparison, a feature film shoots one to two pages a day. A network TV series might shoot up to seven pages in one arduous day; we did twice that," Pedraza says in perspective. "That's nothing short of miraculous, and it's a testament to the teamwork of our cast and crew. We wrapped at 6:27 am on the final day. And that was after starting at about 10 am. Nearly a twenty-hour day."

"By 3 am, our boom mic operator passed out," Gooch also recalls, "and I took over boom mic from then on till sunrise. We were all delirious."

Delirious or not, the crew achieved what they wanted. By the time they wrapped in the early morning, they had finished everything they had set out to do.

The production was tapeless, shooting on P2 flash memory cards. This allowed for quick upload to a computer, and rapid recall of shots. Here, George Takei reviews a recent take with Marc Zicree and co-producer/"digital media wrangler" Winston Engle.

A fter wrapping in Port Henry, there were a few weeks of rest for the L.A. crew before the two days of *Excelsior* shooting in Chatsworth. According to Baldaramos, who by this time Zicree was calling his "secret weapon," they were painting, attaching, and lighting up until the first day of shooting. "When I heard 'action,' and stepped back to see it lit up, I was very amazed; and when I viewed it in its final form at the screening, it was then that I realized what we had accomplished."

Since filming never goes off without a hitch, on the very day scheduled for action, Gigapix wanted to shut the whole thing down. The company had been very generous in allowing Baldaramos the *Excelsior* space for three months and giving up in addition their recording studio for us to convert into Sulu's ready room, but they suddenly realized the enormous expenditure of electricity all the lights powering the graphic screens and the whole set took. The room we were in was windowless and we couldn't keep the bay doors open because of the exterior noise. Hence, all light had to be electrically generated.

Fortunately, Baldaramos was able to renegotiate with Gigapix and bring in a generator at the last minute, and the *Excelsior* shoot went on as planned.

The only disappointment was Sulu's command chair. It wasn't easy to find the properly shaped chair, and when Baldaramos was able to borrow one, he had to recover it in a way that he could undo before returning it. The result was blue material held in place mostly with clamps and gaffer's tape, and there wasn't time or manpower to smooth out its very literal wrinkles.

"For the entire production," Zicree said, "I knew that there would be a moment when the bear ate me. In general, I ate the bear but that was the moment when the bear ate me. On the last day of shooting, when I was there with George Takei, there was the chair with its wrinkles and I called Doug Drexler. I've never, ever said 'we'll fix it in post,' because that is such a cliché. As a director, I always looked for a solution. But in that case, I called Doug and asked, 'Can we fix this in post?'"

When Doug said yes, Zicree was relieved. And ultimately, on screen, it came out fine.

There is one more detail that most people won't notice, but which Zicree put in for visual continuity between the *Enterprise* and the *Excelsior*. "When you see Sulu in his quarters on the *Enterprise*, you see a rather strange '60s kind of lamp, and then when you see his ready room on the *Excelsior*, you see the same lamp. The idea being that he took that with him."

There are approximately 700 special effects shots in WEAT, some of which were created by Joel Bellucci and Doug Drexler, but most were done by the Digital Animation and Visual Effects School, or DAVE School for short, on the lot of Universal Studios Florida. WEAT became their January semester assignment. "It was a great opportunity for the students and for the DAVE School to really get on the map in terms of getting their work viewed by millions of people," Zicree pointed out.

A sequence evolves: storyboard (top); raw greenscreen footage, with lighting flags representing the near side of the shuttle entrance (middle); after the apprentice FX wizards at the DAVE School were done (bottom).

All of the space sequences were totally computer generated, as well as the gravity waves that pass through Young Sulu and Chandris and the force field that surrounds Alana. They created virtual sets for the *Enterprise* shuttle bay and shuttlecraft, and added to the Romulan corridors. Even

the controls under Chandris' fingers were CG.

On a more prosaic level, they painted out a lighting stand accidentally making a cameo appearance in the transporter room... and retroactively exterminated the flies that buzzed through many shots.

When Lia Johnson was unable to go to Florida to film some additional angles of Sulu and Chandris in the Romulan ship against the green screen, Katia Mangani stepped in to wear the silver spacesuit (meticulously re-created from "The Tholian Web"), run around, jump over boxes and pull out her phaser while the visual effects guys directed their actions. The big silver helmet obscured the fact that a body double was being used. Though Katia's face was never seen, she can tell by some of the movements that it is her body in the spacesuit in different spots of the final cut, jumping off the shuttlecraft with Sulu and exploring the damaged Romulan vessel. Ironically, the episode switches back to Johnson just before Mangani makes her second appearance in the sequence, in her footage from Port Henry as a dead Romulan.

It took longer to get in and out of the costume, Katia said, than to shoot the sequence she and Lim did, but it was a lot of fun.

"They used my body but with Rand's head on top!" Katia says of the body replacement she did for Grace Lee Whitney's character, Commander Rand, on the bridge of the *Excelsior,* when the D A V E School needed to correct some unforeseen problems that arose during filming. "It was funny," she continued, "because we had to make a chair from apple boxes to be somewhat similar to the dimensions/proportions of the one in L.A., since we didn't have the chair that Grace Lee Whitney used in her scene. Then the chair was covered completely in a green cloth so they could create the chair on the computer."

Many on the crew wore multiple hats. Here, we see Katia Mangani as extra, clapper, and FX body double (under Grace Lee Whitney's head). She even made the Romulan helmets. And that's beside her main job doing hair and makeup.

The scene was also shot against a green screen to insert the correct background. "But the funniest part for me was that I had to wear a green collar around my neck because this is where they would be attaching Rand's head to my body. They painted a piece of thin cardboard-like paper with green paint and then we taped it around my neck. I thought it was rather comical."

Her task was more difficult than it seems, because Katia had to match Whitney's movements and timing so that, when combined, head and body move in concert. "Grace Lee Whitney tilts her head up a bit and then back down, then she steps and puts her hand on the edge of the captain's chair, and she continues to step/walk around the chair, and then she takes a seat in the chair. This is the sequence that I had to do and try to imitate exactly."

It got easier to do as she got used to the sequence and her muscles remembered it more. "They did not put sensors on my body, like Gollum," Katia exclaims, "but I probably would have thought the same thing had I not done this project first hand!"

"Well, to be pedantic, there wasn't a red carpet," Reaves reveals about the intended red-carpet premiere. "We couldn't get a city permit in time. I've been to premieres of my work before, at places like the Arclight and the Chinese. But all that said, this was extra-special."

George echoed the sentiment: "Well, it was small scale... to me. I've done major feature film red carpets, you know, and the Oscars and the awards shows. So it isn't that, that's for sure. But it was a group of excited and very energized fans. What was best about it was to see the people who I had worked so intensely with, so closely. And produced this wonderful film. We hadn't seen each other for, I think, about a year. There they were, all gathered again. When you work that closely, that intensely, that strenuously, you've spent a good chunk of your life, even though it was a week, and you get to have a real intense feeling about each other." He concludes, "It was a wonderful kind of homecoming, reunion with the actors."

Having brought the production to a successful close, the can-do spirit came up short at the premiere. One of the planned three screenings was canceled late in the game, forcing the merging of the celebrity-studded showing and the one for fans. Without a designated room for luminaries and press to meet in, or an area where producers, crew and cast could comingle, the situation inside was a bit chaotic, and the fans—and a number of crew members—had to wait in line outside until it cleared.

Zicree intended for the premiere festivities, and the episode itself, to stream live on the Internet. The *New Voyages* website had a form to sign up, and thousands did. An unexpected rush at the last minute caused the overtaxed infrastructure to fail. Later on, the episode was made available, streaming on demand.

None of this dampened Zicree's enthusiasm to see something he directed up on a marquee in Beverly Hills and attended by fans from all over the world, as well as *Star Trek* writers like George Clayton Johnson, Alan Dean Foster, and David Gerrold, who were formative influences on him. "To see it projected in high def on a big screen was fabulous," Marc enthuses. "It really held up and for the audience to give a standing ovation, it was really a dream come true."

Feedback from fans that night proclaimed WEAT not only exciting and moving, but one of the greatest *Star Trek* stories ever made by anybody. Appreciation for the quality of this episode is demonstrated in it winning the *TV Guide* Award for best Internet production.

Only one thing matched the standing ovation WEAT got that night for Zicree: "That was when George and I were in Yokohama at the World Science Fiction Convention in front of a thousand people, both Japanese and from all over the world, and they gave it a standing ovation."

Each of us has been left with our own special memories which will stay with us a long time. "The strongest visual memory for me was when we shot George Takei's first scene in the transporter room," Carlos Pedraza recalls. "He just looked so *right* up on the transporter pads, and with the set being almost fully enclosed, you really felt like you were on the *Enterprise*, not a movie set. The strongest emotional memory was when we finally wrapped principal photography and I realized we all, at last, survived."

"I guess the fondest memory will always be Marc calling me from Japan—as he said, 'from the other side of the world,'" Baldaramos remembers, "to tell me how thankful he was, what a good friend I was to have helped him like I did, and most of all, 'I couldn't have done it without you.' Also, George Takei surprising me with, when I introduced myself on the set: "So you're Don Baldaramos, I've heard so much about you, and all you've done! This set looks fantastic!""

For Zicree, his favorite memory is the climactic scene between Sulu and Alana near the end of the episode. "It is an astonishingly emotional, wrenching, powerful scene and the writing on it—I was very proud and pleased with how it read on the page. People would just burst into tears when they read it… She did this amazing, amazing scene where she was in tears and all of us were in tears, and it was just phenomenal… It was one of the most moving moments, I think, in all of film and television history."

Katia adds that for her, "the most special moment was the entire experience, if that makes any sense. It was amazing to see so many people come together, volunteering their time and money, skills and talents, and pouring their heart and souls into this project. It was amazing to see so many people come together for one purpose... to see how much people really cared. And it was amazing to see how a person/people can start from having a dream, a desire, a vision, a passion, to having it actually materialize... come true!"

Looking back on the episode's long journey from pitch to premiere, Michael Reaves notes, "If anyone had told me back then that in 2006, a professional Elvis impersonator would get all the neighborhood kids together and put on a show in the barn—or that I'd co-write and co-produce it, and it would get standing ovations all over the world... well, I'd probably be getting my meds reviewed pretty thoroughly."

But he sums up all of our feelings when he says he was immensely proud of "World Enough and Time," and quips, "And it ain't over yet..."

Epilogue

James Cawley later renamed *Star Trek New Voyages,* calling it *Star Trek Phase II,* after the early name for the aborted 1978 series, and activated the website www.startrekphase2.com. WEAT is available there streaming and for download.

Phase II has since shot several episodes, including its first two-parter, "Blood and Fire," directed by David Gerrold and based on his unproduced story and script from the first season of *Next Generation.* Carlos Pedraza converted the

script into a vehicle for the *Phase II* crew, and the final shooting script was a collaboration between Pedraza and Gerrold.

"World Enough and Time" was nominated for science fiction's two most prestigious awards: the Nebula, in the category of best script; and the Hugo, for best dramatic presentation, shortform.

The Nebula nomination raised some controversy. The rules require that a nominated script was professionally produced, and there were heated arguments on both sides as to whether WEAT qualified. The production blurred traditional boundaries: a fan-run project involving several paid professionals, and allowed but not overseen by CBS-Paramount. Ultimately, this very haziness, and the lack of an official definition in the Nebula rules, kept WEAT on the ballot. New rules for 2009 explicitly allow all Internet productions.

While traditional productions won both awards *(Pan's Labrynth* taking the Nebula, an episode of *Doctor Who* the Hugo), the nominations, and indeed the controversy, mark the arrival of a new kind of production model. In the age of streaming video, Final Cut, and desktop CGI, a dedicated group without much money can boldy go where only studios and networks could go before. • • •

CRYSTAL ANN TAYLOR is a published writer (TV/Film, short story, novella), researcher, script coordinator, journalist, actor, and former magazine editor. Her recent articles can be found online at **TVGuide.com: Fireside Chats from Hollywood** *(http://community.tvguide. com/blog/Fireside-Chats-Hollywood/ 700152230) and* **Wordpress.com: This Writer Wrote** *(http://gollysunshine. wordpress.com/). And she can be contacted through her blog: CAT Scratchings (http://dannygirlpaceyjack.blogspot. com/) or* **This Writer Wrote.**

A Gift Though Small

by Melinda M. Snodgrass

Illustrated by Don Anderson

"I could go. I could do it!"

Tracy's face is flushed and blotchy, and his shoulders are hunched in an attitude that is both defensive and threatening. My mind goes skittering away to the meaningless thought that it has always been a struggle to fit a coat across those narrow shoulders. He looks absurdly young to me, and I remember scraped knees and holding a cold, wet washcloth to his forehead while he knelt in front of the toilet, puking from the flu.

There is the smell of moist cloth, steam, and starch as Bajit continues pressing an order of custom dress shirts. It's always hard to accurately interpret an alien's expression, but the long bony face with its wide set dark eyes seems sympathetic. The mane of black hair that runs from the center of his forehead to the small of his back hangs limp in the humidity of the work room. I've given up trying to get him to wear a shirt, he complains so bitterly about the discomfort. I just make sure the door to the shop is closed when customers come.

We're on the shop floor, surrounded by expensive custom suits and military uniforms. Since my dear Amanda died, I have limited myself to only making gentlemen's attire. She always knew just the right furbelow to place on a dress to make it perfect. The empty garments hang on the walls like an observing audience, enjoying a fight. I curse the people who will eventually fill out those scraps of material. They have brought us to this.

Beyond the shop door is the lounge, and the measurement and pinning area. I spent more than I should have on the umber carpet and chocolate dark sofas, but I had hoped to attract a certain kind of clientele. It was all part of the plan. Moving us from a backwater planet to Hissilek, the capital of the Solar League. Working seven days a week, sixteen hours a day. Finally earning enough to hire an employee. Dressing the members of the Five Hundred, and the officers of the Fleet.

All for Tracy.

"No you couldn't. You're not one of them and never can be. They're quality."

"I'll make them see... I'll show them... that I'm just as good... no, *better* than all of them."

"No, you're not. We are what we are, and it's time, past time, you accepted that, and your lot in life."

He looks around the shop, and his face twists with disgust.

"Yes. Your little kingdom," The words are laced with acid. "Well, this may be enough for *you,* but I'm going. Your little ambitions won't stop me."

My eyes go to the carved wood and glass front door. Outside, an ornate bronze sign reads, *Belmanor & Son, Fine Tailoring.* I point at the door.

"If you walk through that door, you will never come back," I bellow.

"Fine. I hope I never see you again."

He stalks to a rack, and jerks down a cadet's uniform from among all the other uniforms. Unlike its fellows, it is a pale blue with silver piping, and constructed from cheap, synthetic material.

Each clack of Tracy's heels on the stone floor of the sewing room as he walks away is like a blow to me. The sound dies as he steps onto the carpet. The bell over the door rings madly as he jerks it open. A slam as he leaves. A ghostly chime from the bell hangs for a long moment in the overheated air, then fades.

He's gone.

And I reflect on how I've come to this.

*H*eat haze dances above the pavement and the buildings seem to sway from the humidity. The rays of Hissilek's distant blue-white star flash and glitter in the windows of towering office buildings. Overhead the sunlight sparkles on the bright paints of the flitters. They look like metallic dragonflies.

Ahead of me, the buildings are smaller, none above four stories, and shabby. Between Pony Town and Downtown there is a no man's land where humans come to slum and aliens oblige them in the interest of making a Regal.

A limo floats near the doors of one financial palace. I place the elaborate coat of arms—the house of C. de Vaca. A Hajin chauffeur stands next to the back door of the vehicle. His mane is thick gold and he looks hot and uncomfortable in the elaborate livery. The widening of his dark eyes gives me a warning, but it's not enough for me to move completely out of the way before the front doors open, and the marquès emerges.

I bow and scuttle back toward the wall of the building, but the marquès has to slow his pace. One of the phalanx of bankers surrounding the nobleman glares at me. A few moments later and the limo is soaring away, and the bankers have returned to their crystal and mahogany sanctums. I'm grateful to have avoided a reprimand, and I hurry away.

A few minutes later and I'm on restaurant row. The pungent scent of herbs, spices, roasting meat, and grease hang in the moist air. Tracy and I meet here on Friday afternoons after he's done with school. The food is cheap and exotic, and it's a chance to hear about his week without being interrupted by calls and clients.

Seven Tiponi Flutes are hooting and swaying beneath a portal, playing their incomprehensible math-based game. Humans and computers have analyzed the arrangements of sticks, how they change with each move and still have no idea of the rules or what constitutes victory. I would love to hire a Tiponi accountant—they're genius with numbers—but I can't afford one. Thank God for Tracy, he's a whiz at math and has kept my books since he was nine.

Two streets over there are strip clubs and brothels, though they hide beneath other names—lounge, jazz bar, massage parlor, fortune teller, hair stylist. Sex between humans and aliens is strictly forbidden out of fear of the mysterious Cara and their ability to manipulate DNA. But the Cara have vanished from known space, and fears have faded, and sex is a potent drive. Now the police only enforce the ban as a political weapon, when a politician had fallen out of favor with the emperor.

There's a faint trembling beneath my feet. I look north to see a liner lifting off from the Cristóbal Colón Spaceport. We've only travelled on a great ship once—when we immigrated from Reichart's World to Hissilek shortly after Amanda's death. Tracy was five. He'd wanted to go up to the observation deck and look out, but we were caught part way there by a supercilious steward, and sent

back down to dorm quarters.

As if my thoughts have summoned him, I see Tracy hurrying toward me. The strap of his black book bag is slung across his chest like a bandolier. As usual it is overly full. The front of his blue tee shirt is dark with sweat, and his hair hangs limp across his skull. There's an odd expression on his face, and his eyes seem overly bright. I lay a hand on his forehead. He pulls away impatiently.

"I'm fine, Dad."

But I know he's high strung and can work himself into fevers and headaches. Still, I don't argue. I know something is going on, but he'll tell me in his own time.

"What are you in the mood for?" I ask.

He points toward an Isanjo restaurant. I sigh because the food is highly spiced, and my old gut just can't take it anymore. We settle into woven rope chairs. Our waiter races across the lines that have been hung across the ceiling like an elaborate spider web, and lands with a heavy thud beside the table. The wide eyes seem like dark pools nestled in the golden fur on the broad face. A slow blink, and the up-tilted corners of the mouth cock even higher. His order pad is hung around his neck. He lifts it, taps it to life and says,

"Drink?"

"Milk," I say.

"Enchata," says Tracy, asking for the beverage distilled from flowers on the Isanjo home world.

The alien drops a menu, a bowl of dipping sauce and a plate of bread between us, and leaps back up into the tangle of ropes gripping them with his hands and prehensile feet. The pungent scent of the sauce sets my eyes to watering.

Tracy is rummaging in his bag. He pulls out an official-looking envelope. I feel my stomach close down into a tight ball. When the government sends you mail, it's never good news. I glance at his face, and note the blotchy flush that is sweeping up his neck and reddening his face.

"What?"

"Open it," he says.

I note how my precise child has carefully lifted the flap so as not to leave a ragged tear. I pulled out the heavy, watermarked paper. There is a blue, gold, red and green striped ribbon attached by a large metallic gold seal at the bottom.

We are pleased to inform you... selected... deserving... High Ground.

My eyes are frantically racing down the page, catching only a word here and there, as my brain struggles to comprehend what I'm reading. I realize the page is rattling because my hand is shaking.

"This is... they're talking about... the Academy."

"Yes." But there is no excitement in his voice, just tension and a thread of anger. He lifts the letter out of my hands. "Apparently," he scans the page. "I'm one of the deserving poor who has shown academic *promise.*" His tone provides the quote marks, "and they're condescending to admit me."

I feel as if another ship is launching, but it's an emotional shaking. I don't understand what I'm hearing. I have to step carefully. "Well, they're right to do so. You're quite the smartest student in your school. Actually the whole district. Principal Narrano told me—"

"I'm not going." He stares at me defiantly. "There's no merit involved. The Fleet is filled with rich men's sons who get in because of birth and patronage." He dips a piece of bread into the sauce, chews and swallows before adding, "It's a wonder we ever won a battle."

My gaze is pulled out the door and into the street where Hajin, Tiponi, and Isanjo sell craft goods and food from shops and booths. I nod toward the aliens. "They might not agree with you."

He jerks up one bony shoulder. I don't know how teenagers can communicate so much contempt with just a shoulder. "Oh, that was hundreds of years ago."

"Back when humans weren't all weaklings?"

He gives me a reluctant smile. "So maybe it's us deserving poor who are winning the battles."

"Which might be an argument for you going," I offer mildly, but his face closes down, tight with anger.

The Isanjo returns, running lightly across the ropes, and carrying a tray with our beverages. We order our food, and try to find another topic of conversation. But the invitation to the High Ground lays like a boulder in a stream, choking off all flow. I show him the tickets I've bought to a Areñal game to celebrate his graduation. He seems pleased, but he begins to carefully refold the letter, making certain the ribbon is tucked neatly away before sliding it back into the envelope.

"Why aren't you going? Really."

"I won't give them the satisfaction. I looked it up on the grid. Eighty-eight percent of all the scholarship students wash out. It's a sham to make ordinary people feel like we have a chance to be one of them." His face is flushing again. "Well, I refuse to be a damn token! They just let us in so they can prove to themselves that they're superior to anybody who's *not* in the FFH. Well, this will show them how I feel about them."

I bite back the sarcastic rejoinder. *Yes, don't go, that will sure show them.* But I remember similar feelings when my father had lost all his holdings on Reichart's World to a member of the Five Hundred. When a Hidden World is discovered, the League resettles good League citizens on the planet, and gives them the local populace's assets. My father had won one of these grants. If he'd been wiser, or the

FFH less cunning, I would be a wealthy man today.

Instead all he had left me with was a tailor shop on a backwater planet. And now I had a tailor shop in the capital, and my life hadn't fundamentally changed. I had more clients. I made a bit more money. But none of it had been life-changing. The life-changing event had happened back on Reichart's when Amanda died.

But this opportunity could be life-changing for Tracy. Yes, the odds were daunting, but I knew he was brilliant, proud and stubborn. If he enters the portals of the High Ground I know he would finish. I look up at the blue sky streaked with cloud streamers. Far above the darting flitters and the clouds, something seems to glint and I imagine it to be the space station that houses the Fleet Academy.

I just have to get him there.

*I*n the wide world there was shock and consternation when the League learned that the Emperor had decreed that his eldest daughter—Mercedes de Arango, the Infanta—and a handful of her ladies would be attending the High Ground. Women had never before been allowed in our elite military academies, but His Most Serene Highness had been cursed with nine daughters and no sons. Every Emperor of the League must be a military leader, and rather than see the throne fall to a male cousin, the Emperor is going to turn his daughter into a soldier. An absurd notion, but it was less grandiose news that had our neighborhood buzzing.

A story running in the *Solar Times* reported a barony would be bestowed on the man we all called the Flitter King. The idea of the big-bellied, balding Flitter King becoming one of the FFH was hilarious and the source of many jokes. The word in the *Alibi*—Hissilek's independent weekly paper—was that the man was selling the flitters at below cost to the government.

It became very personal, and a lot less funny, when a few days later an "error" was discovered in the grading of Tracy's final paper in history, which dropped his GPA one tenth of one percent behind the Flitter King's son. And coincidentally a correction on Prince Flitter's test raised his solidly B performance to an A. Tracy was supposed to have been the valedictorian, but this "error" meant the newly-minted knight's son had that honor. Tracy became even more silent after that blow, and threw himself into preparing applications for university.

Despite my vow, I've made little progress convincing Tracy to attend the High Ground. In fact I haven't brought it up at all. *I'm totally ineffectual.* I keep telling myself that I'll figure out how best to broach the topic after he's heard back from the universities.

It's mid-summer and the city is like a great panting beast. There's been a rate increase for utilities. I keep air conditioning running in the lounge and fitting area, but I can't afford to run the coolers in the shop or in our apartment upstairs.

The young gentlemen have begun to arrive for their uniform fittings. I'm standing in the shop, unrolling a bolt of chimera silk. I tap it and it changes from blue to white. The material lays rich across my palm, and flows like slick water between my fingers. Good material just feels right to the hand, and because of this wondrous material the wealthy cadets will have both summer and winter dress uniforms in one suit.

The buzzer on the back door sounds. Bajit answers and returns carrying a large box. His long drooping lips have trouble with Tracy's name, and it comes out sounding like "Pacy" as he says,

"It's for master Tracy, sir. Shall I put it in his room?"

"Let me see it." It's from the High Ground.

I shouldn't. It's his box, but I can't help myself. I open it. It contains a cadet's uniform, but it's pale blue rather than the normal midnight blue. The material is a cheap synthetic and the silver piping is already beginning to flake. My eyes go to the bolt of chimera silk on the cutting table.

There is a letter with the uniform stating that while technically a cadet is required to have both a summer and winter dress uniform, the High Ground makes accommodation for scholarship students. They can simply wear this special blue at all times.

And that won't set them apart, heavens no. If Tracy went to the High Ground he would be clothed by the largesse of the academy. The deserving poor, but obviously they are only *so* deserving.

Thrusting it into Bajit's hands I say, "Lay it on Master Tracy's bed."

I start to cut the fabric, and lose track of time. I mustn't make a mistake with material this expensive. Bajit returns and starts to clean up the scraps. I stop him before he reaches the trash can.

"Save those. I can use them for cuffs or lapels."

Tracy comes in. His face is tight and his expression closed off, but there's a vulnerability to his mouth. His mother used to do the same thing. Press her lips together and think I wouldn't notice them trembling.

Tracy yanks three pieces of paper from his book bag and flings them at the cutting table. They flap like wounded and hysterical birds trying to break from cover, and miss the table altogether. They come to rest on the floor.

Bajit hurries to pick them up. The Hajin tries to hand them to him, but Tracy recoils. I take them. There's a printout of an email from the admissions office at New Oxford, one from SolTech, and the third is from Caladonia.

They are happy to accept Tracy as a student, but decline to provide any financial aid, since records indicate he has been offered a full scholarship to the High Ground. Of course we can't afford for him to attend university without a scholarship. Rage is a flare of pain behind my eyes, but I have no where to direct it. *Ineffectual.*

He sits down behind a sewing machine, and tries to summon a knowing, cynical smile. "Oh, it's a grand racket. They admit me to a school where everyone from my social class will flunk out. They won't let me in their other schools *until* I've flunked out, and then they'll use the fact I flunked out as a way to deny my application when I come back to them."

A bit of lyric from an old Earth song comes unbidden to my mind. *...in my set could never pass... you occupy a station in the lower middle class.*

R age and grief and despair form an almost palpable atmosphere in the shop. I try to talk to Tracy, but he's so angry even the most innocuous comment is answered with a vicious retort. I've got to get out.

I've completed formal evening attire for Pal Edan Mayer Fairleigh, Duque de Oxton y Dupont, who is also the Chancellor of the Exchequer. I'll use that as my excuse to flee from my child.

The subway is stifling. The air conditioning is moving the air, but any cooling seems to be at best negligible, at worst imaginary. A train pulls in. I look at the faces staring with blank eyes through the window of the cars, and I flash on a memory from childhood.

We had just arrived on Reichart's World. I was maybe six at the time, and my father was eager to start squeezing a profit out of his property grant on the recently discovered Hidden World. The citizens of Reichart's largest city had been loaded onto transport flitters to be hauled away to the spaceport, and from there to be scattered among the planets of the Solar League. The bean counters on Hissilek had determined if you relocated one third of a population of a Hidden World, and took away one hundred percent of their children below the age of eleven, you removed any possibility of an insurgency.

The faces in the subway this afternoon have that same expression of tamped down rage overlaid with a layer of defeat and despair. I clutch the long box more tightly beneath my arm, and scan the cars. An alien car is only a few feet to my left. There's nothing that says a human can't ride in an alien car, just that aliens can't ride in a humans-only car. There are seats available since only Flutes are riding and they don't bend. I jump aboard as the doors whoosh open.

The Flutes honk softly at me and sway in greeting. I give them a curt nod and take a seat. Actually I'm happy to be among them. The car is actually cool, and the flutes give off a strange minty smell. Far more pleasant than the smell of rank humans.

Five stops later I'm climbing out of the subway. I'm three blocks away from mansion row. This way the inhabitants of these houses don't have to see their staff, human and alien, arriving for the day's work. There are small walkways behind the mansions that lead to the servants' entrances, and larger ones where flitters can pull up to off-load food and drink, decorations for parties and balls, new furniture when la Marquésa or Duquesa becomes bored with her current interior design.

I have never seen the front of these homes in person. Only in pictures on the mediavid when the breathless members of the press would show us pictures of debutante balls, or aristocratic weddings.

Fairleigh favors human servants to alien, and I'm known to the butler. I follow Ignatius up the backstairs to the Duque's dressing room. The Chancellor is a tall, spare, gray-haired man with stooped shoulders. I can't tell if he's worn down from the burden of government service or if it's a habit of some extremely tall men to try and seem smaller.

He tries on the evening wear and I'm pleased to see it fits perfectly. The angled mirrors offer a view from all sides. On the wall with the door and to either side are polished wood drawers, and shelves for shoes. On another wall hang custom shirts. On the third are the day-wear suits. On the final wall is formal wear. I still fuss and complain about how the coat is laying across the shoulders, and offer to accept no payment for such inferior work, but he waves away my apologies and proposal.

"It's quite perfect. Stop fussing, Belmanor." He sighs. "Frankly I'd rather not be wearing it. I hate these events, but I can't avoid this one. My daughter is getting engaged."

I bow. "Congratulations, your Grace. This must be a very joyful time."

He starts to nod, then stuns me by saying, "Actually, I hate it. I had wanted her to go to the university." I try to hide it, but he sees my surprise at this admission. "Yes, I know it's unusual, but I think it's time, past time, for us to start utilizing our ladies. In the early days of exploration and colonization it made sense to protect our wives and daughters, but it's been four hundred years."

I don't care about politics or ancient

history, but it resonates with me that this member of FFH has the same problem with a child as myself. It's presumptuous of me, but I speak up,

"Do they always do the opposite of what we wish, Your Grace?" I ask.

A brief smile touches his mouth. "Invariably. Perhaps I should have picked the most elderly and loathsome member of our set and promised her to him. I might have provoked a rebellion." He pauses and smiles at me again. I'm overwhelmed by the honor. "Not a parent's usual desire, eh?" I nod in agreement. The smile quickly dies, and he adds almost to himself, "But I didn't want her to think I was cruel."

*B*eauregard Honorius Sinclair Cullen, Vizconde Dorado Arco, Knight of the Shells, Shareholder General of the Grand Cartel, heir apparent to the 34th Duque de Argento y Pepco stands on the riser between the three mirrors. Tracy huddles at his feet, chalk in hand, tape measure looped around his neck, adjusting the length of the pants.

Even though the sleeves on his dress uniform are too short, and the pants lack their cuffs, Cullen is a picture from a recruiting poster. His coloring is vibrant, every strand of black hair perfectly coifed, his eyes a brilliant green. My son seems like a washed out ghost next to him.

But my Tracy had gotten into the Academy, too.

Another young cadet is sprawled on the sofa sipping a glass of champagne. I keep it for the really aristocratic clients, and because of their class it has to be good. At the rate they're going I'm going to have a to open a second bottle. I curse them mentally, but I must do it: Arturo Espadero del Campo, Vizconde Agua de Negra, is a cousin to the Emperor himself. This is the first member of the royal family that has

ever entered my shop. I take a leaf from the Flitter King and decide I won't charge del Campo for his uniform.

Cullen drains his glass, and thrusts out his hand. Bajit minces over to refill it. In order to maintain appearances I have to have my alien serving them rather than a fellow human. Which means Bajit is not in the shop sewing, which means I am falling behind schedule on my orders, which means Tracy and I will not be sleeping for several nights.

"Good God, Arturo, military victories? Don't be so conventional," Cullen says. "Military governor, that's what you want. You can make a fortune when you have a planet to squeeze. Especially if you land a Hidden World. The government doesn't care how much you bleed them."

"I don't need money," del Campo says. HIs voice is a soft drawl, and there's something secretive about it. There is actually something smooth to the point of untouchable about the man, from his sleek brown hair to his perfect golden skin, to the shadowed dark eyes. "I want the people's love."

"Why? Are you planning on going into politics after you leave the Fleet?" Cullen asks, and laughs.

He shifts position, and Tracy gives a hiss of pain as Cullen steps on his fingers. Cullen seems to notice Tracy for the first time. "Watch what you're doing," the aristocrat says, and only then does he move his foot off my son's hand.

Tracy ducks his head. "I beg your pardon, sir." I'm proud of him. I've taught him well how to speak to Quality, and his accent is very good. There is scarcely a hint of town in his speech.

The tips of his fingers are a bit red where Cullen has stepped on them. He gives his hand a quick shake, and reaches into the pin box. And then Cullen bellows in pain. Air deserts my lungs as Tracy lifts his head and stares challengingly up at the vizconde. The silence seems to stretch into hours. *Apologize! Apologize!* But he remains stubbornly mute. Tracy slowly pulls the pin out of the fabric, and presumably out of the vizconde.

"If I didn't already have a competent servant I'd hire you so I could have the pleasure of beating you until you became less of an oaf. Do you think you could learn to be less of an oaf?" Cullen's words are edged with contempt and amusement. "Maybe not. You seem slow."

...I didn't want her to think I was cruel...

In a flash I see how it can be done. I cross the floor in two quick strides and slap Tracy hard across the face. The bitter pleasure fades from his gray eyes, replaced with a look of betrayal. I can see where my hand has left a red mark on his cheek. Alarmed, Bajit resorts to the usual Hajin defense mechanism—flight. He goes charging back into the shop, slopping champagne from the bottle.

"How dare you! You will apologize to the vizconde. *Now.*" Grabbing him by the hair, I literally drag him to his feet. "I should give him to you, my lord, to teach him manners and how to behave toward members of the FFH. But you probably wouldn't want him." I give Tracy a shake as if displaying some particularly unpleasant bit of trash.

Cullen is smiling. It makes him a lot less handsome. "You're right. I don't want him. I'm not sure even *I* could carry off having him for a servant." He gives a Tracy a careless shove with his forefinger. I feel my boy's muscles clenching beneath my hands. I give him a another hard shake. "Now say you're sorry," Cullen says.

Tracy ducks his head and mutters, "I beg your pardon, sir, for my clumsiness."

"Still too proud. Whine. Make me pity you."

I risk a glance at Tracy. His profile reveals a face as white as bone and lips gone bloodless from shock and shame. The silence stretches on and on. A glint deep in the vizconde's green eyes shows he is actually becoming angry. This is no longer a game for the rich man.

It is the royal cousin who rescues us. "Oh, leave it go, Boho. He's not worthy of your effort. And I wanted to get a ride in before Lady Estella's party."

The vizconde rips off his jacket and flings it at us. "I should take my custom elsewhere, Belmanor. But I'll give you another chance. Make sure my uniform is perfect and I won't blacken your name to the entire FFH." He walks toward the small dressing room and pauses with his hand on the curtain "But don't expect payment. That will be your punishment for your son's churlish behavior."

A few minutes later and they have left. The bell over the door is still vibrating. The discarded jacket is balled against Tracy's stomach as if he's using it to hold back vomit, or perhaps to hold himself together. I want to hug him. Instead I step away.

"See what you've cost us? I bought that material on credit from Dunlap's. You were right not to go to the High Ground. You haven't got the skills—socially, emotionally, or scholastically."

He flinches at my final words. "I couldn't help what happened. They cheated me... I told you."

God forgive me.

"So *you* said." The words seem like poison and ice as they pass my lips. If he flinched before, this time it is a recoil.

"Papa, why—"

I turn my back on him, and enter the shop. Bajit is frantically ironing shirts. Steam rises from the presser. Tracy follows me in. Tosses away Cullen's jacket. It hits the floor and turns white.

"I could go. I could do it."

"No you couldn't. You're not one of them and never can be. They're Quality."

"I'll make them see... I'll show them... that I'm just as good... no, *better* than all of them."

"No, you're not. We are what we are, and it's time, past time, you accepted that, and your lot in life."

He looks around the shop. At the array of suits and uniforms. He's never complained, but in this vulnerable moment it all shows—his hatred of this place, of the work, of the people we serve.

"Yes. Your little kingdom," The words are laced with acid. "Well, this may be enough for *you,* but I'm going. Your little ambitions won't stop me."

"If you walk through that door, you will never come back," I raise my voice. Perhaps a yell will cover the true emotion behind the words. Not rage, but life-crushing grief.

"Fine. I hope I never see you again." He's spitting out the words, but I can hear the thickness of unshed tears.

He stalks to the rack, yanks down the cheap uniform, and leaves. It's suddenly very quiet except for that damn bell like the ring of the sanctus bells during Mass.

Bajit stops pressing, reaches beneath the workbench and pulls up a pile of folded chimera silk. "Here's the extra I shaved off the bolts, sir," the alien says.

*A*rturo Espadero del Campo is seated in a chair in his quarters on the High Ground. I'm sitting on the bunk, repairing a tear in the shoulder seam by hand. The floating study lamp is very bright, and turns the tiny needle into a flashing point of silver as I stitch. Next to me on the bunk is a garment bag. The Orientation banquet is only a few hours away. When parents and cadets will mingle and say farewell before their parents relinquish

them into the hands of SpaceCom.

My Tracy's room will look like this. Of course, it won't have the antique buffet bolted to the deck and filled with an array of fine liquors and crystal glasses, or the equestrian sculpture in the corner. I glance at the face of the bronze horseman. Yes, it is del Campo.

I finish, give the coat a shake, and hold it while he slides into it. "These dress coats are not designed for vigorous activity, my lord. I can see you are a man of action," I nod toward the statue, "but for today you must behave as if you are in your mother's drawing room."

"Thank you, Belmanor, for making this trip. My batman will see you to the shuttle."

"I... I have another delivery to make, my lord."

He studies me for a long moment. His eyes drift to the garment bag and back to my face. "Your son is the charity scholarship, isn't he? The one who stuck Boho with a pin." I incline my head. "Will you be staying for the banquet?" He sounds bored.

"No, my lord, it wouldn't be appropriate."

"Your son isn't *appropriate* either." He nods toward the garment bag. "Is that a uniform you've brought for him?" I nod again. I don't trust myself to speak. "Remember, tailor, you can take the uniform out of the shop, but you can't take the shop out of the uniform."

He rings a bell by the door. His batman appears. He's an older man with a missing ear on the left, and the side of his face slick and frozen from some terrible conflagration.

"Show the tailor to Cadet Belmanor's quarters, and see to it he's paid for his trouble."

The batman nods. I bow, gather up my sewing kit, and Tracy's uniform, and follow the veteran out of the room.

I use my fee from del Campo to bribe the shuttle pilot to delay leaving for just a few hours. It's not hard to avoid notice aboard the massive space station that houses the academy. There's a large support staff, and I lose myself among them.

A sympathetic cook has set me up by the doors that lead into the great dining hall. Every time a waiter enters or leaves I get a glimpse of the room beyond. The kitchen is steamy and redolent with the smell of roasting meat and fowl, the sharp scent of spices, the tang of grilling seafood, and the comforting smell of baking bread.

And then it's time. The doors are almost always swinging open and I can see amazingly well. The hall is massive, curving pillars along the walls formed from the struts of fold ships lost in battle. Hanging from the ceiling are hundreds of colorful silk battle banners. Some are charred and blackened, damaged, along with their ships, in battles with the elusive and mysterious Cara.

Four long tables of polished star-wood form a square, and there's another table on a raised dais for the professors. Light from the chandeliers glitters, pulls rainbow colors from the crystal, china and silver. The hammered silver and crystal doors at the far end are thrown open, and the parents and cadets enter. In the lead is the Emperor. *The Emperor!* And I'm only fifty feet away!

His daughter walks at his side. She's not as pretty as she looks in sims and vids. I'm vaguely disappointed. Then I see how terrified she looks. Poor thing. They enter in order of rank and precedence, which means del Campo and his family are right behind the royal pair. Then Cullen. I lose interest and start straining to see back toward the doors. There is a tall blond man,

he looks older than the other cadets, and last of all... my Tracy.

He looks wonderful in the chimera silk uniform constructed from cadged pieces off bolts of fabric. His head his up. His expression is proud.

He ends up sitting alone. But he's here.

I've seen enough. I pull back, use a back exit from the kitchen, and go in search of the shuttle bay.

I'm walking past a wide viewport when it strikes me. I'm looking away from Hissilek, and the sun is behind the station's hub. The stars are like scattered diamonds against black velvet. I realize how many of these observation windows I've passed in my wanderings. It's as if the High Ground wants the young officers to focus on their legacy.

Finally my Tracy is going to get to see the stars. • • •

MELINDA M. SNODGRASS wrote the highly-regarded Next Generation *episode "The Measure of a Man," amongst others, and served as story editor and executive script consultant on the series.*

She has written scripts for many other television series, as well as the Circuit *trilogy of novels.*

PALLADIUM
BY DIANE DUANE

Illustrated by Don Anderson

Tillik remembered his dad saying to him a long, long time ago: "Just remember, son, any job in which you're not mistaken for a grave robber is a good job." But that had been so long back, and considering what his dad had done for a living, it had been a joke. Now he could just hear his dad saying, "You never did listen to me. How did you get yourself into this, you—"

The darkness was near-total. Tillik was holding absolutely still, intent on not making a sound, not doing anything that could possibly trip a sensor. Some meters away from him in the darkness, he could just barely hear Elindeh's breathing. It sounded unconscionably loud, but then she had twice as many lungs as he did, and couldn't help it.

Something made a tiny soft sound, a click. It seemed so loud that Tillik jumped at it, suppressed a very bad word, and concentrated on being still again.

"It's all right," Elindeh whispered. "We're done."

"You sure?" Tillik whispered back. Even in a culture as relatively far down the technological scale as this one, life could be full of little surprises.

"Absolutely. The analysis completed just as we anticipated. The target finished transit just now."

He swallowed. "And you're sure it's where it's supposed to be?"

"Yes. It couldn't possibly be missed."

"Then can we have some light?"

From nearby in the darkness came an exasperated hiss. It was all very well for Elindeh: like some of the birds on the ancient Homeworld, she could see the magnetic fields associated with everything around her, and had less use for light than some. But, supremely confident in her own abilities as most of her people tended

to be, she sometimes forgot that not everybody had the same advantages.

A little gleam of reddish light showed down near the floor: all that a smart operative would use in a situation like this—*if there is any situation like this,* Tillik thought, rolling his eyes. He kept holding still, waiting for his eyes to get used to the light. All around them, in vast gloom, shadows towered, long curved walls reaching up toward an invisible ceiling: much closer, the light glowed on the undersides of Elindeh's wings, dyeing the silver of their fine down the color of Tillik's blood. *Something I'm not eager to see...*

Elindeh stood up in the darkness, a silhouette against the dim red light that now seemed to be filling more of the big room as she turned slowly, scanning, and narrowly eyeing the little vidlink she held. The space the two of them stood in was bounded all around by high curved walls in some dark sandstone, graven with faintly-visible murals and panel after panel of thorny-looking alien script—a surprisingly large space for someplace buried so far underground. *And this was made a long time before these people had any powered digging technologies,* Tillik thought. *Must have taken them centuries to mine all these caverns out, smooth the walls, do the carving...* Though water had done the initial work – centuries' worth of deep-tunnelling runoff from one of the planet's greatest waterfalls. It was a very wet planet, Salimash—big oceans covering three-quarters of the planet, lots of rivers, and a climate that reminded Tillik of the endless summertime of his native world, Ondaga: gray skies, dripping skies, skies with never a hint of sun.

Here, at least, it was dry. But far off, in galleries and caves less thoroughly improved than this one, the faint tinkle and drip of water could still be heard echoing in the silence. Tillik, now carefully standing up to brush himself off after having spent the last ten minutes or so crouching on the dark, dusty floor while Elindeh worked, disliked the depth of those echoes. They were too clear a reminder of how far underground they were at the moment, well out of range of the ship's dissimulator technology if anything went wrong. *Which I can't believe hasn't happened yet. What's she waiting for—*

"Well?" he said softly, working to keep the impatience out of his voice. "What about it? How much longer?"

"Only a few minutes," Elindeh said, intent on the readout from her vidlink sender, and roused her wings in a distracted sort of way. Dust flew; she sneezed. Until that moment she had looked like some dark and threatening bird of prey, but the sneezing ruined the effect. Tillik smiled. He remembered the warnings from a few of his teammates when he had been matched up with Elindeh for this mission. *Watch out, she's a predator at heart. Don't let the civilized ways fool you. One day you'll say the wrong thing and she'll take the head off you when you least expect it....*

Tillik rolled his eyes at the memory, even as he looked all around them into the darkness, alert for any sound besides the small ones Elindeh was making. To distract himself from his nerves, he got out his own little linkscreen and touched it alive, stroking the glow right down as soon as it came on, so as not to ruin his readjusting night vision.

His mouth was dry for the first second he stared at the little screen; but then, it always was. The screen was his link to the functions readouts of the vessel officially known as LS *Pertuvaithin,* but which Tillik usually thought of as "Perturbation," because that was what she routinely produced in some official organization or other in the systems where she made starfall. Always when Tillik woke the screen up, he half expected to see that their little ship had something desperately wrong with it: the dissimulation drivers gone unstable again, the life support systems wasting energy or (weirdly) not expending enough of it, the computer acting up in some new and interesting way. But none of that seemed to be happening at the moment; all the little bar-graphs were holding steady, well within their "nominal" levels. *And if things can just keep going that way for another few hours, until we've finished what we're supposed to be doing here—*

"You don't trust me," the ship's computer whispered in his ear, "that's the problem."

Tillik let out another breath as he watched Elindeh turning slowly, finishing her sweep. "If I didn't know better," he said, subvocalizing so as not to disturb her, "I'd think you were going telepathic on us. They warned us after that last upgrade—"

"You leak neuronal discharge like the aft convenience leaks water," the computer said, absolutely without rancor. "I hardly need telepathy to tell what you're thinking. Your thoughts are daubed all over your cortex like Tancreddi wall-scrawlings. How is she doing? Are you ready yet?"

Tillik glanced over at Elindeh. She looked up at him, the big dark-gold eyes catching a moonshine glimmer from her vidlink's screen as she did so. "About thirty seconds," she said.

"Three be praised," Tillik muttered. "I hate caves. Can't wait to get out of here." He touched the link dark again and was just pocketing it when, without warning, the darkness all around them began leaking a dim orange-yellow light around the edges. From the next cavern along and from the cavern behind Tillik, there was a sudden mutter of voices, rising to a hubbub, and then, as the owners of the voices burst into the cavern, to a roar. Torches fluttered in the darkness; Tillik looked around behind him and caught, in the flickering torchlight, the glitter of unsheathed weapons.

He let out a long nervous breath. *Here we go...* Tillik thought.

The foremost of the crowds rushing down on them from either side ringed them around, with a lot more of that gleam of naked metal showing at the edges of the circle: knives and swords, spears and the peculiar arm-length edge-ended club that the Salimasht favored. They were a handsome people as hominids went: routinely a couple of meters tall, with fine dark chiseled features and a fondness for long sweeping cloaks and robes in cheerful, brilliant colors. But the crowd now pressing in around them didn't look at all cheerful. One of the tallest of them—one of the very few not carrying a weapon, for he had other people to do it for him—now pushed in to stand towering over Tillik, glowering down at him. Others in the crowd pushed Elindeh hastily over until she was crowded up right against Tillik. Her beak knocked up against his head, and for a moment Tillik saw stars and not the angry face leaning down over him.

"Why are you down here?" shouted the angry voice that went with the angry face. "What are you doing you in the holy place of the Motikh? Did you think we would not know you'd come?"

"They're here to steal it!" came a shout from the back of the crowd. "They mean to steal the Motikh away into the sky and destroy our land!"

A growl went up from the crowd surrounding them. Tillik drew himself up straighter to attempt to conceal how nervous that sound made him. Normally, when you heard that particular low growl, it was time to run for the ship. But that was a thought he really disliked, especially when he and Elindeh hadn't yet finished the job for which they'd been sent here. Angry crowds were one thing, but an angry evaluation committee when you got back could really ruin your health.

"I assure you, Lord Amaswith," Tillik said with as much dignity as he could muster while feeling the points of several weapons prodding him from various angles, "we have absolutely no intention of stealing your sacred relic—"

The growl got louder. Clearly local opinion found this concept difficult to swallow.

"We are peaceful emissaries," Elindeh said, "explorers and researchers. Why ever would we want to do such a thing?" She was trying as always to sound like the essence of sweet reasonableness, but in such moments of stress, her genetics tended to assert themselves, and what the casual listener heard was the raw, edgy voice of a bird of prey trying to fight its way through the words.

"Who knows what you'd do?" Lord Amaswith said. "You're aliens! You come out of nowhere in your skyboat and start talking nonsense about other worlds and alliances with creatures even more freakish and weird than you are, you go on and on about trade and alliances and networking and who knows what other nonsense when we're in the middle of a war, and we very politely listen to you when you don't have anything more to show of your intrastarrish conglomeration than—"

"Interstellar Aggregation," Elindeh said, now starting to sound slightly cranky.

Lord Amaswith took an involuntary

step back from her as she turned her large golden gaze on him. Then he held his ground, seeing that someone else was holding her. "Whatever you call it. A nonsense, reasonable people call it, no matter what the Aldive says, may the gods save him: so sheltered as he's been all his life, it's not his fault that he thinks like a child. But the rest of the High Council have put up with your blathering for weeks now. And at the end of it all, what do we find? We find you down here, unescorted, in the single place in our land that's most important to us, right outside the chamber that protects the holiest thing we own, the only thing that keeps us safe from the enemies who want to destroy us!" He turned away in disgust, waving at the people around them. "Take them," he said. "Strip them of their magic trinkets and put them somewhere safe. We've got to call the council and decide what to do with them." And he stalked off into the dark, back toward the far cavern.

Tillik found himself surrounded more closely by the unfriendly faces, while he was prodded much more pointedly from behind by spears and swordpoints. He sighed and reached carefully into his pocket, and handed over his vidlink—being careful to disable it with the quick sequence of coded fingerpresses on its case that would make it just a flattened metallic oval with one shiny side and one matte. One of the Salimasht in front of him took the vidlink out of Tillik's hands hastily, then hurried away with it while wearing an uncomfortable look, like a man who suspects he may be carrying a bomb.

The other Salimasht surrounding Tillik and Elindeh began hustling them off in the same direction Lord Amaswith had gone. Tillik found that he had one burly Salimasht to each arm; Elindeh had the same, though Tillik noticed that the same

people were taking great care to avoid touching his colleague's wings, while giving them uneasy looks. Tillik had to restrain a smile at that, for if trouble had any reason to start, whoever was holding Elindeh's arms would shortly find out they were holding entirely the wrong parts of her. *But it hasn't come to that. Not yet. And if we're lucky, it won't.*

Elindeh glanced over at him as the two of them were dragged out of the main cavern and into the lower adjoining one, more like a rough-walled corridor. "Well," Elindeh said under her breath, "I thought that went well…."

Tillik gave her a look. Elindeh's sense of irony came and went without warning, and when it did turn up, it took strange shapes. But for the moment he wasn't entirely in disagreement with her, though this wasn't the time or place to tell her so. They were marched along through cavern after cavern, uphill all the way. It took some minutes before they came to a more finished area, where the rough stone of the walls was replaced by fitted slabs of sandstone, and the gritty ramps underfoot gave way to flights of stairs leading steeply upward. Ahead of them, daylight grew, replacing the smoking cressets in the walls; and at last Tillik and Elindeh and their escort came out through a cordon of spear-armed guards into the light of day.

There everyone paused briefly, some of them puffing quite hard: many of the crowd who had come down to witness their arrest, Tillik suspected, were bureaucrats and other functionaries who rarely had so much physical exercise in the course of a day. Tillik glanced around them at the great circular plaza at the heart of the main Salimasht city of Durshi. It was a handsome place, its architecture solid rather than airy: pairs of slender spires stood up before each of the great low-domed buildings surrounding the plaza—the Aldive's Palace, the Great Council, the Lesser Council, the Courts of Divine Justice. That building was possibly the grandest of them all, a vast circular pile domed and crowned with the symbol of the major Salimashti religion, the Mirror of the Sun. The Salimasht were partial to their gods, possibly because they felt their gods were partial toward them. *That,* Tillik thought, *being part of the problem....*

Having recovered its collective breath, the crowd around them started to move forward again, making for the building that belonged to the Great Council. Its three-story facade occupied the northeastern quarter of the circular plaza, as the Aldive's Palace occupied the northwestern one: the relationship was meant to be suggestive of a kinship between these two parts of the government, though also of a separation between them. Well ahead of the group escorting Tillik and Elindeh, Tillik could see the annoyed Lord Amaswith heading for the great doors in the central portico of the Great Council's building. Under the arches, he paused to speak with a gaggle of people awaiting him there, waving back in the general direction of Tillik and Elindeh and their escort.

"And now it gets interesting," Tillik said. Silently, subvocalizing again, he said to the computer, "Have you got a fix? Just in case anything untoward starts to happen."

No answer came back.

Tillik felt the sweat begin between his shoulderblades. "Did you read that?" Tillik said.

Nothing.

Tillik commanded himself to calm down, set his expression to "neutral," and let their escort lead them in the wake of Lord Amaswith, under the porticoes, into

the Great Council building, and then down many high-ceilinged and beautifully decorated corridors. Tillik spent this walking time proposing himself many good reasons that the computer might have for not answering him, while not really believing any of them. The words DISSIM FAILURE! kept painting themselves behind his eyelids every time he blinked. And all the while, the corridors through which they walked got smaller and narrower and lower-ceilinged and less decorative, and the walls acquired that mute, grim look that somehow says just one word: thick. Finally, in front of a narrow metal-bound door, which also said thick just by its looks, their escort stopped. A beam that looked to Tillik to be the diameter of a small tree was slid back in its massive metal sockets: the door was unlocked with a great metal key and swung open, and Tillik and Elindeh were pushed in.

Inside, the room was clean and bare: stone walls, stone floor, a single high barred window, a couple of stone benches. Tillik turned to the people who were still crowding outside the door, blocking the view of the far wall. "Well," Tillik said to the nearest of them, a green-robed Salimasht man who was holding the cell's massive key, "now what?"

"Now you wait for your trial to begin," the official said.

Or what they call a trial, Tillik thought. "How long?"

The official looked surprised. "About an hour," he said. "Or so I believe. The council room has to be ritually cleansed if the Motikh's to be brought in."

The news that that was going to happen made Elindeh's eyes go wide. Tillik, though, was thinking other thoughts. "Is that usual?" he said. "I mean, a trial happening so quickly."

The official suddenly looked upset.

"Yes," he said, "when there's going to be an execution...."

He hurriedly left the room; behind him the guards shut the door, and the sound of the bolt shooting home seemed very, very loud.

Elindeh sat down on one of the benches, hunched over, her fingers laced together and hanging down between her knees where her dark-green uniform kilt had ridden up; she looked very much the big, sad bird in a cage. For a moment Tillik just stood there, watching, feeling a bit sorry for her. She was literally crestfallen, the pale creamy feathers laid down hard along the centerline of her shapely skull. Tillik suspected she too had been trying to speak to the ship's computer, and failing. A few seconds of depression she could safely be allowed; she was a youngster yet, by either human reckoning or that of the Malaktha, her people. But that was all Tillik was going to spare her. It was Elindeh's job to learn how to handle situations like this. For all that they were a labile people, liable to what in other species would have been taken for profound mood swings, Malakthana were far longer-lived than Tillik's branch of humankind. The experience Elindeh garnered while working in the field with senior operatives like Tillik would stand her in good stead for centuries. *Always assuming she survives.*

And assuming I keep my wits about me and help her do it....

"So then," Tillik said, wandering over to the wall in which that high window was let, and gazing up at the cloudy daylight. "At least we're getting a trial."

Elindeh glanced over at him, and her crest came up just a little at his casual tone. "Remember that 'trial' on Dahlain the year before last?"

He had to chuckle. "Who could for-get?" Tillik said. After catching them out at night doing some illegal observational astronomy, the Dahlainu had taken him and Elindeh and tossed them into an ancient, arid meteor crater, leaving the two of them to have what was meant to be an improving and terminal discussion with a flightless carnivorous avian. *And the improvement was supposed to be strictly dietary,* Tillik thought, *on the avian's side.* Fortunately the creature had been more intelligent than the Dahlaini had ever suspected, so that after some linguistic experimentation, it and Elindeh had been able to find common ground. Now the avian was living at an AG facility on Melanogast, working for a Sentient Resources department there, and Tillik and Elindeh had escaped Dahlain with their skins and a mild reprimand from AG Upper for "disruption of a local status quo."

That was the problem with Upper. They hated "disruption". *Even at the cost of their own operatives' skins,* Tillik thought. Yet at the same time, the system worked. *Mostly. It can seem madness, identifying a broken culture and sending to fix it not a big force of people, well armed and equipped, but just a couple of operatives with a little ship....*

Yet if it makes us think harder about how we get our results, find ways that are more about helping the culture find its own way out of its problems...then maybe it's worth it in the long run.

It's the short run I'm worrying about today. "Computer, where in the Three's names are you?"

No answer.

"The problem in situations like this," Elindeh said, sounding plaintive, "is that half the time they don't take us seriously. If we could just say we came from the Such-and-such Star Empire, people would pay attention!"

"You wouldn't like Upper to hear you saying that," Tillik said, sitting down wearily. "It'd play hell with your next evaluation. They'd cite you for bad attitude."

"Let them find themselves in more situations like this," Elindeh said, the harshness showing in her voice a little, "and maybe they'll understand the attitude a little better."

There was no arguing with that. It didn't help, Tillik supposed, that your organization's very name suggested that you came, not from a mighty interstellar empire that would come in after you with guns blazing, but from some kind of mild-mannered, self-effacing bureaucracy. With only fifteen star systems and the odd independent trading station involved, the Coalition was by no stretch of the imagination an empire—though it had a few empires as neighbors, and mostly kept its relationships with them strictly along the line of trade alliances, while watching them closely to make sure they weren't getting any acquisitive ideas.

Even the name of the organization differed widely depending on which of its fifteen official languages it was translated into; there was no one name that had become particularly widespread among either friends or enemies. Some of the names for the organization translated into terms such as "sortiment", "association," "grouping", or "concatenation"; and there was a plethora of acronyms that Tillik had long since given up on trying to keep track of—that was what computers were for. The word Tillik's own people used was "Aggregate," and they called unfortunate government workers like him, with gentle derision, "Aggies" or "Aggros." That suited Tillik. People who made fun of you, no matter how affectionately, were also likely to underestimate you…. And that often came in handy.

"Still," Elindeh said, looking around her with some approval, "this is a nice cell. Much more comfortable than the last one."

Tillik restrained a grim smile. Elindeh's personal gift for finding the best in anything usually brought out this response in him, and he was always at some pain to keep it to himself—mostly because it was his particular gift to look for, and find, the worst. Upper apparently felt it was important to balance teams this way, one optimist and one pessimist, so that each member could (theoretically) compensate for the other's blind spot. There were other balances—routinely male/female, of course (though rarely the same species), or math-gifted/humanities-gifted, or techie and psych-friendly. The team members, though, were rarely told by Upper into which category they fell. Figuring it out for yourself was one of those ways you spent those long afternoons and evenings in transit between jobs. And the balance also often manifested itself as a constant tension between opposites… which, if you weren't of a philosophical turn of mind, could be something that kept you up all night, either brooding or simmering.

Fortunately Tillik was philosophical—possibly something to do with his previous background in the diplomatic corps. All the same, the look that Elindeh was bending on him now brought him out of philosophical mode. "Do you really think we can stop it?" she said. "The war that's coming?"

"We'd better have," he said, just as softly. "Not much of a chance for this world otherwise."

She looked at him, noting the difference in the tenses they'd been using. "The work's done," Tillik said, "regardless of what happens to us. The paradigm has no choice but to change, now." The only question now is… will we see it—?"

"I can't leave you two alone for a moment before you're giving up all hope, can I?" the computer whispered in Tillik's ear.

Across the room, Elindeh's bowed head came up, whipped around toward Tillik, quick as a hunter sighting prey. Her crest went up in a questioning gesture: are you getting this too?

Tillik nodded. "Tell me about it," Tillik said, subvocalizing, and collapsing onto the bench in absolute relief. "I thought the link was down—"

"Standard evaluation precautions," said the computer. "The other location was secure enough. But once they moved you, I had to make sure the Salimasht tech staff could not detect the dissimulation carrier."

"And they can't?"

"I wouldn't be talking to you otherwise."

Tillik burst out in a sweat of relief. The dissimulator technology handled nearly every function of any importance aboard their ship: in-system motive power, the farjump vortex, the vortex's short-range function that let them get into and out of a planet's gravity well, the duplication technology that let them rearrange limited masses of matter into new configurations… everything. But now he was able to breathe again.

"Not that they have anything sufficient to interfere with me," the computer said. "Vacuum tubes and crude diodes are about their speed. But I had to be sure."

"What's a vacuum tube?" Elindeh said, also subvocalizing.

"Nothing you need to worry about," Tillik said. "Nothing that can threaten us, anyway. They might use a technology based on it to hear that our ship was overhead, if they knew what frequencies to seek for. But I doubt they do. And they wouldn't be able to hear anything more than that, not without encryption keys that they're not equipped to manipulate."

Elindeh sighed. "So now what do we do?" she said aloud.

Tillik put his feet up on the bench, though he could just hear his mother saying, *What's got into you? Were you raised in a barn?* "Now," he said, "we wait."

Elindeh gave him a shady look. "We don't have to do it here," she said silently.

Tillik sighed. It would be easy enough to do what she was suggesting—let the computer use the dissim-based people-mover to bring them up to the ship, then monitor communications and personal movements down here until someone came for them. But he shook his head. "No," he said. "Tell me: how'd they know we were down there, outside the Motikh's secure storage?"

Elindeh put her crest down. "…I'm not sure. Scan didn't show anyone nearby."

"There you have it," Tillik said. "Peepholes? Light conduits? Echo chambers? Who knows. So, equally, we can't be sure what method they're using to keep an eye on us here. Let's sit tight and do what we came here for: let them use us to solve their problem. When the Aggregate has a problem that needs guns and obvious solutions like superseding a species' technology with our own, they send a minifleet. But when they have a problem that needs to look like the locals solved it themselves…."

"If they will," Elindeh said, not sounding very certain about the prospect.

"Then they send us," Tillik said. "And we do our best…. Which we've done. So let's give it a chance to pay off."

And they waited.

It was actually about two hours before the new group of guards came for them and brought them down into the council room.

The room itself was far more splendid

than one would normally have expected of a council chamber. Tillik remembered, from one of the tours he and Elindeh had been given when they were new to the city and still something of a sensation, that the core of this building was one of the older palaces: the new structure had been built around the old one, since due to its contents it was too sacred to interfere with.

The specific contents that made it so were down at the end of this white, long, high, cold stone room, the bare floor of which was now filled with what seemed like about a thousand courtiers. Far beyond them all, under a very handsome geometrically-patterned stained-glass skylight, was a dais. The dais had a long stone-topped table running the width of it. But behind the dais rose a steep flight of steps, running up one side of a square-sided pyramid, and at the top of that pyramid was a throne.

It was a work of art, really, though in what Tillik's people would have considered a somewhat barbaric, if energetic, idiom — high-backed, broad-seated, carved from a single piece of some dark wood that was (their guide had said) nearly as hard as stone, and which was also used industrially in modern times to make ball bearings. Tillek had thought at the time, and thought now as he and Elindeh were marched up toward it and the dais, that ball bearings were probably the last things on the mind of the ancient artisans who made that throne. It was inlaid with arabesques and obscure runic phrases in precious metals, and where inlay was lacking, the throne was carved all over with eyes, apparently the eyes of the gods, staring in all directions. Many of these carvings were deeply set with precious gemstones, themselves carved and inset with other gemstones to look like genuine eyes. The effect was most peculiar, especially when you got close enough to the throne to feel stared at.

For his own part, Tillik was already feeling quite stared-at enough, for there in the centermost chair of the dais, in the first-among-equals position with three other impassive Salimasht nobles seated on each side of him, sat Lord Amaswith, watching the two prisoners as they approached. A few meters from the dais and the table, the escort stopped: but they did not let go of Tillik or Elindeh.

Amaswith rose, and the room went quiet. "As Chief Lord of the Great Council," Amaswith said, looking out across the room, "I stand before the Throne of the Last King, in the place of the Lordship that is Lost, and in the Aldive's name, with the most senior councillors of the Salimasht, to do justice. We do justice on those who come to destroy our people, to threaten the safety and stability of our world, to orphan our children and bereave our world of its proper maintenance, which the gods have given into our hands."

The silence grew deafening. "Well," Elindeh said privately to Tillik, "two out of four's not bad."

He raised a wry eyebrow at her, but said nothing. *Her irony's back,* he thought. *Always a good sign....*

"Let the instrument and fount of all justice be here with us," Lord Amaswith said, and signaled to the back of the room. Silently, the doors down at the end of the room opened.

Six Salimasht women in blue robes came pacing slowly in. The crowd parted before them, and, looking down through the open space, Tillik could see that the middle pair carried between them a curiously carven box of some dark wood. As the women passed, every Salimasht made a curious gesture, holding up a hand with the palm outward, then clenching the hand into a fist. The guards holding Tillik and Elindeh did the same, and pulled them a little to one side.

Before the dais, the six women stopped; the two with the box stepped forward. Two of their colleagues came up beside them and reached down to lift the lid of the box; a third stepped up to reach into the box and lift out an object, then turned and held it high.

It was a gleaming lump of some silvery metal, rounded and blobbed and a little scorched on its surface, as if it had been molten at some time. It had a faintly human shape—if you looked at it long enough, you could make out a head, a torso, arms pressed to the torso's sides, legs pressed together. At the sight of it, all around the rooms breaths were indrawn, eyes went wide.

Tillik flicked a glance at Elindeh, but Elindeh had no eyes for him at the moment, only for the metal shape reverently held up, and now reverently lowered. As the woman in the blue robe slipped the object back into the box, Lord Amaswith looked over at the two of them.

"In the deeps of time," he said, "there were many small countries hereabouts. Telenda, Warish, Muruven, Latoun, Ravith, Mitigart: a hundred names, a hundred little city-states, endlessly squabbling for power and land. But finally the gods took counsel among themselves and decided to end the strife by making one land foremost among the others, unconquerable among the nations."

He looked down at the box as it was closed. "So one night," Lord Amaswith said, "the Goddess of War and her hosts stood high in heaven and rained their burning spears down on the world. All the nations looked up in terror that night. All save Salimasht, for it was on one of the hills outside this city that the Motikh fell. The Goddess spoke a word in a Salimasht prophet's ear, telling him to go out and seek for the image of her that had fallen from the sky. Once that image was found, it should be brought into the city; and once it was safe inside our walls, Salimasht would never fall, and could never be conquered in battle."

Lord Amaswith looked down at the box with an expression of profound satisfaction. "And so the event has proven," he said, "a hundred times. Over the centuries, nation after nation went up against us, and was destroyed. Now only we and the Arinhen remain—our nearest neighbor and oldest enemy, most intransigent and resistant to the obvious will of the gods. Eventually they too will be gone, and we will be masters of the world. But in the meantime, there are still occasional dangers to our security."

He turned and glared at Tillik and Elindeh. "Such as you. You were trying to steal the Motikh, as a thousand others have before you. But you were not even able to enter the outer sanctuary, were you? Much less the inner one, the Hall of Mysteries where the Motikh is kept safe."

He fell silent, staring at them.

Tillik cleared his throat. "I'm sorry," he said, "but was that meant as an invitation to speak?"

"For as much good as it's likely to do you," said Lord Amaswith, "yes."

Tillik drew himself up straight. "Then as the senior member of this mission to your world," he said, "and the delegated representative of the Aggregate to you and the other political entities here, I must protest our treatment in this matter."

"You may protest all you like," said Lord Amaswith, "as long as you explain what you were doing."

"Investigating," Elindeh said. "The carvings down there, for example, which we never had a chance to look at in any detail when we arrived. Investigation of such cultural and geological resources is one of our functions. As resource identification specialists—"

"Spies, you mean," said Lord Amaswith.

"I must protest your putting such a prejudicial construction on the concept!" Tillik said. "You have no evidence to support—"

"You can protest whatever you like for the little time you have left," said Lord Amaswith. "But I think we have heard enough for everyone here to understand what you were up to, and draw their own conclusions. You were looking for a way to steal the Motikh. I'm sure I don't care why, so don't bother telling me reasons! But you failed, and we found you in the act of failing." His smile was very unpleasant. "I'm sure you'll understand that there is only one punishment for such an offense—"

"I doubt we will understand it," Elindeh said, her eyes flashing scorn, "but I'm sure we can guess what it will be."

"Good," said Lord Amaswith. "That saves us some time. It is therefore my duty in the name of the Aldive—"

"Yes," Tillik said. "And while we're on the subject, just where is the Aldive?"

"That is none of your concern," said Lord Amaswith. "Now if we can just get on to the main—"

"No, I think he has a point," said a voice from the back of the room. "Don't you?"

A look of the purest shock went over Lord Amaswith's face. Tillik turned and saw, through the suddenly parting crowd, a short roly-poly shape standing at the back of the room, not entirely surrounded by a small crowd of personal functionaries—but they had learned over time, Tillik suspected, not to block their master's view. Among his fellow Salimasht, the

shape standing in the open doors was an incongruous one, a patch of somber color—grey and tawny and white robes— amid all the flagrant color of his entourage and the mass of other functionaries in the room. But Nalaidu Ongweina Mirrivun Alalsar Salima, last scion and heir of the ancient family that was all that was left of the Lost Kings, did not need anything more to set him apart from the crowd except his face. That face was carved into every end-wall of every house in the city, for which he served as a sort of minor tutelary deity, and would until he died and his face was replaced by—*Who, I wonder?* Tillik thought, and his glance went to Lord Amaswith. *I bet I can guess.* But, comparing the two faces—the round, bland, cheerful one, and the one almost as hawklike as Elindeh's but without her pensive, sympathetic quality—Tillik could guess which one he would prefer at his house's gable-end.

As the Aldive approached, Lord Amaswith got up rather hurriedly. "Royal Master," he said, "while you do us great honor by attending this routine meeting, there is no need for you to remain. The business at hand is merely one of routine housekeeping—"

"Housekeeping?" said the Aldive, looking mildly at the six blue-robed women and the dark carved box that sat on the floor in the midst of them. "What, did the Hall of Mysteries need dusting all of a sudden?"

Lord Amaswith's expression suggested that he had jostled off his line of discourse. He recovered himself with a little difficulty. "Royal master, none of us would want to distract the Luck of the City from his duties to deal with a mere business of petty theft by—"

"Theft? Of what? Nothing petty, that's for sure. That kind of thing is what you've been giving me to deal with since I was twelve, once a month at people's-court in the palace." The Aldive turned on Lord Amaswith an expression that was completely guileless, on the surface of it. But Tillik caught a flash of it in passing, as the Aldive went past him, and was suddenly alert.

"Royal Master—" said Lord Amaswith as the Aldive paused before the dais.

"And here are the noble representatives of the Aggregate," said the Aldive. "It's been weeks since I saw you two at the Palace; what have you people been up to? It was archaeology when I saw you last. Something about standing stones out by the city boundaries."

Now his full regard was turned on them. The face was friendly, almost child-like, and the Aldive's manner was blithe, as it had been every time they'd met with him so far: like someone without a care in the world. But Tillik, looking at him full on in the cool morning light falling through the high windows, in this charged atmosphere very different from the silk-hung cocoon of the Palace, suddenly knew that something else entirely was going on. A great jolt of adrenaline ran through him. *This is it,* he thought. *What we came for actually has a chance of getting done.*

If we can just steer what's going to happen in the right direction....

"Sir," Tillik said, bowing, "as always, we are very glad to see you." Beside him, Elindeh spoke one of the ritual greetings of her people, a long soft croaking phrase, and bowed as her people did, with wings instead of body, spreading them out to their furthest and then drooping them to the ground.

This caused some trouble to the people who were holding her arms, as Elindeh was not entirely gentle about the way she spread her wings out; her restrainers both abruptly found themselves sitting on the floor. The Aldive managed to seem to be looking at Tillik when this happened, so that only Tillik caught the noticing sideways flicker of the Aldive's eyes, and the way he then turned and seemed to be surprised.

"Let those people go," the Aldive said loudly, looking around him then. "What do you think they are, some kind of skittish riding-beast? They're hardly going to bolt out of the room, not with all these guards. Why, even the Aldive of the City could hardly get in."

And he looked up at the dais. The tone of voice in which this statement was made was mild enough, but Tillik could hear the barb in it. And if he could, so could Lord Amaswith, who (Tillik saw, stealing a glance) had gone positively pale, a difficult task for one so dark.

"And it's not as if they're interested in bolting anyway, I'd think," the Aldive said. "It was they who came to us, remember. Though perhaps after this I'd understand if they'd had a change of heart."

The Aldive looked around him. "Well?" he said after a moment. "Must I stand?"

All the people on the dais looked very uncomfortable. The one nearest the end of the dais picked up his chair and brought it down to the Aldive, and the Aldive seated himself. "Now," he said, and the room went very very quiet. "I see that our guests—for in such wise we welcomed them, not so long ago—are suddenly being tried for their lives. Otherwise the Motikh, the gods' custodian of the lives of the city, would hardly be here. What are they supposed to have done?"

"Royal Master," said Lord Amaswith, "they were found outside the Hall of Mysteries, and they were—"

From the back of the room came a dull booming sound. Everyone looked at the closed doors.

"You really are having a bad time with procedure today, my Lord Amaswith," said the Aldive, standing up and craning his neck. "What in the Mirror's name—" He moved out toward the clear space through the crowd, but it was already closing up as everybody standing on either side of it started moving inwards to get a clear view of the doors.

"Ah me," said the Aldive, and turned to step up onto the dais. The Salimasht nobles all hurriedly stood as he came up, but the Aldive waved them back into their seats, himself standing beside Lord Amaswith's chair and peering toward the back of the room. "So who is that?" he shouted. "Let them in!"

The surprised guards at the back of the room bowed to their master and opened the doors. Beyond them was revealed a crowd of people, standing close together and looking uncertain. "Come on," the Aldive shouted to them, "come right up here!"

Lord Amaswith looked quite stricken at the sudden collapse of protocol. The Aldive sat down in Amaswith's chair, while all the other senior lords stood staring, uncertain what to do. The Aldive ignored them, watching the group coming up through the crowd. "Everything else is strange today," the Aldive said in a matter-of-fact way. "Why not this as well?" And he glanced down at Tillik.

Fleeting though it was, there was something unusual about the expression. Tillik suddenly found himself wondering. *How long has this man been pretending to be an unengaged innocent,* he thought, *the next thing to a simpleton?* For the look in the Aldive's eye was that of a man who was expecting Tillik to do something. *It's as if he's been waiting for us,* Tillik thought. *And possibly waiting for us to do something in particular.*

And Three be praised, we may be able to oblige him.

Tillik's heart was pounding. He watched, as everyone else did, the small group of figures making their way up through the Salimasht who lined the way to the dais. They were dressed somewhat differently from the Salimasht. Their overrobes were shorter, and most of these were patterned: their underrobes went only to the mid-shin, and all the people approaching, men and women alike, were booted. All of them had the same hairstyle, shorn off square just above the shoulders, as opposed to the Salimasht hair style, which tended either to be quite short or quite long.

The little group—there were only six of them—walked up to stand before the dais. Five of them bowed, but one stood straight and locked eyes with each person sitting at the dais, one after another. Finally his eyes came to rest on Lord Amaswith.

"I am the Voice of the Demal of Arinhen," he said. "I am the Demal's hand, and her sword. And I come today to require you to surrender, for the gods have done a great miracle, and given us mastery over you."

Silence hung in the air for a moment. Then, slowly, laughter started. It grew until the rafters of the great room rang with it. And one of those laughing the most loudly was Lord Amaswith.

Eventually the laughter ebbed a little. "Oh, indeed!" said Lord Amaswith. "It must be quite a miracle, to put such mad words in your mouth, such crazed thoughts in your brain!" There was some more laughter in reaction to this. "Tell us, then, what this great miracle might be! And then get you gone, for we have more pressing business today."

The Voice of the Demal of Arinhen had

stood there, going dark of face, even for a Salimasht, with what Tillik thought was probably anger. But now the Voice smiled. It was such a small, thin smile that anyone with a scrap of sense, Tillik thought, should have gone cold at the sight of it.

The Voice turned to one of the silent aides behind him and put out a hand. The aide reached into her robe and brought out something wrapped in a dark cloth. This she handed to the Voice. The Voice turned around, unwrapped the cloth with some care, and then held it up in one hand, with difficulty, as if the object was very heavy. It was a gleaming lump of some silvery metal, rounded and blobbed and a little scorched on its surface, as if it had been molten at some time. It had a faintly human shape: a head, a torso, arms pressed to its sides, legs pressed together.

It was the Motikh.

Tillik glanced over at Elindeh and watched her slowly, slowly lower her lids over her great eyes. Tillik briefly gave thanks that no one around them knew what a Malakthana's smile looked like. Then he let out a whole month's worth of sigh, trying not to look too obvious about it. Their mission wasn't quite done yet, but this moment was what it had all been about.

And something occurred to him. "I forgot to ask you," he said silently to Elindeh, "when you finished the analysis. What exactly was the composition of the metal?"

"Meteoric," Elindeh said, "as we thought. But not much of the usual iron-nickel material. Oh, there were traces—that's what's made the bronzing you see on the surface. Tin, carbon, traces of silicate. But the rest was noble metals. Two percent gold, twelve percent silver, and the other eighty-six percent palladium."

Tillik's eyebrows went up. "Really,"

Tillik said, and he was unable to restrain the smile. "Is that so...."

As far as the smile went, no one noticed it at all, because everybody was shouting—everybody except Lord Amaswith, who stood with a terrible set look on his face, the expression of a man doing his utmost not to reveal fear.

After a moment he actually laughed, though to Tillik's eye there was a forced quality to it. "A fake," Amaswith said. "The true one is here."

The Voice gave Lord Amaswith a completely unconvinced look. "I think not," he said. "I think the true one has been taken from you by the gods, as punishment for your arrogance and pride. And in its place they have left you with a worthless thing with no power to it, a duplicate that will not protect you from anything—much less the avenging armies of Arinhen, when we come to stand before your walls, and your gates are breached, and your once-proud city falls before us!"

Then the real madness broke loose. Lord Amaswith came down from the dais and pushed the women aside who were guarding the dark, carven box. He threw its lid open and snatched the Motikh up out of it, and tried to pull the other Motikh out of the Voice's hands. The Voice kept hold of it, laughing in Amaswith's face, and then started shouting at him. All around the room, voices were raised in a hubbub of fury and fear.

Now, Tillik thought.

"Ladies and gentlemen!" he cried.

Many eyes turned to him in shock, but there wasn't enough quiet yet for him to be heard. "Ladies and gentlemen, if you please!!"

People stared. "Ladies and gentlemen," Tillik said, "can't you tell what has happened here? Don't you understand it?"

The muttering that spread through the

crowd suggested that understanding was in short supply.

"It's a miracle!" Tillik said. "Look at the Salimasht Motikh! Look at the Arinhen one! They are absolutely identical! Don't you see that the gods mean you not to know which one is the first one, the Motikh whose possession meant certain victory? That way neither side can ever be sure that it's the one that's going to win a war!"

"And neither side," Elindeh said, "can be sure that the other side is the one that's going to lose!"

Lord Amaswith had for some moments been trembling with rage. Now he whirled in a storm of robes and practically ran up to Tillik, and actually shook the Motikh he was holding in Tillik's face. "Do not seek to play games with us!" he shouted. "Do not try to hide your culpability! You are responsible for this, this sacrilege!"

"How?" Tillik said, allowing himself to look amused for the moment. "You just said we failed to steal anything! Now what are you accusing us of?" Amaswith's mouth moved, but no sound came out; his face went dark with fury. "Whatever you come up with," Tillik said, "I have a feeling you're not going to have any more evidence for it than you had for us stealing anything."

Amaswith just stood there and shook, while the hubbub in the room grew. The Aldive, though, looked down from the dais, just watching, manifesting a strange kind of calm. Slowly, eyes began to be drawn to him; slowly, people started to catch his quiet.

"Our stranger-guests," the Aldive said after a few moments, "may be able to see some truth in this matter that we are blind to, being too close to it. Madam—Linde, was it?"

She bowed to the Aldive again, her wings right out. "Elindeh, may it please the City's Luck."

Tillik threw her a brief approving look, for it was the phrasing a local citizen would use when greeting the Aldive in the public road, or asking him to accept testimony in an informal lawsuit.

"Madam Elindeh, would you do me the courtesy of examining our Motikh, and—the other one"—there was kind of a gasp around the room—"and telling me whether you can find any difference between them."

"Royal Master, I must protest—!" Lord Amaswith cried. "These creatures cannot touch the holy Motikh, their mere contact with it would—"

"Oh come now, my Lord Amaswith," said the Aldive, sounding very dry. "You were within an inch of stuffing the holy Motikh up Master—Tillek, is it?"

"Tillik, if it please the Luck."

"—Up his nose, in any case," said the Aldive. "So be still. Show the lady the Motikh. Noble Voice, I would be obliged if you would do the same. Madam, am I right in thinking that you have devices to exactly measure objects for their weight, size and so forth?"

"I have had such, may it please the Luck," said Elindeh, "but mine was taken from me when we were brought here."

"And yours too, Master Tillik? Indeed. Restore their equipment immediately," said the Aldive to the room in general.

This was done, though it took a moment to find where the vidlinks had been put, and in whose charge. Tillik was most amused to see the frantic and frustrated toolmarks on the casing of his link when it was put back into his hands; but it was otherwise intact. He looked up from it to see Elindeh most professionally scanning the Motikh in Lord Amaswith's trembling hands. "Very good, my Lord," she said, and went over to the Voice. "Sir, please hold it up—I thank you."

She finished the scanning, and turned back to the dais. "May it please the Luck of the City," Elindeh said, "I am finished."

"And what have you found?"

"These two items are absolutely identical, may it please the Luck," she said. "They are the same length and width, the same mass to the microgram, and exactly the same shape in every respect. Their physical composition, their density, and even the composition of the scorchmarks and other markings on their surfaces are exactly the same."

"I see," said the Aldive. "So which is the real one? Or perhaps I should say, the original?"

Tillik kept his face quite straight at this phrasing. "I regret to say there is no way to tell, may it please the Luck," Elindeh said, though the regret in her voice was, frankly, minimal. "And probably there never will be."

Tillik privately thought that this might be a canard. Unquestionably Elindeh was an artist at the use of the dissimulator technology's restructuring and matter duplication functions. But even her delicate touch would not be able to prevent the very best high-end electron shell analysis proving one of the two Motikhs to be significantly younger than the other in terms of actual duration-in-space. However, there was no way the Aldive's people would have the technology to know which one for many, many years. *By which time,* he thought, *it'll be too late, because they'll have learned to live with each other. At least a little....*

"So it is a miracle," Tillik said. "And you should all be thanking your gods for it! After centuries of wars, centuries of your people killing each other without end, they're tired of it at last! But maybe they've come to their senses. After all, the more of you die, the fewer worshippers they have! And that has to annoy them. So

now, without depriving one side of its holy of holies... the other side too has been given a sign of the gods' favor. Possibly the most certain sign of it. The chance of peace...."

The Voice looked up at the Aldive with a dubious expression, as if unsure that there could ever be too few of the other side, no matter what the gods might have put down in writing. But the Aldive sat absolutely still, looking down at Tillik and Elindeh, waiting.

"My associate speaks a truth," Elindeh said, spreading her wings wide. Her gravity and her imposing and exotic appearance went a long way, Tillik thought, to distracting any listener from the fact that she had said "a" and not "the." And as she glanced around with those huge golden eyes, which had to look a little crazed to anybody who didn't know how rational she was, Tillik was sure he could just hear them thinking: *What a quaint idiom she has. How long are those talons? Don't I have somewhere to be?*

"Royal Master," said Lord Amaswith, his voice shaking, though whether the tremor was more caused by anger or fear, at this point, was impossible to tell. "This is a moment of greatest danger for our people. We have been posed this awful conundrum, and it is important beyond all belief to pause, to take thought, to not act precipitately in the face of our ancient enemies and of strangers who will doubtless benefit by our destabilization! We must do nothing without consideration, without taking time for mature counsel to—"

"Thank you," said the Aldive. "Be silent."

Utterly astonished, Lord Amaswith became so.

"Good," the Aldive said. "My lords, my ladies and gentlemen, and you noble guests of various types— The gods, too, have been silent this long time. Now they've spoken, and I agree with the emissaries of the Aggregate: the message is one of peace. You'll forgive me, therefore, if I do this."

And the Aldive turned and started to walk up the stairs behind the dais.

The room fell utterly silent. It was a steep climb, but the Aldive went up it steadily, never looking back. On the topmost step he stood, looking down at the ancient throne before him: the ornate carvings of it and the many all-seeing eyes, the symbols and the runes, the jewels and the gold. Then the Aldive bent over and dusted off the wide stone seat. And finally he turned and sat himself down.

The room's silence held. It was as if at least half the occupants were giving lightning a chance to strike. Tillik looked around at the shocked Lord Amaswith, who stood absolutely trembling with voiceless rage.

The Aldive leaned back in the great throne, looking out over the crowd. Then he stretched out his legs, looking entirely comfortable, and smiled at those who watched.

"So much better a view," the Aldive said, looking out across the shocked crowd. "Yes, this is a great improvement. Ladies and gentlemen and nobles of all kinds and both our lands: am I not the scion of the Lost Kings? I think there is no argument about that. But who lost the Kings, exactly? Their blood was much watered down by battles, endless battles, no matter that we won them! And I am all there is left of that blood. Perhaps it has been traditional for these many years to let others bear the actual rule of Salimasht. Well, in a time of miracles, traditions must sometimes be set aside. I will start with this one."

He looked down at Tillik and Elindeh.

"There will be no executions today," the Aldive said. "These explorers, or researchers or whatever they are, have been privileged to be present at a great miracle. If they were in the Hall of Mysteries, or outside it, what matter? Today our peoples are released from our long punishment. So I release the strangers too, to go or stay as they please. And as for us, let us put the two Motikhs away safe, as an earnest of the gods' new will for us. There will be no more wars of Salimasht against Arinhen. Those days are done."

"Royal master," said Lord Amaswith, striding to the bottom of that steep flight of stairs, "you cannot do this. You will not do this! It is a position that, with your lack of experience, you cannot possibly maintain—"

"Why not?" the Aldive said. " I have an army, haven't I? Especially since, by the grace of the kindly gods, my poor soldiers can now stop going to war with our neighbors, and live long enough to collect on their funeral plans. Which has been a rare enough circumstance in recent years."

The soldiers at the back of the room, looking up at the Aldive, slowly fell to their knees.

"Royal Master!" shouted Lord Amaswith in absolute outrage. Then he looked horrified.

Slowly the Aldive nodded. "Yes," he said. And he stood up and looked out across the room. "Since on this day of miracles I've sat in the throne of my ancestors and not been blasted—as some have been eager to tell us would happen—" He stared down at Amaswith. "Am I master here?"

There was a long breathless silence in the room. Then, toward the back of the room, people began going down on their knees. The wave of respect, or at least uncertainty, progressed right up to the front of the room: and Tillik, never one to spoil a moment, bowed low. Elindeh, beside him, did the same.

Slowly, with the utmost reluctance, Lord Amaswith knelt.

Silence.

"Good," said the Aldive. He looked out over the crowd. Bowing also—and pointedly not on their knees—were the representatives from Arenhel. "Noble Voice," said the Aldive to their leader, "you and your people have had a hard drive from your city. Perhaps you would do me the honor of staying the night. We can talk tomorrow, if you please, about how things shall go between our lands henceforth."

The Voice looked up at the Aldive. "Noble Aldive," he said, "nothing would please us more."

"Guards, escort them with honor to the Red Wing of the palace, and give order for their every comfort," the Aldive said. "Nobles, ladies and gentlemen, a great change is upon us. We must all take time to thank the gods for their gift, and think how to use it best. For now, go your ways."

The doors at the back opened: the room began, with surprising speed, to empty. The lords on the dais were quick to follow.

"Well," Elindeh said under her breath, "I thought that went well."

Tillik just nodded, and stood where he was, watching.

Almost everyone was gone before the Aldive rose from his throne. He came down the steps carefully, then onto the dais, and finally stepped down from it and walked around to where Elindeh and Tillik were standing some feet away from the rigid Lord Amaswith.

"Better," said the Aldive as he joined them. "I was beginning to think the air was thinner up there, the way it is in the mountains. Got a nosebleed once when I was young, on a trip up those mountains.

I wouldn't care to repeat that."

"Royal Aldive," said Tillik, "it has been a momentous afternoon. With your permission, we will withdraw."

The Aldive put a hand on Tillik's arm. "Stay," he said.

Lord Amaswith joined them, his face dark as thunder. "Royal master—"

"Out," said the Aldive.

"Royal Master, you—"

"Out," said the Aldive, looking up into the set, dark, angry face. He did not raise his voice or move a muscle; but in Lord Amaswith's face, something changed.

He turned and walked from the hall in a whirl of bright robes. The three of them stood, silent, until the doors closed behind Amaswith, and silence fell.

The Aldive looked from Tillik to Elindeh: and very slowly he bowed to them.

Tillik was astounded. Elindeh was actually shaking; Tillik could see it in the down at the edges of her wings. "Sir," she said, "there is no need."

"There is," said the Aldive. "A long time now I have been praying the gods to send us help."

"Oh, but sir—" Tillik said.

The Aldive held up a hand. Tillik fell silent. "But it is contingent on us to recognize such help when it comes," he said, "and not to throw it away once it arrives. So you must forgive me for doing nothing in particular when you came. And for seeming to understand little, when you spoke. I didn't dare change the way I had been behaving for so long, since I was being so closely watched. I knew that for you to do whatever you had come to do, things must seem to proceed as they had always done."

Tillik nodded.

"Sir," Tillik said. "One thing I must learn. What brought you here at this particular moment in time?"

The Aldive glanced around him. "You

would like me to say," he said, "that a little voice spoke to me out of the air and told me to come. And indeed, a voice did speak."

Tillik glanced at Elindeh, and saw her slowly lower her lids over her great eyes again.

"But I have other means of hearing what goes on in the world, and some other voices I listen to as well," the Aldive said. "Some of them not even Lord Amaswith knows about. A concept that would have shocked him, and one I have been concealing until, one way or another, the gods should speak and tell me the time was right. And when all the voices agree that I should be somewhere—well."

Tillik nodded, and smiled.

"So," the Aldive said. "Much will now happen. Therefore I think you should go. Indeed I think you should go as quickly as possible, as things are likely to become lively around here. Lord Amaswith will not let this afternoon's doings pass entirely without some action. But afterwards... you should come back. In six of our months, or so, let us say. Then the Voice and I will be able to greet you on far more equal terms, and arrange a joint trade alliance of some kind with the Aggregate. But not—"

He paused. Outside in the great plaza, there was a far-off noise as of the shouting of many voices.

"Not today," he said. "So go."

They both bowed to him. Without another word, the Aldive made for the great doors, to join those of his people who were waiting outside to conduct him to safety.

"So are you done now?" the computer said.

"I'd say so," Tillik said. "Did you get all that?"

"Every moment captured in sound and moving image," the computer said, "for you to gloat over all the way home."

Tillik glanced down the hall, seeing the doors shut behind the Aldive. "Then bring us up," Tillik said.

The cold white room shimmered out of existence around them.

That evening, as they sat in their little commonroom aboard *Pertuvaithin* after reports were transmitted, and dinner cooked and eaten, Elindeh looked up at Tillik from the screenbook she was reading. "I meant to ask you," she said. "What did you mean when you said that this had happened before?"

"Oh." Tillik got up and went over to the realignment hatch, touched the controls. The machinery hummed softly, rearranging the carbon and oxygen and hydrogen atoms in its buffer tank into a new configuration; a moment later, a cup of chai was standing there. He took it out, blew on it, went to sit down again. "An old story," Tillik said, sipping, and burned his mouth. He put the cup down, and put his hands around it to warm them. "From the oldest of the human homeworlds. There were several versions of it, I believe. Something falls from the sky, and the gods say 'As long as you have this, you're safe...' One version of the story says the thing was made of wood. Another said it was metal: precious stuff. A different metal was named after it, a long while after." He cocked an amused eye at her.

"What, palladium?"

"Yes. That's why I laughed." He turned the cup around on the table, warming his hands on a different part. "But the story's a tragic one, in that old version. Everybody in it spends months or years trying to steal the magic thing that fell from the sky and made the city unconquerable. And meanwhile, outside the walls, an old bloody war drags on and, and people die and die until everyone gets used to the idea that the dying is just another fact of life, something that's going to go on forever." Tillik shook his head. "A vile concept."

"Which is why you knew what to do about this problem the moment that Upper described it to us four moons ago," Elindeh said.

Tillik shook his head and picked up the cup again. "Not at all," he said. "The right conditions had to be in place. There was no way to tell if they were until we got here and did our research. And half the result was always going to be contingent on whether the people here were ready for the solution."

"Or the person," Elindeh said. "The Aldive...."

Tillik nodded. "Without him we would have been executed."

"Oh, come on now," Elindeh said, "that's overreacting, surely. The computer would have pulled us out of there without any trouble."

"Of course," Tillik said, picking up the cup again and sipping more carefully. "But execution is how it would have been reported outside that room. Enemies of the gods, magically destroyed by the gods!" He gave her an amused look over the rim of the cup. "And everything would have gone back to 'normal'—the dying would have continued. Or worse, it would have gone on until the Salimasht did finally succeed in completely destroying their enemies. They would become the only viable culture on this planet...and as such, they would begin to stultify... or self-destruct. Because what happens to a culture based on superiority, when there's no one left to be superior to? Or one based on warfare, when there are no enemies left? It starts running downhill... or manufactures them from inside, and tears itself apart out of habit."

He drank, appreciating the good hot chai in silence for a moment.

"I have a message for you from Upper," said the computer.

The sweat broke out between Tillik's shoulder blades again. "Well?"

"They say, 'Don't bother coming back.'"

Tillik's eyes went wide with shock. Elindeh, though, flung her arms and wings out wide, and laughed out loud. "You idiot," she said, "they mean we don't need to debrief."

"She's right," said the computer. "You're being sent straight to Amaranth."

"What's wrong there?" Tillik said, relieved.

"A boundary treaty negotiation has fallen apart in the system's second asteroid belt," said the computer, "and the miners are threatening to strike if the two planets on either side of the belt don't get things sorted out."

"Then let's for all sakes get out there," Tillik said. "Let us know when the vortex math is done."

"Working now," said the computer.

Elindeh put her book aside and got up. "I'll start getting things locked down," she said, and went aft.

Tillik let out a breath, looking down for the last time in a while at the watery globe of Salimash, and he smiled. *At least,* he thought, *nobody's said anything about a wooden horse....* • • •

DIANE DUANE co-wrote the **Next Generation** *episode "Where No One Has Gone Before" with Michael Reaves. She is one of the most popular* **Star Trek** *novelitss, revolutionizing the portryal of the Romulans—or, rather, Rihannsu. She also worked on DC's* **Star Trek** *comics series. She has written many more novels and scripts outside the Franchise, including the (to date) nine-volume* **Young Wizards** *series.*

I CANNA CHANGE THE LAWS OF PHYSICS!

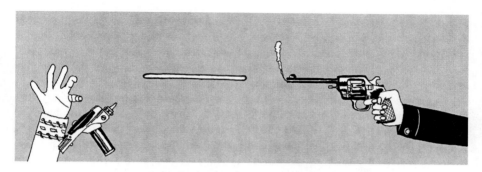

A SCIENCE ARTICLE BY ADAM WEINER

Everyone knows that when you see a good sci-fi movie, you have to buy into the world of the film. For example, even though it's highly improbable that space travel over the vast distances portrayed in *Star Trek, Star Wars,* and other icons of the space adventure genre could ever be achieved, it wouldn't be much fun if we were shouting in outrage every time a space ship engaged its "warp drive." It would be pretty hard to sit through several seasons of the *Enterprise* in transit to the nearest star without it. Its "five year mission" might get pretty boring and effectively destroy any possibility of a sequel. The really cool way-out stuff like transporter systems, holodecks, and warp cores are things that make wish we could be part of that imaginary future, and keep us coming back for more.

And *Star Trek* in general does a pretty fair job of attempting as much as possible to explain these amazing products of technological and scientific fancy by using real ideas from the world of modern physics—or when all else fails, they at least use the jargon. (When using the term *Star Trek,* of course, I refer to the entire television and feature-film canon, through *Enterprise* and *Nemesis.)*

Much has been written on "the Physics of *Star Trek,*" probably most notably by Lawrence Krauss, author of the book of the same title. In that book Krauss does an entertaining job of discussing, from a physics perspective, the issues relevant to the possible existence of all of these neat gadgets, cosmological phenomena, and strange entities that form the meat of a typical episode.

Recently I rented some DVD's with episodes from the original series and *TNG.* I hadn't seen these in quite a while and had forgotten how, underneath all of the fancy attempts to connect the forefronts of modern physics to the *Star Trek* universe, we find that some very simple fundamental principles often get violated or overlooked somehow on a *Trek* episode. Let's focus on a few of these and assess them with some basic physics.

Do not be alarmed, however. I am a great fan of the *Star Trek* phenomenon, I admit to a particular, even reverential, fondness for the original series, and would never presume to denigrate the shows except in the spirit of a good natured ribbing. So with that in mind let's proceed:

The weapons of the future

I magine being suddenly whisked off to an alien planet. Thankfully, it is "class M" so you don't suffocate, but coming over the ridge, you spot a scary hostile creature with an insect-like face pointing his phaser directly at you. You, however, are armed only with a semi-automatic handgun typical of early 21st-century Earth. You're under-gunned. If you get hit by the phaser beam you'll be vaporized! But are you really at a disadvantage? It has always been glaringly apparent to me how slowly phaser beams actually move when unleashed on a typical *Trek* episode. You can easily see the beam move from phaser to target. (How you could see the beam at all is another matter since, if it really is electromagnetic radiation like they say, you would never see the beam until it hit you in the eye—like a flashlight.)

At one point in *The Next Generation* episode "Hide and Q," Commander Riker tests his weapon by shooting an innocent rock no more than 30 meters away. I took out a stop watch and timed the beam several times to get an estimate of the phaser beam velocity. It took well over a second (about 1.4s on average) to cover the distance. This gives the beam an approximate speed of:

$$V = d/t = 30m/1.4s = 20 \text{ m/s}$$

...or 45 miles per hour. It is perplexing that in the *Star Trek: The Next Generation Technical Manual,* phasers are described as emitting electromagnetic energy (which always propagates at the speed of light), yet every time you actually watch a phaser being fired on the show, the beam pokes along at the incredibly modest speed calculated above. What's the deal? Amazingly, the phaser beams on the original series travel much faster than those

on TNG. While you can still see them move from one point to another, they're three or four times as fast as the newer models. (At least they're too fast to time with a simple stopwatch!) Is this some mysterious 24th century technological oversight?

In any case, the muzzle velocity of a bullet exiting a semi-automatic handgun is commonly over 1,000 miles per hour, and it's a lot harder to see than phaser fire. While the phaser is going to do a lot of damage if it hits you, it's not that hard to step out of the way... as we see later in the same *TNG* episode when Worf dodges some enemy fire with a casual step to his right. Try doing that with a barrage of bullets. 24th century phaser or 21st century gun? You decide.

The full stop maneuver

M any times over the course of a season in one of the *Trek* shows, usually during some exciting battle scene, or other emergency situation, the command is given by Kirk or Picard (or whoever is captain of that particular series) to bring the ship to a "full stop." (To achieve this, they often then initiate "reverse thrust" before coming to rest.) Contained in such a seemingly simple maneuver, however is a fundamental misconception of physics. The question we have to ask is: a full stop *relative to what?*

What does it mean to be at rest? According to Newton's First Law of Motion, there is no experiment you could do to distinguish between being at "rest" from being in motion at constant velocity. I remember once I was on the train between San Diego and L.A. I dozed off for a few minutes and when I woke up I thought we had come to a stop. I had absolutely no sense of motion, and was starting to get irritated that we might be late due to the apparent delay when the train hit a bump, and I realized that we were still moving at 70 miles per hour (relative to the ground). All non-accelerating or *inertial* frames of reference are equivalent.

So what does it mean to be in motion then? If the Earth and ground suddenly disappeared, as a passenger on the train, I would have no way to know whether I was in motion or not, since all motion is relative to a *frame of reference*. I can say that I am moving at 70 miles per hour relative to the stationary ground frame of reference just as correctly as you might say that I am stationary and the ground is moving at 70 miles per hour relative to my frame of reference.

So when the *Enterprise* comes to a full stop, relative to what frame of reference is it stopped? Now sometimes we might be able to reason that it is relative to some other object. For example when Q surrounds the *Enterprise* with a giant chain link fence from the same episode mentioned in the previous section, we can assume that the full stop is relative to the fence. O.K., fair enough. But lots of times it doesn't work that way. Sometimes they encounter an enemy ship far from any other reference points. Maybe Kirk calls for a full stop. Perhaps he means relative to the enemy ship, but if that's true, then the ship would have to also be at rest relative to the *Enterprise*. The implied (incorrect) assumption here is that there is some absolute spatial frame of reference to which all motion is relative. Of course, if the ship is traveling at some velocity, then presumably that must be relative to the frame of reference of where they started their voyage (Earth maybe), but coming to a "full stop" in deep space is ambiguous at best.

Inertia and tractor beams

D espite all of the fancy modern and pseudo-modern physics in many an episode, regular everyday old Newton's laws get a little dicey on *Star Trek*. Let's look at the concept of the tractor beam for a moment. The tractor beam must grip the object it intends to tow by exerting a force on that object. According to the Third Law, the object exerts an equal and opposite force back on the *Enterprise,* tending to pull it backwards towards the object it is towing. (Imagine standing on a skateboard while pulling on a rope attached to your friend on roller skates.)

Of course, *if* the impulse engines are applying *thrust* when the tractor beam is engaged, then everything can still accelerate forward. (Get off the skateboard and use the force of friction between your feet and the floor to accelerate you and your friend forward.) It is never explicitly stated that when they engage the tractor beam, the impulse engines are also engaged but let's give them the benefit of the doubt. So far so good.

But here's the mystery. Once the object is in tow and moving with the Enterprise, *why do you need to leave the tractor beam on at all?* This is Newton's First Law again. "An object in motion at a constant velocity, or at rest, will remain in that state unless acted on by a net outside force." Newton's Second Law says that if there is a net outside force, then the object of mass m will *accelerate* according to the equation $F_{net} = ma$. So once the ship you're towing is moving at the same speed as the *Enterprise,* why not simply turn off the tractor beam and save energy? It will move right along with the ship!

It is a common misconception that a force is required to keep an object in motion because on Earth, the *force* of friction acts to slow objects down. In fact, to maintain constant velocity, what is required is a complete *absence* of a net force.

Net force means the effective sum of all the forces acting on an object. To have zero net force requires that either no forces act on an object, or alternatively, several forces are acting that cancel each other out. For example, if you want to push a box along the floor at a constant velocity, the force with which you push must be exactly equal to the opposing force of friction. Your pushing force is only greater than friction when you are speeding up. If there is no friction, once the box is in motion (relative to you of course—since we need to remember that all motion is relative) you don't need to apply any force to keep it in motion.

The writers of *Star Trek* often seem to fall for the quaintly Aristotelian view of physics that force is required to maintain a state of motion. The view is reinforced by the impression that whenever the *Enterprise* is "in motion," the engines are on. Of course, a supply of energy, and therefore engine power, would be required when traveling at warp speeds, since the warp drive seems to work by stretching and compressing space-time (according to Einstein's Theory of General Relativity), rather than by applying an actual forward directed force or thrust. But traveling at a constant "sub-light" or impulse velocity would require the complete absence of thrust. Question: Without friction or other disturbing force, what do you need to do to *maintain* constant velocity? Answer: Nothing! (And don't turn on those engines unless you want to accelerate.)

Inertial dampers

H ere's where the creators of *Star Trek* realized they had a problem and got busy. What is that problem? Well consider: on a typical leisurely day in space, the *Enterprise* may need to engage its impulse engines. Full impulse usually means a velocity of one fourth the speed of light, or 7.5 x 10⁷ m/s. So let's say the *Enterprise* is leaving spacedock at Starbase 10 and accelerates to full impulse (relative to the starbase). It seems that typically it takes maybe 20 or 30 seconds to get up to speed. What acceleration is required? Well, we can do a very simple calculation, assuming it takes 30 seconds to achieve full impulse. Acceleration is equal to the rate of change of velocity:

$$a = \Delta v/\Delta t = (7.5 \times 10^7 \text{ m/s} - 0 \text{ m/s})/30 \text{ s}$$
$$= 2.5 \times 10^6 \text{ m/s}^2$$

or about 250,000 "g's." Well that's a pretty big acceleration. What might that do to a human body? We can calculate the force exerted on an average-sized crew member having a mass of about 80 kg using Newton's Second Law:

$$F = ma = (80\text{kg})(2.5 \times 10^6 \text{ m/s}) = 2.0 \times 10^8 \text{ N, or about } 23,000 \text{ tons.}$$

I'll let you decide what it might feel like to experience a force of 23,000 tons.

Recognizing the problem inherent with accelerations and forces of these magnitudes, the creators of *TNG* cleverly incorporated into their 24th century technology the idea of "inertial dampers," which are somehow able to nullify the effects of these tremendous accelerations. Because anything with mass has inertia, or a resistance to a change in motion, a force is required to accelerate a mass. However, if somehow you could eliminate inertia, it wouldn't take any force to accelerate you! How these work, we really couldn't say, but at least the producers are acknowledging a very real physics issue.

Sound in space

Do we even need to say it? Everyone knows this one but still it bears repeating. Ready? *Sound cannot propogate through a vacuum.* It needs a medium made of matter to travel. Space is a vacuum. Photon torpedoes should be seen, not heard. Space battles (from a vantage point outside the ship) would be conducted in dead silence. We should not hear the *Enterprise* whooshing by when it engages the warp drive. Only from inside the ship can you hear sound. This is the most common and egregious cinematic sci-fi error, and completely unnecessary in my opinion. Imagine the dramatic tension of a space battle, where all the silent action viewed from outside the ships is juxtaposed with quick cuts back to the deafening chaos inside an embattled star cruiser. Now, that is a scene that I would love to see, but unfortunately never do.

Artificial gravity and jostling ships

Some of the best moments from the original *Star Trek* occur when the *Enterprise* is jostled by Klingon weapons fire, or by contact with some type of energy field, and Captain Kirk, Mr. Spock and the rest of the bridge crew are flung (fling themselves?) around the set in an overly dramatic and slightly comical way.

Now, presumably everyone is able to stand comfortably on the ship's decks due to some form of artificial gravity. In the *Star Trek: The Next Generation Technical Manual,* there is some vaguely comprehensible gibberish about using gravitons (the actual theoretical, although not yet discovered in the real world, particles that transmit the gravitational force). And this is a fine example of using real theory to justify something on the show.

However, it is amusing that the artificial gravity always seems to point "straight down" in the *frame of reference of your television screen,* which seems to be the normal frame of reference for the *Enterprise,* and perhaps constitutes some absolute reference frame, because whenever the ship "tilts" due to a violent attack, everyone falls down the incline and crashes into the instruments. In *Star Trek II: The Wrath of Khan,* there is even a gauge on the bridge that shows the ship's orientation relative to some absolute "horizontal." You would think that the ship's designers would have found it a lot simpler to make the artificial gravity maintain a constant direction relative to the ship.

So where does this all leave us? Have the producers, writers, directors, and technical advisors of *Star Trek* overlooked some fundamental laws of physics in the day-to-day grind of creating a string of popular hit series? Well, yes. But does that detract from our enjoyment of the shows. I think not! And for some of us, investigating the idiosyncrasies in the physics actually augments the experience.

Finally, remember how much fun it is to watch those old episodes? Recall that fever pitch of dramatic tension that Kirk, Spock, McCoy and company achieve as they spiral towards a high voltage climax (something at which none of the sequels has ever fully succeeded in my opinion)? In the heat of all of that excitement, let us not forget Scotty's powerful and classic admonition "I canna change the laws of physics!" Well, sometimes they do anyway, but I wouldn't have it any other way.

ADAM WEINER is a physics teacher and author of Don't Try This at Home! The Physics of Hollywood Movies *(Kaplan Publishing). He has also written articles on Hollywood science for the* Popular Science *online magazine. He is a big fan of the original* Star Trek.

MOON OVER LUNA

BY DAVID R. GEORGE III

Illustrated by Mishi McCaig

It appeared in the sky with no warning at all, and with no explanation.

I didn't see it at first. When I turned our car into the apartment complex where we live, though, I noted that several people had congregated at the far end of the parking lot. The group stood between two of the four buildings in the development. Everybody peered in the same direction, their backs to us, their chins raised as they all gazed upward into the gathering dusk. Whatever the object of their attentions, it seemed hidden from our view by Building #4.

"What are they doing?" asked my daughter from the front passenger seat. At eleven years old, Cassie had begun the sixth grade last month. Just as I now do every Monday and Wednesday during this first quarter of the school year, I'd stayed at work half an hour later today so that I could pick her up from field-hockey practice on my way home; on Tuesdays and Thursdays, she meets with the debate society and I have to leave early to get her. "Is it a new plane, Dad?"

"I don't know, honey," I said. "Maybe." I'd actually had the same thought. They call Wichita the *Air Capital* because of the numerous aircraft manufacturers that have called the city home throughout the years: Boeing, Cessna, Beechcraft, Learjet, and others. It's not unusual to spy unmarked planes overhead from time to time as they're taken on shakedown flights.

I pulled our car into an open parking space, into the veritable canyon formed by the mammoth sport utility vehicles that rose high on either side. With oil prices skyrocketing for years now, I couldn't believe that people still drove such gas-guzzling behemoths. Then again, our entire family consisted of only one adult and one child, so we didn't have much need to tote around many passengers or a lot of cargo.

As Cassie collected her knapsack and field-hockey stick from the back seat, I reached in for my briefcase. I didn't usually carry it to and from work, instead leaving it in my cubicle, but today I'd had to cart home a couple of manuals, a few relevant program printouts, and the department cell phone, since I'd be on call this week. I liked my job for the most part—designing and coding computer solutions to the real-world issues facing the company can be genuinely satisfying—but I dreaded those after-midnight emergencies when some technical error took down one of the nightly batch processes. The shrill chirp of the cell phone would rouse me so that somebody from operations could fill me in on the problem. Even a quick resolution—and rarely did any fix require less than two or three hours worth of work—would leave me feeling foggy and sleep-deprived for days.

Cassie and I stepped up onto the sidewalk and started for our building. The weather had grown markedly cooler this past weekend, and right now, Indian summer continued its retreat, the brisk twilight promising a chilly night. I put a hand on Cassie's back as we headed for our apartment, but then she looked back over her shoulder and said, "Can we go see?" She gestured with her field-hockey stick toward Building #4—we lived in #1—toward where the small crowd had assembled. After a long Monday and now confronting the prospect of interrupted slumber tonight and in the coming week, I wanted nothing more than to go home, to have dinner with my daughter, and then later, after putting her to bed, to fall asleep in my own room while watching Letterman or maybe reading a book. But I hesitated just enough for Cassie to squeeze in an extra entreaty—"Please, Dad"—and as with so many of the little things in her young life, I couldn't say no to her.

"All right," I agreed. I took the field-hockey stick from her and tucked it under my other arm, then reached for her hand. We strolled together along the walkway that ran alongside the parking lot before it curved in between Buildings #3 and #4. As we approached the people there, I saw the familiar faces of tenants, including one of whom I'd taken particular notice recently. With Cassie in tow, I made my way toward Jill, our new, attractive, and decidedly single next-door neighbor. Before we reached her, though, I spotted the manager of the complex, Mrs. Crenshaw, standing frozen, her mouth agape. The old woman's mien of amazement halted me in my tracks. Only after Cassie stopped beside me and began to look around did I become aware of the abnormal silence about us. It struck me as peculiar that not only did I not hear the far-off roar of aircraft engines, but not a single person around us spoke.

As I regarded the quiet, motionless people intently peering upward, Cassie asked, "What's *that?*" Clearly puzzled, she released my hand and pointed toward the sky, toward where everybody else stared. I followed the direction of Cassie's finger and found myself gazing at the Moon. Unintentionally mimicking Mrs. Crenshaw, I felt my own jaw drop.

Full and silvery white in the crisp autumn air, the Moon held its place in the heavens as it had for all of human history and before. The bright sphere remained as unchanged as ever, but it no longer traced its orbit alone. A second white orb had joined the scene, hovering inexplicably beside the only natural satellite that the Earth had ever known.

Until now.

Standing in the alley, Julian Palleros could not turn away from the sight of the dual moons. He tried to envision some means by which the late-afternoon Los Angeles sky could have been gimmicked to provide such a spectacle, but even in Hollywood, the land of professional make-believe, he couldn't. A feeling of astonishment gripped him, mitigated only by a measure of personal relief.

Just a few minutes earlier, Palleros sat in his dressing room, reading through his copy a second time as he attempted to make sense of the lead news item. *Reached for their opinions,* the final paragraph began, *astronomers at the Palomar Observatory would offer no statement at this time on the precise nature or possible origins of the object. Additionally, they declined comment on whether any of the observatory's telescopes would now be employed to study the mysterious globe. When questioned about the chances of extraterrestrial life being involved—*

Palleros dropped his arm heavily onto the sofa, the sheets of the script in his hand creasing noisily as he did so. "'Extraterrestrial life,'" he said disgustedly, his voice loud in the small room. "ET's and mysterious objects."

He suspected another ill-conceived prank. How else could he justify such a ludicrous story? Last month, one of the news writers had slipped into his pages a fabricated report of an escaped python in

La Jolla that had swallowed whole two dogs, a cat, and a bicycle. Palleros had carried the fictitious account out to the anchor desk with him, and when the teleprompter had failed during the broadcast—somewhat suspiciously, he would later think—he'd nearly gone live with the outrageous item. To his embarrassment, Regina, his co-anchor, had glanced at his text during a commercial break and had come to his rescue, pointing out the gag. Though no one had confessed to the misguided deed and no culprit had been unmasked, Palleros had complained bitterly about the incident to the executive producer, who in turn had made it clear to the entire writing staff that they'd all lose their jobs if anything like that happened again.

"And yet here this is," Palleros muttered to himself, waving the obviously bogus story through the air. He checked the clock hanging on the wall beside the sofa and saw that he had twenty minutes until air. *Plenty of time for heads to roll,* he thought with some satisfaction.

Script in hand, Palleros stalked out of his dressing room, intending to find the exec. Instead, he nearly ran headlong into Josh Durgin, one of the news writers. "What is this?" Palleros demanded without preamble, brandishing the pages of his copy out before him. "An unknown object suddenly appearing next to the Moon?" he scoffed. "Should I also tell viewers that it's actually the eye of a giant snake that's going to devour the Moon?"

Palleros watched as Durgin transitioned through a series of recognizable expressions: surprise, confusion, and finally comprehension. "Julian," Durgin said, motioning to the script, "that story is *real.*"

"It... what?" Palleros replied weakly. He'd anticipated resistance, argument, even outright denial, but not a brazen ef-

fort to sustain this practical joke conducted at his expense.

"You don't have to believe me," Durgin said. "Just go outside and look for yourself." Then he edged past the news anchor and strode down the corridor.

Palleros stood quietly for a moment, peering after Durgin as he walked away. When the writer had rounded the corner at the end of the hall and passed out of sight, Palleros chose to heed his suggestion, ridiculously unnecessary as it seemed. Once he had done so, once he had gone outside and put the lie to the twin-moons tale, he would add Durgin's counterfeit advice to the list of the writers' transgressions.

Palleros paced to the nearest stairwell and pounded down a half-flight to a pair of metal doors. He stiff-armed the crossbar and pushed out into the fall afternoon, into the alleyway running along the back of the studio. He set his eyes on the Moon at once, the grayish white disk dull but distinct in the fading daytime light.

He also saw the new mass in the sky.

Now, a solid minute of scrutiny became two. The full Moon looked to Palleros no different than he'd ever seen it, the pale planetoid mutely regarding the Earth with its vaguely face-like aspect. Above it and to the left floated the second orb, similarly white with ashy patches. It largely resembled the Moon, though it appeared much smaller in size.

Palleros didn't know what he should think or how he should feel. Curiosity and wonder mixed in his mind with incredulity and fear. His concerns about a sabotaged news script quickly vanished, such personal considerations plainly insignificant. Instead, the sight of the second moon—or whatever it turned out to be—enthralled him. He reflected on what he knew about the solar system, and he could only assume that a rogue asteroid had been captured by the Moon's—or perhaps the Earth's—gravitational field.

But aren't asteroids usually smaller and irregularly shaped? he asked himself. And if an asteroid, wouldn't scientists have been tracking its approach for some time now? As a newsman, Palleros surely would have learned of such efforts.

A door slammed off to the left, down the alley. Palleros turned to see that several people from the building had come outside. A woman he didn't recognize lifted her hand to the sky, while a man—one of the lighting technicians, he thought—chattered excitedly.

His reverie broken, Palleros realized that he had just a few minutes before airtime. He stole a final glimpse of the spatial intruder, then returned inside and headed for the set. Almost immediately, he had to take his place behind the anchor desk with Regina, where he prepared to deliver to the greater Los Angeles area the few details known to that point about the day's events.

"Our top story," he intoned at the top of the hour, "a large astronomical body has appeared in the skies above our planet." On his monitor, he saw over his right shoulder an inset depicting the unexplained globe along with the words *NEW MOON?* "Accounts of the previously unknown and as yet unidentified object first turned up in the Central Time Zone, where people reported seeing it start to emerge from behind the Moon approximately two hours ago. The spherical body has now come completely into view and seems to be in orbit about the Moon."

The picture on the monitor changed, this time showing a full-screen image of the Moon and its counterpart. Palleros paused, the surreality of the current circumstances abruptly threatening to overwhelm him. Making an effort to keep himself steady, he focused on the 'prompter and forced himself to continue.

"Officials at the National Aeronautics and Space Administration estimate the size of the object at five hundred miles in diameter," he said, "about a quarter that of the Moon. Though they would not immediately speculate on its mass, they did indicate the possibility that it could have some impact on the tides and weather systems here on Earth."

Just what we need, Palleros thought. *First global climate change, now this.*

"In Washington, D.C.," he went on, "the White House has yet to issue a formal statement, but the President is expected to address the nation later tonight. Meanwhile, a spokesman for the Department of Homeland Security has urged citizens to stay calm, insisting that the country is in no immediate danger. At the same time, he added that the government has not ruled out the involvement of terrorists in this matter." Palleros suppressed the impulse to shake his head at the outlandish notion that Islamic extremists—or anybody else, for that matter—might have had something to do with the unforeseen arrival of a new moon above the planet.

He finished the opening story for the newscast, concluding by raising the idea of alien beings being involved, a question about which astronomers at Mt. Palomar refused to conjecture. Palleros then threw the feed over to Kim Wong, one of the station's field reporters. The caption at the bottom of the screen showed that she'd taken to the streets of Pasadena for the broadcast. One after another, clips played of Kim asking ordinary individuals for their reactions to Earth's "second moon." Most revealed shock and bewilderment, unable to offer even any wild guesses about how or why this had happened. One young man, though, proposed that a movie studio might be conducting an extreme marketing campaign in support of some new science-fiction film premiering soon, while an older man wondered aloud if China might somehow be behind it all.

The relatively calm demeanor of the interviewed people surprised Palleros. For all anybody knew right now, the world might be facing terrible danger. Still, he heard nothing truly meaningful until the last person with whom Kim spoke. The woman, identified on-screen as *Amy from La Cañada,* gave voice to the thought—to the feeling, really—that had grown in Palleros's mind ever since he'd first seen the baffling new object hanging above the Earth. "I don't know what's going on up there," said Amy from La Cañada, her gaze drifting skyward, "but I don't think things are ever going to be the same again."

Palleros could not have agreed more.

◎ ne evening in late December, around the holidays, the government confirmed a rumor that had been circulating for two months, ever since the appearance of Earth's second moon.

At the time I learned of this, Cassie and I sat on opposite sides of the coffee table in our living room, surrounded by the Christmas decorations we'd put up the previous weekend. Festooned with garlands, sparkling white lights, and ornaments, our short but full tree stood at the end of the room, in front of the sliding glass doors that led out onto our small, second-floor balcony. The scent of pine filled the apartment, and the strains of carols drifted up from the radio. Cassie sat cross-legged on the floor, while I perched on the edge of the couch. Between us on the oaken tabletop lay a tape dispenser, two pair of scissors, and several rolls and discarded scraps of colorful gift paper, as well as a stack of presents that we'd spent the afternoon wrapping.

"Well, kiddo, that about does it," I said, tired not just from the afternoon's efforts, but from weeks of shopping and decorating and preparing for the holiday season. "And not a moment too soon," I observed. The next morning, we'd be heading over to the home of Cassie's Aunt Barbara— my former sister-in-law—where we would join Barb, her husband, and her two children in celebrating Christmas.

In point of fact, I suppose that Barbara remains my in-law, even though the link that connected us together—my wife, her sister—is gone now. After the accident, it just seemed easier to think of Barb as Cassie's aunt rather than as Gwen's sister. Even well more than two years later, it still seemed easier.

"What about this one?" Cassie asked, pulling out a long, narrow box from beneath the table. Through clear, hard plastic, I saw the gold-shirted action figure of the character who I had in my youth watched command the starship *Enterprise.* We'd picked up the Captain Kirk toy for Charlie, Barb's thirteen-year-old son.

"Oh no," I said, dropping sideways onto the couch, exaggerating my fatigue. I peeked over at the pile of wrapped gifts. "Maybe we already have enough presents for Charlie," I jokingly suggested.

"Da-ad," Cassie said, drawing the word out into two long syllables. "You know he loves *Star Trek.*"

"I know, I know," I said. I eyed the heap of gifts we'd already finished. "But if I have to wrap one more present..." I let my voice trail off.

"Oh, Dad," Cassie admonished me, reaching for a roll of red paper adorned with snow-covered wreaths. "I can do it."

"That's a good girl," I told her, sitting up straight again and leaning forward to ruffle the auburn hair she'd inherited from her mother. She swatted my hand away, then set to wrapping Charlie's gift. "While you're doing that, I'll go start dinner for us."

"That's a good boy," Cassie said without looking up. I laughed at the remark, delighted by my daughter's blossoming sense of humor. As I began to rise, the urgent notes of "Carol of the Bells" came to a close, giving way to a news summary. I sat back down to listen.

"This afternoon, the National Aeronautics and Space Administration announced its intention to send a spacecraft to Aurora." In the days after the initial sighting of the new moon, numerous names had arisen for it: Gemini, Selene, Eos, Luna II, and plenty of others. Astronomers had provided their own official designation—JE1335 or something like that—but neither the media nor the public at large had accepted the technical appellation for general usage. Eventually, the name Aurora—in Roman mythology, goddess of the dawn and sister of Luna—had gained favor.

"According to NASA Administrator Adrienne Finestra," the report went on, "final production and testing of the Ares V heavy-lift vehicle will be accelerated in order to meet a launch window in May of next year. Although consideration was given to a manned expedition, Finestra indicated that the first of what will probably be a series of missions will be automated, in the interests of both safety and the swiftness with which the operation can be undertaken. The project has been named Artemis."

I understood the need for safety, considering that no credible explanation for the existence of Aurora had yet been found; several scientific hypotheses had been advanced, but none had survived serious examination. For the same reason—having an unexplained object materialize out of the blue so close to the Earth—speed seemed like a sensible aim as well. If Aurora posed a threat, better to discover that sooner rather than later.

Across from me, apparently paying no attention to the broadcast, Cassie worked a pair of scissors through the wrapping paper. "The governments of Russia and China," continued the news reader, "have vowed to lodge formal protests through the United Nations about the U.S. decision to exclude the international community from its plans. Member nations of the European Union are also expected to register a joint objection.

"In other news—"

As I picked up the remote control for the stereo system and began scanning through the stations, I wondered for a moment why other countries would oppose a strictly American mission to Aurora. No other nation or group of nations had accomplished as much beyond the Earth as the United States had. Further, the U.S. had conducted its nonmilitary space program with an unparalleled level of transparency, something likely to continue in this case, given the open disclosure of the coming Aurora mission. Still the only country ever to land human beings on the Moon and return them safely to Earth, America had time and again demonstrated its benign—

The Moon, I realized. Though I couldn't remember the exact details about it—if I'd ever known them—I did recall the existence of an international treaty that restricted the use of the Moon to peaceful purposes; I think it also prohibited the extraction of resources by individual nations. To this point, I'd heard of no such accord being established for Aurora. Perhaps other countries feared that the United States would take advantage of the situation and claim the new world for itself.

On the tuner, I located another station featuring Christmas songs, so I discontinued the scan. On the floor, Cassie worked at folding the wrapping paper around Charlie's gift. "Dinner will be in about half an hour," I said as I climbed to my feet and headed for the kitchen. There, I opened the refrigerator and pulled out a ham steak and the fixings for a salad, then plucked two different packages of vegetables from the freezer.

As I set to making our evening meal, my mind returned to the radio report. Word of the U.S. sending a mission up to Aurora had circulated for some time among the general populace, so NASA's announcement hadn't come unexpectedly. It occurred to me, though, that I had been looking forward to a manned expedition. As with just about everybody else on Earth, I wanted to know how and why Aurora had come to orbit the Moon, what effect it ultimately would have on mankind, and really, just what it was.

A rock, I told myself. *Merely an undistinguished mass of minerals floating through space, snared by the Moon's gravity.* Except that astronomers hadn't observed Aurora approaching the Earth, nor had they been able to detect any indication of it at all in any of the routine recordings made of the skies in the days leading up to its arrival. Perhaps of greater note, orbital mechanics could identify no flight path that would have resulted in Aurora's current circular course about the Moon.

I put down the bag of frozen peas I'd just opened and moved to the sink, to the small window above it that looked out the back side of our apartment. I peered out across the span of snow that stretched from our building out toward Rock Road. Though it wasn't even six-thirty yet, the winter night had already fallen. Patchy clouds interrupted the starscape here and there, but I did not see the Moon or its

companion. I leaned in over the sink and craned my neck, first to one side, then to the other. Finally, I caught sight of the paired orbs, though they showed not as disks, but as a larger and a smaller crescent.

Even all these weeks after seeing Aurora for the first time, I hadn't grown accustomed to its place in the sky. In truth, it stirred me, not in some intellectual vein that could be explained by the mystery surrounding it, but in a visceral way. Aurora *felt* like an intruder, and therefore like a threat, but it also seemed like something more. I couldn't account for it, but something nagged at the back of my thoughts, like a long-known fact that defies recollection. It troubled me, weighed on me, yet I hadn't been able to name it, let alone give it voice.

"Dad?"

I jumped a bit, startled out of my woolgathering. I turned to see my daughter standing at the threshold of the kitchen, in front of the small table where we shared our meals. "Yes, honey, what is it?"

Cassie held up Charlie's gift, now wrapped. "I just wanted to tell you that I finished," she said. "I'll put all the other presents in shopping bags, so we'll be ready to go tomorrow."

"Great," I said. "I'll call you when dinner's ready."

Cassie nodded her head, but she made no move to leave. Finally, she asked, "Are you all right?"

"Yes," I answered automatically. No matter what happened in my life, as Cassie's lone parent, I had to be all right all the time. She needed me, and I knew that.

Except I could see that Cassie could tell something bothered me. Though still more than a year away from being a teenager, she had already developed a strong intuition, an ability to read emotion in other people, including adults, even if she didn't always understand the emotions involved. She stood there and regarded me with her young eyes, and I knew I needed to say more.

"I was just looking at the Moon," I offered.

"At the Moon?" Cassie said, putting Charlie's present on the counter and walking over to where I stood at the sink. "Or at Aurora?"

"Well... more at Aurora," I admitted. I glanced out the window again, bending in over the double basin until I once again saw the thin arc of Earth's instant second moon.

In that moment, I thought of Gwen.

I often did. In February, Cassie and I would mark the third anniversary of the accident that had taken her from us, but I honestly couldn't assert that there had been a single day since then when I hadn't thought of my departed wife. It didn't help that my daughter grew with each passing day to look more and more like her.

Still, the loss had gotten easier to bear with time, to the point where I had not only begun to notice other women, but to finally consider the possibility of dating again. I certainly didn't envision remarrying, or even becoming too seriously involved, but recently I'd ruminated about how nice it would be just to share an evening with somebody—to go to dinner, see a movie, sit and talk, that sort of thing.

But gazing up at Aurora, memories of Gwen recurred strongly to me, almost as though she had something to do with the mystifying object, or it with her. I should have felt haunted, but I didn't. Instead of my normal lingering sadness, I experienced a rising hope.

Beside me, Cassie stood on tiptoe and pulled herself up across the sink, obviously attempting to peer out at the Moon and Aurora. I stepped back and swept her up, holding her out toward the window so that she could see too. After a few seconds, she asked, "Does Aurora bother you, Dad?"

"Does it *bother* me?" I repeated, unsure what to make of the question. Day by day, I'd avidly followed the news reports about Aurora. Not a week passed without scientists positing some new theory to account for it. None had been particularly compelling, and not a single one had stood up under analysis. "I'm very curious about it, but I wouldn't say it bothers me," I told Cassie, setting her back down on the floor. "What do you think about it?"

Cassie shrugged. "It's just Aurora," she said. It was somewhere else, and now it's here." She spoke with little inflection, giving no indication that she had any real interest in the subject.

"But what do you *think* it is?" I asked. I wondered if her impassive manner might belie an underlying discomfort, perhaps something like the uneasy association my own mind had drawn between Aurora and Gwen.

"I don't know," she said. "It is what it is." She shrugged again. "It doesn't even matter anyway. People won't agree, and once it's gone, they never will."

"Wait," I said. "You think Aurora will go away?"

"I guess," Cassie replied. Apparently wanting to say nothing more about it, she retrieved Charlie's present from atop the counter. "I'll go put this and the others in the shopping bags, then I'm going to read my book until dinner." Gwen and I had cultivated in Cassie a love of reading.

"Okay, honey," I said. "I'll call you to set the table."

Cassie left, and I turned my attention to preparing our dinner. As I emptied the bag of frozen peas into a pot, a wave of disappointment washed over me. Aurora had seized my imagination in several different ways, but it evidently had failed to engage my daughter much at all. For some reason, it pained me not to be able to share this with her in a more meaningful way.

I placed the pot of peas on the stove, then couldn't resist moving back to the sink and taking one last glimpse out the window. The two tapering wisps of light looked as though they formed an element of the backdrop from a sci-fi movie. Decades worth of memories of the night sky told me that the smaller arc didn't belong there, but for the first time, I thought it added beauty to the panorama.

And again, unaccountably, I thought of my dead wife.

s instructed, the studio audience clapped. Melanie Astor found her mark and took her place as the stage manager counted her down from five. She watched the burly man hold up the appropriate number of fingers until he reached one, and then he pointed at her. Atop the stage-left television camera, the red in-use indicator light flashed on.

"Welcome back to *The Melanie Astor Show,*" Astor said, her voice reining in the audience, the sound of their applause diminishing like a heavy rain coming to a swift stop. "Our topic today," she said, speaking into her handheld wireless microphone, "is what the unmanned Artemis mission will find when it heads to Aurora four months from now. So far, we've spoken with cosmologists from the University of Chicago, who view Earth's second moon as nothing more than a captured asteroid. Our next guests, though, have a very different opinion." She paused, allowing time for her last sentence to provoke both those in the studio and those watching at home. Then, raising her empty hand in the direction of the talk-show set at center stage, she said, "Would

you please welcome Doctor Amala Shastri and Doctor Douglas Linders."

A man and a woman walked out from backstage, and the studio audience dutifully brought their hands together once more. Astor padded toward the three easy chairs arrayed around the low, circular coffee table, but stopped short of the platform upon which they sat. She waited for her guests to take their seats before saying, "So, Doctor Shastri, Doctor Linders, why don't you tell our audience what it is you do?"

The man and the woman looked at each other, as though to determine which of them should speak first. After just a moment, Shastri looked over at Astor and said, "We're both psychologists specializing in social dynamics."

"Psychologists," Astor repeated, emphasizing the point. She noted that neither Shastri nor Linders seemed nervous, despite this being their first appearances on television. Through the years she'd been hosting her own show, Astor had seen most neophytes betray some level of anxiety; those who didn't, she'd learned, felt an intense compulsion to be there. Whether the two psychologists simply sought their fifteen minutes of fame or they truly wanted to get their message out remained to be seen.

"So, from your professional vantage," Astor went on, "what can you tell us about the sudden advent of this second moon above us?" She motioned to a point just behind the guests, to where the most famous photograph taken during the past three months appeared on a large screen. In the picture, the Moon floated full and tinted slightly orange above the nighttime Manhattan skyline, and with it, so too did Aurora. Both Shastri and Linders glanced back over their shoulders at the nocturnal landscape.

"This," Linders said, turning back to

face the audience, "is a delusion."

Confused murmurs percolated up in the studio. Astor and her producers had expected such a reaction—had *wanted* such a reaction. Discussion of interesting issues helped keep the cameras rolling, but controversy brought in the real dough. Astor stepped up onto the platform and over to the empty chair, but she did not sit just yet. "A delusion," she said. *"Whose* delusion?" She knew the answer, and that her viewers would never buy it.

Linders held Astor's gaze for so long that she actually thought he might not respond, but then he looked out at the audience. "It's *everybody's* delusion," he said, as though challenging all those assembled. Astor heard several boos surface amid the buzz.

"Now wait a minute," she said, finally sitting down as she cast herself as the spokesperson for her viewers. "Are you saying that this—" she pointed up at image of the Moon and Aurora—"isn't real?"

"It's real," Shastri said, "but only in the minds of those who observe it."

"It is an example of mass hysteria," Linders claimed.

"So the two of you genuinely believe that everybody on Earth, all seven billion of us, are essentially seeing things?" Astor asked. It no longer amazed her that her producers could find people to say the most outrageous things on national television.

"We don't know for a fact that *everybody* on Earth thinks that they see Aurora," Shastri pointed out.

"Well, no, I suppose not," Astor allowed, "but isn't that really a distinction without a difference? Certainly millions, billions, of people do see Aurora."

"That seems to be the case," Linders agreed.

"Let me ask you this," Astor said. "Do

you see Aurora?"

Linders smiled. "Yes," he admitted, "I do."

"And so do I," Shastri added.

he audience responded with a mixture of gasps and snickers. Astor herself might have had to suppress a smile of her own had the revelation not angered her. She had no problem interviewing publicity hounds, but she needed them to at least put up something of a sustained argument. "Then how can you even suggest that this is all a delusion?" she demanded. "I mean, if you perceive Aurora, then what reason do you have to think that it's not actually real?" The idea seemed absurd on the face of it.

"We can make this claim," Shastri said, "because of a pattern of behavior in our society, not just here in the United States, but all around the world."

"One of the chief components required for mass delusion is for there to be prevailing socioeconomic ills throughout the region affected," Linders said. "Certainly the state of affairs in the world today is precarious at best, what with all of the wars being waged, the genocides being perpetrated, the extreme weather conditions brought about by global climate change, the growing healthcare crisis, and the overall lack of confidence in governmental authorities. Coupled with the ready conduit of twenty-four-hour news channels to propagate word of all these problems, there is ample evidence that conditions are ripe for communal hysteria."

"Additionally," Shastri added, "the inability of astronomers to provide even a functional working theory that would explain Aurora demonstrates the impossibility of there actually being this second moon. That also plays into people's fears and further strengthens the delusion."

Astor saw expressions of disbelief on the faces of the audience, watched them wave away the very idea the two psychologists proposed. She'd seen such reactions before and knew that she was on the verge of losing their attention. She needed either to offer support for the two doctors, or to take the audience's side and seriously challenge them. Since she could see no reasonable way to do the former, she chose the latter. "Even if we agree with all of that—" she started, but she didn't really know how best to argue such an unprovable premise. During her college days, back when she'd planned on a career in journalism and not as a daytime talk-show personality, she'd taken a humanities elective in philosophy. She recalled the account of Bishop George Berkeley, who asserted that because people's interactions with the universe came wholly by way of sensation, which occurred in the mind, humanity therefore could not prove the reality of matter, which existed outside the mind. When faced with the virtually indisputable argument, Samuel Johnson simply put his boot into a stone and famously avowed, "I refute Berkeley thus." Astor decided on a similar tack, rising from her chair and making her way behind the set to where the photograph of Aurora and the Moon still showed on the screen. "Even if everything about the stresses we're all feeling is true," she said, then opened her hand toward the picture, "what about *this?*"

"It is akin to the UFO phenomenon," Shastri said, "in which not only individuals but entire communities have reported seeing flying saucers or alien spacecraft."

"But there are planes and helicopters in the skies that can be mistaken for other things," Astor said, walking out toward the audience, putting physical distance between herself and the two psychologists. "There aren't wayward moons buzzing about the Earth."

"Ms. Astor," Linders said with an attitude of forbearance, "there have been numerous documented cases of mass hysteria throughout human history. There have never been witches, and yet the trials in Salem in the seventeenth century found many men and women guilty of sorcery. Nineteen of them were put to death for their imagined crimes."

"But that's different too, isn't it?" Astor said, surprised to see in Linders an intensity that showed that he actually believed his claims. "I mean, you're talking about a handful of people in a community who believed in the supernatural to begin with, and we're talking about billions of people seeing one single, particular thing in which nobody believed until three months ago."

"It is different only in magnitude," Linders said. "In Salem and the surrounding villages in the sixteen hundreds, people believed that they had witnessed men and women exercise magical powers. In this case, people believe that they're seeing a new moon."

"And as a recent poll discovered," Shastri said, "a large majority of people think that Aurora poses a significant threat to humanity."

"I see," Astor said. "So you must think that when Artemis reaches Aurora—or the point in space where we all believe Aurora to be—the sensors on the ship will prove you right. There won't be anything there for Artemis to land on."

"No, there won't be," Linders said, "but the delusion may well continue. The technicians at NASA monitoring the flight expect that the ship will land on Aurora, and so they may read their instruments in such a way that those expectations are borne out."

Astor smiled, seeing even more parallels with Berkeley's idealistic philosophy.

"So even if it appears that Artemis lands on Aurora, you still won't be convinced of Aurora's existence," she said, shaking her head, wondering how this supposedly scholarly argument could be anything but a put-up job. "How did the two of you come to all of this?"

"We did so separately," Shastri said, obviously bristling at the implication that she and Linders were not legitimate. "We were not colleagues prior to this, but our observations and research led us to the same inferences. We're now working on a technical paper outlining our evidence, as well as suggesting how best we might deal with the situation."

"All right then," Astor said. She glanced at the show clock to confirm the time, then turned toward the nearest camera, waited for the in-use indicator to light to wink on, and spoke into it. "When we come back, we'll take questions here in the studio and phone calls from you at home. Aurora: is it real or all in our heads? When we come back."

She waited for the in-use light to go dark and the stage manager to confirm that the show had gone to a commercial break, then she looked back over at Linders and Shastri. Astor had welcomed all manner of guests to her program in the four years she'd been on the air, many of them downtrodden or troubled in some way, most far less educated than the two psychologists sitting on the stage, and quite a few of them had made outrageous claims about their own lives. But never before had Astor wanted to ask the question that now occurred to her. *Do you really believe all of this,* she wanted to know of the doctors, *or did you just want to be on television?*

Astor chose not to ask the question. For one thing, it would be discourteous. For another, she realized that she didn't want to know the answer. She couldn't counte-

nance what Shastri and Linders were claiming, but at the same time, something about their arguments nagged at her. *What if they're right?* she thought suddenly and unexpectedly. *What would that say about humanity?*

I sat in the booth across the table from Jill, feeling more than a little out of place. I couldn't quite figure out how to sit comfortably or where to put my hands. The vision of Jill's bright blue eyes gazing back at me, of her lovely face framed by her shoulder-length blonde hair, set me staring down at the tabletop or out the window to my right. But as I watched a curl of snow flutter across the pond beside which the restaurant stood, I resolved to conquer my restiveness. With an effort, I folded my hands together in front of me, then looked over to regard my date.

My date, I thought with some amazement as Jill smiled warmly at me. I hadn't been out with a woman—let alone on Valentine's Day—since my wife had died three years ago, and if going to dinner or the movies with Gwen didn't qualify as dating, well, then it had been more like fifteen years, back before our wedding. *And it shows,* I scolded myself. After depositing Cassie with Barbara and her family for an overnight stay, I'd knocked on Jill's door, then had spent the drive to the restaurant talking about the relative mildness of this year's winter, about how on many days in the past months the temperature had risen into the sixties and even the seventies. Not exactly scintillating conversation, I knew.

"So, Jonathan," Jill said, "did you grow up in Kansas?" She had apparently decided not to wait any longer for me to take the lead on our date. Maybe she even sensed my discomfort. *Probably* she did.

"No, I'm a transplant," I said, and even revealing that minute bit of information about myself seemed strange. Gwen, of course, had known virtually everything about my life. "I'm from the East Coast originally," I explained, forcing myself to go on. "Upstate New York. But I went to college in Indiana, then got a job straight out of school in Kansas City. My job got outsourced about six years ago, which is when we moved to Wichita." I stumbled over the word *we*.

"Cassie's adorable," Jill said. She and my daughter had become fast friends when Jill had moved in to the complex last year. If Cassie hadn't mentioned Gwen's death to her, I'm sure that at least one of the neighbors must have done so. Regardless, casual observation would have told Jill that Cassie and I lived by ourselves, otherwise I'm sure that she never would have suggested having dinner together.

"She's terrific, but obviously I'm biased," I said. "She really likes you."

"I'm glad," Jill said, smiling again. She really had a nice way about her, I thought, not to mention being very attractive. At forty-two, I was six or seven years older than Jill, but she looked even younger than her mid-thirties. I had initially judged her to be in her late twenties, and I'd only deduced her actual age from references she'd made when we'd run into each other in and around the apartment complex.

The waiter brought our glasses of Chianti and our appetizer—a *caprese* salad—and I decided to use the distraction to turn the conversation away from me. As we sipped our wine and started to eat, I asked Jill the same question she'd asked me. I knew from previous discussions that she managed a real-estate office—with the ongoing upswing in foreclosures and the corresponding downturn in housing prices, business must've been difficult—but I didn't know where she'd been born and raised. "What about you?" I said.

"Are you originally from Kansas?"

"I'm a native," Jill said. "I spent my childhood in Hutchinson, but I went to school at K-State."

"Who in Kansas didn't?" I joked. Kansas State University had about twenty-five thousand students, a fairly sizable number for a small state in terms of population. The town of Manhattan probably wouldn't even exist without the presence of the college and the army base, Fort Riley.

Jill and I talked for a while about her life and family in Kansas. Back at KSU, she'd earned a degree in business management with an eye toward Wall Street, but then had discovered that she had no burning desire to abandon her home state, which she loved. She thought that Kansas embodied so much of American life, not just in actuality, but metaphorically as well. She thought it perfect that the state sat in the physical center of the continental U.S., declaring that if you wanted to pick up the country and balance it on the point of a pin, that pin would necessarily have to be beneath Kansas.

Our entrées eventually arrived, and as we continued to talk, I found myself feeling more at ease. I asked Jill a lot of questions about herself, first, because I wanted to learn more about her, but second, because I didn't want to talk about myself. It happened anyway, and I just kept hoping that Jill wouldn't want to know about Gwen. I didn't know if I could face that. I might not have been married anymore, but what I hadn't really appreciated until that night was that I still *felt* married.

Overall, my nerves calmed during the meal. I liked Jill, and I could definitely see becoming close to her, but only as a friend. At least for right now, I understood that I could offer nothing more than that.

While we waited to share a dessert, I glanced out the window. Darkness had descended, but the mantle of snow on the ground and out across the frozen pond shined brightly beneath a gibbous moon—*two* of them, actually. Aurora transited its larger companion, its shadow blotting out a circle on the Moon's surface. In the four months since its arrival above the Earth, I hadn't lost my fascination for it, perhaps because none of my questions about it had been answered. I wasn't alone: the American public—and no doubt the rest of the world too—clamored for the seventeenth of May, the date on which the Artemis lander would alight on the mysterious orb.

Across the table, Jill followed my gaze. "Pretty amazing, isn't it?" she said.

"It is," I said, watching the brace of moons in their slow-motion dance. "I just..."

"What?"

"I don't know," I said, looking over at Jill. "I think... it seems like there must be something significant... some deep meaning... in what's going on up there, but I can't see it, I can't figure it out."

Jill appeared to consider this, then shrugged. "Maybe there's not," she said. "Maybe it's simply the random workings of a clockwork universe."

"Maybe," I said, though that answer did not satisfy.

"You know what my brother thinks?" Jill said, leaning in over the table and lowering her voice to a secretive whisper. "He thinks Aurora's an alien spaceship."

I'd heard rumblings of this myself, mostly around the office, and somebody had told me that an abundance of sites dedicated to that conviction had proliferated all over the Internet. "I suppose it's possible," I said. "But I don't know. A spaceship five hundred miles in diameter?"

"If aliens have the technology to travel light-years to our planet," Jill said, "then building a ship that big would probably be no big deal."

"I suppose," I said again, my tone noncommittal. The argument seemed self-fulfilling: it could be a ship that large because if it was, then the aliens who built it must have come from far away and would therefore be very advanced.

"Well, science doesn't have an explanation for it," Jill said. "Nobody detected any asteroids getting close to Earth beforehand, and if Aurora was an asteroid, none of the physics adds up. Nobody can figure out how it could have been caught by the Moon's gravity or how it can be going around in its circular orbit."

"But if it's a spaceship..." I said, following Jill's train of thought.

"If it's a spaceship," Jill said, "then the pilot could have flown it here in a way that kept it hidden behind the Moon as it got closer to Earth. And they could also direct their ship into whatever orbit they wanted."

The appearance of Aurora through the efforts of an advanced alien species would indeed provide answers to many of the questions people had. At the same time, it raised plenty of other issues. First and foremost, it would require the existence of extraterrestrial life, something a lot of people believed in, but which had never even come close to being proven. And also—"Why would they come here and orbit the Moon?"

"I don't know," Jill said.

"And if they came all this way, why wouldn't they make contact with us here on Earth?" I persisted

"Who knows?" Jill said. "They're *aliens.*"

"Right," I said, still not satisfied, but recognizing that I wouldn't be until I actually learned the truth about Aurora. Speculation only strengthened my desire to know.

Our discussion of Aurora ended when the waiter arrived with our dessert, a hazelnut chocolate torte, over which we *ooh*ed and *aah*ed. Afterward, I drove us back to the apartment complex and escorted Jill to her door. She invited me in for a nightcap and some more conversation, but I demurred. As well as our date had gone, I think she realized what I had come to realize, namely that I wasn't yet ready for anything more than a friendship—with Jill or any other woman. I kissed her chastely on the cheek, then made my way along the building to my and Cassie's apartment.

As I walked through the cold night air, I kept my head down, alert for patches of ice. I didn't look up at Aurora, but I felt the weight of its presence above me. Whether an asteroid or a spaceship, whether the product of chance in a vast universe or the design of an alien intelligence or something else entirely, I craved an explanation.

Inside, alone, I carried the stepstool from the kitchen into my bedroom. There, I climbed up to pull down one of the boxes stored on the upper shelf of my closet. I quickly found what I was looking for.

Sitting on the edge of my bed, I paged through my and Gwen's wedding album.

oe Wyandotte strung the new black lace through the eyelets on his sneaker, also new and black, just like all of the clothing he wore. He had trouble with the simple task because his hands shook. As this day had neared, he'd anticipated it with an ever-clearer mind, with a hardening certainty that he had chosen well for himself. Now that the time had finally come, he literally trembled with excitement.

When he'd finally finished lacing and tying his sneakers, Joe stood from one of the two cots that had been set up in the small bedroom. He'd shared this space for the last few weeks with Brother Bill—Joe didn't know his surname—and would until the appointed time of thirty-three minutes past eight o'clock this evening, just a few hours from now. At that point, Aurora would reach its zenith in the sky and appear directly in the center of the Moon. The Golden Moment, as Brother Tanner called it.

Joe straightened the black bedclothes, which had been impossible to purchase in stores, and which they'd eventually had to order via the World Wide Web. The Net, in fact, had been extremely useful for the Order of Aurora Bliss. It had been through a chat room that Joe had first learned of the movement. Back then, just a month after Aurora had arrived at Earth, he'd still been living in Muncie, Indiana, working as a night watchman at one of the downtown office buildings. In the four months since then, he'd quit his job, sold almost all of his belongings, moved out of his apartment, and relocated two thousand miles across the country to San Jose, California. After moving into the compound—a central courtyard surrounded by a group of four three-bedroom condominiums, all of them rented by Brother Tanner—Joe sold his car for forty-five hundred dollars. He would need no more money beyond that.

Out in the living room, Joe saw that the

four cots belonging to the brothers who stayed there had all been neatly made up, just like his. As well, the ceremonial candles—black, of course—had been set up on the counter that divided the dining area—two more cots there—from the kitchen. Joe walked over and found the one into which he'd etched his name—not his old name, not his *earthly* name, but the new, celestial one he'd selected: Rel-dren. He couldn't help but smile at the sight of his eternal identity.

"Brother Joe," Brother Donald said. He stood with Brother Alan in the kitchen, the two of them at the counter preparing the evening's special victuals. Two large jars of applesauce sat open before them, along with a dozen small plates and at least as many prescription pill bottles. Brother Donald held a serving spoon, Brother Alan a mortar and pestle.

Joe nodded. "How is it coming along?" he asked.

"We are very nearly ready," Brother Donald said, a beatific smile decorating his face.

"We'll be done before the final Offering," Brother Alan added.

Joe nodded again. He had already completed his own assigned tasks, which had included readying the courtyard for this evening, as well as tidying his room and donning his ebon garments. Brothers Donald and Alan hadn't dressed yet, but he knew they would as soon as they'd finished their duties.

Moving to the end of the dining area, Joe pushed open the sliding glass door and stepped out into the courtyard. As always at this time of the evening, mats had been laid out in rows for each of Brother Tanner's forty-one disciples. Some, Joe saw, had already taken their places, sitting cross-legged on the black pads. Several held their eyes closed, clearly meditating, but others peered upward into the twilit sky, looking toward the point where the signal would finally come for salvation. No one spoke.

Joe took a deep breath. Just a few days old, the spring had brought with it warm days and temperate nights. The scent of fresh blooms filled the air with a sweetness that seemed to carry the spirit of the occasion. Joe's entire life—each year, each month, each day, each instant—had been leading him to this time and place. Had he not turned one corner, had he not taken one path, had he not made one decision or another, he would have missed out on all this time with Aurora Bliss, and on all the time yet to come.

I'm so lucky, Joe thought.

He looked over at the single mat that sat on its own in front of the other, but Brother Tanner had yet to assume his place, from which he guided the Order. Beside his mat, though, the begrimed hibachi had already been set in position, the red glow of burning coals visible within. The handle of the short branding iron jutted out beyond the lip of the metal appliance. Next to it sat a large pitcher.

Ready for the last rite to begin, but still an hour or so away, Joe decided to try to settle himself, to temper his enthusiasm. He navigated around the mats until he reached his own, in the fourth row, right on the end. He kneeled down, bowed his head in humility and appreciation, then folded himself into a modified lotus position.

At first, Joe closed his eyes and concentrated on regulating his breathing. He succeeded in quieting his body, even as he failed to tame his runaway emotions. In the temple of his mind, he roared and danced and dreamed, his elation impossible to contain. He raised his head and opened his eyes, and as though the moment had been crafted specially for him, the vista included the freshly risen Moon, low in the smoldering sky, with Aurora already starting its journey in front of it. The universe was his.

An hour later, after everybody in the Order had come out into the courtyard, Brother Tanner arrived. The last orange-red tendrils of dusk had decamped for the night, surrendering to the deepening blue-black of infinity. Against a backdrop of glittering stars, the Moon and Aurora had risen high in the firmament. The setting could not have been more perfect.

"My brothers," the great Tanner said, seated atop his own mat, "our time is finally at hand." Though small of frame, he still cut a striking figure, with dazzling gray eyes and a halo of bright white hair ringing his head. Like the other brothers, he wore sneakers, socks, slacks, and a vest, all of them jet black. "Through the years, I have searched for the Sign that would point the way to the everlasting paradise we all so fervently seek in our lives. Five months ago, I found it." Brother Tanner turned to peer over his shoulder at the rising Moon and its charge. Every member of the Order likewise lifted their own gaze to look upon the final development of the Sign.

"Now then," Brother Tanner said, "for the last time here on Earth, let us share with one another and with the powerful forces of the universe the path to redemption that each of us has taken." As he always did, Brother Tanner looked to the first mat in the first row, to the person of Brother Richard, who had followed him the longest.

"My path began in Philadelphia," Brother Richard said, reciting the phrase with which he always began, the phrase with which, in some form, each member of the Order always began. The statements that would be delivered that night

had already been recorded onto videotape, in private, with only Brother Tanner present to perform and witness the filming. Everybody had placed their personal tape beneath their pillow. "I started out miserable and unloved, angry and violent," Brother Richard admitted, as he always did, and then he quickly narrated events from his life that helped capture the essence of that life. It required less than two minutes, at the end of which he stood and walked over to Brother Tanner, who administered the Sign of the Sign. Then Brother Richard returned to his mat.

When his turn came, Joe started his story in Hastings, Indiana. He touched on his absent mother and his brutal father, his fractured early life and misspent youth. He briefly described his lifelong yearning for happiness and the steps along the way that had brought him to the present, to the threshold of all he had ever sought in his twenty-seven years of existence.

Once Joe had finished, he rose from his mat, his joints making popping sounds as he did. He made his way around the group until he stood before the leader of the Order. Joe dropped to his knees and leaned forward, waiting until he felt the touch of Brother Tanner's forehead on his own. Then Joe held out his bare arm, offering in supplication his longing to be marked with the Sign, to know the Sign, to follow the Sign.

Brother Tanner grasped the handle of the branding iron, lifting the metal rod from the shimmering heat of the coals. "Here and now, Brother Joe," he said, "I humbly bestow upon you the Sign of the Sign, representing the ultimate guidepost that will take us all to our endless glory." He pressed the red-tipped end of the iron onto Joe's upper arm, onto the eye-shaped scar tissue already etched into Joe's flesh by repeated applications over the past months.

For just a second, the pain shattered Joe's peace of mind, but his discipline prevented him from screaming. In the next moment, he controlled the experience completely, the throbbing of his re-made wound pushed away. He smelled the sickly sweet scent of his own singed skin, and all at once, the totality of the time he'd spent in the compound recurred to him: his tentative arrival, his acceptance by Brother Tanner and his acolytes, his repeated trials to ensure his worthiness for the journey ahead.

Brother Tanner set the branding iron back down, and Joe picked himself up and went back to his mat. There, he watched and listened to the final Offerings of the rest of Order. When the last of them had received the Sign of the Sign and retreated to his mat, Brother Tanner took hold of the pitcher and doused the ritual coals. Then he turned and looked high up into the sky. All eyes followed his.

Joe didn't know the precise time, but he could see that it must be closing in on eight thirty-three. The Moon had almost reached its apex, and Aurora neared the very center of the lunar disk. A surge of adrenalin rushed through Joe's body. He wanted to jump up and shout his jubilation, but he waited. There would be all the time for joy soon enough.

Seconds before the Golden Moment, Brother Tanner stood up, and the rest of the Order followed suit. Finally, the Moon attained as high a point in the sky as it ever would, and Aurora hung above its center point. It looked for all the world like a great eye casting its gaze upon the members of Aurora Bliss. It could not have been a more obvious Sign.

Brother Tanner spun on his heel. "The time is upon us," he said. The gathering dissolved, everybody moving quickly to the building in which they lived. Inside, Joe took his place in line with the others as they snaked into the kitchen. When he reached the counter, he took a spoon from an untouched plate and devoured three large mouthfuls of the applesauce admixture. Then he retrieved his ceremonial candle and carried it to the room he shared—at least for the next few minutes—with Brother Bill.

Joe set his candle on the floor at the foot of his cot, found the book of matches he'd placed there earlier, and lighted the wick. The flame guttered and almost went out, but then steadied. Joe climbed onto his cot and lay on his back. He entwined his fingers together across his midsection, then closed his eyes. He heard Brother Bill come in and strike a match, then listened to the squeak of springs as his erstwhile roommate crawled onto his own cot.

Joe waited expectantly. His breathing slowed, even as his exhilaration knew no bounds. He felt immeasurably grateful to Aurora for signaling the Golden Moment, for providing the signpost that would lead to an eternity of bliss.

Joe never opened his eyes again.

felt my feet shifting unsteadily beneath me. I looked down, but the solid ground had gone, replaced by fine gray sand. Startled, I surveyed the terrain around me and saw that wherever I had been before, I now stood in the middle of a desert. Dunes rose and fell like the arid waves of a waterless ocean.

With deliberate steps, I strode forward, pulling my feet from the clutch of the sand and setting them heavily back down. I heard no sound but that of the fine grains slipping from my shoes and flowing back onto the desert wasteland. I knew that I was lost, but that if I didn't keep moving, I would die.

Up ahead, a great shadow skimmed across the desolate tracts of sand. I stopped and regarded the sky, expecting to see clouds scudding along, intermittently blocking the sunlight, but I saw instead the velvety spread of a starry but moonless night. How can there be shadows then? *I wondered.*

I looked forward again, but the changing umbral patches had become permanent. Not shadows then, *I realized,* but *features* of this barren world. *As though to confirm my location, the blue-white ball of the Earth peeked over the horizon. I stared in awe as it ascended, until the much larger arc of the Moon also appeared. In no time at all, it dominated the sky, fully eclipsing the Earth.*

Aurora, *I thought.* I'm on Aurora.

In the unnatural silence, I gawked at the Moon. I didn't know why or how I had come to be here. I remembered my many errant thoughts of Aurora, the many emotions I'd felt as—

A whisper of movement caught my attention. Peering back down at the sands, I saw, five or so yards away, a column rising slowly upward from the gray banks. Delicate granules poured from it as it climbed to a height of five feet, perhaps six. I watched as the falling sand drained away, revealing the form beneath. A reddish-brown mane showed through first, and then shoulders and arms wrapped in white. A torso came next, and a waist, and legs—

I didn't need the last diaphanous curtain of sand to slide from her face to recognize my wife, but I waited until then to speak. She wore her wedding gown.

"Gwen," *I said, my voice lonely amid the emptiness of this strange world. In that one word, that familiar name, I could hear everything that I felt. Delight blended with desperation, hope with loss, relief with fear. I could not believe that the love of my life had come back to me, and I could not trust the reality of the situation.*

"Jonathan," *Gwen said, though I could only see the movement of her lips, the shape they made to form my name. I heard no voice.* "Welcome." *Still no sound.*

"Welcome?" *I said.* "To what? What is this place?" *The words seemed to leave my mouth and tumble to the desert floor, dust upon dust.* "Why are we here?" *I wanted to know.*

Gwen reached around behind herself and took hold of the train of her dress. With an elegant flourish, she lifted it, then bent deeply at the knees. My heart ached at the gentle beauty of her.

With her free hand, Gwen reached out toward the gray sand and pressed a finger into its yielding surface. Slowly, a splash of color spread from the point of contact. I saw rich browns and bright greens flow outward as though imbuing the surroundings with a greater reality. Other hues appeared as well, reds and yellows and blues, and with them, textures. The browns became soil, the greens became grass and other plants. Gwen looked up and studied me as the geography transformed. She smiled at me, and in that moment, I would have been content to die, to end my days with my eyes fixed upon the loving countenance of my sweet Gwendolyn.

Or maybe I already have, *it suddenly occurred to me. I lifted one foot and then the other, slogging as best I could toward my wife.* "Gwen," *I said, my urgency plain,* "what's happened? Where are we?" *I knew what I wanted the answer to be, though part of me worried about Cassie. How would she handle a second devastating loss in her life? How would she fare as part of Barb's family?*

"Gwen," *I said again, heaving myself forward, my momentum weakening the sand's resistance on my legs. I needed to reach her, to touch her, to hold her.*

Just an arm's length away, exhausted by

my efforts, I stopped. "It's all right, Jonathan," she told me, and now, finally, I heard her voice. It might as well have been music, so much did it stir my soul. "Look around you," she said, spreading her arms wide.

I did look. We now stood in a meadow, but not just any meadow. I recognized The Lagoon in Swope Park, the boathouse on its shore, and the stretch of grass where Gwen and I had picnicked all those years ago. We'd been dating for less than a year, but we both had known. We couldn't have an open container of alcohol in the park, so we'd brought a bottle of sparkling apple juice instead. When I'd poured out two flutes for us, I'd secretly slipped the engagement ring into Gwen's. In the park that afternoon, we'd laughed and cried from the happiness we both felt so strongly that it could not be restrained.

I turned back to Gwen. "Here we are again," she said, as though pointing out the most obvious fact. "Here and wherever we want to be, for now and ever. Together."

Tears streamed down my face. I wasn't much of a religious man, though I'd always believed in God. I don't know whether I'd ever truly accepted the reality of an afterlife, but I had hoped for it, had prayed for it.

I thought of Cassie again, but this time found contentment in the certainty that she would be all right. I don't know how I knew, but I did. All things, it now seemed, were possible.

"I love you, Gwen," I said.

"I love you, Jonathan."

I reached for my wife tentatively, fearful that if I attempted to touch her, she would vanish, that all of this would vanish. My hands came up along the sides of her upper arms. I hesitated, but I had to know. I tried to embrace Gwen—

—and my joy redoubled when I felt the physical truth of her body. I pulled her close and embraced her, her own arm encircling my back and holding me tightly. I began to kiss her hair, her neck, the side of her face, each delivered peck a miracle. I felt filled up by the wondrous majesty of what the universe offered.

And at last, my lips found Gwen's. My flesh quivered. My heart soared. I closed my eyes and saw stars, brilliant pinpoints of light illuminating all of creation. I heard bells, echoing through the void, satiating the need to banish the silence. My ears rang and rang and—

—and the fourth ring, perhaps the fifth, finally woke me. I sat up in the darkness, disoriented at first, but the next peal of the department cell phone engaged my reflexes. I reached to where it lay on my nightstand and picked it up. It rang one more time before I flipped it open and answered the call from operations.

As Hamid detailed the night's problem for me, I threw back the covers and sat up on the edge of the bed. I turned on the light, then blearily scratched out some notes on a pad. When the conversation had ended, I grabbed my laptop and took it out into the dining area. There, connected wirelessly to the Internet, I logged in to my workstation at the office.

But my dream—the dream I'd just now woken from and the dream I obviously harbored deep in my heart—remained with me. "Aurora as heaven," I said mockingly, irritated with myself for entertaining such a foolish notion, even subconsciously. I knew better, didn't I?

But as I started to type again, I decided that I wasn't yet ready to let the idea go.

ebbie Ostray hoisted the sign up, resting its wooden haft against her right shoulder. "Don't believe what you hear," she chanted, "Aurora is a lie... don't let RocketSys Corp... spend our country dry." She pumped her arms up and down as she walked along the National Mall in Washington, D.C., hoping to draw the attentions of passersby. The news organizations, such as they were, had already come by earlier in the afternoon—at least those few that deemed civil protest newsworthy had come by. As best she could tell, that had included reporters from the not-for-profit public affairs channel, C-SPAN2, which almost nobody watched, and from the local public broadcasting station, which even fewer people watched.

"Don't believe what you hear," Ostray called, adding her voice to those of the sixteen individuals from the group who'd shown up that day. "Aurora is a lie." Humans Outraged about Aurora eXploration—aptly shortened to the acronym HOAX—now boasted nearly a thousand members throughout the United States, and half again that number around the rest of the world. "Don't let RocketSys Corp..." Ostray had hoped for a larger showing, but in truth, it didn't surprise her that so few had been willing to travel to the nation's capital for the event. "...Spend our country dry." People had families and busy lives, and many lived from paycheck to paycheck, so the time and money it cost to travel to D.C. could easily trump the need to speak out against governmental malfeasance and corporate graft. Societal issues often could not compete for attention with the personal issues of the citizenry.

To her left, Ostray saw the poignant figures of patrolling soldiers that together composed the Korean War Veterans Memorial. The idea that men and women had fought, been wounded, and died to safeguard the freedom of the American people only served to underscore her resolve in marching to help spotlight the high crimes of the current administration. Genuine

philosophical differences between the political parties didn't trouble her, but the blatant funneling of funds to the cronies of those in power usurped the will of the public and undermined democracy. For Ostray, greed seemed the worst possible motive to betray the interests of your country.

She reached the corner of the Reflecting Pool nearest the Lincoln Memorial and followed the others around to the right, along the short border of the water. They all continued chanting, but while the beautiful April day had brought many visitors out to the Mall, few paid the HOAX members any mind. Ostray felt tired—she and Ronnie had driven all the way from Tennessee to be there for the protest—but she would not allow that to deter her enthusiasm for the cause.

The group had chosen that day, the seventeenth of April, for their demonstration because it marked exactly one month before the Artemis spaceship would land on Aurora—or so the administration would have the population believe. Once the second moon had supposedly appeared in the sky and the government had vowed to explore it, enormous no-bid contracts had been tendered to several companies. Though nominally American firms, they had paid virtually no corporate income tax last year, or for many of the preceding years. RocketSys had received the most lucrative contract, valued at three-point-one billion dollars. In all, the administration had committed eight-point-seven billion to the project to just four companies, all of them with ties to numerous political officials.

Ostray followed Ronnie around the next corner and started down the long side of the Reflecting Pool. Though her throat had begun to feel a bit rough, she refused to stop her chanting. "Don't believe what you hear...."

Contrary to how the so-called new media characterized HOAX—when they characterized the group at all—the members did not oppose space exploration. Nor did they rail against all corporate involvement in the business of the people. They generally objected to the unregulated apportionment of public funds to private companies, and specifically to the billions paid out for the launching of an expensive rocket on an unnecessary mission.

Aurora, she and others had discovered, did not really exist. The four letters painted in red across Ostray's sign—*HOAX*—represented not only the name of their organization, but also the implementation by the administration of a plan to defraud the American taxpayer. While the rest of the country had with amazement accepted the arrival of a second moon, Arnie Chesbro had not. When astronomers and cosmologists had again and again failed to offer any reasonable explanation for Aurora, and when the government had then chosen to disburse to a quartet of corporations the equivalent of more than the gross national product of scores of countries, Arnie had grown suspicious.

A contractor in the information-technology industry, Arnie had begun to employ his computer expertise in formulating a model for Aurora—a model that showed how the *image* of another moon could be created so that it would be seen by people all over the Earth, even in the absence of a real second moon. Over the course of the past few months, Arnie had devised no less than four means by which such a deception could be achieved. The most convincing design, at least to Ostray, involved a large gas-filled lens positioned in orbit of the actual Moon, off of which a series of earthbound lasers would bounce in order to form the faux Aurora.

Up ahead, Ostray spied a three-person news crew: reporter, camera operator, and sound technician. For a fleeting moment, she thought that they might cover the HOAX protest, but they quickly moved off in the other direction, toward the World War II Memorial. It didn't matter. Ostray felt resolved to maintaining the fight against the avarice permeating the confines of the capital, no matter how little attention the media paid the cause.

One month, Ostray thought. *One month, and then maybe we'll have something.* Since Aurora did not physically exist, the Artemis rocket obviously would not be able to land on it. Ostray fostered no illusions about the lengths to which the federal government would go to preserve their fraud. Some people believed that Apollo 11 and its successors had never reached the Moon, and though Ostray did not share such a contention, she did not doubt the ability and willingness of certain politicians to deceive. Still, it seemed likely to her that the world would see a broadcast of an ersatz Artemis landing, justifying the extreme expense in allegedly conducting the mission—and probably justifying future expenditures as well.

Once that took place, though, things could be different. The corporations benefiting from the administration's largesse might actually deliver the goods for which they'd been contracted: an Ares rocket, a guidance system, fuel, and the rest. For that reason, the number of individuals involved in the conspiracy might so far be limited. It would take quite a lot of people, though, to fake a rocket launch, telemetry, transmissions from space. And when that happened, Ostray was sure, somebody on the inside would talk.

"Don't believe what you hear..." she bellowed, fulfilled by her efforts to bring the truth to the American public. She would not give up. Whether anybody knew it or not, the country needed her.

he time had come, and so I tore my gaze away from the sight of Aurora as it circled the full Moon. I stepped from our balcony back into the apartment, sliding the glass door closed behind me. I moved to the couch and sat down, expecting Cassie to join me soon.

On the television, which I'd left on, graphics announcing the Artemis mission flashed colorfully across the screen, but I'd muted the sound for the time being. It would still be a few minutes before the lander's cameras would be deployed and it started its descent to the surface of Aurora.

Though I sought to remain outwardly calm, I felt an amalgam of anticipation and dread. I didn't know what Artemis would find when it touched down on Aurora—the natural material of an asteroid, the machined exterior of an alien spacecraft or artifact, or something else—but I suspected what it would not find: my wife, alive in some form even after she'd been killed in a car accident three years ago, living in a place where she could revisit the best times of her life—of *our* lives. I wanted that to be true, and I had ever since the dream, so vivid, that I'd had last month.

Perhaps, now that I thought about it, the wild idea had been born earlier than that. Hadn't I peered up at Aurora and thought about Gwen almost from the beginning? Yes, I suppose that had been the case after all.

I'd said nothing to Cassie about my dream or about the crazy fantasy that my mind refused to abandon. I knew with great conviction what the cameras aboard Artemis would *not* see tonight. And still, I had to admit, my hopes, unfounded and unreasonable, remained.

On the television screen, a counter appeared in the upper right-hand corner. "Five minutes until they have a live picture from Artemis," I called to Cassie.

"I'll be there," Cassie called back from her bedroom.

Whatever happened tonight, I wondered how my daughter would remember it. In the last week or so, I'd come to realize that people mark the passage of time in their lives by a relatively small number of events. Watching Cassie in the days since this first occurred to me, I'd also come to understand that the quantity of episodes chalked up for the purpose of measuring a lifetime is, counterintuitively, greater for a child than for an adult. For Cassie—and remembering back to my own youth, for me—so many seemingly meaningful occasions arise: birthdays, holidays, family vacations, the starts and ends of school years and summers and sports seasons.

For adults, though, such experiences tend to fade in the memory before too long. A man or a woman might recall something wonderful—or something terrible—that happened on their birthday, but when you reach your twenties and thirties and forties, there have been so many birthdays that they merge together in recollection, and in that, they lose their significance. Youth itself becomes just one incident, the days and months and years agglomerated into a single point— childhood—on the measuring stick of life. It is mostly the later, singular events that linger: a marriage, a divorce, the birth of a child, the death of a parent.

With those unique, or at least momentous, times in life necessarily come *before* and *after*. I look back on the days *before* I got married, and on the days *after*. My forty-two years can be neatly divided into those prior to my wedding and to those subsequent, into those prior to my daughter's birth and to those subsequent. Now, I suspected, there would be the time before Aurora graced the skies of the Earth, and the times afterward—not just for me, but for a lot of people, and for humankind as a whole.

"I'm here," Cassie said as she walked into the living room. She flopped down onto the couch beside me, her hair still wet from the bath she'd just taken. She wore her pink pajamas, the ones with the unicorns and castles, which I hadn't seen in quite a while. "Has it started yet?"

"Not yet," I told her. I pointed to the counter onscreen. "Thirty-five seconds to go."

"Okay," she said. She leaned back and looked around the room, her indifference palpable. Over the past seven months, I'd tried to speak with Cassie on a number of occasions about Aurora, but I'd been unable to really engage her.

When the counter on the television reached zero, the graphic disappeared, replaced by a gray-white expanse. On the left side of the screen, what seemed to be a metal strip stretched obliquely from top to bottom. I couldn't quite make sense of the scene, and then I remembered that I had turned off the sound. I picked up the remote from the coffee table and pressed the *MUTE* button again.

"...looking at is the actual surface of Aurora," a voice said. I stared more closely at the TV and detected movement in the sweep of grayish white filling most of the screen. "The narrow band of metal along the left-hand portion of your picture is, we're told, a piece of the mount for Artemis's external camera, which was deployed just moments ago. We're going to switch now to a live audio feed from Mission Control at the Johnson Space Center in Houston, Texas."

A few seconds of silence followed, and then an official-sounding voice said, "Artemis onboard computers confirm thirty seconds from PDI." A banner across the bottom of the screen explained that PDI stood for Powered Descent Initiation. "Standing by for ullage." Again, text appeared detailing the firing of the Artemis lander's thrusters in order to settle the fuel in the tanks prior to ignition. "Five seconds...we have ullage."

I felt myself leaning forward on the couch, as though about to leap up from excitement. My palms were sweating. I strained to see the surface of Aurora as it passed below the camera, but it must have been too far distant yet for me to make out details.

"Counting down to PDI," announced the voice of Mission Control. "Five, four, three, two, one... ignition. Craft attitude is optimal. DPS tank reads green." DPS: Descent Propulsion System. "The Artemis lander has begun its eight-minute journey down to its destination."

As the craft dropped from space toward Aurora, I hunted for any surface features that might become visible. I saw only the ashy patches discernible from the Earth. No dunes, no indication of sands, and no colors.

The voice of Mission Control continued to narrate the technical details of Artemis's flight. I could not take my eyes from the scene. Seven minutes into the descent, the surface of Aurora revealed itself in gentle peaks and troughs—like banks of sand in a desert.

I gasped, the memory of the gray, arid wastes of my dream foremost in my mind. At seven and a half minutes, just thirty seconds from touchdown, the lander's thrusters began kicking up dust—or finely granulated sand.

My heart pounded in my chest. "Twenty seconds," proclaimed the man from Mission Control, and then, "Ten seconds." I watched as the tiny, hoary particles whipped into a frenzy below the lander. *"Five seconds, four, three, two, one—"*

The voice cut off abruptly, and on the television, the surface of Aurora vanished, replaced by a field of stars. "What?" I said, confused. "What happened?" I raised the remote, thinking that the station had lost its feed, but I did nothing.

"We have RCS shutdown," said the voice of Mission Control, *"but we cannot confirm landing."* Seconds of silence passed.

"What happened?" I said again, and this time I glanced over at Cassie. She shrugged.

"I guess Aurora's gone," she said.

My mouth formed into an *O* as I looked at her, and I recalled having a similar reaction the first time I'd ever laid eyes on Aurora. I couldn't believe what she'd suggested, but—

I jumped to my feet and raced to the balcony, throwing open the sliding glass door and striding outside. In the sky, full and silvery white, the bright orb of the Moon held its place in the heavens as it had for all of human history and before. The Moon remained as unchanged as ever, but it no longer traced its orbit in tandem with any other astronomical body.

Aurora was gone.

I felt pressure behind my eyes and knew that tears threatened. I fought them back, a reflex I'd developed long ago to shelter my daughter. I wanted to cry, but I wouldn't. Instead, I breathed in and out deeply several times in an attempt to calm myself. Once I had, I went back inside.

Cassie still sat on the couch. She looked not at the television, but at me. "It *is* gone," I told her, and suddenly I remembered that months ago, Cassie had essentially predicted that Aurora would not stay here, beside the Earth and its Moon. "How did you know?" I asked her.

Cassie pointed at the television. "We just saw it disappear," she said.

"No," I said, "not that." I walked over to the couch and sat down beside my daughter. "A while ago, you told me that you thought Aurora would go away." I paused, trying to fathom how Cassie possibly could have known, or even intuited, that this would happen.

"I don't know," Cassie said, lifting one shoulder up in a half-shrug. "It came here when nobody expected it to, so why wouldn't it leave the same way?" The thought seemed logical, but Aurora's arrival had made no sense, and now, neither did its departure.

We watched the television for another hour, but nobody could explain what had taken place. The Artemis lander, deprived of Aurora's gravitational pull, had been caught instead by that of the Moon. The scientists on TV predicted that it would crash into the lunar surface several days from now.

"I'm going to bed," Cassie said a short while later. I shook off the daze I felt enough to manage a smile for her.

"Good night, honey," I said. I stood up and hugged her tightly, then kissed the top of her auburn-tressed head.

"Good night, Dad."

And as I watched her leave, I knew that I understood almost nothing about the universe. Not nothing, but almost.

ivuli Ngaiza approached the cropland that he and his family farmed in the Morogoro Region of eastern Tanzania. He hadn't been able to sleep, and his restlessness and concerns had brought him out into the dry night. The long-rains season had so far proven irregular, and Kivuli feared a poor harvest. If they could not bring enough of their vegetables to market, he might have no choice but to uproot his wife and children and their extended family so that they could try to find a more dependable climate.

As he neared the southern border of the one and a half hectares they worked, he looked up to the sky. The full Moon shined brightly back at him, but now it did so alone. The other orb that had accompanied it since the beginning of the last short-rains season had gone now, though Kivuli had seen it just yesterday.

Maybe it's just hiding, he thought, knowing that sometimes the little moon traveled behind the usual Moon. Somehow, though, he knew that wasn't the case now. That meant something, he told himself, and he eagerly waited through the rest of the night, forgoing sleep in search of the omen he and his family so desperately needed.

Hours later, by the time the Moon had set, its smaller companion had not shown itself. That hadn't happened since the little moon had first appeared seven months ago. Kivuli could draw only one conclusion: the little moon had gone for good. And that could only be a sign of a fine harvest to come.

He was sure of it. • • •

DAVID R. GEORGE III had co-story credit on the first season Voyager *episode "Prime Factors." Since then, he has become a prolific* Star Trek *novelist, including the* Crucible *trilogy, and reached the best-seller lists of the* New York Times *and* USA Today.

DARK ENERGY FOUND STIFLING GROWTH IN THE UNIVERSE

WASHINGTON—For the first time, astronomers have clearly seen the effects of "dark energy" on the most massive collapsed objects in the universe using NASA's Chandra X-ray Observatory. By tracking how dark energy has stifled the growth of galaxy clusters, scientists have obtained the best clues yet about what dark energy is and what the destiny of the universe could be.

These new X-ray results provide a crucial independent test of dark energy, long sought by scientists, which depends on how gravity competes with accelerated expansion in the growth of cosmic structures.

Scientists think dark energy is a form of repulsive gravity that now dominates the universe, although they have no clear picture of what it actually is.

"This result could be described as 'arrested development of the universe,'" said Alexey Vikhlinin of the Smithsonian Astrophysical Observatory in Cambridge, Mass., who led the research. "Whatever is forcing the expansion of the universe to speed up is also forcing its development to slow down."

The results show the increase in mass of galaxy clusters over time aligns with a universe dominated by dark energy. It is more difficult for objects like galaxy clusters to grow when space is stretched, as caused by dark energy.

"For years, scientists have wanted to start testing how gravity works on large scales and now, we finally have," said William Forman, a co-author of the study from the Smithsonian Astrophysical Observatory. "This is a test that general relativity could have failed."

When combined with other clues—supernovas, the study of the cosmic microwave background, and the distribution of galaxies—this new X-ray result gives scientists the best insight to date on the properties of dark energy.

The study strengthens the evidence that dark energy is the cosmological constant. Although it is the leading candidate to explain dark energy, theoretical work suggests it should be about 10^{120} times larger than observed. Therefore, alternatives to general relativity, such as theories involving hidden dimensions, are being explored.

—from NASA press release, December 16, 2008

F■■■

G round cars shrieked to a halt. Muffled curses sounded. Pedestrians jumped back, eyes widened, mouths spread into incredulous O's.

A great shining metal sphere had appeared out of thin air right in the middle of the intersection.

"What? What?" bumbled a traffic controller, leaving the fastness of his concrete island.

"Good heaven!" cried a secretary, gaping from her third story window. "What *can* this be?"

"Popped outa nowhere!" ejaculated an old man. "Outa nowhere, I'll be bound!"

Gasps. Everyone leaned forward with pounding hearts.

The sphere's circular door was being pushed open at that moment.

Out jumped a man. He looked around interestedly. He stared at the people. The people stared at him.

"What's the meaning?" ranted the traffic controller, pulling out his report book. "Looking for trouble, eh?"

The man smiled. People close by heard him say, "My name is Professor Robert Wade. I've come from the year 1951."

"Likely, likely," grumbled the officer. "First of all get this contraption out of here."

BY RICHARD MATHESON

Illustrated by Kevin Farrell

"But that's impossible," said the man. "Right now anyway."

The officer stuck out his lower lip. "Impossible eh?" He stepped over to the metal globe. He pushed it. It didn't budge. He kicked it.

"Please," said the stranger, "that won't do any good."

Angrily, the officer pushed aside the door. He peered into the interior.

He backed away, a gasp of horror torn from paled lips.

"What? What?" he cried in fabulous disbelief.

"What's the matter?" asked the professor.

The officer's face was grim and shocked. His teeth chattered. He was unnerved.

"If you'd..." began the man.

"Silence, filthy dog!" the officer roared.

The professor stepped back in alarm, his face a twist of surprise.

The officer reached into the interior of the sphere and plucked out three objects.

Pandemonium.

Women averted their faces with gasps of revulsion. Strong men shuddered and stared. Little children glanced about furtively. Maidens swooned.

The officer hid the objects beneath his coat quickly. He held the lump of them with one trembling hand. The other he clapped violently on the professor's shoulder.

"Vermin!" he shouted. "Pig!"

"Hang him, hang him!" chanted a group of outraged old ladies, beating time on the sidewalk with their canes.

"The shame of it," muttered a churchman, flushing a bright vermilion.

The professor was dragged down the street. He tugged and complained. The shouting of the crowd drowned him out. They struck at him with umbrellas, canes, crutches, and rolled-up magazines.

"Villain!" they accused, waving vindictive fingers. "Unblushing libertine!"

"Disgusting!"

"Sickening!"

But in alleys, in vein bars, in pool rooms, behind leering faces everywhere, squirmed wild fancies. Word got around. Chuckles, deeply and formidably obscene, quivered through the city streets.

They took the professor to jail.

Two men of the control police were stationed by the metal globe. They kept away all curious passersby. They kept looking inside with glittering eyes.

"Right in *there,*" said one of the officers again and again, licking his lips excitedly. "Wow!"

High Commissioner Castlemould was looking at licentious postcards when the tele-viewer buzzed.

His scrawny shoulders twitched, his false teeth clicked together in shock. Quickly he scooped up the pile of cards and threw them in his desk drawer.

Casting one more inhaling glance at the illustrations, he slammed the drawer shut, forced a mask of official dignity over his bony face and threw the control switch.

On the telecom screen appeared Captain Ranker of the control police, fat neck edges oozing over his tight collar.

"Commissioner," crooned the captain, his features dripping with obesiance. "Sorry to disturb you during your hour of meditation."

"Well, well, what is it?" Castlemould asked sharply, tapping an impatient finger on the glossy surface of his desk.

"We have a prisoner," said the captain. "Claims to be a time traveler from 1951." He looked around guiltily.

"What are you looking for?" crackled the Commissioner.

Captain Ranker held up a mollifying

hand. Then, reaching under the desk, he picked up the three objects and set them on his blotter where Castlemould could see.

Castlemould's eyes made an effort to pop from their sockets. His Adam's apple took a nose dive.

"Aaah!" he croaked. "Where did you get those?"

"The prisoner had them with him," said Ranker uneasily.

The Commissioner drank in the sight of the objects. Neither of the men spoke for gaping. Castlemould felt a sensuous dizziness creep over him. He snorted through pinched nostrils.

"Hold on!" he gasped, in a high cracking voice. "I'll be right down!"

He threw off the switch, thought a second, threw it on again. Captain Ranker jerked his hand back from the desk.

"You better not touch those things," warned Castlemould, eyes slitted. "Don't touch 'em! Understand?"

Captain Ranker swallowed his heart.

"Yes sir," he mumbled, a deep blush splashing up his fleshy neck.

Castlemould sneered, threw off the switch again. He jumped up from his desk with a lusty cackle.

"Haah haah!" he cried. "Haah haah!"

He hobbled across the floor, rubbing his lean hands together. He scuffed the thick rug delightedly with his thin black shoes.

"Haah haah! Aah haah haah haah!"

He called for his private car.

Footsteps. The burly guard unlocked the door, slid it open.

"Get up, *you,*" he snarled, lips a curlycue of contempt.

Professor Dade got up and, glaring at his jailer, walked past the doorway into the hall.

"Turn right," ordered the guard. Wade turned right. They started down the hall.

"I should have stayed home," Wade muttered.

"Silence, lewd dog!"

"Oh, *shut up,*" said Wade. "You must all be crazy around here. You find a little..."

"Silence!" roared the guard, looking around hurriedly. He shuddered. "Don't even say that word in my clean jail."

Wade threw up imploring eyes. "This is too much," he announced. "Any way you look at it."

He was ushered into a room which spread out behind a door reading, "Captain Ranker—Chief of Control Police"

The chief got up hastily as Wade came in. On the desk were the three objects discreetly hiden by a white cloth.

A wizened old man in funereal garb looked at Wade, a shrewd deductive look on his face.

Two hands waved simultaneously at a chair.

"Sit down," said the chief.

"Sit down," said the Commissioner.

The chief apologized. The Commisioner sneered.

"Sit down," Castlemould repeated.

"Would you like me to sit down?" Wade asked.

Apoplectic scarlet splattered over Chief Ranker's already mottled features.

"Sit down!" he gargled "When Commissioner Castlemould says sit down, he means sit down!"

Professor Wade sat down.

Both men circled him like calculating buzzards preparing for the first swoop.

The professor looked at Chief Ranker.

"Maybe you'll tell me..."

"Silence!" snapped Ranker.

Wade slapped an irate hand on the chair arm. "I will not be silent. I'm sick and tired of this asinine prattle you people are talking. You look in my time chamber and find *these* idiotic things and..."

He jerked the cloth from the objects which the cloth had shielded.

The two men jumped back and gasped as though Wade had torn the clothes from the backs of their grandmothers.

Wade got up, throwing the cloth on the desk.

"Now for God's sake, what's the matter?" he growled. "It's food. *Food.* A little food!"

The men wilted under the repeated impact of the word as though they stood in blasts of purgatorial wind.

"Shut your filthy mouth," said the captain in a choked wheezy voice. "We refuse to listen to your obscenities."

"Obscenities!" cried Professor Wade, his eyes widening in disbelief. "Am I hearing right?"

He held up one of the objects.

"This is a box of crackers!" he said incredulously. "Are you telling me that's obscene?"

Captain Ranker closed his eyes, all atremble. The old Commissioner regained his senses and, pursing his greyish lips, watched the professor with cunning little eyes.

Wade threw down the box. The old man blanched. Wade grabbed the other two objects.

"A can of processed meat!" he exclaimed furiously. "A thermos-flask of coffee. What in the hell is obscene about meat and coffee?"

Dead silence filled the room when Wade had ended.

They all stared at one another. Ranker shivered bonelessly, his face suffused with excited fluster. The Commissioner's gaze bounced back and forth between Wade's indignant face and the objects that were back on the desk. Cogitation strained his brain centers.

At length, Castlemould nodded and coughed meaningfully.

"Captain," he said, "I want to be alone with this scoundrel. I'll get to the bottom of this outrage."

The captain looked at his superior and nodded. He hurried from the room wordlessly. They heard him stumbling down the hall, breathing steam whistles.

"Now," said the Commissioner, dwindling into the immensity of Ranker's chair, "just tell me what your game is." His voice cajoled; it was half joking.

He picked up the cloth between sedate thumb and forefinger and dropped it over the offending articles with the decorum of a minister throwing his robe over the naked shoulders of a strip teaser.

Wade sank down in the other chair with a sigh.

"I give up," he said. "I come from the year 1951 in my time chamber. I bring along a little... food... in case of slight emergency. Then you all tell me that I'm an obscene dog. I'm afraid I don't understand a bit of it."

Castlemould folded his hands over his sunken chest and nodded slowly.

"Mmm-hmm. Well, young man, I happen to believe you," he said. "It's possible. I'll admit that. Historians tell of such a period when... ahem... physical sustenance was taken orally."

"I'm glad someone believes," Wade said. "But I wish you'd tell me about this food situation."

The Commissioner flinched slightly at the word. Wade looked puzzled again.

"Is it possible?" he said. "that the word... *food...* has become obscene?"

At the repeated sound of the word something seemed to click in Castlemould's brain. Eyes glittering, he reached over and drew back the cloth. He seemed to drink in the sight of the flask, the box, the tin. His tongue flicked over dried lips.

Wade stared. A feeling close to disgust rose in him.

The old man ran a shaking hand over the box of crackers, as though it were a chorus girl's leg. His lungs grappled with air.

"Food." He breathed the word in bated salacity.

Then, quickly, he drew the cloth back over the articles, apparently surfeited with the maddening sight. His bright old eyes flicked up into Professor Wade's. He drew in a tenuous breath.

"F... well," he said.

Wade leaned back in his chair, beginning to feel an embarrassed heat sluicing through his body. He shook his head and grimaced at the thought of it all.

"Fantastic," he muttered.

He lowered his head to avoid the old man's gaze. Then, looking up, he saw Castlemould peeking under the cloth again with all the tremor of an adolescent at his first burlesque show.

"Commissioner."

The ratty old man jerked in the chair, his lips drawing back with a startled hiss. He struggled for composition.

"Yes, yes," he said, gulping.

Wade stood up. He pulled off the cloth and stretched it out on the desk. Then he piled the objects in the center of it and drew up the corners. He suspended the bundle at his side.

"I don't wish to corrupt your society," he said. "Suppose I get the facts I want about your era and then leave and take my... take *this* with me."

Fear sprang up in the lined features. "No!" Castlemould cried.

Wade looked suspicious. The Commissioner bit off his mental tongue.

"I mean," he glowed, "there's no point in going back so soon. After all—" he flourished his skinny arms in an unfamil-

iar gesture—"you *are* my guest. Come, we'll go to my house and have some..."

He cleared his throat violently. He got up and hurried around the desk. He patted Wade's shoulder, his lips wrenched into the smile of a hospitable jackal.

"You can get all the facts you need from my library," he said.

Wade didn't say anything. The old man looked around guiltily.

"But you... uh... better not leave the bundle here," he said. "Better take it with you." He chuckled confidentially.

Wade looked more suspicious. Castlemould stiffened the backs of his words.

"Hate to say it," he said it, "but you can't trust inferiors. Might cause terrible upset in the department. *That,* I mean." He glanced with effected carelessness toward the bundle, and his narrow throat suffered an honest contraction. "Never know what might happen. Some people are unprincipled, you know."

He started for the door to avoid arguments. He turned, fingers clawed around the knob.

"You wait here," he said. "I'll get your release."

"But..."

"Not at all, not at all," said Castlemould, springing out into the hallway.

Professor Wade shook his head. Then he reached into his coat pocket and drew out a bar of chocolate.

"Better keep this well hidden," he said, looking about, "or it's the firing squad for me."

As they entered the hallway of his house, Castlemould said, "Here, let me take the package. We'll put it in my desk."

"I don't think so," Wade said, keeping back laughter at the Commissioner's eager face. "It might be too much of a... temptation."

"Who, for *me?*" cried Castlemould. "Haah. Haah haah! That's funny." He kept holding onto the Professor's bundle, his lips molded into a pouting circle.

"Tell you what," he bargained furiously. "We'll go in my study and I'll guard your bundle while you take notes from my books. How's that, haah? Haah?"

Wade trailed the hobbling old man into the high-ceilinged study. It still didn't make sense to him. Food... he tested the sound of it in his mind. Just a harmless word. But, like anything else, it could have any meaning people assigned to it.

He noted how Castlemould's vein-popping hands caressed the bundle, noted the acquisitive shifty-eyed look that swallowed up his dour old face. He wondered if he should leave the... he smiled to himself. It was getting him too.

They crossed the wide rug.

"Have the best book collection in the city," bragged the Commissioner. "Complete." He winked a red-veined eyeball. "Unexpurgated," he promised.

Wade said, "That's nice."

He stood before the shelves and ran his eyes over the titles, surveying the parallel rows of books that walled the room.

"Do you have a..." he started, turning. The Commissioner had left his side and was seated at the desk. He had unwrapped the bundle and was looking at the can of meat with the leer of a miser counting his gold.

Wade called loudly, "Commissioner!"

The old man jumped wildly and dropped the can on the floor. Abruptly, he slid from sight and emerged above the desk surface a moment later, dripping with abashed chagrin, the can tightly gripped in both hands.

"Yes?" he inquired pleasantly.

Wade turned quickly, his shoulders shuddering with ill-repressed laughter.

"Have you... have you a history text?"

His voice was shaky.

"Yes sir!" Castlemould burst out. "Best history text in the city."

His black shoes squeaked over the floor. From a shelf overladen with dust, he tugged out a thick volume, blew off a cloud and proffered it to Professor Wade.

"Here we are," he said. "Now you just sit right here—" he patted the cracked leather back of an armchair—"and I'll get you something to write on."

Wade watched him as he hustled back to the desk and jerked out the top drawer. May as well let the old fool have the food, he thought.

Castlemould came back with a fat pad of artipaper.

"Now you just sit right here and take all the notes you want," he said. "And don't you worry about your... f... don't you worry."

"Where are *you* going?"

"Nowhere! Nowhere!" the Commissioner professed. "Staying right here. I'll guard the..." His Adam's apple dipped low as he surveyed the three articles again and his voice petered out in rising passion.

Wade eased down into the chair and opened the book. He glanced up once at the old man.

Castlemould was shaking the flask of coffee and listening to it gurgle.

On his seamed face hung the look of a reflective idiot.

Wade began to read: "The destruction of Earth's f___-bearing capacities was completed by the overall military use of bacterial sprays. These minute germinal droplets permeated the earth to such a depth as to make plant growth impossible. They also destroyed the major portion of m___-giving animals as well as ocean edibles, for whom no protectional provision was made in the last desperate germ attacks of the war.

"Also rendered unpalatable were the major water supplies of Earth. Five years after the war, at the time of this writing, the heavy pollution still remains, undiminished by fresh rains. Moreover..."

Wade looked up from the history text, shaking his head grimly.

He looked over at the Commissioner. Castlemould was leaning back in his chair, juggling the box of crackers thoughtfully.

Wade went back to the book and hurriedly finished the selection. He completed his notations and closed the book. Standing, he slid the volume back into its place and walked over to the desk.

"I'll be going now," he said.

Castlemould's lips trembled, drawing back from his china teeth.

"So soon?" he said, close to menace hovering in his words. His eyes scanned the room, searching for something.

"Ah!" he said. Gently he put down the box of crackers and stood up.

"How about a vein ball?" he asked. "Just a short one before you go."

"A what?"

"Vein ball." Wade felt the Commissioner's hand clutch his arm. He was led back to the armchair. "Come along," said Castlemould, weirdly jovial. Wade sat. No harm, he thought... I'll leave the food. That will mollify him.

The old man was wheeling a cumbrous wagon-like table from one corner of the room. From its dialed top rose numerous shiny tendrils that dangled over the sides to end in stubby needles.

"Just one way of—" the Commissioner glanced around like a salesman of illicit postcards "—drinking," he finished softly.

Wade watched him pick up one of the tendrils.

"Here, give me your hand," said the Commissioner.

"Will it hurt?"

"Not at all, not at all," said the old man. "Nothing to be afraid of."

He took hold of Wade's hand and jabbed the needle into the palm. Wade gasped. The pain passed almost immediately.

"What does it..." Wade started. Then he felt a soothing flow of muscle-easing liquors flowing into his veins.

"Isn't that good?" asked Castlemould.

"This is how you drink?"

Castlemould stuck a needle into his own palm.

"Not everyone has such a deluxe set," he said proudly. "This vein wagon was presented to me by the governor of the state. For my services, y'know, in bringing the notorious Tom-Gang to justice."

Wade felt pleasantly lethargic. Just a moment more, he thought; then I must go. The flow of warmth kept coming.

"Tom-Gang?" he asked.

Castlemould perched on the edge of another chair.

"Short for—ahem—Tomato Gang. Group of notorious criminals trying to raise... tomatoes. Wholesale!"

"Horrors," said Wade.

"It was grave, grave."

"Grave. I think I've had enough."

"Better change this a little," Castlemould said, rising to fiddle with the dials.

"I've had enough," Wade said.

"How's that?" asked Castlemould.

Wade blinked and shook his head to clear away the fog.

"That's enough for me," he said. "I'm dizzy."

"How's this?" Castlemould asked.

Wade felt the warmth increasing. His veins seemed to run with fire. His head whirled.

"No more!" he said, trying to rise.

"How's this?" Castlemould asked, drawing the needle from his own hand.

"That's enough!" Wade cried. He reached down to pull out the needle. His hand felt numb. He slumped back into the chair. "Turn it off," he asked feebly.

"How's this!" cried Castlemould. Wade grunted. Someone played a hose of flames through his body. The heat twisted and leaped through his system.

He tried to move. He couldn't.

He was inert, in a liquored coma, when Castlemould finally turned down the dials.

Wade was sagged in the chair, the shiny tentacle still drooping from his palm. His eyes were half closed. They were glassy and doped.

Sound. His thickened brain tried to place it. He blinked his eyes. It was like compressing his brain between hot stones. He opened his eyes. The room was a blurry haze. The shelves ran into each other, watery streams of book backs. He shook his head. He thought he felt his brains jiggling.

The mists began to slip away one by one like the veils of a dancer.

He saw Castlemould at the desk.

Eating.

He was bent over the desk, his face a blackish red as though he were performing some rabidly carnal rite.

His eyes had glued themselves to the food spread out on the cloth.

He was apart. The thermos-flask banged against his teeth. He held it in interlocked fingers, his body shivering sensuously as the hot fluid drained down his throat. His lips smacked ecstatically.

He sliced another piece of meat and stuck it between two crackers.

His trembling hand held the sandwich up to his wet mouth. He bit into their crisp layers and chewed loudly, his eyes glittering orbs of excitement.

Wade's face twisted in revulsion. He sat staring at the old man.

Castlemould was looking at postcards while he ate. His eyes shone. He gazed at them, jaws moving busily, then looked at what he was biting, then looked at the cards again while he chewed.

Wade tried to move his arms. They were logs.

He struggled and managed to slip one hand over the other. He drew out the needle, a sigh rasping in his throat. The Commissioner didn't hear. He was lost... absorbed in an orgy of digestion.

Experimentally, Wade shifted his legs. They were numb. If he stood he knew he'd pitch forward on his face.

He dug nails into his palms. At first there was no feeling. Then it came slowly, slowly, at last flaring up in his brain and clearing away more fog.

His eyes never left Castlemould.

The old man shivered as he ate, caressing each morsel.

Wade thought, he's committing an act of love with a box of crackers.

He fought to regain control.

Castlemould had polished off the cracker box. He was nibbling on the bits of crumb that remained. He picked them up with a moistened finger and popped them into his mouth. He made sure there were no remaining scraps of meat. He tilted up the flask and drained it. Practically empty, it was suspended over his gaping mouth. The remaining drops fell drip-drip into the white-toothed cavity and rolled over his tongue and into his throat.

He sighed and set down the flask.

He looked at his pictures once more, his chest laboring. Then he pushed them aside with a drunken gesture and sank back in the chair.

He stared in sleepy dullness at the desk, the empty box, the can and flask. He ran two weary fingers over his mouth.

After a few moments his head slumped forward. His rattling snores echoed through the room. The festival was over.

Wade struggled up. He stumbled across the floor. It tried to heave itself up in his face. He got to the side of Castlemould's desk and held on dizzily. The old man still slept.

Wade edged around the desk, leaning against its solid surface. The room still spun.

He stood behind the old man's chair, looking down at the shambles of violent dining. He took a deep ragged breath and held onto the chair with eyes closed until the spasm of dizziness had passed.

He opened his eyes and looked once more at the desk.

He noticed the postcards. He stared incredulously.

They were pictures of food.

A head of cabbage, a roast turkey, a loaf of bread. In some of them, partially unclad women held desiccated lettuce leaves, lean tomatoes, dried up oranges; held them out in their hands in profane offering.

"God, I want to go back," he muttered.

He was halfway to the door when he realized he had no idea where his chamber was.

He stood weaving on the threadbare rug, listening to Castlemould's snores ring out.

He went back then and squatted dizzily by the side of the desk. He kept his eyes on the open-mouthed Commissioner as he slid out the desk drawers.

In the bottom drawer he found what he wanted, a strange gun-like weapon. He took it. "Get up," he said angrily, rapping the old man on the head.

"Aaah!!" cried Castlemould, starting up. His midriff collided with his desk. He fell back in the chair, the wind knocked out of him.

"Get up," Wade said.

A confused Castlemould stared up. He tried to smile and a crumb fell from his lips.

"Now, look here, young man."

"Shut up. You're taking me back to my chamber."

"Wait—"

"Now!"

"Careful! Don't fool with that thing. It's dangerous."

"I hope it's very dangerous," Wade said. "Get up now and take me to your car."

Castlemould groaned to his feet. "Young man, this is..."

"Oh, be quiet, you stupid senile goat. Take me to your car, and keep hoping I don't pull this lever."

"God, don't do that!"

The Commissioner suddenly stopped halfway to the door. He grimaced and bent over as his stomach began to protest against its violation.

"Oh! That food," he muttered wretchedly.

"I hope you have the belly ache of the century," said Wade, prodding him on. "You deserve it."

The old man clutched at his paunch. "Ohhhh," he groaned. "Don't shove."

They went into the hall. Castlemould spun against the closet door. He clawed at the wood.

"I'm dying!" he announced.

Wade ordered. "Come on!"

Castlemould, heedless, pulled open the door and plunged into the closet depths. There, in the stuffy blackness, he was very sick.

Wade turned away in disgust.

At last the old man stumbled forth, face white and drawn.

He shut the door and leaned back against it.

"Oh," he said, weakly.

"You deserved that," Wade said. "Richly."

"Don't talk," begged the old man. "I may die yet."

"Let's go," Wade said.

They were in the car. A recovered Commissioner was at the wheel. Wade sat across the wide front seat, holding the weapon level with Castlemould's chest.

"I apologize for..." started the Commissioner.

"Drive."

"Well, I don't like to appear inhospitable."

"Be quiet."

The old man made a face.

"Young man," he said tentatively. "How would you like to make some money ?"

Wade knew what was coming. "How?" he said flatly.

"Very simple."

"Bring you food," Wade finished.

Castlemould's face twitched.

"Well," he whined, "what's so bad about that ?"

"You have the gall to ask me that," Wade said.

"Now, look, young man. Son..."

"Oh, God, *shut* up," Wade said sourly. "Think about your hall closet and shut up."

"Now, son," insisted the Commissioner. "That was only because I'm not used to it. But now I—" his face became suddenly clever and evil—"I have a taste for it."

The car turned a corner. Far ahead Wade saw his chamber.

"Then lose your taste," he said, never taking his eyes off the old man.

The Commissioner looked desperate. His scrawny fingers tightened on the wheel. His left foot drummed resolutely on the floorboards.

"You won't change your mind?" he said.

"You're lucky I don't shoot you."

Castlemould said no more. He watched the road with slitted, calculating eyes.

The car hissed up beside the chamber and stopped. "Tell the officers you want to examine the chamber," Wade ordered him.

"If I don't?"

"Then whatever comes out of this barrel, you'll get right in the stomach."

Castlemould forced a brisk smile to his lips as the officers came up.

"What's the meaning... oh, Commissioner," the officer said, sliding unnoticeably from truculence to reverence. "What can we do for you?" He doffed his cap with a face-halving smile.

"Want to look over that... thing," said Castlemould. "Want to check something."

"Yes *sir,* sir," said the officer.

"I'm putting the gun in my pocket," said Wade quietly.

The Commissioner said nothing as he opened the door. The two of them got out and approached the chamber.

"I'll go in first," Castlemould said loudly. "Might be dangerous in there. Wouldn't have you take a risk."

The officers murmured appreciatingly. Wade's mouth tightened. He contented himself by thinking how hard he was going to boot the old man right out into the street.

The Commissioner's bones crackled as he reached up for the two door rungs. He pulled himself up with a teeth-clenching grunt. Wade gave him a shove and enjoyed the sound of the old Commissioner staggering against the steel bulkhead inside.

He reached up his free hand.

He couldn't make it with just one hand.

He needed both rungs. He grabbed them and swung in quickly.

Castlemould was waiting. The moment Wade entered a scrawny hand plunged into his pocket. The weapon was jerked out.

"Aaah *haah!*"

The high-pitched voice echoed shrilly inside the small shell.

Wade pressed against the bulkhead. He could see a little in the dimness.

"What do you think you're going to do now?" he asked.

The white teeth flashed. "You're taking me back," Castlemould said. "I'm going with you."

"There's only room for one person in here."

"Then it'll be me."

"You can't operate it."

"You'll tell me," Castlemould ordered, waving the weapon.

"Or what?"

"Or I'll burn you up."

Wade tensed himself.

"And if I tell you?" he asked.

"You stay here till I come back."

"I don't believe you."

"You have to, young man," cackled the Commissioner. "Tell me how it works."

Wade reached for his pocket.

"Watch it!" warned Castlemould.

"Do you want me to get out the instruction sheets or not?"

"Go on. But be careful. Instruction sheets, haah?"

"You wouldn't understand a word of them."

Wade reached into his pocket.

"What's that you've got?" Castlemould asked. "That's not paper."

"A bar of chocolate," Wade breathed the words. "A thick, sweet, creamy rich bar of chocolate."

"Gimme it!"

"Here. Take it."

The Commissioner lunged. He fell off balance, and the weapon pointed at the floor.

Wade stepped to one side and grabbed the old man by the collar and the seat of the pants. He hurled Commissioner Castlemould out through the doorway. The old man went sprawling into the street.

Shouts. The officers were horrified.

Wade tossed the chocolate bar after him.

"Obscene dog!" he roared, as the bar bounced off Castlemould's skull.

He jerked the door shut and turned the wheel until it was sealed. He strapped himself down and flipped switches, chuckling at the thought of the Commissioner trying to explain the bar of chocolate so he could keep it.

Outside, the intersection was suddenly empty, except for staring people and a few wisps of acrid smoke.

There was only one sound in the dead stillness.

The rising wail of a hungry old man.

The chamber shuddered to a halt. The door opened and Wade jumped out. He was surrounded by men and students who came flooding from the control room.

"Hey!" said his friend. "You made it!"

"Of course," Wade said, feeling the pleasure of understatement.

"This calls for a celebration," said the friend. "I'm taking you out tonight and buying you the biggest steak you ever... hey, what's the matter?"

Professor Wade was blushing. • • •

RICHARD MATHESON wrote the original series episode "The Enemy Within." Movies based on his work include **The Incredible Shrinking Man, Duel, What Dreams May Come,** *and most recently, adapted for the third time,* **I Am Legend.**

COLUMBUS
OF THE
STARS:
A TREK NOT TAKEN?

Stop me if you've heard this one.

In 1964, a successful writer begins shopping around Hollywod a pitch for a science fiction series of a new kind.

Unlike previous such series, which have tended to be either anthologies, or else cheap daytime fare for children, this is a series for prime time with continuing characters, aimed at an adult audience.

It's the story of a starship and her crew. Their assignment is to survey for undiscovered planets, to contact alien beings and cultures, to probe into reaches never visited by mankind.

I'm sure you're ahead of me. The writer is, of course, Ib Melchior, and the series is *Columbus of the Stars.*

No? Well, that *other* series pitch did have the advantage of selling. Although its synchronicitous sibling never left the launch pad, it's interesting to consider that sometimes, an idea may only seem unique in retrospect because it succeeded, while other iterations of the notion did not.

If things had gone a little differently, might this be an issue on *Columbus of the Stars,* with an article about a forgotten and somewhat similar pitch with the unlikely name *Star Trek?*

At the time, the safer bet might have been *Columbus of the Stars.* Ib Melchior had worked in television since 1948, and wrote for the series *Men into Space.* He was a published science fiction author. He had moved to the big screen, writing and directing *The Angry Red Planet.* In 1964, he had two films in the pipeline: *Robinson Crusoe on Mars,* which he wrote, and *The Time Travelers,* again as writer-director. (*Crusoe's* Friday, Vic Lundin, developed *Columbus of the Stars* with Melchior.)

Gene Roddenberry had impressive television credits, with scores of produced scripts and a Writers Guild award, but his only science fiction was an anthology episode, "The Secret Weapon of 117," in which a covert alien invasion falls to that little human thing called love. He had recently become a showrunner with *The Lieutenant,* but did better provoking conflict with the Marine Corps, which withdrew its production support in midseason, than in drumming up ratings. The network had not picked the show up for a second season.

Imagine yourself a network executive in 1964, and this crosses your desk. Might you have given it a shot?

—The Editor

SERIES FORMAT BY
IB MELCHIOR
AND VIC LUNDIN

COLUMBUS OF THE STARS

A One-Hour Science Fiction Adventure Series.

Many years ago a dauntless young captain under the patronage of a great queen embarked upon a courageous voyage of exploration and adventure across uncharted seas towards unknown worlds. The three vessels of his command suffered untold hardships and dangers. One of the ships became disabled; they all had to elude grim, hostile forces; a frightening meteor from space beyond crashed down, narrowly missing the little fleet; strange, inexplicable happenings affecting their vital equipment drove fear into the hearts of the crew; the deadly Sargasso Sea threatened to imprison and swamp them, and signs of impending success turned out to be mere mockery, until finally a man-made artifact found drifting in the deep, alien waters restored lost faith and spirit. And before long landfall was made. One vessel was lost, but a new world was discovered... a world of great beauty, wonder and riches. The name of the captain of this intrepid voyage was Christopher Columbus. Five centuries later, another young captain embarks upon an equally courageous, adventurous and vital voyage of exploration—a voyage into deep, uncharted galactic space itself. This young Captain may well be known as—

COLUMBUS OF THE STARS

—and the fabulous adventures and exploits of this young space explorer, his crew and his ships... on new and alien worlds, in space, in the unimagined elements of the unknown... are the stories and episodes of the series.

SYNOPSIS OF THE SERIES FROM WHICH SOME OF THE STORIES WILL SPRING...

For some time, the sun has gone through unprecedented phases of sunspot concentrations, cosmic ray flares and disturbing variations in solar eruption activity, with damaging results from freak meteorological conditions on Earth. Careful and knowledgeable study of these unusual phenomena has led an eminent astronomer to a spine-chilling conclusion. The sun is becoming unstable; it exhibits all the characteristics of a nova in the making! Within a couple of centuries, it will flare up in one gigantic eruption of pure, searing energy—instantly vaporizing the entire solar system in its mighty death throes. Mankind has two hundred years to exist before being utterly annihilated—unless a new home is found in the galaxy, and the means to reach it in a total evaculation are created!

But the scientist finds little support for his dire belief among other astronomers, who would rather attribute the sun's worrisome behavior to matters other than certain doom... And besides—it is a long time off!

When the astronomer insists upon his predictions, he is derided as just another crackpot prophet of doom and mercilessly ridiculed. So great is the scorn and mockery heaped upon him that he suffers a near-fatal stroke—and no longer is able to champion his cause...

However, the old man has a son, Chris, a young officer in the U.S. Astronaut Corps, who upon his return from an exploration trip to one of the near planets learns of his father's fate—and the reasons for his collapse. Angrily, bitterly, he takes up his father's cause—and succeeds in rallying about him other men and women of farsighted concern from the world over. And finally, he and his follow-ers manage to persuade the First Lady of the United States of America to prevail upon the President to make an explorative expedition possible: an attempt to find an-other solar system with an Earth-like planet, to which mankind can migrate—just in case...!

Three ships are made ready, each with a complement of about twenty astronauts, including female technicians, and chosen by careful computer analysis of their char-acteristics and abilities. If a New Earth is found, colonization can thus begin at once. The nearest star system, where the probability of a solar system with a habit-able world is high, is that of Alpha Cen-tauri, four point three light years away. The expedition will be gone from Earth for many earth years, although to the crews aboard the ships, travelling at speeds close to that of light itself, and by means of an advanced space/time warp drive, only a fraction of that time will seem to have passed, following the proven Einstein time paradox effect.

On the flagship of the little fleet, com-manded by the young astronaut officer, Chris, a scientific observer is placed by the President, to whom he will report di-rectly upon the return of the expedition. This man is most sceptical both as to the reasons for making the journey, and its ul-timate success. As a result, an air of strain and increasingly bitter verbal clashes de-velop between him and the young cap-tain...

Once escaped from the Earth's gravita-tional pull, the three ships try to link up according to plan—and the first mishap is discovered. One of the ships has sustained damage—and a precarious and dangerous repair job is required. Supervised by Chris himself, it is performed in space—but it is considered an ill omen for the journey...

Finally the ships link up, so that the crews have access to the entire cluster; the time warp drive is activated—and the vast, incredible journey begins in earnest...

From the start the journey is beset by misadventures and near calamity...

...Leaving their own solar system, still building up velocity and passing close by the mighty planet Jupiter, the fleet runs into a magnetic space storm, which nearly sends the expedition crashing to oblivion on the lethal mass of the monster planet... A hit by a meteor creates a near-cata-strophic emergency... Sabotage by hostile factions back on Earth is discovered only in the barest nick of time... The trip seems to leap precariously from crisis to crisis... Tempers run short, and not even the more pleasant aspects of the journey, the luxu-rious ray health baths, the awe-inspiring celestial sights, and the natural closeness of the young people can avert what finally threatens to become near mutiny, even as the expedition grows close to its first goal—almost within a distance at which a solar system might be observed... if it exists... Only a sudden, terrifying devel-opment causes the space-exhausted crew members to snap out of their dangerous space-kafar...

The ship cluster is already decelerating from its maximum speed—when it runs into a gigantic space dust cloud... The in-dividual ferrous particles are small enough to be handled by the meteor shield, and far enough apart not to create a menace—but another, frightening and wholly unforeseen fact is suddenly appar-ent—and threatens to destroy the entire expedition!

When the ship cluster passed through the magnetic storm near Jupiter, it was it-self magnetized! It is now a huge, incred-ibly strong magnet, hurtling through the dust cloud! And instantly, the tiny iron particles are inexorably attracted to it—and before long, a thick coat of clinging space dust is formed around the ship's hull, growing ever thicker and heavier—coating and clogging all observation instruments, and even the space drive itself! The ship no longer can decelerate nor maneuver at all! Blindly, they hurtle on towards the blazing alien sun—ultimately to fall in towards its infernal mass, being seared to super-hot vapor in an instant!

But Chris and the observer scientist—forced to close co-operation by grim necessity—together reason out a possible escape... Feverishly, the entire crew labors to carry out the plan... The outer meteor shield of the ships, linked together as one, is made into one huge electro-magnet... and by shooting fantastic charges of alternate electric current through the metal shield, the polarity is changed, and the ferrous dust particles are made to catapult themselves from the stricken vessel—leaving it clean and clear to escape the embrace of the deadly space dust cloud...

And then—when close observation is restored, and while the distant observation equipment is being repaired—a wondrous sight can suddenly be seen... There, drifting in space, is a derelict, a space ship wreck swimming serenely in the void—cold and dead! A ship of an obviously alien design! Where did it come from? Who built it?? The earth expedition may be closer to success—or even further from it than ever before, if the dead and broken ship is itself an unsuccessful explorer!

Reluctantly, Chris decides not to board the derelict; too much power would be wasted, and the all-important mission is still to be fulfilled... and at that moment, a jubilant report comes from the observation center. The equipment is repaired; the alien solar system before them can be clearly seen and four bright, Earth-sized planets can be made out orbiting the sun!

The first of the planets to be explored by the expedition is the one nearest to the blazing sun; but it is too near. The boiling, seething surface can be observed in fiery turbulence on the view screens. It is obviously unsuited for any life...

Next, the planet furthest away is explored. The flagship lands there—but the world is a frozen world: barren rock fields, poisonous atmosphere, ammonia snow covered peaks...

The third planet also looks desolate and dead; and when the exploration ship sets down, it topples and is totally wrecked when a solid-appearing plain turns out to be a quicksand-like pumice dust lake... The planet is arid, scorched and spectacularly thermal-eroded, and it is a herculean task to rescue the stranded crew of the crippled ship, but it is finally done without loss of life.

But spirits are low. No habitable planet has been found—and there is only one more... the second planet from the alien sun...

The three ships all land—and kneel in thanksgiving when they, to their awe and wonder, find a planet as close to Earth at its best as is at all possible...! Lush, rolling, green fields; verdant groves of trees; meandering brooks... but no animal life whatsoever!...

And then they receive a fantastic shock. There—upon the far horizon—they see a huge, fabulous city, sprawled comfortably under a gigantic, transparently shimmering, dome-like covering...!

And a party led by Chris himself sets out to explore this alien city...

It is a breathtaking, awe-inspiring place; the dome is a titanic force-field protecting the city beneath... but the place is utterly dead and deserted... The whole expedition is joined in the city, examining the pictorial records of the ancient, long dead alien race... A beautiful, humanoid people of strange, unearthly grace, and with a vast fund of knowledge and science...

The expedition has found a perfect future home for mankind!

And then it happens.

They are not alone!

Suddenly, they are attacked by a horde of lumbering, massive, insensitive creatures—and manage to escape imminent annihilation only in the last possible moment by taking refuge in a vault-like room...

And a pathetic, ironic fact becomes clear from the records found in the vault... The alien race is indeed extinct—has been for many centuries, as is all animal life on the planet... That billion-to-one chance overtook them so quickly that countermeasures were impossible; their planet passed through the tail of a huge, wandering comet... a tail of poisonous, inescapable gasses that wiped out all life... The unearthly attackers, even now trying to reach the trapped expedition, are in fact the last few of a host of self-repairing servo-robots protecting the property of their long dead masters against the intruders!

And the robots break through...

It is a savage, brawling battle that ensues; the massive robots are nearly indestructible—even with the fantastic laser weapons of the expedition—and the desperate fight is not without its tragic toll of injury—and death...

But at last it is over.

The New Earth is secure...

When the weary expedition force returns to the ships, they are met with a vital message from Earth...

The astronomers and scientists of Earth have finally recognized the inexorable danger to the planet and mankind; Chris is implored to do everything in his power to achieve success—the future of mankind depends on it... even now the entire population of Earth is co-operating in building the titanic fleet, which will take man away from his dying sun...!

But the new-found planet has been made uninhabitable for any kind of animal life over a prolonged period of time by the poisonous comet—and reluctantly Chris leaves the beautiful world behind...

And on goes the search of the young—

COLUMBUS OF THE STARS

COLUMBUS OF THE STARS will have as its continuing characters these personalities:

COMMODORE CHRISTOPHER, a brilliant, forceful, imaginative young space captain in his early thirties, who commands the expedition. He is tall, with virile good looks without being stereotyped, and he is wholly dedicated to his all-important mission and its ultimate success...

The three ships of Commodore Christopher's command each has a complement of twenty astrocrew members, including a captain. There are fourteen women technicians, serving as computer feeders and records staff, divided equally between the three ships, except for the Flagship, which—being slightly larger—has two extra technicians. Here, too, is the Female Officer under whose command the women spacecrew serve. This woman officer is also one of the continuing characters of the series.[1]

---

1. Yes, this does seem sexist today, but keep in mind that *Star Trek* wasn't very forward-looking on gender roles, either. The three females in its regular and semi-regular cast were, in essence, a nurse, a personal assistant, and a telephone operator. —*The Editor*

Also aboard the Flagship is the Chief Scientist, a mature man perhaps 45 years of age. Because of certain basic differences, there is conflict between this man of science and the young commodore, although at the same time the two men hold one another in great respect. This man will also be a continuing character.

In addition, there is a young Astro-Engineer, a real firebrand, reckless and hotheaded, but a genius in his vital field. He does cause trouble and crisis—but always acts out of his own convictions, faulty though they may occasionally be...

And there are others... And, too, there are many possibilities for the important guest star parts to come from the crews of the Flagship and her two companions, as well as from the alien cultures and existences the Earth explorers may encounter.

Some Points About—

COLUMBUS OF THE STARS

...It is today an accepted scientific belief that there are literally millions of inhabitable planets within our own galaxy. These—and the vast space between them—are the field of action for the series.

...The action-adventure story possibilities in subject and scope, excitement and drama are limited only by the imagination. The elements of human conflict, humor and drama will be provided by the series characters...

...The series will forever be "new"—and yet have the vital audience identification possibilities lacking in an anthology because of its continuing characters, who can capture the loyalties of the viewing audience...

...In addition, the series will possess the magic and century-long "exploitation" of the Columbus name...

...In the matter of production, the three identical ships will provide an important asset in permanent sets and effects. Imagination and ingenuity in story and execution will be substituted for elaborate production costs...

It turns out that *Columbus of the Stars* and *Star Trek* did not lead entirely separate lives. Melchior and Lundin's series proposal reached Gene Roddenberry at least once, and possibly twice.

Vic Lundin reports that he gave a copy of the *Columbus of the Stars* pitch bible to Byron Haskin, director of *Robinson Crusoe on Mars,* during post-production on that film, in early 1964. Haskin subsequently served as associate producer on the first pilot episode of *Star Trek.* Might he have shown *Columbus of the Stars* to Roddenberry earlier, when the writer was formulating his own series pitch?

Certainly, there are some elements in common between the *Columbus* pitch bible and the undated *Star Trek* pitch bible reprinted in the book *The Making of Star Trek.* Besides the central element of a starship on an exploration mission in deep space, both documents try to sell their series along similar lines.

1) It will have the varied settings of an anthology, but the audience-identification qualities of an ongoing series with continuing characters.

2) Extensive standing sets, representing the various functional areas of the starship(s), will help keep overall costs down by allowing plenty of shipboard action.

3) The series' possibilities are only as limited as the number of habitable worlds—and a recent study suggests there may be millions. Radio astronomer Frank Drake formulated his famous equation in 1960, estimating the number of communicating civilizations in the galaxy (and estimating the number of habitable worlds as part of the process). This is probably the equation Roddenberry admits in *The Making of Star Trek* that he failed to track down in time, and made up a fake placeholder for instead.

This could all, of course, be coincidence, the sort of thing any savvy would-be science fiction series creator of 1964 might figure a network would want to hear: why this new series type will work, why it will have the "legs" for a long run, and why it won't cost a fortune to make. Similar series ideas have shown up independently before. Some even made it to the air together: *The Munsters* and *The Addams Family, Chicago Hope* and *ER*.

Ib Melchior and Vic Lundin shopped *Columbus of the Stars* around to producers and studios. Melchior and Lundin had named *Columbus of the Stars* according to the "combine something familiar with something futuristic" pattern that had worked with *Robinson Crusoe on Mars.* (Melchior also had pitches at the time called *Space Family Robinson* and *Treasure Asteroid.)*

This time, the formula didn't seem to work. Melchior and Lundin went straight futuristic, renaming their project *Starship Explorers.* This time, the population explosion was a more immediate motivating factor for the mission, and the crew was an international one, occupying a single starship. In a letter to television executive Herb Sussan, Melchior mused over adding an android to the cast. The captain's relationship to him/it would be "almost a friendship, certainly an attachment such as most people form for a faithful car or boat!" (Roddenberry later explored similar ground in his pilot *The Questor Tapes* and, of course, with the character of Data on *Star Trek: The Next Generation.)* Most interestingly, the short pitch document is billed at the top as "AN IDEA... ...for a TV Series about a Starship and its Crew, roaming the Galaxy in search of New Worlds..."

Meanwhile, Desilu had picked up *Star Trek,* and Byron Haskin suggested Vic Lundin to Gene Roddenberry for the role of Spock. When Lundin met with Roddenberry, he brought along documents about *Starship Explorers,* including concept illustrations, and left them with the producer. More than two years later, when *Star Trek* finally reached the air, Lundin was stunned to find an *Enterprise* bridge he felt suspiciously similar to the one designed for his and Melchior's series. He thought his later role as the series' first Klingon in "Errand of Mercy" may have been an attempt to pay him back.

Again, it may well have been a similar answer to a similar question. And *Star Trek* certainly had elements of its own that contributed to its success: the half-alien first officer, the transporter, an existing human presence in the galaxy (further expanding the types of stories they could do).

Whether or not *Star Trek* borrowed from *Columbus of the Stars/Starship Explorers,* it's fascinating to see that something that has become enshrined in the common culture was not as unique as it seemed. One can scarcely help looking at this stillborn twin, this shadow sibling, and wondering, what if...? —*The Editor*

Float Like a Butterfly

by
Norman
Spinrad

Illustrated by Kevin Farrell

YOUR DREAMMASTER 301

Since the dawn of time, the lives people lived in their dreams were far more exciting than those in the waking workaday world, but quite unpredictable, and also limited by their own unconscious imagination.

No more! Now the DREAMMASTER 301 allows you to not only program your dreams but to enjoy dreams beyond your own imagination created for you by the masters of this great new artform.

And it's easy to use too! Even children above the age of ten can easily use the simple controls. Parental guidance is advised.

THE CARAVAN OF DREAMS CATALOG

THE WORLD'S LARGEST SELECTION OF DREAMCHIPS
and at prices that can't be beat!!!

Tired of paying high prices for our competitor's limited selection of dreams adapted from moldly old video games and third-rate movies? CARAVAN OF DREAMS takes your Dreamtime to the next level, and at prices we guarantee can't be beat.

CARAVAN OF DREAMS has *no* production costs, no rights purchase costs, because we do not produce the dreamchips in our catalog. Instead, we offer a wide and ever growing selection of dreams created by *independent* dreamchip producers, and pass the savings on to *you!*

By offering independent dreamchip creators a means for getting their product to you without dream shops and their distributors, THE CARAVAN OF DREAMS CATALOG slashes retail prices even further.

And in conjunction with the American Association of Dreamwriters, we have created the AAD Rating Code, modeled on the film industry's rating system. The AAD Rating Code on every dreamchip we offer guarantees no unpleasant Dreamtime surprises.

The **G** rating guarantees no death, pain, foul language, sexual content, or nudity. Suitable for all ages.

GP dreamchips allow limited nudity, violence, and some erotic content. Parental guidance is advised.

MA rated dreamchips are for Mature Adults only. Terminal violence, but not to your Dreamtime Avatar. Full frontal nudity. Explicit sexual content short of penetration or actual orgasm. Adult language and images.

UR—Unrestricted dreamchips are not available at this time due to existing state and pending federal legislation.

Take advantage of our special introductory offer and save even more. Order three dreamchips and get a fourth one free!

• • •

*Y*ou are in a basketball gym decorated for the Senior Prom with red, white and blue streamers, a revolving mirrorball, a refreshment table under a canopy of the same colors. A four-piece band vaguely resembling a modestly-punked version of the early Beatles, with neon red, green, blue, and yellow Fab Four

hairdos and black leather shirtless suits open to the waist, plays a dance version of "I Wanna Hold Your Hand," as teenagers in tuxes and ballgowns whirl happily around the floor.

One boy dances within a glorifying cone of golden light as if being followed by an overhead spot. He's wearing a black prom tux with a golden ruffled shirt and a heavy gold chain in place of a bowtie. He's got a mane of golden surfer hair, a face reminiscent of Jim Morrison played by Leonardo DiCaprio, the body of any red-blooded girl's dreams, and he dances like the Michael Jackson of *Thriller.*

He's dancing with a busty blonde wearing the top half of a tight ballgown and a cheerleader's skirt revealing the legs of a Vegas showgirl. Her face is straight from a Hollywood plastic surgeon's catalog except for the triumphantly possessive smirk.

You can't take your eyes off them, and as they glide by you, he gives you a sympathetic shrug and sweet little smile whose smarmy ruefulness stabs at your heart as you sit there in your wheelchair, all dressed up and no way to go.

"Hey you, don't be blue, your fairy godmomma's gonna look after you," a voice like Tina Turner rapping Mohammed Ali sings in your ear. She's wearing a gown of fluff and feathers every color of the pastel rainbow and she's got wings that cloak her shoulders done up like glitter-dusted peacocks' tails. Hair as white as Andy Warhol's done in a crown of Rasta dreads and the face of an elder Princess Di from uptown Jamaica.

"Listen up, girl, I say pay attention to me, you gonna float like a butterfly when I set you free. "

She produces something that looks like an airline ticket in a gold foil jacket. "Time to fly, now move your ass, here's your most frequent flyer pass. Once around the world, that's the dish, and when you get back, you get one big wish. Wish for the Moon, wish for the guy, or a lifetime supply of no-cal cream pie."

You take the ticket and—

You're a butterfly.

You're a bright orange and black Monarch butterfly flitting around above the dancers, whirling, swirling, dancing in the air to "Lucy in the Sky with Diamonds." No diamonds in the high school gym sky, but your fairy godmomma's up there with you, a Rasta Tinkerbell from Woodstock hovering on iridescent dragonfly vanes.

"Good karma make you larger, bad cess make you small, touchin' terra firma and you gonna take you one big fall. There's always a catch, so here's the thing. Like an Air Force flyboy, gotta earn your wings."

You're high in the Wild Blue Yonder, a tiny butterfly circling before a rainbow that fills the clear blue sky before you, and within, a million hummingbirds zip around like cartoon helicopters. "Off ya go, give it your best, time for the solo license test. Can't throw you to the dogs like a cat's little mouse, so this one time it's on the house."

*A*nd now *you* are a hummingbird, wings whirring, your little body thrumming like a juiced-up two-stroke lightweight motorcycle engine as you pass through into the world Beyond the Rainbow. It's a great big world to little you, but not so wide. Tree trunks seem to tower into the stratosphere above you, the flowers on bushes as tall as mountains are mostly as big as you are, below gambol doggies and pussycats as big as dinosaurs, and it's all brilliantly colored, like a tv screen with the hue control cranked way up, the blue of the sky, the green of the fo-

liage, the red and yellows and purples of the flowers, even the dun-brown of tree trunks and limbs, positively glowing.

And it's a loud world too, your fellow hummingbirds like formations of helicopters, huge cawing crows hopping around the fields below, dogs barking like firecrackers exploding, bees and hornets zipping around like World War II prop fighter planes.

Smell and taste combine in one delightful sense. You're awash in the fragrances of sweet honeys and chocolates, the taste of roses, morning glories, orchids, intoxicating. You flit and hover from flower to flower, siphoning up nectars from the floral smorgasbord with your long hollow beak.

You drop down to a big bush of red roses where half a dozen hummingbirds are already feasting and sample the nectar which tastes of rosewater and cola and fills you with energy. There are a few bees doing likewise, but they pay you and your fellow hummingbirds no heed until—

More and more and more of them arrive from the hive hanging from a tree limb far above, descending to claim and occupy the prize, dozens, scores, what seems like hundreds, and in moments the rose bush is fairly covered with bees, two, three, four, five to every flower, buzzing threateningly, angrily, evicting the hummingbirds by sheer force of stinger-armed numbers. Your fellow hummingbirds hover uncertainly around the swarming bees, some of them making unsuccessful dives at the roses. But you're not among them. You look up at the hive, hover for a moment, and then make for it, your beak straight ahead like a threatening sword.

The swarm of bees on the roses rises en mass to pursue you, to defend their hive. But you're too fast for them, and you lead them on a merry chase, spiraling up and around tree trunks, into the tree crowns, over hill and dale, and finally up and beyond the trees, up, and up, and up, until you feel your strength waning, and—

*Y*ou become a big black raven, with long powerful wings which carry you higher and higher with every slow easy stroke. The bee swarm can no longer follow you. They buzz below in angry frustration. You caw at them laughingly. They give it up. If you had a nose, you would thumb it.

Onward you fly, following the afternoon sun westward. It takes a lot less effort to cover a lot more ground when you're a raven, your wings working slowly but steadily, flying high over fields of golden grain towards the purple majesty of the mountains that begin to peer up over the western horizon.

Not much aerial traffic up here over the plains, no bugs at your altitude, just crows and what are maybe sparrows or starlings poaching the grain, the odd hawk or kite circling way up higher than you are.

You pass over a farmstead. There's something coming up at you, and you swoop lower to have a look. There's a little boy down there waving and shouting, and then you see why. What's coming up at you, or at least trying to, is an ungainly half-grown chicken, a chick really, having escaped from somewhere and trying none-too-gracefully to try out its wings, flapping the stubby things valiantly but frantically, slipping and sliding through the air like a puppy on ice.

It's cute, it's funny, but what isn't is the circling falcon high above whose attention the silly fuzz and aerial flopping has attracted. It folds its wings and goes into a stoop straight at the struggling pet chick. It's not a big bird, in fact its not as big as a tough burly raven like you, it's got a raptor's sharp curved beak and talons, but your beak is much bigger and strong enough to crack walnuts, so—

You zip into a flying dash to intercept it and then you're under the falcon's dive trajectory, flapping your big black wings as you fly tight circles in its downward path, cawing raucous raven threats, and shrieking mocking challenges.

The falcon has to spread its wings and break its stoop or collide with you, and it does, and for a mad moment, the two of you confront each other hanging there in the air. The falcon stares at you with its fierce little raptor's grin and its cruel beady little eyes. You stare back. It cocks its head back and forth, a challenge maybe, but also a mime of outraged perplexity. You stare it down. You clack your beak once, twice, thrice, making sounds like a nutcracker splintering little skulls.

It's no way, José, as the falcon turns and makes off for the nearest thermal.

You spiral down to where the chick is still trying to teach itself how to fly, innocently and none-too-brightly unaware of the fate you have saved it from. With an avian shrug, you circle tight around it, herding it back downward. It takes a while for the silly thing to get the message, but it finally does, being probably exhausted by then anyway, and flops back down into the kid's waiting hands.

He blows you a grateful kiss, and you head back up and westward, turning into a vulture as you hit a thermal like a great but gentle hand. You're a big vulture. In fact you're a condor, member of an endangered species maybe, but the biggest flying bird there is. You won't win any avian beauty contest, maybe, but your wings are six feet across, you ride the thermals effortlessly as a sailplane with them, and your eyes can see for miles and miles with crystal clarity like a camera's zoom lens.

And what you see is a mighty range of mountains blocking the way before you, their crowning peaks miles high.

*B*ut you're a condor, you're the 747 of birds, you know the highways and byways of the mountain skyways, you ride the foothill ridgeline thermals, circling up them with your great wings outstretched, your telescopic vision seeking out a pass into the upper reaches, and easily enough finding it.

You soar into the mountains from thermal to thermal above the slopes of the branching canyons, into the main cordillera, meandering with them ever westward, through forested shoulders and rocky snowcapped peaks that tower high above even your imperial flight path. It's great fun, it's like a three-dimensional roller-coaster ride, but silent and graceful, without the thrills and chills, the wind of passage playfully ruffling your feathers, the thermals passing you on from hand to invisible hand, you could soar like this forever, glissing through the winding skyways at the top of the world.

And then you're through the mountains, flying over a searing desert that's paradise for thermals, you're up there with the airliner flight paths as you soar over a lesser mountain range; indeed you see a 737 flying *beneath* you.

In a twinkling, you're on the coast, with the broad blue Pacific stretching out before you. Hang gliders ride the updraft of a seaside cliff above a sandy beach packed with sunbathers. Surfers ride the crests of meager waves among the swimmers. Time for a little fun.

You drift down low enough towards the beach for the throngs down there to get their first good look at the mighty but elusive condor. You skim up and down the strand to the wondering delight of the onlookers pointing fingers and gawking up at you. You execute a few tight circles, show off a couple of loops, cap this act of

the performance with a perfect Immelmann, then ride the beach thermal up to where the hang gliders fly.

At first, their riders are startled and maybe a little frightened to suddenly find a condor among them, your wings are about as wide as theirs—you are, after all, a species of grim-looking vulture met face to face in midair, and they scatter around you.

But you soar after a half dozen of them, dip below them, come up the other side, do it again and again, fly in front and below them to come up facing them. You're floating on a thermal and so are they, it's soft and slowly gentle flight, almost a mutual hover, as the boys and girls hanging in their harnesses regard you with bewildered amusement now. You waggle your wings and bank left, right, left, right, in the universal flyboy greeting.

In the quiet sky, you can hear their laughter and cries of delight. A couple of the hang gliders attempt to return the greeting, nowhere as easy a feat for canvas wings as it is for yours. You turn away and fly a slow easy curve back over the beach towards the cliffside thermal. One, two, three, and then all four of the hang gliders are following you, raggedly at first, but then forming up, two by two into a wedge formation behind you like migrating geese playing follow the leader.

You're the expert at getting the best out of thermals, no mere human hanging from some pipe and canvas contraption, what they're still learning, you do what comes naturally, and you lead your little flock up, up, up, higher above the beach than any of them have probably been before. Seeing this, other hang gliders join the flying wedge, and soon every hang glider in the area joins in, and you're flying point for a flock of a couple of dozen laughing, cheering, joyous humans doing their best to maintain formation.

You lead them up and down the ridge-line thermals for a few high altitude passes until they all get it and you've gained their confidence sufficiently enough to try some air show stunts. They can't fly loops like you, so you lead the formation in a swooping dive into a level glide low over the beach, but not so low that momentum won't carry their unflap-pable wings back to the ridgeline ther-mals.

You can hear the people below clap and cheer and see the scintilations of snap-shots being taken with pointless flashes. You lead your wedge of hang gliders back to the thermals to recover altitude, and then do it again, this time sweeping in a little curve out over the sea for the surfers, a few of whom wave up at you, standing easily enough on their boards in the light surf.

One more trip to the thermals, and back again you come, not so low this time, high enough so that they can maintain safe al-titude as you lead your flying circus in three complete turns of a perfect circle over the beach, drifting out over the surfers on the last one. Coming out of it, you waggle your wings as you head back over the beach to the cliffs, the hang glid-ers follow suit, and then the flying wedge is waggling its collective wings in unison in an extro salute to the cheering audience as it passes over them.

Up the thermal you lead them, higher and higher you circle, higher than mere hang gliders can follow, as they circle fur-ther and further below you, cheering you on—

—and onward west, for now *you* are one of them, you are a hang glider, the mother of all hang gliders, with the body of a human but arms that are helium-filled balloons in the shape of broad wings thirty feet across. You're lighter than air.

You can float up here effortlessly for-ever. But there are propellers on either wing, and as you dangle not from a chaf-ing harness but directly from your own wings, your feet rest on bicycle pedals. And you can move your legs, they're strong and supple enough to pedal the propellers.

*Y*ou're an aerial trail bike and biker combined as you peddle out over the blue Pacific, only this is much, much better, for there are no hills to climb, it's like an endless effortless downhill ride when you don't feel like peddling, which is more of the time than not, for all you have to do is pedal yourself from wester-ing breeze to westering wind and let them carry you onward like a clipper ship under full flying sail.

Tropical isles drift by beneath you. The wakes of outrigger canoes. An ocean liner. A whale breaches. Schools of flying fish skim and bounce along the surface of the sunlit waters. On and on and on until a large land mass looms up on the western horizon. As you approach, you can see a waterfront city in the distance, and—

There's a ship below you, a rusty little freighter lying dead in the water, its open decks covered here and there with makeshift tenting, every inch of space crammed with people. They all wave their arms frantically at you, and you can hear them shouting up at you in a language that must be something like Chinese from the look of them.

You circle over the boat. They point up at you, then towards the city on the shore, shouting words you don't understand. But the meaning is plain enough. You head off towards the shore. When you reach the city, you see that it must be a Chinese city, curving peaked roofs, ornate pagodas, skyscraper towers in fantastic shapes and brilliant colors out of some sci-fi magazine cover, red banners, flags, and bunting, waving everywhere.

Half the waterfront is given over to a naval base. An aircraft carrier. Slim gray frigates and destroyers. A couple of submarines. And many, many smaller craft; gunboats, patrol boats, speed boats, harbor tugs.

You attract military attention down there as you fly over, mostly men in blue uniforms standing on the docks, pouring out of buildings to gawk up at you, though there seems to be some sudden purposeful action on the aircraft carrier flight deck as you fly over it to do a quick tourist turn over the city.

Crowds stand and gape below, babbling and shouting, you can hear a raucous symphony of car and bicycle horns, sirens, gongs. Now that you've attracted the attention of the citizenry, you waggle your great balloon wings, turn back towards the shore, circle back over the city again, once, twice, thrice, and then you're flying back to the naval base with a huge crowd following you through the crowded streets below.

When you arrive, you find yourself bracketed by three loudly clattering helicopters, left, right, behind. Their noses bristle with machine guns. The draft from their vanes bounces you about. Fuselage doors are open on the sides of the choppers flanking you. Armed men crouch there shouting at you. But you can only see this, you can't hear them over the engine din, and they couldn't hear you if you shouted. And you're not equipped with a radio. And you have no hands to gesture with.

You try to fly out to sea, but the choppers easily block you. You waggle your wings, and try again. Again they block you. One of them flies up above you, hovering angrily there, the downdraft of its vans pushing you lower. The other two box you in, and the three of them herd you like sheepdogs towards the carrier flight deck.

You peddle furiously but of course you can't escape, and you can see the men in the open fuselages of the choppers flanking you laughing uproariously. You stick your tongue out at the them and mime laughing back. They start sticking out their tongues at you. You're laughing. They're laughing.

You thrust your tongue out, pull it back, thrust it out again, long strokes, short strokes, the repeating pattern of the international SOS. Finally, something has been communicated. You can see some of them shouting something forward to the pilots.

You waggle your wings in the same manner, then make a try at heading out to sea again, and this time they finally let you, following above and to the sides but at more courteous distances now, keeping you out of their turbulent wakes. It's not long before three fast patrol boats and a small gunship are pacing the aerial rescue procession on the sea below.

You reach the derelict freighter and hover over it. Your helicopter escort hovers with you. There's chaos on the decks below. Some of the people are pointing up at you with beaming grins of relief. Others are jumping up and down. Some can be seen gathering up possessions. But many seem to be trying to duck for cover that doesn't exist.

The coast guard flotilla arrives on the scene. The three patrol boats surround the freighter a hundred and twenty degrees apart. Armed men appear on their decks. The gunboat moves in closer and lowers a motorized skiff. The skiff makes for the freighter with an officer in a blue uniform standing in the prow. A rope ladder is lowered and he climbs to the freighter's deck.

He's immediately surrounded by shouting gesticulating refugees. He doesn't appear happy and as he starts shouting, neither do they. There's an argument going on, the officer against everyone else, he's barking orders and pointing back out to sea with angry thrusts of his right arm, they're screaming, and crying, and obviously pleading. A man naked to the waist but wearing a dirty white captain's cap knees and elbows through the crush to confront the coast guard officer, seeming to speak in a less confrontational manner, as he points to whatever lies below decks, to the stern, shrugging. He starts to make pleading gestures. Everyone within earshot down there is crying and pleading in terror. Women hold up small children and babies.

The officer folds his arms across his chest. He makes some sort of short speech in this posture, then storms off to the rope ladder and climbs back into the skiff. The skiff returns to the gunboat and is winched aboard.

The gunboat's idling engine comes to life. It executes a turn, and heads back to the docks, followed by the patrol boats. The helicopters depart with them, leaving you floating alone over the freighter lying dead in the water, awash with despairing people abandoned to their fate.

You explode in outrage.

Quite literally. A blinding flash of light, the smell of fireworks gunpowder, a lordly ear-splitting roar, the feeling of unfolding like an enormous bird bursting full grown from the egg into the sky, and now you are a dragon, bellowing in Godzillan fury in the direction of what should have been the rescue flotilla.

*Y*ou are a big dragon. As big as a major dinosaur, flapping huge leathery wings and angrily swishing your great sinuous crocodile tail, coal locomotive smoke steaming out of your nostrils.

The people on the freighter deck below mostly cringe in fear. Some of them bang on round brass gongs. There's a great shout of relief below as you head off towards the fleeing boats.

You're as fast as an A-380 superjumbo and just as large, you catch up to the boats in nothing flat, fly a few score yards ahead of them, and hover just above the waves confronting them.

You huff, and you puff, and you breathe out a great plume of bright orange-red flame that blocks their passage. And another, and another.

The gunboat turns and tries to get by you on your port side, but you pirouette in the air with lordly reptilian grace, and block it yet again with a great gout of fire. Its engines die to an idle. The patrol boats huddle around it like terrified ducklings.

You fly around above them, breathing out a continuous barrage of fiery breath, faster and faster and faster, encircling them in a wall of flame.

Sailors come out on the decks. There's pointing. There are arguments.

You break off circling and breathing fire and head off back towards the freighter, but when you see that the boats aren't following you, you come back, and do it again. Once, twice, thrice, and on the third go-around, they finally get the message, rev up their engines, and follow you at top speed back to the freighter.

You circle above the freighter, blowing fire harmlessly into the air as skiffs and lifeboats are lowered just as a reminder that you're still around and in charge. You remain there as they shuttle back and forth between the coast guard boats and the derelict freighter until you get a sign from an officer on the gunboat bridge indicating that all the refugees are safely aboard. Only then do you allow the boats to depart for the shore, flying above them all the way to the docks. There's a great crowd of people from the city gathered up and down the quays beyond the perimeter of the naval base now and so you hover above the docks flapping your great leathery wings, blowing fountains of flame high into the air for the wondering attention of the crowd to pass the time while the boats unload the refugees.

The crowd is pressed against the perimeter fence, held raptly in place by the apparition of a legendary dragon putting on this show for them, which also serves to make them bear witness to the arrival of the refugees and the manner in which they are treated. Which, taking place before thousands of witnesses, including their guardian dragon, is businesslike and respectful.

The crowd cheers and applauds, whether for you, or the rescue, and probably both, and when the last of the refugees is ashore and they are gathered huddled on the dock surrounded by armed troops, you drop down lower and hang directly above them, holding them in the protective embrace of the shadow of your wings, roaring and blowing plumes of flame skyward to make the threatening message to the authorities plain.

Then you zoom high up into the air, execute a victory roll, turn a fire-breathing double loop, and fly a little above skyscraper level over the city, where you put on an exuberant pyrotechnic aerobatics display, treating every quarter of the city to loops, somersaults, rolls and tight dipping turns around the tops of the towers, breathing bright plumes of flame, even a few shaky smoke rings, bellowing uproariously, filling the air with the sharp celebratory tang of fireworks smoke.

The city below picks up the mood, and an impromptu fiesta is called into being. Tinny gong music. Dancing and surging in the streets. Laughter and shouting and

rhythmic clapping. Then a long sinuous *paper* dragon cakewalks out into an open plaza from a side street, at least a score of people inside a paper tube that's all red, and yellow, and gilt, with the pop-eyed, gape-jawed head of a cartoon dragon, bobbing up and down in time to the mad music of gongs, trumpets, electric guitars, as, amidst strings of firecrackers going off like machine-gun bursts, the dragon dance is performed in your honor.

You fly low over the paper dragon, and manage to snap your wings together three times overhead by way of applause, then climb up into the sky heading westward.

H°igher and higher, faster and faster, soaring at supernatural supersonic speed, up through a light cloud deck into the bright blue sky, higher still, and the heavens deepen towards purple, and though the sun remains as a richly glowing orange sphere, a brilliant panoply of stars comes out, and there's a full silvery Moon above you.

The face of the Man in the Moon winks at you, yes he does, and then you find you are not alone up here in the Land of Aerial Legend beyond the Wild Blue Yonder.

Something with the body of a lion soars by you on eagle's wings. White-robed angels fly in a distant chorus playing golden harps. World War I biplanes stage mock dogfights, shooting streams of water in lieu of bullets. A great black bird big as you are, holding an Arabian-garbed sailor in gentle talons. The *Graf Zeppelin* lumbers below. Captain Nemo's Victorian gingerbread flying fortress. The *Spruce Goose*. A flying elephant blows you a salute with his trunk.

There's music in these spheres. Angels' harps playing harmonic chords. Canary song and bouncy brass band military airs. The steady all-but-subsonic bassline of the planets in their orbits. Gongs and a mantric drone.

You are in your true dragonly element up here, borne on wings of leather and wings of song, a legendary flying wonder of the aerial highways above the skyways among your fabulous peers. Onward west you soar, your reptilian body warmed to blood heat by the music, by the gamboling presence of your fellows, flying free towards your distant goal beyond the eternal sun.

The aerial symphony coalesces into a single piercing theramin tone wailing up and down the scales, like the intro to some schlocky sci-fi flick, and yes, a flight of flying saucers appears. Seven featureless silvery Frisbees in V-formation.

The left-hand trailing saucer breaks off and heads for you, tacking wildly in an impossible series of zig-zags. Then it's pacing you only a few feet below your taloned feet. It extrudes a fat white-gloved hand. The cartoon hand beckons insistently. It points to you, it points to the saucer, it makes a fist with the thumb upraised, inviting you to hitch a ride, but the flying saucer is not even half your size.

The theramin music rises to a crescendo and becomes a brassy fanfare as a distant mighty drum bangs out a Tah-TAH, and you're falling down towards the silvery saucer.

You're no longer a dragon, you're human, you're *you*, and you're not really falling, you're landing atop it with the springy leg grace of a circus tumbler. You can stand! You can jump! You move towards the leading edge of the flying saucer just to prove to yourself that you can also walk. The surface of the thing is slick as glare ice, but it grips the soles of your feet like velcro.

You laugh, you shout, and off you go on your flying saucer ride, surfing the invisible waves of the ether to an electronic instrumental version of "Good Vibrations."

The saucer swoops lower as if riding the curl of a wave breaking on the beach, and you're back in a blue sky over the land. The saucer zigs and zags, but you don't fall off, you can't fall off, even when it's rolling through the air sideways like a wheel, even when it buzzes a foothill town flying upside down.

Over towns, over cities, over mountains and plains, stunting its way ever westward, startling the tourists in Red Square, scattering the holding stack over Frankfurt International Airport, pacing skiers on the slopes of the Alps, miming wheelies, buzzing the aerial traffic, flapping its leading edge up and down like a fancy low-rider hot-rod promenading along Hollywood Boulevard and showing its stuff.

It swoops down over Paris at Notre Dame, follows the Seine to the Eiffel Tower, flies through the Tower legs, fluttering as if it's about to fall, comes out the other side, scattering terrified tourists, as you laugh aloud at the prank.

You can't help laughing, hooting, giving off Rebel Yells, as you bend this knee and that, shift your weight, realizing that you've not just been along for the ride, you're flying this puppy, it's Saturday night, and you're the low-riding Silver Surfer of the skies!

Over the Channel to London, terrorizing more tourists as you whip along low above the roadway of Tower Bridge, turning wheelies as you pass between the huge stone uprights. Southeast to Brighton, where you put on a show above the carnival strand, and then it's out over the ocean.

Crossing the Atlantic is like riding one big long breaker, surfing the crest of a tsunami through the sky, and then you're over New York, miming a cartoon dog-fight with a King Kong atop the Empire State Building.

And at last, west across the heartland, heading triumphantly home.

A great rainbow rises over the western horizon as you gliss through the air towards it. Then it fills the sky before you with glowing pastel glory, and you glide through it into—

The gondola of a hot air balloon. The heater is hissing to a Reggae beat. The balloon above is a great big yellow Smiley Face. Long red, white, and blue streamers from the wicker gondola basket are blowing in the wind.

*A*nd your fairy godmomma's up there with you, dragonfly wings wrapped around her body like an iridescent cloak against the cooling breeze of drifting passage, and beaming at you like your favorite teacher at her prize pupil.

"Welcome home kiddo, now that wasn't so bad, betcha the best fun you ever had."

From within the sheath of her dragonfly wings, she produces a live yellow canary. "You done done the right things, so now here's your wings!"

The canary flits across to you, bumps gently against the breast pocket of your airline captain's blue and burgundy uniform and turns into a solid gold pilot's wings pin.

Your fairy godmomma turns off the burner and the balloon begins to silently descend. It's after midnight, but a million stars are out, and the light of a full Moon beams down like a kleig light to illumine the object below.

Which is your high school. Most of the lights in the building are dark. The Prom is letting out. Boys and girls in tuxedos and ball gowns are giddily filtering into the parking lot, arm in arm, shoulder to shoulder, couples snuggling together and smooching.

"The ball's over Cinderella, and there goes that floozy off with your fella, now's when you make your one big wish, but love ain't magic, now ain't that tragic, I don't do romance, no windows neither, take your time you need a breather."

A spotlight from above picks out your would-be surfer god beau walking hand-in-hand with his tawdry cheerleader queen towards his daddy's souped-up black SUV.

"Gotta say the word so I do my stuff, mooning like little miss lonely heart ain't enough."

You look down at the prom-goers climbing into their cars, at your would-be-never-was high school sweetheart being dragooned out of your life by bouncy boobs and a hank of probably per-oxided blond hair.

And you give your fairy godmomma your one and only wish, leaping out of the gondola.

"For this one night in the land of the free, let everyone here fly like me!"

You glide like Peter Pan on invisible strings down over the parking lot, hover in midair like Tinkerbell. You pirouette in the air like a ballerina, you waltz around in circles, you rock and you roll to "Girls Just Wanna Have Fun."

You've got an audience down there, staring up goggle-eyed, boys forgetting their girls, girls forgetting their boys, as they bounce up and down to the beat. Every bounce takes them higher and higher, until they begin to notice that their feet are no longer touching down.

They're walking on air, and then they're dancing on air, it's the wildest post-Prom party in the history of the world.

You drop down into it, boys dancing like heavy metal butterflies with their chosen girls, girls dancing alone, whoops and hollers and yelps of joy.

You bop and roll through the aerial dance floor, the queen of this hop, and there he is in his rock star tux, his golden mane rolling like the sea in the wind, doing the all too funky monkey with his Barbie doll moll.

You go over to a quick-time tango, fandangoing through the air, bends, and sweeps, and then outstretched arms, and with this gesture, you've got him. He takes your hands, and you whirl each other high up into the sky above the high school world.

Little Miss Vegas hangs there furiously in the air with her hands on her hips.

If anyone cared, her look could kill.

But *he* only has eyes for *you*. • • •

NORMAN SPINRAD wrote the original series episode "The Doomsday Machine" and the unproduced "He Walked Among Us." His novels include the proto-cyberpunk **Bug Jack Barron** *and* **The Iron Dream,** *which takes the form of a novel by an alternative-universe Adolf Hitler, and a critical analysis thereof.*

ROCK—A—BYE BABY, OR DIE!

BY
GEORGE CLAYTON JOHNSON

Illustrated by Michael Okuda

When a TV writer "pitches" to a series, he brings several story ideas. Here's one from the same session that produced "The Man Trap." —The Editor

The ship in space, hurtling toward Minerva—a planet. Mission: To pick up two ruthless criminals. They have been judged criminally deranged and must be taken to a hospital planet. Several persons have been badly wounded apprehending the two and a starship doctor is needed.

Abruptly, a glowing speck on the viewscreens, swift, radiant, headed toward the ship on a collision course. Evasive action. The speck follows. Pressor beams. Phaser weapons. All fail to destroy the tiny hunk of matter. All hands brace for impact. The ship rocks savagely as the tiny speck of matter hits it.

Close on the communications console: a switch flips up of its own accord. All hands react to a strange sound that reverberates throughout the ship: The sound of a baby squalling! As Kirk reacts to this incredible infant wail:

Star Trek—Credits

ACT ONE:

A search of the ship reveals no baby. Instead, there is evidence to assume the ship is alive! The glowing speck of matter was an entity, a soul—trying to be born—to become—to exist. It found a host—the complex circuitry of the ship. There seems to be no way to separate the entity from the ship. To Mr. Spock it is a scientific marvel. To Kirk it is a responsibility—something to take back to Earth for the experts to examine. To Dr. McCoy it is a nuisance—something that stands between himself and his patients on Minerva. To Uhura, the ship is frightening. Her switchboard is the baby's voice. The crying disturbs her.

Kirk puts Spock and Scott to work to locate the offending circuits. Spock's advice: Save the ship at any cost. The complication: There is evidence that the "baby" is growing at an accelerated rate. In the first five minutes the ship has apparently aged one year. It is beginning to explore its body and environment—working doors, elevators, the propulsion system. It is developing an awareness of self.

The crying is getting on everyone's nerves—is interfering with intraship communication. How do you soothe a crying baby? Uhura's answer: "Soothe it. Get it to sleep." "Do that," says Kirk. She comforts the "baby." "There, there. It will be all right." She feels foolish doing this. She sings: "Rock-a-bye baby, in the treetop..." The "baby's" sobs become softer. It is working. Somewhere a crewman drops a wrench. With the clang of the wrench the baby shrieks. Kirk's orders: "Silence on the ship." He too feels foolish. Everyone walks on eggs as the baby sleeps.

Spock and Scott isolate the "awareness" of the baby. It is located in the complex circuitry of the ship's computer. Can they turn this section of the ship off? No!

The computer is responsible for many aspects of the ship's function. Without the computer the ship would be disabled—life support systems, warp drive, helm, navigation, engineering—all are dependent on the computer in the same way a human is dependent on his automatic nervous system to keep his heart going.

The baby is growing even as it sleeps, absorbing information automatically from the ship's library. Wonders Spock: "What will the baby be like when it wakes?"

Approaching Minerva. The baby wakes. It sees Minerva's sun—an unholy brightness at this close distance. "Pretty, pretty," says the baby. It takes control of the ship, wrenching it from its course. It heads for the sun as a human baby might crawl toward a bright toy. One difference: This toy is capable of killing all aboard if they cannot gain control of the ship in the next few minutes. The heat rises steadily. "Pretty, pretty!" says the baby.

END ACT ONE.

ACT TWO:

A frantic effort to regain control of the ship. Kirk orders the circuits connecting the computer with the drive cut. Torches brought into play. The wires severed. As they watch, the wires creep back together. Elevators refuse to carry officers and crewmen to destinations. Doors refuse to open and close. The ship rocks in angry tantrum as Kirk tries to wrest control of the ship from the baby. Heat rising. Crewmen collapsing. Refrigeration systems overloading. Kirk's question? How does a baby learn not to play with fire? Answer: Once burned, twice shy. Kirk orders high tension lines connected to the ship's outer hull. A surge of current. The ship flinches, cries out. Again. The ship falters in its rush to the sun. Again. The ship veers away from the sun. The baby has learned that suns are dangerous.

In a way, says Spock to Kirk, since you are the captain of the ship you are the baby's father. "What is a father?" asks the baby. Kirk flinches.

If Kirk is the father, Spock is the teacher. Spock tries to answer the question. Already the ship exhibits the questing mind of a five-year-old with the endless litany of *Why?* Why am I different? Why do the crewmen call me monster? Why doesn't Uhura sing to me anymore?

Why is Kirk mad when I call him "Father?"

And now the ship takes up an orbit about Minerva.

When Kirk and Doctor McCoy prepare to transport down, the transporter refuses to work. The baby won't let Kirk leave the ship.

"Don't leave me alone," says the baby. "Don't go away, Father."

END ACT TWO.

ACT THREE:

Kirk fumes. He is a captive aboard his own ship. Yet, it is imperative he transport down and pick up the prisoners. "Why?" asks the ship. "Because it is my duty," says Kirk. "What is duty?"

And now begins a simplified explanation of the concept of duty, of responsibility, of moral imperatives.

Kirk promises he won't be gone long—that he'll come back. And now the baby is a six-year-old—brave—like a child who takes pride in the fact that it isn't afraid to cross the street alone—to go to school without holding on to mother's hand.

It allows Kirk and the burning McCoy to transport to the planet where they take

charge of Nolan Russell, a psycho-killer and his side-kick, Ray Francis. The inhabitants of Minerva are non-human, alien—unpretty by human standards. Russell and Francis had embarked on a program of extermination against the "crocs" who are a gentle and pacifist people. Fortunately for the people of Minerva, there was a sizeable colony of Earth people who were not pacifistically inclined. They took a hand and apprehended the two vicious killers. Unfortunately, several humans were injured capturing the two killers. Unfortunate also that Minervan doctors were not accustomed to treating human injuries, thus the need for McCoy. He immediately sets to work on his patients—a half dozen people. Kirk leaves him to care for the injured and transports the prisoners to the ship.

The two killers are put in the ship's brig.

Kirk goes to check on the progress of the "baby."

He finds that the baby has continued to mature at a rapidly increasing pace.

Meanwhile, in the brig, the two prisoners examine their cell. A childlike voice: "Who are you? What are you doing here?"

The two don't realize who the owner of the voice is, but they recognize the childlike tones. They quickly con the baby. They are victims. Innocent! They merely protected themselves from monsters who were trying to kill them. Kirk was lied to by the inhuman monsters on Minerva. They are to be taken back to earth to be executed. They wring the baby's heart with their pitiful tale.

The door clicks open. The baby has believed them and is trying to help them escape their cruel fate. Already the baby's voice is that of a young, idealistic teenager.

Down the hall the two prisoners overcome a crewman and take his phaser. Now they are armed. Says Rusell: "Wait till I get my hands on Captain Kirk. I'll kill him like a croc."

END ACT THREE.

ACT FOUR:

Kirk is preparing to return to Minerva via transporter when the two killers break into the transporter room. He tries to resist but is clubbed down by Russell. The killer places the phaser to Kirk's temple and is about to trigger it when Francis points out the fact they can use the captain to gain access to the bridge. Once on the bridge they can force the crew to take them to another planet. Russell is furious at being balked from killing Kirk, but recognizes the logic of Francis's argument. Together, supporting Kirk they make their way to the elevator. A voice: "What's wrong with Father?"

They explain they are taking the Captain, who is sick, to the bridge, so his friends can take care of him. The ship assists them to the bridge where they cover the officers and demand to be taken to another planet.

Spock, realizing the danger to all, orders Sulu to set a course away from Minerva.

Kirk recovers consciousness. The baby realizes what is going on. In a contrite, grief-stricken voice it manfully tells Kirk how the prisoners escaped from their cell. It is sorry. What can it do to make things right again?

Apparently nothing. The criminals have the upper hand. But Kirk's earlier talk about duty and responsibility have had their effect. The baby knows the responsibility for freeing the prisoners was his. So also must be the responsibility for rectifying the mistake.

The ship takes control of the helm.

"What's happening?" cries Russell.

It quickly becomes apparent what is happening. The ship has altered course and is diving toward the sun.

"Why?"

The sun is dangerous to humans. The criminals are human. If they don't want to be harmed they must give up their weapons to "Father." If they don't they will die.

The criminals try to regain control of the ship but as was the case earlier, cut wires heal themselves. Equipment is obstinate. The ship demands they give up their weapons. The heat becomes unbearable. Only Mister Spock can function with any efficiency in the blazing heat. The viewscreen is a solid sheet of white-hot flame.

The criminals recognize defeat. They give up their weapons.

However, it is too late. The ship is caught in the grip of the sun, unable to pull free. As the ship's officers, including Kirk, grow weaker, the ship dives to its doom. "I'm sorry, Father," cries the ship. Spock uses full power trying to free the ship, but it is no use. The *Enterprise* and all hands on board are apparently doomed.

With his last bit of energy Kirk raises himself. Spock has given up. Logic dictates that the ship hasn't the power to pull free. Spock has accepted the inevitable.

But Kirk has not.

He calls out to the ship. "It's up to you," he says. No pilot or helmsman has the absolute control of all elements of the ship.

No Captain or first officer can override programmed circuits or get the last available erg of energy from the ship. But perhaps the ship itself can.

"I'll save us, Father," cries the ship. And now the ship begins its fight for life. Circuits burn out and repair themselves. Main drive and auxiliary drives function simultaneously. Even the pressors and phasers come into play to add their thrust to the ship's drive.

Staring at the instruments, Spock sees the impossible happening. The ship is winning the battle. It is pulling away as circuits overload, sparks flash from consoles, lights blink and burn out. Kirk rouses himself with an effort. "Good boy!" he cries. "Good boy!"

And then there is a scream. The ship. The voice of the ship weakens. It is in bad trouble. It is dying. "Did I do well, Father? Are you proud of me?"

And now the ship is in the clear, pulling away.

"I'm proud of you," says Kirk. "Very proud."

The voice is a whisper. "Goodbye, Father."

Kirk shouts: "Hold on! Fight!"

But it is too late. Faintly. "Goodbye."

"Dead," says Spock.

And on the surface of Minerva, Dr. McCoy, unaware of what has happened aboard the ship, is very busy. He is delivering the child of a young pregnant woman who was gunned by the two killers, Russell and Francis, in their attempted escape.

Simultaneously with the death of the ship, a child is born. It cries lustily.

And only we know that the sound of the baby's cries are identical to the newborn sound of the cries heard aboard the *Enterprise* when the ship was born. As we:

FADE OUT.

END ACT FOUR. •••

GEORGE CLAYTON JOHNSON wrote the episode chosen by NBC for the premiere of the original series, "The Man Trap." He also wrote numerous episodes of the original Twilight Zone, *and the story of the original* Ocean's Eleven. *He is the co-author, with William Nolan, of the novel* Logan's Run, *of which a second film adaptation's on-again-off-again development is currently on again for a 2010 release.*

by James Trefil

The red part of the strawberry isn't the fruit. It's actually a modified part of the stem. The fruit is the little yellow thing sticking to the side.

A cubic foot of limestone can yield fifty thousand fossil shells—the remains of small animals living on the continental shelves.

There are about ten trillion cells in the human body.

When you see something that looks like a puddle of water on the highway, what you are actually seeing is light that was moving from the sky toward the highway, but has been bent around by refraction in the air until it comes to your eye.

The famous German philosopher Immanuel Kant first speculated that there might be other galaxies in the universe. He first used the term "island universes" to refer to them.

THE TELEVISUALIZER
Reviews of Science Fiction for the Home Screen

BY SCOTT ASHLIN

*H*orror and sci-fi movies from the 1950's have not generally been especially well-served by the DVD industry. This is not to say that there is a paucity of films available in the format—there most assuredly isn't!—but rather that the discs themselves tend to be bare-bones presentations, all too often using ragged-out television prints or fuzzy, pan-and-scan VHS transfers as their source material. Warner Brothers' recent "Cult Camp Classics, Volume 1: Sci-Fi Thrillers" is an admirable step toward correcting that situation. The set not only collects three movies that have been somewhat difficult to obtain at sane prices in recent years (all of them, oddly enough, pictures distributed originally by Allied Artists and dating from 1958), but gives them some of the highest-quality packaging of any comparable films yet released on DVD. All three are taken from cleaned-up prints and are presented in what look like their original aspect ratios, with all feature cover art derived from their original theatrical one-sheets (far preferable, in my mind, to the sterile Photoshop compositions one sees so often these days). And what is perhaps most noteworthy, all carry audio commentaries in addition to the usual trailers. Let's open up the box now, and see what's inside…

*I*n 1957, Universal International Pictures made a pretty big stir with *The Incredible Shrinking Man.* Director Jack Arnold was in those days the studio's foremost specialist in inexpensive sci-fi/horror movies, having previously helmed such hits as *It Came from Outer Space, Creature from the Black Lagoon,* and *Tarantula.* Screenwriter Richard Matheson adapted the script from one of his own most potent novels, and the special effects crew included men who had done impressive work on *This Island Earth* and the more comedic entries in the old *Invisible Man* series. It was a formidable concentration of talent, and while a comparison between the print and celluloid versions of the story is likely to leave one frustrated at how much of the novel's cinematic potential was left unrealized, that apparently wasn't an issue for the average late-50's movie-goer. *The Incredible Shrinking Man* was a success at the box office, and in the years since, it has acquired a reputation as one of the last truly classic science fiction films of the 1950's. Naturally, it was ripped off almost immediately.

The man most responsible for that rip-off was one whose works have inspired at least as much love among B-movie fans as that for Jack Arnold, albeit for very different reasons. Whereas Arnold had a knack for winning respectable results from modest resources, independent producer/director Bert I. Gordon is justly remembered as the driving force behind some of the most endearingly goofy and misbegotten monster flicks of a decade in which goofy and misbegotten monster flicks were thick on the ground. Gordon's answer to *The Incredible Shrinking Man* was *The Amazing Colossal Man,* which inverted Matheson's premise to yield a much more conventional monster romp, rendered with a degree of persuasiveness that was similarly opposite to what its inspiration had offered. *The Amazing Colossal Man* nevertheless made a decent amount of money for distributors American International Pictures, enough so that a sequel—*War of the Colossal Beast*—followed in 1958. Meanwhile, a different independent producer weighed in with a rip-off of the rip-off.

Attack of the 50 Ft. Woman (1958; this DVD, 2007)
Allied Artists (Warner Home Video)
Director: Nathan Juran
Writer: Mark Hanna
Producers: Jacques Marquette, Bernard Woolner
Cast: Allison Hayes, William Hudson, Yvette Vickers
B/W; 66 minutes; unrated; aspect ratio: 1.33:1
Extras: Theatrical trailer, commentary by Yvette Vickers and film historian Tom Weaver
Available individually, or as part of *Cult Camp Classics 1—Sci-Fi Thrillers* box set

That second-order rip-off artist was Jacques Marquette. Marquette was a cinematographer of substantial ability, but his short career as a producer is notable mainly for the John Agar anti-classic, *The Brain from Planet Arous,* and for *Attack of the 50-Foot Woman.* Both of those pictures were made in collaboration with director Nathan Juran (who took screen credit for them under the pseudonym "Nathan Hertz"), with Marquette himself running the camera, and both are somewhat difficult movies to assess. On the surface, they are cheap, shoddy absurdities, riddled with illogical plot developments and hampered by special effects that are occasionally breathtaking in their insufficiency. But at the same time, Juran and Marquette brought to them a degree of subtle craftsmanship that somehow manages to counteract the foolishness of the proceedings while simultaneously calling attention to it, and *Attack of the 50-Foot Woman,* specifically, benefits as well from some shockingly insightful characterization courtesy of writer Mark Hanna (who also co-wrote *The Amazing Colossal Man)* and lead performers Allison Hayes, William Hudson, and Yvette Vickers.

Hayes plays Nancy Archer, heiress to the $50 million Fowler fortune; Hudson is her parasitic, two-timing husband, Harry; and Vickers is Honey Parker, the scheming honky-tonk hussy with whom Harry is currently cheating on his wife. Nancy has a history of both alcoholism and mental instability, so she is not widely believed when she returns from a drive through the desert one night, raving about a UFO and a giant alien. Harry and Honey are thrilled at first with what they take to be evidence of Nancy's impending final crack-up, but the frazzled woman is telling nothing but the truth. A second encounter with the humongous spaceman transpires when Harry is around to witness it, and the son of a bitch speeds off in Nancy's car, leaving her to her own devices against the alien. The sudden disappearance of his filthy-rich wife nearly lands Harry in an immense amount of trouble with the law, but he's actually even worse off after a naked and comatose Nancy curiously turns up on the roof of her pool house, defusing the impending legal action. (The cops plausibly conclude that she simply wandered up there on a bender before succumbing to alcohol poisoning.) Whatever the alien did to Nancy, radiation from its body is transforming her into a giant, too, and she's going to want to have words with both Harry and Honey just as soon as she emerges from that coma.

Modern audiences are likely to be just a little bit irritated with *Attack of the 50-Foot Woman,* on the grounds that Nancy doesn't launch her retributive rampage until the last ten minutes of this 66-minute film. Until then, the movie focuses instead first on the triangular relationship among the main characters, and then on the efforts of the local authorities to find and deal with Nancy's space giant. This is probably the point on which *Attack of the 50-Foot Woman* most closely resembles *The Amazing Colossal Man.* Although Colonel Glenn Manning did at least become huge relatively early in the latter movie, he didn't actually do anything until the final reel, either. In any event, it means that a person must watch the bulk of the film for something other that what they presumably came to it for, and the alternate sources of engagement are something of a mixed bag.

The hunt for the alien is an occasion for much hilarity, in essentially the way one would expect from a movie with this title and this pedigree. It's funny enough when the use of simple double exposures instead of real matting renders the alien and his ship transparent in the shadowed portions of their bodies. The revelation that the gargantuan astronaut's spacecraft is scaled on the inside to the comfort of creatures perhaps one tenth his height, and that this representative of a hyper-advanced extraterrestrial civilization dresses like an extra in an Italian Viking movie, is something else again. The sharp-eyed will also get a chuckle out of the fact that the same actor plays both the titan from space and the owner of Honey Parker's favorite bar.

On the other hand, however, *Attack of the 50-Foot Woman's* relationship-drama elements are strangely powerful and engrossing—as well they should be, considering that they're really the secret heart of the film. Mark Hanna's writing (and Allison Hayes's acting even more so) captures with disturbing accuracy the love-hate dynamic of a deeply dysfunctional, abusive relationship. I have been very close to someone in a similar situation, and it was like a punch in the stomach for me when the drunken Nancy followed up an embittered tirade, asking how she could have been so stupid as to take Harry back after his last round of infidelities, by collapsing, sobbing, into his arms and begging him not to leave her. William Hudson is never called upon to do anything quite that intense, but his rendition of a cowardly, self-interested, small-hearted slimebag is equally effective in its quieter way.

As for Yvette Vickers— well, let's just say there's a reason why she spent most of the 50's playing one sexually predatory bad girl after another, from her early delinquent pictures like *Juvenile Jungle* and *Reform School Girl,* all the way to her scene-stealing performance as a female answer to Harry Archer in *The Giant Leeches.* The way Vickers herself tells it on the audio commentary track to this edition of *Attack of the 50-Foot Woman,* she got to be such a specialist at parts of this type that it started to affect her real-world social life. She couldn't go to a party without every woman in the house literally grabbing hold of their men in an effort to keep them away from her!

That commentary track, which Vickers shares with film historian Tom Weaver, is somewhat less satisfying than one might have hoped. Vickers and Weaver do manage to keep a conversation rolling fairly steadily (a fact which alone puts their commentary somewhere in the right tail of the bell curve), but unfortunately, they do it mostly by talking about everything in the world except *Attack of the 50-Foot Woman.* You want to hear about Vickers' father, and his career as a composer and performer of elevator music (excuse me— "smooth jazz")? About the reason why Jacques Marquette always gave his name as "Jack" when signing in for a table at a restaurant? About what it was like for Vickers to work with people who weren't in *Attack of the 50-Foot Woman,* on projects related to it only by her presence in the cast? Then this is the commentary track for you.

A handful of relevant and enlightening anecdotes (like the aforementioned bit about Vickers's reception at Hollywood parties) do surface over the course of the commentators' hour-long chat, but I personally would normally be inclined to give up on it after fifteen minutes at most. But as I said earlier, extras of any kind are rare enough with B-movies of this vintage that all concerned deserve kudos simply for trying.

O f the three films in the set, *The Giant Behemoth* was the one that had me most excited, for I had read about it for years without ever managing to see it. This, of course, meant that I was well

The Giant Behemoth [aka *Behemoth the Sea Monster]* (1958; this DVD, 2007)
Diamond Pictures Corp., distributed in U.S. by Allied Artists (Warner Home Video)
Writer/Director: Eugene Lourie
Producer: David Diamond
Cast: Gene Evans, Andre Morell, John Turner
B/W; 80 minutes; aspect ratio: 1.66:1
Extras: Theatrical trailer, commentary by Dennis Murren & Phil Tippett
Available individually, or as part of *Cult Camp Classics 1—Sci-Fi Thrillers* box set

aware of its reputation—not many people have a whole lot to say about *The Giant Behemoth,* and what they do have to say almost uniformly isn't good. Now, perhaps the resultant low expectations had something to do with this, but I enjoyed *The Giant Behemoth* rather a lot. It is, as you may have heard, extremely derivative, but it gets most of what it recycles far more right than a great many 1950's monster-rampage flicks, and there is at least one instance in which it actually improves upon its most likely source of inspiration.

The behemoth of the title is a made-up, aquatic sauropod dinosaur called a Paleosaurus. Evidently hanging out peacefully unnoticed at the top of the bathypelagic food chain for the last 130 million years, it eventually winds up the final repository for all the radioactive contamination in its ecosystem (wait a minute—were there any A-bomb test-firings in the Atlantic Ocean?) and... I don't know, gets pissed off, or something. The point is, it starts making a pest of itself all up and down the southern and southeastern coasts of England, and finally swims straight up the Thames to wreak stop-motion havoc courtesy of Pete Peterson and Willis O'Brien.

Meanwhile, a couple of the usual white-coats follow along a step or two behind it, endeavoring to figure out what sort of monster they're dealing with, and how it might possibly be stopped. Matters are complicated by the fact that the radioactive contamination of the creature's flesh mandates a perfectly clean kill—no bombs, no shells, no anything that might splatter irradiated blood and meat all over half of downtown London. Dr. Karnes (Gene Evans), the visiting American (funny how, even in British monster movies, it's always the Yank who takes the lead), determines that the monster is already dying of its own radioactivity, and has the brilliant idea to hasten the process along a little with the help of a radium-tipped torpedo.

Sounds rather familiar, and there's every reason why it should. It's practically the same story as *The Beast from 20,000 Fathoms,* but with the action relocated from the northeast coast of the Americas to Cornwall and London. In making the transplant, writer/director Eugene Lourie was doing no more than Ishiro Honda, Shinichi Sekizawa, and Takeo Murata had done with *Godzilla: King of the Monsters* (which started life as an unapologetic bid to cash in on the success of *The Beast from 20,000 Fathoms* in Japan), but there was one major, telling difference— Lourie himself had directed *The Beast*

from 20,000 Fathoms! And in fact even this second go-round was not enough to work the idea out of his system, for he would make essentially the same movie yet a third time as *Gorgo* in 1961. It makes one wonder, especially given that those three films together comprise 75% of Lourie's output as a motion picture director. (Lourie also did a bit of directing for television, but was primarily an art director and production designer.)

Furthermore, *The Giant Behemoth* goes so far as to copy a few other notable copies of Lourie's earlier film. The monster's ability to concentrate its radioactivity into a sort of area-effect death-ray (mind-bendingly explained as a fortuitous development of its natural capacity to generate and discharge electricity, like a torpedo ray or an electric eel) is obviously akin to Godzilla's atomic breath, while the scene in which the Paleosaurus tears its way through a line of high-tension electrical towers is also plainly lifted from *Godzilla.* And the climactic duel beneath the surface of the Thames between the dinosaur and a midget submarine armed with a single, specially modified torpedo owes a great deal to the showdown against the monster octopus in *It Came from Beneath the Sea* (although this version is handled with far more excitement and suspense). There's a whole lot of déjà vu going on here, even before you factor in the unfortunate frequency with which Lourie tries to economize by replaying bits of special-effects footage with different frame-cropping, or with the film flipped to create a mirror image of itself.

I did, however, say that I enjoyed *The Giant Behemoth,* and I didn't mean simply that I had a good laugh at its expense. There were numerous such laughs, obviously (and I haven't even mentioned the terrible hand-puppet that represents the monster when only its head and neck are visible emerging from the water), but there is more to this movie than might initially meet the eye. Special effects veterans Dennis Muren and Phil Tippet dismiss all the non-monster material as boring in their audio commentary, but to a close observer of 1950's monster movies, it is in the human story that *The Giant Behemoth* really shines.

I can think of few other such films that are so utterly sensible in their progression from a series of strange incidents in an isolated locale to a large-scale governmental and military operation in the heart of a major population center. For one thing, it's honestly rather amazing to see an ostensible science fiction movie from the late 1950's in which the scientists ever practice anything recognizable as genuine science. When Karnes and his British colleague, Dr. James Bickford (Hammer horror regular Andre Morell), begin their investigation of the earliest creature incidents, they proceed in exactly the manner you would expect of real-world marine biologists. They collect testimony from witnesses; they examine the scenes of the events; they take water samples and wildlife specimens, which they then subject to authentic tests that really would detect the sort of phenomena for which they are searching. In short, they go out into the field to gather and sift the evidence, like scientists are supposed to. And when their investigations lead them outside of their areas of competence, they turn to recognized experts in the relevant fields. What's more, when the markedly eccentric paleontologist (a wildly overacting Jack MacGowran) shows up to examine photographs of the monster's footprints, his automatic assumption is that the colossal tracks are newly discovered fossils, rather than the spoor of a living dinosaur; it brought a smile to my face

when I realized that MacGowran's character didn't immediately grasp the true significance of what he was seeing.

The uncommonly careful approach to science in this movie even extends to the monster to a certain extent. Yes, the notion of an air-breathing marine animal as massive as the Paleosaurus somehow going unnoticed, even in the open ocean, until the late 1950's is absurd, and the notion of a carnivorous, electric, salt-water sauropod is equally so. However, the idea that the Paleosaurus has become radioactive as a consequence of the geometrically progressive concentration of toxins at each higher level of the food chain is dead on. It's exactly the same process that has brought the California condor to the brink of extinction, and that makes the livers of top predators like the great cats lethally poisonous to humans. Let us also not lose sight of the fact that this particular atomic monster is slowly dying from its irradiation, or that its worsening sickness is at one point explicitly raised as a possible explanation for its violent, erratic behavior. And as stupid as that "bioelectricity as atomic death-ray" business is, the movie redeems it just a little during the fight against the submarine, when we see the Paleosaurus using low-level discharges as a navigational aid, exactly the way electric fishes do in the real world.

Finally—and this may be the most shocking thing of all about *The Giant Behemoth*—there is no perfunctory romance. I repeat, *there is no perfunctory romance!* Though it seems at first that Jean Trevathan (Leigh Madison), the daughter of the creature's first victim, and her boyfriend, John (John Turner), are destined to be the movie's love interest, both characters disappear from the narrative fairly early on. Some might hold that against the movie (Muren and Tippett certainly seemed to in the commentary track), but I score it instead as another manifestation of *The Giant Behemoth's* unusual realism. After all, why the hell would a Cornish fisherman's daughter and her dock-hand boyfriend remain involved in the hunt for a radioactive dinosaur after they've told the investigating authorities what they know? Jean has a father to mourn, and John has to earn a living. Nor do they have anything more to contribute once they've relayed their respective stories about Jean's father's death and the weird things that washed up on the beach a day or two afterward. If Eugene Lourie sees no need to keep a girl around just so that there'll be somebody for his hero to kiss in the final shot, then I say more power to him.

There is one minor complaint I feel

Queen of Outer Space (1958; this DVD, 2007)
Allied Artists (Warner Home Video)
Director: Edward Bernds
Screenplay: Charles Beaumont
Story: Ben Hecht
Producer: Ben Schwalb
Cast: Zsa Zsa Gabor, Eric Fleming, Laurie Mitchell, Lisa Davis
Color; 80 minutes; aspect ratio: 2.35:1
Extras: Theatrical trailer, commentary by Laurie Mitchell & Tom Weaver
Available individually, or as part of *Cult Camp Classics 1—Sci-Fi Thrillers* box set

honor-bound to make about the presentation Warner Brothers have given *The Giant Behemoth* for this DVD, a nit that insists upon being picked. The back of the box claims a running time of 90 minutes, but the movie is actually a full ten minutes shorter than that. Otherwise, what we have here is very much on par with the *50-Foot Woman* disc, although it would appear that in this case nobody with any meaningful connection to the film was available for the commentary track.

Muren and Tippett's credentials are that they both did a lot of stop-motion work, and that Muren owns the original Paleosaurus props; that's probably good enough for a movie of *The Giant Behemoth's* stature, nearly 50 years after its release. About halfway through the film, Muren and Tippett's commentary takes on sort of a snarky, *Mystery Science Theater 3000* vibe, which is alternately entertaining and grating—entertaining because these are a laid-back and witty couple of guys, and grating because they unabashedly reveal just how little preparation they did. I understand that two hard-working professional effects artists are probably too busy to pour hours and hours into research and reflection for a project like this one, but watching the movie through once before hitting "record" would have been a good start. As for the first half of the commentary track, it is in some ways almost the opposite of what Tom Weaver and Yvette Vickers recorded for *Attack of the 50-Foot Woman*. Whereas Weaver and Vickers were smoothly conversational but also rambling and frequently irrelevant, Muren and Tippett are stilted and labored for their first 40-odd minutes, sometimes lapsing into silence for uncomfortably long periods, but when they are talking, their stories are invariably germane and informative.

*T*hus far, the "Cult Camp Classics" set has distinguished itself with a remarkable lack of camp. *Attack of the 50-Foot Woman* and *The Giant Behemoth* were both intended seriously by their creators, and can be considered campy only in the sense that a certain amount of inadvertent mirth will almost inevitably result when naïve premises and inadequate resources collide. With *Queen of Outer Space,* however, the camp label is fully justified.

While the details of its earliest genesis are subject to some dispute, director Edward Bernds has been quoted as saying that he, at least, meant *Queen of Outer Space* as a spoof of earlier "girl planet" movies like *Cat-Women of the Moon* and *Fire Maidens from Outer Space.* Astute observers would likely have suspected as much, anyway, simply from the casting of the famous-for-no-obvious-reason Zsa Zsa Gabor as the female lead. Having Zsa Zsa head up a movie you were serious about would make roughly as much sense as casting Paris Hilton (Gabor's step-great - granddaughter, appropriately enough) in a serious film that doesn't involve her getting a huge iron spike driven through her head. Unfortunately, like most modern movies that come by their cheesiness deliberately, *Queen of Outer Space* is more an endurance test than anything else.

It is now 1985 (the passage of time has rendered this point far more amusing than any of the movie's actual jokes), and after 22 years of construction, there is a fully functioning space station orbiting the Earth at a distance of 10,000 miles from the surface. A trio of astronauts (wearing uniforms recycled from *Forbidden Planet)* are supposed to be taking the scientist who designed the station (recycled from *World Without End)* aloft to visit it (in a rocketship recycled from *Flight to Mars),* but they never make it to their destination. This is because the station is destroyed by just about the chintziest death-ray you ever did see, which is then trained on the rocket in turn. Strangely, two direct hits fail to destroy the vessel (one sufficed for the much larger space station), but merely cause it to crash-land on Venus. The movie acknowledges that this is an astonishingly unlikely turn of events, but conspicuously fails to offer any meaningful justification for the rocketship's 26-million-mile death-dive.

Venus, of course, is inhabited solely by beautiful women (or at any rate, by women whom we may presume to have been beautiful by 1950's standards), plus the occasional crummy giant spider. These women are ruled by the usual evil queen (played by Laurie Mitchell, who accompanies Tom Weaver on the sporadically delivered but nicely focused commentary track), who has banished all of the Venusian menfolk to an orbiting space-dungeon. Zsa Zsa is a scientist who secretly leads a pro-male revolutionary front, and when the Earth men are captured and imprisoned on charges of espionage, she springs them from the lockup in exchange for their aid in overthrowing the queen. And naturally, all the astronauts will have their pick of alien girlfriends, even though two of them are even more annoying than the comic-relief electronics technician in *Destination Moon.*

Lots of people seem to love *Queen of Outer Space,* but I'm not one of them. Few things are as displeasing to me as failed comedy, for the simple reason that a failed comedy has nothing to fall back on. Approached seriously, *Queen of Outer Space* could have been as clumsy and stupid as it is, and still have been solidly enjoyable. In fact, it was during one of the few completely straight-faced scenes—an attack by a giant spider upon the protagonists during an escape attempt—that the movie finally got a laugh out of me. The scene begins with stock monster footage from *World Without End,* progresses to one of the comic-relief jackasses having a completely immobile rubber bug dropped on him from above the frame, and ends with the impressively unimpressive spider prop bursting into flames under the Fearless Space Captain's *Forbidden Planet*-surplus raygun. *Queen of Outer Space* is never half that funny when it's actually aiming for a laugh.

Director Edward Bernds had previously flexed his comedic muscles by calling the shots on both the Bowery Boys and the Three Stooges, and while the comic sensibility here is on a level marginally above that, Bernds' background should nevertheless give you the general idea. The moment when one astronaut expresses his incredulity over an all-female society by making reference to women drivers pretty well encapsulates the whole film—it's like having your most unimaginatively chauvinistic octagenarian uncle bombard you with dumb-broad jokes for 80 minutes, only in Cinemascope and DeLuxe Color. Apart from the spider scene, the only fun I had came from trying to trace the origins of all the sets, props, and costumes that had been raided from earlier movies' closets. Of course, what this really means is that it's with *Queen of Outer Space* that Warner Brothers have shown their true mettle. I simply must applaud any company willing to give so classy and respectful a release to a film that deserves as little respect as this one. • • •

SCOTT ASHLIN—also known to his internet readers as El Santo—is the writer of the website 1000 Misspent Hours and Counting (www . 1000misspenthours . com).

HUBBLE CAN HUNT FOR TRACES OF LIFE OUTSIDE SOLAR SYSTEM

WASHINGTON—NASA's Hubble Space Telescope has discovered carbon dioxide in the atmosphere of a planet orbiting another star. This breakthrough is an important step toward finding chemical biotracers of extraterrestrial life.

The Jupiter-sized planet, called HD 189733b, is too hot for life. But the Hubble observations are a proof-of-concept demonstration that the basic chemistry for life can be measured on planets orbiting other stars.

"Hubble was conceived primarily for observations of the distant universe, yet it is opening a new era of astrophysics and comparative planetary science," said Eric Smith, Hubble Space Telescope program scientist at NASA Headquarters in Washington.

Mark Swain, a research scientist at NASA's Jet Propulsion Laboratory in Pasadena, Calif., used Hubble's near infrared camera and multi-object spectrometer to study infrared light emitted from the planet, which lies 63 light-years away. Gases in the planet's atmosphere absorb certain wavelengths of light from the planet's hot glowing interior. The molecules leave a unique spectral fingerprint on the radiation from the planet that reaches Earth. This is the first time a near-infrared emission spectrum has been obtained for an exoplanet.

"The carbon dioxide is the main reason for the excitement because, under the right circumstances, it could have a connection to biological activity as it does on Earth," Swain said. "The very fact we are able to detect it and estimate its abundance is significant for the long-term effort of characterizing planets to find out what they are made of and if they could be a possible host for life."

Astronomers look forward to using the James Webb Space Telescope, after it is launched in 2013, to look spectroscopically for biomarkers on a terrestrial planet the size of Earth or a "super-Earth" several times our planet's mass.

—from NASA press release, December 9, 2008

dark energies

by Larry Niven

Illustrated by Michael Okuda

The Ventura Freeway was accursed.

This was Emery's show. Even so, Wendell Braun wondered what he was doing here. He said, "We're going nowhere fast. Four-thirty on a Thursday. How far is this lab of yours?"

"The workshop's about twenty-five miles west," Gordon Emery said.

It was still possible that there might be money in this, Braun thought, but the odds weren't good. Emery had a four bedroom house, a little overgrown yard, and a one-car garage he kept spotless. He wasn't getting rich off his discoveries. Braun kept an open mind. *Let's see the workshop.*

A bulge of nonstandard equipment was taking up some of Braun's knee room. He wriggled a bit. "How long have you been at this?"

"Took me fifteen years," Emery said. "I was running out of money. I'm near broke now."

Braun thought he should not have admitted that. He said, "You bet fifteen years of your life? Emery, how did you know you *could* do this thing? I grew up *knowing* antigravity isn't possible. They taught me *that* much at Dartmouth: relativity theory says gravity only goes one way."

"Mr. Braun, I'm older than you. *I* grew up *knowing* we'd have flying cars. Didn't you? Every so often something would turn up, like a plane you could turn into a boxcar by folding back the wings. What we all expected was the cars in *Back to the Future II."* The Lexus hybrid braked hard as red taillights flared. "Sorry. Then there was the filamentary nature of the universe."

"Say what?"

"The newest telescopes, Hubble and the like, show the universe as chains of galaxies, vast linked filaments with vast empty spaces between. It's like a handful of soap bubbles. Seeing that—from inside the universe, you know, and over such distances—that was a major triumph for astronomy. Explaining it—well, nobody else could. I thought I had something."

Braun waited.

"Then there was dark energy. You've *got* to know about dark energy."

"Heard of it."

"Dark energy causes the universe to expand. Masses move away from each other. Dark energy is antigravity operating over a large scale—and it *is* classic Einstein, even if he wanted it for something else entirely. Albert wanted a jigger factor to stop the universe from falling in on itself."

"Okay, dark energy." Braun was getting a little seasick, the way traffic surged and braked. "Nothing to bet your lifestyle on."

"Then there was the accident at New Bell Laboratories. Part of the particle accelerator pulled right out of the ground in a big loop. I guessed that they'd focused dark energy. I thought I could do it too."

"But you didn't have two miles of particle accelerator."

"But they published their results. By

then—" Emory braked hard. "Sorry."

"Mr. Emery, don't you know somebody you wouldn't want at the wheel of a flying car? I sure do."

"Okay, it's a point."

"That's what stopped us. That's why we don't have the flying cars. Can you picture Senator Ted Kennedy at the wheel of a great big flying limousine, and no cops willing to arrest him? Damn!" Braun's hands came up to brace him against the dashboard. The seat belt cut into him; blood flooded into his cheeks, nose, ears.

"Awful, isn't it?" Gordon Emery reached for a switch on the widgetry that was taking up too much of Braun's knee room. The car lifted.

"Oh my God," Braun said.

The car lifted. It was a Lexus 400h, a hybrid SUV, not otherwise remarkable. The Lexus coasted above an eighteen-wheeler truck and settled in, thirty feet up, moving at around forty miles per hour.

Cars behind the Lexus brushed each other. Braun could hear tearing metal.

"It's not very fast," Emery said, "but it's faster than them!"

"That cop car sees us. There go the lights."

Emery laughed. "How can he reach us?"

"Okay. New Bell Labs. You think they focused dark energy and the equipment went *up."*

"Yeah. Then I knew that it could be done with equipment I could find in this, *this* civilization, not some alien factory a hundred million light years away. Once you know something can be done, you're halfway there. But it really came back to the filamentary chains of galaxies. Can't you see what's been happening?"

Braun shook his head. He hoped Emery was watching his driving. There was little to hit up here—a powerful selling point, once they got down to business—but

Emery's eyes weren't focused, and his smile was dreamy.

He said, "If I use up the energy in a battery, it's gone, right? If a whole civilization uses huge quantities of dark energy—and if they've got antigravity—well?"

"Cheap spaceflight. Really cheap."

"The force pushing galaxies apart, it would get used up. It would go away. The wizards, they'd expand through the universe. One galaxy, then another. The galaxies around them would stop receding. You'd get chains of galaxies like stepping stones. We're way behind, Mr. Braun, starting way late. Everywhere across the universe, chains of galaxies where the universe stopped expanding hundreds of millions of years ago. Once I knew it could be done—"

"Helicopter. Police helicopter."

"The thing is, I need backing. Are you willing to put up some money? Because when this hits the evening news, I might be able to find someone else. *And* I just got us a lot of free publicity."

"Not free. You're going to get a ticket. You don't have an aviator's license for *this.*"

Emery turned right where there was no turn. Streets flowed below. He crossed the 405 freeway and settled smoothly onto Sherman Way. The helicopter was over them; then they were in the tunnel that runs under Van Nuys airport. Emery matched course with the traffic.

"I'll back you," Braun said, "if you give up the flying car."

"Give it up?"

"We're going to have to think about markets," Braun said. "I grew up with a guy—anyway, everybody knows someone—a cousin, a neighbor—someone who *should not* be given a flying car. *You,* Mr. Emery, you shouldn't have one either. Maybe our market really is the civilian

space program, if NASA gets out of our way. What do you think?"

"I just wonder," Emery said, "if we're back to where we used to be when I was a boy. If enough civilizations are using dark energy, you could see the expanding universe slow and stop and then collapse. What do you think?"

"Keep the car. Keep it hidden. One day it'll be in the Smithsonian. How much do you need?" • • •

LARRY NIVEN is a master of hard science fiction. He won both the Hugo and Nebula awards for his novel Ringworld, *and four additional Hugos for shorter works. He adapted his novella "The Soft Weapon" into the animated* Star Trek *episode "The Slaver Weapon," and wrote for the syndicated* Star Trek *comic strip. He has also written for the original* Land of the Lost *and the revival of* The Outer Limits.

ARENA

by Fredric Brown

Illustrated by Kevin Farrell

FARRELL

Carson opened his eyes, and found himself looking upward into a flickering blue dimness.

It was hot, and he was lying on sand, and a sharp rock embedded in the sand was hurting his back. He rolled over to his side, off the rock, and then pushed himself up to a sitting position.

"I'm crazy," he thought. "Crazy—or dead—or something." The sand was blue, bright blue. And there wasn't any such thing as bright blue sand on Earth or any of the planets.

Blue sand.

Blue sand under a blue dome that wasn't the sky nor yet a room, but a circumscribed area—somehow he knew it was circumscribed and finite even though he couldn't see to the top of it.

He picked up some of the sand in his hand and let it run through his fingers. It trickled down onto his bare leg. *Bare?*

Naked. He was stark naked, and already his body was dripping perspiration from the enervating heat, coated blue with sand wherever sand had touched it.

But elsewhere his body was white.

He thought: Then this sand is really blue. If it seemed blue only because of the blue light, then I'd be blue also. But I'm white, so the sand *is* blue. *Blue sand.* There isn't any blue sand. There isn't any place like this place I'm in.

Sweat was running down in his eyes.

It was hot, hotter than hell. Only hell— the hell of the ancients—was supposed to be red and not blue.

But if this place wasn't hell, what was it? Only Mercury, among the planets, had heat like this and this wasn't Mercury. And Mercury was some four billion miles from—

It came back to him then, where he'd been. In the little one-man scouter, outside the orbit of Pluto, scouting a scant million miles to one side of the Earth Armada drawn up in battle array there to intercept the outsiders.

That sudden strident nerve-shattering ringing of the alarm bell when the rival scouter—the Outsider ship—had come within range of his detectors—

No one knew who the Outsiders were, what they looked like, from what galaxy they came, other than that it was in the general direction of the Pleiades.

First, sporadic raids on Earth colonies and outposts. Isolated battles between Earth patrols and small groups of Outsider spaceships; battles sometimes won and sometimes lost, but never to date resulting in the capture of an alien vessel. Nor had any member of a raided colony ever survived to describe the Outsiders who had left the ships, if indeed they had left them.

Not a too-serious menace, at first, for the raids had not been too numerous or destructive. And individually, the ships had proved slightly inferior in armament to the best of Earth's fighters, although somewhat superior in speed and maneuverablility. A sufficient edge in speed, in fact, to give the Outsiders their choice of running or fighting, unless surrounded.

Nevertheless, Earth had prepared for serious trouble, for a showdown, building the mightiest armada of all time. It had been waiting now, that armada, for a long time. But now the showdown was coming.

Scouts twenty billion miles out had detected the approach of a mighty fleet—a showdown fleet—of the Outsiders. Those scouts had never come back, but their radiotronic messages had. And now Earth's armada, all ten thousand ships and half-million fighting spacemen, was out there, outside Pluto's orbit, waiting to intercept and battle to the death.

And an even battle it was going to be, judging by the advance reports of the men of the far picket line who had given their lives to report before they had died—on the size and strength of the alien fleet.

Anybody's battle, with the mastery of the solar system hanging in the balance, on an even chance. A last and *only* chance, for Earth and all her colonies lay at the utter mercy of the Outsiders if they ran that gauntlet—

Oh yes. Bob Carson remembered now.

Not that it explained blue sand and flickering blueness. But that strident alarming of the bell and his leap for the control panel. His frenzied fumbling as he strapped himself into the seat. The dot in the visiplate that grew larger.

The dryness of his mouth. The awful knowledge that this was *it*. For him, at least, although the main fleets were still out of range of one another.

This, his first taste of battle. Within three seconds or less he'd be victorious, or a charred cinder. Dead.

Three seconds—that's how long a space-battle lasted. Time enough to count to three, slowly, and then you'd won or you were dead. One hit completely took care of a lightly armed and armored little one-man craft like a scouter.

Frantically—as, unconsciously, his dry lips shaped the word "One"—he worked at the controls to keep that growing dot centered on the crossed spiderwebs of the visiplate. His hands doing that, while his right foot hovered over the pedal that would fire the bolt. The single bolt of concentrated hell that had to hit—or else. There wouldn't be time for any second shot.

"Two." He didn't know he'd said that, either. The dot in the visiplate wasn't a dot now. Only a few thousand miles away, it showed up in the magnification of the plate as though it were only a few hundred yards off. It was a sleek. fast little scouter, about the size of his.

And an alien ship, all right.

"Thr—" His foot touched the bolt-release pedal—

And then the Outsider had swerved suddenly and was off the crosshairs. Carson punched keys frantically, to follow.

For a tenth of a second, it was out of the visiplate entirely, and then as the nose of his scouter swung after it, he saw it again, diving straight toward the ground.

The ground?

It was an optical illusion of some sort. It *had* to be, that planet—or whatever it was—that now covered the visiplate. Whatever it was, it couldn't be there. Couldn't possibly. There *wasn't* any planet nearer than Neptune, three billion miles away—with Pluto around on the opposite side of the distant pinpoint sun.

His *detectors! They* hadn't shown any object of planetary dimensions, even of asteroid dimensions. They still didn't.

So it couldn't be there, that whatever-it-was he was driving into, only a few hundred miles below him.

And in his sudden anxiety to keep from crashing, he forgot even the Outsider ship. He fired the front braking rockets, and even as the sudden change of speed slammed him forward against the seat straps, he fired full right for an emergency turn. Pushed them down and *held* them down, knowing that he needed everything the ship had to keep from crashing and that a turn that sudden would black him out for a moment.

It did black him out.

And that was all. Now he was sitting in hot blue sand, stark naked but otherwise unhurt. No sign of his spaceship and—for that matter—no sign of *space*. That curve overhead wasn't a sky, whatever else it was.

He scrambled to his feet.

Gravity seemed a little more than Earth-normal. Not much more.

Flat sand stretching away, a few scrawny bushes in clumps here and there. The bushes were blue, too, but in varying shades, some lighter than the blue of the sand, some darker.

Out from under the nearest bush ran a

little thing that was like a lizard, except that it had more than four legs. It was blue, too. Bright blue. It saw him and ran back again under the bush.

He looked up again, trying to decide what was overhead. It wasn't exactly a roof, but it was dome-shaped. It flickered and was hard to look at. But definitely, it curved down to the ground, to the blue sand, all around him.

He wasn't far from being under the center of the dome. At a guess, it was a hundred yards to the nearest wall, if it was a wall. It was as though a blue hemisphere of *something*, about two hundred and fifty yards in circumference, was inverted over the flat expanse of the sand.

And everything blue, except one object. Over near a far curving wall there was a red object. Roughly spherical, it seemed to be about a yard in diameter. Too far for him to see clearly through the flickering blueness. But, unaccountably, he shuddered. He wiped sweat from his forehead, or tried to, with the back of his hand.

Was this a dream, a nightmare? This heat, this sand, that vague feeling of horror he felt when he looked toward that red thing?

A dream? No, one didn't go to sleep and dream in the midst of a battle in space.

Death? No, never. If there were immortality, it wouldn't be a senseless thing like this, a thing of blue heat and blue sand and a red horror.

Then he heard the voice—

Inside his head he heard it, not with his ears. It came from nowhere or everywhere.

"Through spaces and dimensions wandering," rang the words in his mind, *"and in this space and this time I find two peoples about to wage war that would exterminate one and so weaken the other that it would retrogress and never fufill its des-*tiny, but decay and return to mindless dust whence it came. And I say this must not happen."*

"Who... what are you?" Carson didn't say it aloud, but the question formed itself in his brain.

"You would not understand completely. I am—" There was a pause as though the voice sought—in Carson's brain—for a word that wasn't there, a word he didn't know. *"I am the end of evolution of a race so old the time cannot be expressed in words that have meaning to your mind. A race fused into a single entity, eternal—*

"An entity such as your primitive race might become"—again the groping for a word—*"time from now. So might the race you call, in your mind, the Outsiders. So I intervene in the battle to come, the battle between fleets so evenly matched that destruction of both races will result. One must survive. One must progress and evolve."*

"One?" thought Carson. "Mine, or—?"

"It is in my power to stop the war, to send the Outsiders back to their galaxy. But they would return, or your race would sooner or later follow them there. Only by remaining in this space and time to intervene constantly could I prevent them from destroying one another, and I cannot remain.

"So I shall intervene now. I shall destroy one fleet completely without loss to the other. One civilization shall thus survive."

Nightmare. This had to be nightmare, Carson thought. But he knew it wasn't.

It was too mad, too impossible, to be anything but real.

He didn't dare ask *the* question—which? But his thoughts asked it for him.

"The stronger shall survive," said the voice. *"That I cannot—and would not change. I merely intervene to make it a complete victory, not"*—groping again—

"not Pyrrhic victory to a broken race.

"From the outskirts of the not-yet battle I plucked two individuals, you and an Outsider. I see from your mind that in your early history of nationalisms battles between champions, to decide issues between races, were not unknown.

"You and your opponent are here pitted against one another, naked and unarmed under conditions equally unfamiliar to you both, equally unpleasant to you both. There is no time limit, for here there is no time. The survivor is the champion of his race. That race survives."

"But—" Carson's protest was too inarticulate for expression, but the voice answered it.

"It is fair. The conditions are such that the accident of physical strength will not completely decide the issue. There is a barrier. You will understand. Brain-power and courage will be more important than strength. Most especially courage, which is the will to survive."

"But while this goes on, the fleets will—"

"No, you are in another space, another time. For as long as you are here, time stands still in the universe you know. I see you wonder whether this place is real. It is, and it is not. As I—to your limited understanding—am and am not real. My existence is mental and not physical. You saw me as a planet; it could have been as a dustmote or a sun.

"But to you this place is now real. What you suffer here will be real. And if you die here, your death will be real. If you die, your failure will be the end of your race. That is enough for you to know."

And then the voice was gone.

Again he was alone, but not alone. For as Carson looked up, he saw that the red thing, the red sphere of horror which he now knew was the Outsider, was rolling toward him.

Rolling.

It seemed to have no legs or arms that he could see, no features. It rolled across the blue sand with the fluid quickness of a drop of mercury. And before it, in some manner he could not understand, came a paralyzing wave of nauseating, retching, horrid hatred.

Carson looked about him frantically. A stone, lying in the sand a few feet away, was the nearest thing to a weapon. It wasn't large, but it had sharp edges, like a slab of flint. It looked a bit like blue flint.

He picked it up, and crouched to receive the attack. It was coming fast, faster than he could run.

No time to think out how he was going to fight it, and how anyway could he plan to battle a creature whose strength, whose characteristics, whose method of fighting he did not know? Rolling so fast, it looked more than ever like a perfect sphere.

Ten yards away. Five. And then it stopped.

Rather, it *was stopped*. Abruptly the near side of it flattened as though it had run up against an invisible wall. It bounced, actually bounced back.

Then it rolled forward again, but more slowly, more cautiously. It stopped again, at the same place. It tried again, a few yards to one side.

There was a barrier there of some sort. It clicked, then, in Carson's mind. That thought projected into his mind by the Entity who had brought them here: "—accident of physical strength will not completely decide the issue. There is a barrier."

A force-field, of course. Not the Netzian Field, known to Earth science, for that glowed and emitted a crackling sound. This one was invisible, silent.

It was a wall that ran from side to side of the inverted hemisphere; Carson didn't have to verify that himself. The Roller was doing that; rolling sideways along the barrier, seeking a break in it that wasn't there.

Carson took half a dozen steps forward, his left hand groping out before him, and then his hand touched the barrier. It felt smooth, yielding like a sheet of rubber rather than like glass. Warm to his touch, but no warmer than the sand underfoot. And it was completely invisible, even at close range.

He dropped the stone and put both hands against it, pushing. It seemed to yield, just a trifle. But no farther than that trifle, even when he pushed with all his weight. It felt like a sheet of rubber backed up by steel. Limited resiliency, and then firm strength.

He stood on tiptoe and reached as high as he could and the barrier was still there.

He saw the Roller coming back, having reached one side of the arena. That feeling of nausea hit Carson again, and he stepped back from the barrier as it went by. It didn't stop.

But did the barrier stop at ground level? Carson knelt down and burrowed in the sand. It was soft, light, easy to dig in. At two feet down the barrier was still there.

The Roller was coming back again. Obviously, it couldn't find a way through at either side.

There must be a way through, Carson thought. *Some* way we can get at each other, else this duel is meaningless.

But no hurry now, in finding that out. There was something to try first. The Roller was back now, and it stopped just across the barrier, only six feet away. It seemed to be studying him, although for the life of him, Carson couldn't find external evidence of sense organs on the thing. Nothing that looked like eyes or ears, or even a mouth. There was, though, he saw now, a series of grooves—perhaps

a dozen of them altogether, and he saw two tentacles suddenly push out from two of the grooves and dip into the sand as though testing its consistency. Tentacles about an inch in diameter and perhaps a foot and a half long.

But the tentacles were retractable into the grooves and were kept there except when in use. They were retracted when the thing rolled and seemed to have nothing to do with its method of locomotion. That, as far as Carson could judge, seemed to be accomplished by some shifting—just *how* he couldn't even imagine—of its center of gravity.

He shuddered as he looked at the thing. It was alien, utterly alien, horribly different from anything on Earth or any of the life forms found on the other solar planets. Instinctively, somehow, he knew its mind was as alien as its body.

But he had to try. If it had no telepathic powers at all, the attempt was foredoomed to failure, yet he thought it had such powers. There had, at any rate, been a projection of something that was not physical at the time a few minutes ago when it had first started for him. An almost tangible wave of hatred.

If it could project that, perhaps it could read his mind as well, sufficiently for his purpose.

Deliberately, Carson picked up the rock that had been his only weapon, then tossed it down again in a gesture of relinquishment and raised his empty hands, palms up, before him.

He spoke aloud, knowing that although the words would be meaningless to the creature before him, speaking them would focus his own thoughts more completely upon the message.

"Can we not have peace between us?" he said, his voice sounding strange in the utter stillness. "The Entity who brought us here has told us what must happen if our races fight—extinction of one and weakening and retrogression of the other. The battle between them, said the Entity, depends upon what we do here. Why cannot we agree to an eternal peace—your race to its galaxy, we to ours?"

Carson blanked out his mind to receive a reply.

It came, and it staggered him back, physically. He actually recoiled several steps in sheer horror at the depth and intensity of the hatred and lust-to-kill of the red images that had been projected at him. Not as articulate words—as had come to him the thoughts of the Entity—but as wave upon wave of fierce emotion.

For a moment that seemed an eternity he had to struggle against the mental impact of that hatred, fight to clear his mind of it and drive out the alien thoughts to which he had given admittance by blanking his own thoughts. He wanted to retch.

Slowly his mind cleared as, slowly, the mind of a man wakening from nightmare clears away the fear-fabric of which the dream was woven. He was breathing hard and he felt weaker, but he could think.

He stood studying the Roller. It had been motionless during the mental duel it had so nearly won. Now it rolled a few feet to one side, to the nearest of the blue bushes. Three tentacles whipped out of their grooves and began to investigate the bush.

"O.K.," Carson said, "so it's war then." He managed a wry grin. "If I got your answer straight, peace doesn't appeal to you." And, because he was, after all, a quite young man and couldn't resist the impulse to be dramatic, he added, "To the death!"

But his voice, in that utter silence, sounded very silly, even to himself. It came to him, then, that this *was* to the death. Not only his own death or that of the red spherical thing which he now

thought of as the Roller, but death to the entire race of one or the other of them. The end of the human race, if he failed.

It made him suddenly very humble and very afraid to think that. More than to think it, to *know* it. Somehow, with a knowledge that was above even faith, he knew that the Entity who had arranged this duel had told the truth about its intentions and its powers. It wasn't kidding.

The future of humanity depended upon *him*. It was an awful thing to realize, and he wrenched his mind away from it. He had to concentrate on the situation at hand.

There had to be some way of getting through the barrier, or of killing through the barrier.

Mentally? He hoped that wasn't all, for the Roller obviously had stronger telepathic powers than the primitive, undeveloped ones of the human race. Or did it?

He had been able to drive the thoughts of the Roller out of his own mind; could it drive out his? If its ability to project were stronger, might not its receptivity mechanism be more vulnerable?

He stared at it and endeavored to concentrate and focus all his thougts upon it. *"Die,"* he thought. *"You are going to die. You are dying. You are—"*

He tried variations on it, and mental pictures. Sweat stood out on his forehead and he found himself trembling with the intensity of the effort. But the Roller went ahead with its investigation of the bush, as utterly unaffected as though Carson had been reciting the multiplication table.

So *that* was no good.

He felt a bit weak and dizzy from the heat and his strenuous effort at concentration. He sat down on the blue sand to rest and gave his full attention to watching and studying the Roller. By close study, perhaps, he could judge its strength and detect its weaknesses, learn things that would be valuable to know when and if they should come to grips.

It was breaking off twigs. Carson watched carefully, trying to judge just how hard it worked to do that. Later, he thought, he could find a similar bush on his own side, break off twigs of equal thickness himself, and gain a comparison of physical strength between his own arms and hands and those tentacles.

The twigs broke off hard; the Roller was having to struggle with each one, he saw. Each tentacle, he saw, bifurcated at the tip into two fingers, each tipped by a nail or claw. The claws didn't seem to be particularly long or dangerous. No more so than his own fingernails, if they were let to grow a bit.

No, on the whole, it didn't look too tough to handle physically. Unless, of course, that bush was made of pretty tough stuff. Carson looked around him and, yes, right within reach was another bush of identically the same type.

He reached over and snapped off a twig. It was brittle, easy to break. Of course, the Roller might have been faking deliberately but he didn't think so.

On the other hand, where was it vulnerable? Just how would he go about killing it, if he got the chance? He went back to studying it. The outer hide looked pretty tough. He'd need a sharp weapon of some sort. He picked up the piece of rock again. It was about twelve inches long, narrow, and fairly sharp on one end. If it chipped like flint, he could make a serviceable knife out of it.

The Roller was continuing its investigations of the bushes. It rolled again, to the nearest one of another type. A little blue lizard, many-legged like the one Carson had seen on his side of the barrier, darted out from under the bush.

A tentacle of the Roller lashed out and caught it, picked it up. Another tentacle whipped over and began to pull legs off the lizard, as coldly and calmly as it had pulled twigs off the bush. The creature struggled frantically and emitted a shrill squealing sound that was the first sound Carson had heard here other than the sound of his own voice.

Carson shuddered and wanted to turn his eyes away. But he made himself continue to watch; anything he could learn about his opponent might prove valuable. Even this knowledge of its unnecessary cruelty. Particularly, he thought with a sudden vicious surge of emotion, this knowledge of its unnecessary cruelty. It would make it a pleasure to kill the thing, if and when the chance came.

He steeled himself to watch the dismembering of the lizard, for that very reason.

But he felt glad when, with half its legs gone, the lizard quit squealing and struggling and lay limp and dead in the Roller's grasp.

It didn't continue with the rest of the legs. Contemptuously it tossed the dead lizard away from it, in Carson's direction. It arced through the air between them and landed at his feet.

It had come through the barrier! The barrier wasn't there anymore!

C arson was on his feet in a flash, the knife gripped tightly in his hand, and leaped forward. He'd settle this thing here and now! With the barrier gone—

But it wasn't gone. He found that out the hard way, running head on into it and nearly knocking himself silly. He bounced back, and fell.

And as he sat up, shaking his head to clear it, he saw something coming through the air toward him, and to duck it, he threw himself flat again on the sand, and to one side. He got his body out of the way, but there was a sudden sharp pain in the calf of his left leg.

He rolled backward, ignoring the pain, and scrambled to his feet. It was a rock, he saw now, that had struck him. And the Roller was picking up another one now, swinging it back gripped between two tentacles, getting ready to throw again.

It sailed through the air toward him, but he was easily able to step out of its way. The Roller, apparently, could throw straight, but not hard nor far. The first rock had struck him only because he had been sitting down and had not seen it coming until it was almost upon him.

Even as he stepped aside from that weak second throw, Carson drew back his right arm and let fly with the rock that was still in his hand. If missiles, he thought with sudden elation, can cross the barrier, then two can play at the game of throwing them. And the good right arm of an Earth-man—

He couldn't miss a three-foot sphere at only four-yard range, and he didn't miss. The rock whizzed straight, and with a speed several times that of the missiles the Roller had thrown. It hit dead center, but it hit flat, unfortunately, instead of point first.

But it hit with a resounding thump, and obviously it hurt. The Roller had been reaching for another rock, but it changed its mind and got out of there instead. By the time Carson could pick up and throw another rock, the Roller was forty yards back from the barrier and going strong.

His second throw missed by feet, and his third throw was short. The Roller was back out of range—at least out of range of a missile heavy enough to be damaging.

Carson grinned. That round had been his. Except—

He quit grinning as he bent over to examine the calf of his leg. A jagged edge of the stone had made a pretty deep cut, sev-eral inches long. It was bleeding pretty freely, but he didn't think it had gone deep enough to hit an artery. If it stopped bleeding of its own accord, well and good. If not, he was in for trouble.

Finding out one thing, though, took precedence over that cut. The nature of the barrier.

He went forward to it again, this time groping with his hands before him. He found it; then holding one hand against it, he tossed a handful of sand at it with the other hand. The sand went right through. His hand didn't.

Organic matter versus inorganic? No, because the dead lizard had gone through it, and a lizard, alive or dead, was certainly organic. Plant life? He broke off a twig and poked it at the barrier. The twig went through, with no resistance, but when his fingers gripping the twig came to the barrier, they were stopped.

He couldn't get through it, nor could the Roller. But rocks and sand and a dead lizard—

How about a live lizard? He went hunting, under bushes, until he found one, and caught it. He tossed it gently against the barrier and it bounced back and scurried away across the blue sand.

That gave him the answer, in so far as he could determine it now. The screen was a barrier to living things. Dead or inorganic matter could cross it.

That off his mind, Carson looked at his injured leg again. The bleeding was lessening, which meant he wouldn't need to worry about making a tourniquet. But he should find some water, if any was available, to clean the wound.

Water—the thought of it made him realize that he was getting awfully thirsty. He'd *have* to find water, in case this contest turned out to be a protracted one.

Limping slightly now, he started off to

make a full circuit of his half of the arena. Guiding himself with one hand along the barrier, he walked to his right until he came to the curving sidewall. It was visible, a dull blue-gray at close range, and the surface of it felt just like the central barrier.

He experimented by tossing a handful of sand at it, and the sand reached the wall and disappeared as it went through. The hemispherical shell was a force-field, too. But an opaque one, instead of transparent like the barrier.

He followed it around until he came back to the barrier, and walked back along the barrier to the point from which he'd started.

No sign of water.

Worried now, he started a series of zigzags back and forth between the barrier and the wall, covering the intervening space thoroughly.

No water. Blue sand, blue bushes, and intolerable heat. Nothing else.

It must be his imagination, he told himself angrily, that he was suffering *that* much from thirst. How long had he been here? Of course, no time at all, according to his own space-time frame. The Entity had told him time stood still out there, while he was here. But his body processes went on here, just the same. And according to his body's reckoning, how long had he been here? Three or four hours, perhaps. Certainly not long enough to be suffering seriously from thirst.

But he was suffering from it; his throat dry and parched. Probably the intense heat was the cause. It was *hot!* A hundred and thirty Fahrenheit, at a guess. A dry, still heat without the slightest movement of air.

He was limping rather badly, and utterly fagged out when he'd finished the exploration of his domain.

He stared across at the motionless Roller and hoped it was as miserable as he was. And quite possibly it wasn't enjoying this, either. The Entity had said conditions here were equally unfamiliar and equally uncomfortable for both of them. Maybe the Roller came from a planet where two hundred degree heat was the norm. Maybe it was freezing while he was roasting.

Maybe the air was as much too thick for it as it was too thin for him. For the exertion of his explorations had left him panting. The atmosphere here, he realized now, was not much thicker than that on Mars.

No water.

That meant a deadline, for him at any rate. Unless he could find a way to cross that barrier or to kill his enemy from this side of it, thirst would kill him eventually.

It gave him a feeling of desperate urgency. He *must* hurry.

But he made himself sit down a moment to rest, to think.

What was there to do? Nothing, and yet so many things. The several varieties of bushes, for example. They didn't look promising, but he'd have to examine them for possibilities. And his leg—he'd have to do something about that, even without water to clean it. Gather ammunition in the form of rocks. Find a rock that would make a good knife.

His leg hurt rather badly now, and he decided that came first. One type of bush had leaves—or things rather similar to leaves. He pulled off a handful of them and decided, after examination, to take a chance on them. He used them to clean off the sand and dirt and caked blood, then made a pad of fresh leaves and tied it over the wound with tendrils from the same bush.

The tendrils proved unexpectedly tough and strong. They were slender, and soft and pliable, yet he couldn't break them at all. He had to saw them off the bush with the sharp edge of a piece of the blue flint. Some of the thicker ones were over a foot long, and he filed away in his memory, for future reference, the fact that a bunch of the thick ones, tied together, would make a pretty serviceable rope. Maybe he'd be able to think of a use for rope.

Next, he made himself a knife. The blue flint *did* chip. From a foot-long splinter of it, he fashioned himself a crude but lethal weapon. And of tendrils from the bush, he made himself a rope-belt through which he could thrust the flint knife, to keep it with him all the time and yet have his hands free.

He went back to studying the bushes. There were three other types. One was leafless, dry, brittle, rather like a dried tumbleweed. Another was of soft, crumbly wood, almost like punk. It looked and felt as though it would make excellent tinder for a fire. The third type was the most nearly wood-like. It had fragile leaves that wilted at a touch, but the stalks, although short, were straight and strong.

It was horribly, unbearably hot.

He limped up to the barrier, felt to make sure that it was still there. It was.

He stood watching the Roller for a while. It was keeping a safe distance back from the barrier, out of effective stone-throwing range. It was moving around back there, doing something. He couldn't tell what it was doing.

Once it stopped moving, came a little closer, and seemed to concentrate its attention on him. Again Carson had to fight off a wave of nausea. He threw a stone at it and the Roller retreated and went back to whatever it had been doing before.

At least he could make it keep its distance.

And, he thought bitterly, a devil of a lot of good *that* did him. Just the same, he spent the next hour or two gathering stones of suitable size for throwing, and making several neat piles of them, near his side of the barrier.

His throat burned now. It was difficult for him to think about anything except water.

But he *had* to think about other things. About getting through that barrier, under or over it, getting *at* that red sphere and killing it before this place of heat and thirst killed him first.

The barrier went to the wall upon either side, but how high and how far under the sand?

For just a moment, Carson's mind was too fuzzy to think out how he could find out either of those things. Idly, sitting there in the hot sand—and he didn't remember sitting down—he watched a blue lizard crawl from the shelter of one bush to the shelter of another.

From under the second bush, it looked out at him. Carson grinned at it. Maybe he was getting a bit punchdrunk, because he remembered suddenly the old story of the desert-colonists on Mars, taken from an older desert story of Earth— "Pretty soon you get so lonesome you find yourself talking to the lizards, and then not so long after that you find the lizards talking back to you—"

He should have been concentrating, of course, on how to kill the Roller, but instead he grinned at the lizard and said, "Hello, there."

The lizard took a few steps toward him. "Hello," it said.

Carson was stunned for a moment, and then he put back his head and roared with laughter. It didn't hurt his throat to do so, either; he hadn't been *that* thirsty.

Why not? Why should the Entity who thought up this nightmare of a place not have a sense of humor, along with the other powers he has? Talking lizards, equipped to talk back in my own language, if I talk to them— It's a nice touch.

He grinned at the lizard and said, "Come on over." But the lizard turned and ran away, scurrying from bush to bush until it was out of sight.

He was thirsty again.

And he had to *do* something. He couldn't win this contest by sitting here sweating and feeling miserable. He had to *do* something. But what?

Get through the barrier. But he couldn't get through it, or over it. But was he certain he couldn't get under? And come to think of it, didn't one sometimes find water by digging? Two birds with one stone—

Painfully now, Carson limped up to the barrier and started digging, scooping up sand a double handful at a time. It was slow, hard work because the sand ran in at the edges and the deeper he got the bigger in diameter the hole had to be. How many hours it took him, he didn't know, but he hit bedrock four feet down. Dry bedrock; no sign of water.

And the force-field of the barrier went down clear to the bedrock. No dice. No water. Nothing.

He crawled out of the hole and lay there panting, and then raised his head to look across and see what the Roller was doing. It must be doing something back there.

It was. It was making something out of wood from the bushes, tied together with tendrils. A queerly shaped framework about four feet high and roughly square. To see it better, Carson climbed up onto the mound of sand he had excavated from the hole, and stood there staring.

There were two long levers sticking out of the back of it, one with a cup-shaped affair on the end of it. Seemed to be some sort of a catapult, Carson thought.

Sure enough, the Roller was lifting a sizable rock into the cup-shaped outfit.

One of his tentacles moved the other lever up and down for a while, and then he turned the machine slightly as though aiming it and the lever with the stone flew up and forward.

The stone arced several yards over Carson's head, so far away that he didn't have to duck, but he judged the distance it had traveled, and whistled softly. He couldn't throw a rock that weight more than half that distance. And even retreating to the rear of his domain wouldn't put him out of range of that machine, if the Roller shoved it forward almost to the barrier.

Another rock whizzed over. Not quite so far away this time.

That thing could be dangerous, he decided. Maybe he'd better do something about it.

Moving from side to side along the barrier, so the catapult couldn't bracket him, he whaled a dozen rocks at it. But that wasn't going to be any good, he saw. They had to be light rocks, or he couldn't throw them that far. If they hit the framework, they bounced off harmlessly. And the Roller had no difficulty, at that distance, in moving aside from those that came near it.

Besides, his arm was tiring badly. He ached all over from sheer weariness. If he could only rest a while without having to duck rocks from that catapult at regular intervals of maybe thirty seconds each—

He stumbled back to the rear of the arena. Then he saw even that wasn't any good. The rocks reached back there, too, only there were longer intervals between them, as though it took longer to wind up the mechanism, whatever it was, of the catapult.

Wearily he dragged himself back to the barrier again. Several times he fell and could barely rise to his feet to go on. He was, he knew, near the limit of his endurance. Yet he didn't dare stop moving now, until and unless he could put that catapult out of action. If he fell asleep, he'd never wake up.

One of the stones from it gave him the first glimmer of an idea. It struck upon one of the piles of stones he'd gathered together near the barrier to use as ammunition, and it struck sparks.

Sparks. Fire. Primitive man had made fire by striking sparks, and with some of those dry crumbly bushes as tinder—

Luckily, a bush of that type was near him. He broke it off, took it over to the pile of stones, then patiently hit one stone against another until a spark touched the punklike wood of the bush. It went up in flames so fast that it singed his eyebrows and was burned to an ash within seconds.

But he had the idea now, and within minutes he had a little fire going in the lee of the mound of sand he'd made digging the hole an hour or two ago. Tinder bushes had started it, and other bushes which burned, but more slowly, kept it a steady flame.

The tough wirelike tendrils didn't burn readily; that made the fire-bombs easy to make and throw. A bundle of faggots tied about a small stone to give it weight and a loop of the tendril to swing it by.

He made half a dozen of them before he lighted and threw the first. It went wide, and the Roller started a quick retreat, pulling the catapult after him. But Carson had the others ready and threw them in rapid succession. The fourth wedged in the catapult's framework, and did the trick. The Roller tried desperately to put out the spreading blaze by throwing sand, but its clawed tentacles would take only a spoonful at a time and his efforts were ineffectual. The catapult burned.

The Roller moved safely away from the fire and seemed to concentrate its attention on Carson and again he felt that wave of hatred and nausea. But more weakly; either the Roller itself was weakening or Carson had learned how to protect himself against the mental attack.

He thumbed his nose at it and then sent it scuttling back to safety by throwing a stone. The Roller went clear to the back of its half of the arena and started pulling up bushes again. Probably it was going to make another catapult.

Carson verified—for the hundredth time—that the barrier was still operating, and then found himself sitting in the sand beside it because he was suddenly too weak to stand up.

His leg throbbed steadily now and the pangs of thirst were severe. But those things paled beside the utter physical exhaustion that gripped his entire body.

And the heat.

Hell must be like this, he thought. The hell that the ancients had believed in. He fought to stay awake, and yet staying awake seemed futile, for there was nothing he could do. Nothing, while the barrier remained impregnable and the Roller stayed back out of range.

But there must be *something*. He tried to remember things he had read in books of archaeology about the methods of fighting used back in the days before metal and plastic. The stone missile, that had come first, he thought. Well, that he already had.

The only improvement on it would be a catapult, such as the Roller had made. But he'd never be able to make one, with the tiny bits of wood available from the bushes—no single piece longer than a foot or so. Certainly he could figure out a mechanism for one, but he didn't have the endurance left for a task that would take days.

Days? But the Roller had made one. Had they been here days already? Then he remembered that the Roller had many tentacles to work with and undoubtedly could do such work faster than he.

And besides, a catapult wouldn't decide the issue. He had to do better than that.

Bow and arrow? No; he'd tried archery once and knew his own ineptness with a bow. Even with a modern sportsman's durasteel weapon, made for accuracy. With such a crude, pieced-together outfit as he could make here, he doubted if he could shoot as far as he could throw a rock, and knew he couldn't shoot as straight.

Spear? Well, he *could* make that. It would be useless as a throwing weapon at any distance, but would be a handy thing at close range, if he ever got to close range.

And making one would give him something to do. Help keep his mind from wandering, as it was beginning to do. Sometimes now, he had to concentrate a while before he could remember why he was here, why he had to kill the Roller.

Luckily he was still beside one of the piles of stones. He sorted through it until he found one shaped roughly like a spearhead. With a smaller stone he began to chip it into shape, fashioning sharp shoulders on the sides so that if it penetrated it would not pull out again.

Like a harpoon? There was something in that idea, he thought. A harpoon was better than a spear, maybe, for this crazy contest. If he could once get it into the Roller, and had a rope on it, he could pull the Roller up against the barrier and the stone blade of his knife would reach through that barrier, even if his hands wouldn't.

The shaft was harder to make than the head. But by splitting and joining the main stems of four of the bushes, and wrapping the joints with the tough but thin tendrils, he got a strong shaft about four feet long, and tied the stone head in a notch cut in the end.

It was crude, but strong.

And the rope. With the thin tough tendrils he made himself twenty feet of line. It was light and didn't look strong, but he knew it would hold his weight and to spare. He tied one end of it to the shaft of the harpoon and the other end about his right wrist. At least, if he threw his harpoon across the barrier, he'd be able to pull it back if he missed.

Then when he had tied the last knot and there was nothing more he could do, the heat and the weariness and the pain in his leg and the dreadful thirst were suddenly a thousand times worse than they had been before.

He tried to stand up, to see what the Roller was doing now, and found he couldn't get to his feet. On the third try, he got as far as his knees and then fell flat again.

"I've got to sleep," he thought. "If a showdown came now, I'd be helpless. He could come up here and kill me, if he knew. I've got to regain some strength."

Slowly, painfully, he crawled back away from the barrier. Ten yards, twenty—

The jar of something thudding against the sand near him waked him from a confused and horrible dream to a more confused and more horrible reality, and he opened his eyes again to blue radiance over blue sand.

How long had he slept? A minute? A day?

Another stone thudded nearer and threw sand on him. He got his arms under him and sat up. He turned around and saw the Roller twenty yards away, at the barrier.

It rolled away hastily as he sat up, not stopping until it was as far away as it could get.

He'd fallen asleep too soon, he realized,

while he was still in range of the Roller's throwing ability. Seeing him lying motionless, it had dared come up to the barrier to throw at him. Luckily, it didn't realize how weak he was, or it could have stayed there and kept on throwing stones.

Had he slept long? He didn't think so, because he felt just as he had before. Not rested at all, no thirstier, no different. Probably he'd been there only a few minutes.

He started crawling again, this time forcing himself to keep going until he was as far as he could go, until the colorless, opaque wall of the arena's outer shell was only a yard away.

Then things slipped away again—

When he awoke, nothing about him was changed, but this time he knew that he had slept a long time.

The first thing he became aware of was the inside of his mouth; it was dry, caked. His tongue was swollen.

Something was wrong, he knew, as he returned slowly to full awareness. He felt less tired, the stage of utter exhaustion had passed. The sleep had taken care of that.

But there was pain, agonizing pain. It wasn't until he tried to move that he knew that it came from his leg.

He raised his head and looked down at it. It was swollen terribly below the knee and the swelling showed even halfway up his thigh. The plant tendrils he had used to tie on the protective pad of leaves now cut deeply into the swollen flesh.

To get his knife under that imbedded lashing would have been impossible. Fortunately, the final knot was over the shin bone, in front, where the vine cut in less deeply than elsewhere. He was able, after an agonizing effort, to untie the knot.

A look under the pad of leaves told him the worst. Infection and blood poisoning, both pretty bad and getting worse.

And without drugs, without cloth, without even *water,* there wasn't a thing he could do about it.

Not a thing, except *die,* when the poison had spread through his system.

He knew it was hopeless, then, and that he'd lost.

And with him, humanity. When he died here, out there in the universe he knew, all his friends, everybody, would die too. And Earth and the colonized planets would be the home of the red, rolling, alien Outsiders. Creatures out of nightmare, things without a human attribute, who picked lizards apart for the fun of it.

It was the thought of that which gave him courage to start crawling, almost blindly in pain, toward the barrier again. Not crawling on hands and knees this time, but pulling himself along only by his arms and hands.

A chance in a million, that maybe he'd have strength left, when he got there, to throw his harpoon-spear just *once,* and with deadly effect, if—on another chance in a million—the Roller would come up to the barrier. Or if the barrier was gone, now.

It took him years, it seemed, to get there.

The barrier wasn't gone. It was as impassable as when he'd first felt it.

And the Roller wasn't at the barrier. By raising up on his elbows, he could see it at the back of its part of the arena, working on a wooden framework that was a half-completed duplicate of the catapult he'd destroyed.

It was moving slowly now. Undoubtedly it had weakened, too.

But Carson doubted that it would ever need that second catapult. He'd be dead, he thought, before it was finished.

If he could attract it to the barrier, now, while he was still alive— He waved an arm and tried to shout, but his parched throat would make no sound.

Or if he could get through the barrier—

His mind must have slipped for a moment, for he found himself beating his fists against the barrier in futile rage, made himself stop.

He closed his eyes, tried to make himself calm.

"Hello," said the voice.

It was a small, thin voice. It sounded like—

He opened his eyes and turned his head. It *was* a lizard.

"Go away," Carson wanted to say. "Go away; you're not really there, or you're there but not really talking. I'm imagining things again."

But he couldn't talk; his throat and tongue were past all speech with the dryness. He closed his eyes again.

"Hurt," said the voice. "Kill. Hurt—kill. Come."

He opened his eyes again. The blue ten-legged lizard was still there. It ran a little way along the barrier, came back, started off again, and came back

"Hurt," it said. "Kill. Come."

Again it started off, and came back. Obviously it wanted Carson to follow it along the barrier.

He closed his eyes again. The voice kept on. The same three meaningles words. Each time he opened his eyes, it ran off and came back.

"Hurt. Kill. Come."

Carson groaned. There would be no peace unless he followed the blasted thing. Like it wanted him to.

He followed it, crawling. Another sound, a high-pitched squealing, came to his ears and grew louder.

There was something lying in the sand, writhing, squealing. Something small, blue, that looked like a lizard and yet didn't—

Then he saw what it was—the lizard

whose legs the Roller had pulled off, so long ago. But it wasn't dead; it had come back to life and was wriggling and screaming in agony.

"Hurt," said the other lizard. "Hurt. Kill. Kill."

Carson understood. He took the flint knife from his belt and killed the tortured creature. The live lizard scurried off quickly.

Carson turned back to the barrier. He leaned his hands and head against it and watched the Roller, far back, working on the new catapult.

"I could get that far," he thought, "if I could get through. If I could get through, I might win yet. It looks weak, too. I might—"

And then there was another reaction of black hopelessness, when pain sapped his will and he wished that he were dead. He envied the lizard he'd just killed. It didn't have to live on and suffer. And he did. It would be hours, it might be days, before the blood poisoning killed him. If only he could use that knife on himself—

But he knew he wouldn't. As long as he was alive, there was the millionth chance—

He was straining, pushing on the barrier with the flat of his hands, and he noticed his arms, how thin and scrawny they were now. He must really have been here a long time, for days, to get as thin as that.

How much longer now, before he died? How much more heat and thirst and pain could flesh stand?

For a little while he was almost hysterical again, and then came a time of deep calm, and a thought that was startling.

The lizard he had just killed. *It had crossed the barrier, still alive.* It had come from the Roller's side; the Roller had pulled off its legs and then tossed it contemptuously at him and it had come through the barrier. He'd thought, because the lizard was dead.

But it hadn't been dead; it had been unconscious.

A live lizard couldn't go through the barrier, but an unconscious one could. The barrier was not a barrier, then, to living flesh, but to conscious flesh. It was a *mental* projection, a *mental* hazard.

And with that thought, Carson started crawling along the barrier to make his last desperate gamble. A hope so forlorn that only a dying man would have dared try it.

No use weighing the odds of success. Not when, if he didn't try it, those odds were infinity to zero.

He crawled along the barrier to the dune of sand, about four feet high, which he'd scooped out in trying—how many days ago?—to dig under the barrier or to reach water.

That mound was right at the barrier, its farther slope half on one side of the barrier, half on the other.

Taking with him a rock from the pile nearby, he climbed up to the top of the dune and over the top, and lay there against the barrier, his weight leaning against it so that if the barrier were taken away he'd roll on down the short slope, into the enemy territory.

He checked to be sure that the knife was safely in his rope belt, that the harpoon was in the crook of his left arm and that the twenty-foot rope fastened to it and to his wrist.

Then with his right hand he raised the rock with which he would hit himself on the head. Luck would have to be with him on that blow; it would have to be hard enough to knock him out, but not hard enough to knock him out for long.

He had a hunch that the Roller was watching him, and would see him roll through the barrier, and come to investigate. It would think he was dead, he hoped—he thought it had probably drawn the same deduction about the nature of the barrier that he had drawn. But it would come cautiously. He would have a little time—

He struck.

Pain brought him back to consciousness. A sudden, sharp pain in his hip that was different from the throbbing pain in his head and the throbbing pain in his leg.

But he had, thinking things out before he had struck himself, anticipated that very pain, even hoped for it, and had steeled himself against awakening with a sudden movement.

He lay still, but opened his eyes just a slit, and saw that he had guessed rightly. The Roller was coming closer. It was twenty feet away and the pain that had awakened him was the stone it had tossed to see whether he was alive or dead.

He lay still. It came closer, fifteen feet away, and stopped again. Carson scarcely breathed.

As nearly as possible, he was keeping his mind a blank, lest its telepathic ability detect consciousness in him. And with his mind blanked out that way, the impact of its thoughts upon his mind was nearly soul-shattering.

He felt sheer horror at the utter *alienness, the differentness* of those thoughts. Things that he felt but could not understand and could never express, because no terrestrial language had words, no terrestrial mind had images to fit them. The mind of a spider, he thought, or the mind of a praying mantis or a Martian sand-serpent, raised to intelligence and put in telepathic rapport with human minds, would be a homely familiar thing, compared to this.

He understood now that the Entity had been right: Man or Roller, and the universe was not a place that could hold them both. Farther apart than god and devil, there could never be even a balance between them.

Closer. Carson waited until it was only feet away, until its clawed tentacles reached out—

Oblivious to agony now, he sat up, raised and flung the harpoon with all the strength that remained to him. Or he thought it was all; sudden final strength flooded through him, along with a sudden forgetfulness of pain as definite as a nerve block.

As the Roller, deeply stabbed by the harpoon, rolled away, Carson tried to get to his feet to run after it. He couldn't do that; he fell, but kept crawling.

It reached the end of the rope, and he was jerked forward by the pull on his wrist. It dragged him a few feet and then stopped. Carson kept on pulling himself toward it hand over hand along the rope.

It stopped there, writhing tentacles trying in vain to pull out the harpoon. It seemed to shudder and quiver, and then it must have realized that it couldn't get away, for it rolled back toward him, clawed tentacles reaching out.

Stone knife in hand, he met it. He stabbed, again and again, while those horrid claws ripped skin and flesh and muscle from his body.

He stabbed and slashed, and at last it was still.

A bell was ringing, and it took him a while after he'd opened his eyes to tell where he was and what it was. He was strapped into the seat of his scouter, the visiplate before him showed only empty space. No Outsider ship and no impossible planet.

The bell was the communications plate signal; someone wanted him to switch power into the receiver. Purely reflex action enabled him to reach forward and throw the lever.

The face of Brander, captain of the

Magellan, mother-ship of his group of scouters, flashed into the screen. His face was pale and his black eyes glowing with excitement.

"Magellan to Carson," he snapped. "Come on in. The fight's over. We've won!"

The screen went blank; Brander would be signaling the other scouters of his command.

Slowly, Carson set the controls for the return. Slowly, unbelievingly, he unstrapped himself from the seat and went back to get a drink at the cold-water tank. For some reason, he was unbelievably thirsty. He drank six glasses.

He leaned there against the wall, trying to think.

Had it happened? He was in good health, sound, uninjured. His thirst had been mental rather than physical; his throat hadn't been dry. His leg—

He pulled up his trouser leg and looked at the calf. There was a long white scar there, but a perfectly healed scar. It hadn't been there before. He zipped open the front of his shirt and saw that his chest and abdomen were criss-crossed with tiny, almost unnoticeable, perfectly healed scars.

It *had* happened.

The scouter, under automatic control, was already entering the hatch of the mother-ship. The grapples pulled it into its individual lock, and a moment later a buzzer indicated that the lock was air-filled. Carson opened the hatch and stepped outside, went through the double door of the lock.

He went right to Brander's office, went in, and saluted.

Brander still looked dizzily dazed. "Hi, Carson," he said. "What you missed! What a show!"

"What happened, sir?"

"Don't know, exactly. We fired one salvo, and their whole fleet went up in dust! Whatever it was jumped from ship to ship in a flash, even the ones we hadn't aimed at and that were out of range! The whole fleet disintegrated before our eyes, and we didn't get the paint of a single ship scratched!

"We can't even claim credit for it. Must have been some unstable component in the metal they used, and our sighting shot just set it off. Man, oh man, too bad you missed all the excitement."

Carson managed to grin. It was a sickly ghost of a grin, for it would be days before he'd be over the mental impact of his experience, but the captain wasn't watching, and didn't notice.

"Yes, sir," he said. Common sense, more than modesty, told him he'd be branded forever as the worst liar in space if he ever said any more than that. "Yes, sir, too bad I missed all the excitement." • • •

FREDRIC BROWN (1906-72) worked in all story lengths, but he was especially prized for his short-short stories. The original run of **Thrilling Wonder Stories** *featured seven of his stories, including the classic "Knock," which opened with a two-line ultra-short of its own.*

The Science Fiction Writers of America named "Arena" one of the 20 best science fiction stories written before 1965. It was adapted for the original **Star Trek** *and, as "Fun and Games," for the original* **Outer Limits.**

JUNO MISSION TO TAKE CLOSEST LOOK YET AT JUPITER

WASHINGTON—NASA is officially moving forward on a mission to conduct an unprecedented, in-depth study of Jupiter.

Called Juno, the mission will be the first in which a spacecraft is placed in a highly elliptical polar orbit around the giant planet to understand its formation, evolution and structure.

"Unlike Earth, Jupiter's giant mass allowed it to hold onto its original composition, providing us with a way of tracing our solar system's history," said Scott Bolton, Juno principal investigator from the Southwest Research Institute in San Antonio.

The spacecraft is scheduled to launch in August 2011, reaching Jupiter in 2016. The spacecraft will orbit Jupiter 32 times, skimming about 3,000 miles over the planet's cloud tops for approximately one year. The mission will be the first solar powered spacecraft designed to operate despite the great distance from the sun.

The spacecraft will use a camera and nine science instruments to study the hidden world beneath Jupiter's colorful clouds. The suite of science instruments will investigate the existence of an ice-rock core, Jupiter's intense magnetic field, water and ammonia clouds in the deep atmosphere, and explore the planet's aurora borealis.

"Juno's extraordinarily accurate determination of the gravity and magnetic fields of Jupiter will enable us to understand what is going on deep down in the planet," said Professor Dave Stevenson, co-investigator at the California Institute of Technology in Pasadena. "These and other measurements will inform us about how Jupiter's constituents are distributed, how Jupiter formed and how it evolved, which is a central part of our growing understanding of the nature of our solar system."

Deep in Jupiter's atmosphere, under great pressure, hydrogen gas is squeezed into a fluid known as metallic hydrogen. At these great depths, the hydrogen acts like an electrically conducting metal which is believed to be the source of the planet's intense magnetic field. Jupiter also may have a rocky solid core at the center.

The Juno mission is the second spacecraft designed under NASA's New Frontiers Program. The first was the Pluto New Horizons mission, launched in January 2006 and scheduled to reach Pluto's moon Charon in 2015.

—from NASA press release, Nov. 24, 2008

IN MEMORIAM

SIR ARTHUR C. CLARKE
1917-2008

FORREST J ACKERMAN
1916-2008

Beginning in the 1950's, Arthur C. Clarke was widely considered one of the "Big Three" writers of science fiction, along with Robert Heinlein and Isaac Asimov.

Asimov acknowledged Clarke as the world's greatest science fiction writer, in accord with their tongue-in-cheek Asimov-Clarke Treaty of Park Avenue, while Clarke conceded that Asimov was the world's best science writer.

Nonetheless, Clarke made a lasting contribution in science writing, suggesting in 1945 that satellites in a geosynchronous orbit would be ideal for telecommunications. The International Astronomical Union calls such an orbit a Clarke orbit in recognition.

Clarke made his first professional story sale to *Astounding,* and it was published in 1946. Six of his stories appeared in *Thrilling Wonder Stories* in 1949-51, including the popular "Breaking Strain" (published as "Thirty Seconds—Thirty Days") and "Earthlight," which he later expanded into a novel.

He wrote the novel *2001: A Space Odyssey* concurrently with Stanley Kubrick's screenplay, and rewrote sections after viewing footage—"a rather expensive method of literary creation," as he put it.

Clarke received a knighthood in 1998 from his native U.K., and the highest civil honor of his adopted Sri Lanka, Sri Lankabhimanya, in 2005.

Sir Arthur continued to write until the end of his life, most often novels in collaboration. *The Last Theorem,* with Frederik Pohl, appeared posthumously. • • •

Although he became a professional in the science fiction and horror genres as a writer, agent, and editor, Forrest J Ackerman was known throughout his long life as a fan's fan.

He fell in love with science fiction after buying an early issue of the first regular SF magazine, *Amazing Stories,* and commenced the epic letter-writing that made him famous with a missive published in *Science Wonder Quarterly* in 1929.

By 1934, he was so well known as a fan that *Wonder Stories* made him Honorary Member Number One of their new Science Fiction League, as well as an Executive Director.

He traveled to New York in 1939 with fellow Los Angeles fan Ray Bradbury for the first World Science Fiction Convention, and wore a futuristic costume there—sparking a con tradition.

He founded the magazine *Famous Monsters of Filmland* in 1958, introducing a generation of future filmmakers to movies then only available in infrequent cinema screenings or TV airings, if at all.

He loved playing with words. He popularized the term "sci-fi" (to the chagrin of some). He shortened his nickname to "4e," wrote *Famous Monsters* as "Dr. Acula," and dubbed his eighteen-room home "the Ackermansion."

There, he accumulated a famous collection of science fiction and film books, artwork, magazines, and props, of which he delighted in giving public showings.

He wrote numerous short stories. His first, "Earth's Lucky Day," written with Francis Flagg, appeared in the final issue of *Wonder Stories,* in 1936. • • •

DR. ZOTTS

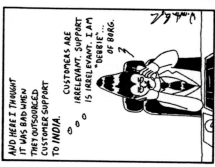

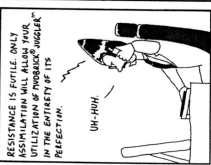

Printed in the United States
139333LV00001BB/2/P